Love for all Seasons

Spring Fling

Summer Lovin'

Falling Into You

The Snowflake Seduction

Love for all Seasons

Spring Fling
by Barbara Keaton

Summer Lovin'
by Sapphire Blue

Falling Into You
by Maureen Smith

The Snowflake Seduction
by A.C. Arthur

Parker Publishing, LLC

Noire Passion is an imprint of Parker Publishing, LLC.

Published by Parker Publishing, LLC
12523 Limonite Avenue, Suite #440-438
Mira Loma, California 91752
www.parker-publishing.com

ISBN 978-1-60043-013-8

First Edition

Manufactured in the United States of America

Dedications

Barbara Keaton

To Dyanne Davis – my true sistah! Thank you for being the frick to my frack—much love to you!

Sapphire Blue

To my husband

Maureen Smith

For all my readers

A.C. Arthur

To all the heartbroken and heartbreakers, love will find a way.

Spring Fling

by

Barbara Keaton

Chapter 1

Just one more week until Spring Break, and then it's sand, beach, sun and plenty of rest in Jamaica, Tavia Joelle Dennison's mind sing-sang as she stood in front of her third class of the day and thought about the great gift her friend and fellow teacher, Joanne Larson, had given her. Well, actually, Joanne and her latest beau were supposed to go, but having broken up two days ago, Joanne asked Tavia to go—the accommodations were already paid for and had been transferred to her. At first Tavia hadn't believed her until Joanne placed a copy of an itinerary in her hand. She had smiled broadly as she read her name on the papers.

"You only have to get your airfare," Joanne had said as she waltzed from Tavia's loft. "And the guide for this exclusive resort will arrive in the mail a week before you leave. So, go get your passport."

Tavia had never been out of the United States, even though she made it a point to visit as much of her own country as she could. A history buff, Tavia had been to nearly every state in the United States, visiting major cities and exploring their history and culture. Her all time favorite had been Charleston, South Carolina, where she'd decided no matter what to visit the city every year in addition to a new state. Tavia had never been to the islands and had always wanted to go, but had never moved past ordering a brochure or stopping in a travel agency to pick up a few travel guides.

"Professor Dennison?"

Tavia blinked several times, her eyes focused to meet the curious gazes of her students.

"My apologies—who's next?" she asked as she forced herself to pay attention to her students in what was one of her favorite classes. Made up of writers of all types—poets, lyrists, journalists, the curious—her creative writing class for the past two years attracted scores of people who enjoyed the free style and creative juxtapositions she allowed the class to go out on. As a tenured professor in the University of Illinois' English Department, Tavia finally got an opportunity to teach a class that she felt broke up the monotony of the other classes she taught: English Composition, English for Teachers, and Comparing the Writings of the Classics, which to her, by far, was the most boring class she'd ever had the displeasure of teaching since she'd received her Ph.D. in English Literature nearly twenty years ago. The class consisted of graduate students who sat around and pontificated on the works of Kafka versus William Shakespeare or Edgar Allen Poe versus Voltaire. She had wondered, up until two years ago, what brain surgeon had created the curriculum on that subject, and then blanched when she found out the Dean of her department, Dr. Walter Braithwaite, was that brain surgeon.

The class was a result of his doctoral dissertation on the widely varied writers, who in Tavia's opinion had very little in common outside of being great writers. Braithwaite had sold the curriculum to the university and its English department as a "necessary component to the future educational well-being of its students." Tavia had wanted to laugh until her sides hurt—until she found herself being assigned to teach the boring class.

"Professor Dennison, I know this is a creative writing class, but why do we have to sit here and listen to his mindless diatribe?" protested Laurina, a senior journalism major, as she pointed a slender finger at the student sitting next to her. And though Tavia was inclined to agree, she was the last person to protest. This was creative writing, with no-holds on what a student could write as long as it was tasteful. And even that clause was subjective. What she considered lewd and lascivious someone else may have found highly erotic and tasteful.

She glanced at Laurina, and then to the subject of her ire, the university's infamous running back and Heisman Trophy hopeful, Devon Harris. Tavia looked at them both and saw the spark of conflict she knew would lead the two to become an item. She'd been teaching collegiate level classes her entire career, and she'd seen the beginnings of many a relationship start out like Devon and Laurina's—combative.

An image of Tavia's last date sprung to mind. Twisting her mouth, she thought of Bruce and wanted to pull her graying hair out at the roots.

Bruce Gordon, the chief of the campus police, had hounded her for weeks to go out with him. She had noticed Bruce, his smooth cocoa complexion, as she walked across the campus one autumn day. He stopped his squad car, exited, then leaned on the hood and watched her as she disappeared down the street. The next day she found him waiting in the same spot, but instead of remaining quiet, he greeted her, nodding his head as she crossed in front of the cruiser. On the third day, he'd been sitting in the vehicle and had the nerve to honk the horn at her and grin. She lifted her head as she rolled her eyes and bit her bottom lip to keep from laughing aloud. She was too damn old, at forty-five, to be honked at; but still, it made her feel somewhat youthful in an oddly appealing way.

Each day thereafter, as she made her daily two-mile trek from her loft condo, in an old renovated warehouse, to the campus, she spotted him waiting for her to pass. After an entire week of the same thing and by the beginning of the next, he had mustered up enough nerve to not only ask her name, but requested her company at a dinner and a show that upcoming Friday night. Tavia agreed. She hadn't had a date in eons and outside of the unwanted crushes and invitations from the male students and the custodial engineer, Ben—she was truly fond of him, but at 79, he was more like a father than a suitor—she hadn't had much male attention.

Her thoughts switched to the math professor whose class was meeting right next to hers for the remaining semester and into the entire following school year while the university built a new Math and Science Building. She'd found herself seeking him out ever since she'd stumbled upon him conducting a math seminar on campus. She had watched him as he stood at the podium, an African king among a sea of white faces. She noted how his deep voice carried across the large auditorium style classroom, the silence palatable as he moved smoothly from one end of a large chalkboard to the next, quickly writing a formula on the board. Tavia had sat in an upper seat and watched in awe as this young professor commanded his audience's full attention. He sported a Cornel West Afro and thick black frames, which in her opinion gave him more of an air of intelligence and not the totally weird moniker she'd heard a few students use to describe him behind his back. As she sat and watched him present a lecture on the Quantum Leap, she was spellbound and quite impressed with his knowledge of what seemed to her a series of complex math equations and theories. He had walked across the stage, his back ramrod straight, the master of this arena. Tavia leaned on the seat in front of her and watched his stealth movements, graceful and poised. He had on a charcoal two-piece suit, a white shirt, dark tie, and black wing tipped shoes. She inhaled deeply when he took off the jacket, loosened the tie about his neck and then rolled up his sleeves. Absently Tavia licked her lips as her eyes trailed down the back of him—the pants hinted at a tight behind and muscular legs. She wanted to know who this brother really was.

Later, Tavia looked him up on the university's internet and was surprised when she found he was ten-plus years her junior.

The sound of Laurina's voice snapped Tavia out of her daydream.

"Professor Dennison, I do not believe that explaining the fluid moves of women should be considered poor taste," Devon said and smiled at Laurina, his eyes glued to her face.

"Laurina, I think we owe it to Devon to hear him out. We don't criticize each other's work in this class. Go ahead, Devon. Read what you've written." Tavia crossed her legs at the ankles and forced back a chuckle. Ever since she'd watched some show on BBC America where a woman, a so-called etiquette expert, insisted it was improper to cross at the knees—that was for men—she had made it a point to never cross her legs. She sat and tried to focus on the words Devon spoke as her mind wandered over thoughts of Bruce.

Bruce, recently divorced with two teenage sons, had insisted he escort her home each and every day. In the beginning she'd found his dead pan humor somewhat refreshing, but later, as she got to know him, she found his biting humor mean and sarcastic, especially when he turned it toward the young professor as he walked past them one day.

"Now that's a sell out right there." Bruce had chuckled as he began speaking about the professor as if he weren't human. "And those clothes. All that money these folks are paying him, and he wears those white boy pants."

"What's wrong with what he's wearing?" she had asked. She noted that her voice had taken on more of a defensive bent than she had meant to display. "They look clean to me, and I see nothing wrong with his attire." Her mind traveled to what he wore the day of the conference. She shivered as her mind replayed the sound of his voice and the way the suit trousers had made promises of a muscular behind and legs as he strolled across the stage.

Tavia reached to her chest as a wave of heat crept up around her neck before snaking downward and settling into the core of her womanhood. She inhaled deeply, almost moaned before she remembered who she was with. She glanced at Bruce but he didn't seem to notice her flash of heat.

"You don't get it," he said as they resumed walking. "But I don't expect you to. You just like him. An egg head."

Tavia huffed out loud, then pulled in her bottom lip and simply nodded her head as she remembered all the times as a kid growing up on the west side of Chicago being teased because her diction was different and she loved to read and write. Back then the kids had called her white. She'd stopped walking and looked up at Bruce. To her, he was no better than those kids, who to her, had settled for mediocrity simply because no one had told them they didn't have to. Her mother had never settled for mediocrity and neither would Tavia. To add to her apprehension about Bruce, he had broached the subject of when they would have sex only a week after their first date.

Tavia had been celebrating celibacy for nearly five years, her last fling so long ago she had forgotten what a naked man with a penis looked like. Maybe that's why she found herself having a heated flash whenever she thought about the young professor, she mused as she thought about the wicked sensation—one she never remembered having, not even when she was married.

Having been divorced for ten years, Tavia decided to skip the dating scene and focus on raising her daughter, Jonetta, and create a life she'd always dreamed of—peaceful and alone! She had just sent Jonetta off to complete her second year in college and had downsized from a three-bedroom house to a two-bedroom loft.

Sure she had been mildly interested in Bruce, but she didn't like him enough to end her drought. But when she thought of the young professor something inside of her stirred—she just couldn't put her finger on why. He was geeky, and his clothes were way too baggy, but each time she had seen him at various university functions, she had been captivated by his voice—a deep resonate baritone that seemed to vibrate off the walls and settle down into the pit of her being.

She tried to picture him with shorter hair, hipper clothes and no glasses, but she just couldn't see the professor the students had nick-named "Weird" in anything hipper than what he tended to wear on a daily basis: ill fitting Dockers, a button down oxford shirt, a blazer and loafers.

Tavia sighed as her thoughts returned to Bruce. He lasted all of one day after she'd told him she intended on remaining celibate. And that was just fine with her because prior to the sex conversation, she'd begun to secretly hope he'd stop calling. Bruce was not only a control freak, but was super bossy and had appointed himself her guardian. Heck, she thought, my momma and daddy are in Chicago. But had she known fifty-year-old men were just as bad as twenty-one year old men, she would have never entertained the thought of going out with Bruce and all his idiosyncrasies. Sadly, according to Jonetta, all men were nuts and she had recently sworn off them. Tavia assumed Jonetta had met someone who hadn't measured up the expectations Tavia had raised her with.

"Professor Dennison?" Laurina cried out in exasperation.

Tavia held up her hand. "Laurina, once more, this is creative writing. And in this class, Devon has a right to express himself in any written media he so chooses as long as we aren't offended. Are you offended at his comparison of killer ants and women's movements?" Tavia tilted her head to the right and watched with detached amusement as Laurina folded her arms across her chest and sighed loudly. Tavia waved her hand at Devon, signaling for him to continue to read. Silently, she admitted the topic was totally off base, had no merit and was simply boring, and she wondered what drink this man-child had consumed lately.

"Excuse me, Professor Dennison," came the voice from the classroom door. "May I borrow your erasable board? My room is missing one."

Tavia's head slowly turned to face the door. Her breath hitched, and the heat she'd felt before began its descent from her face, across her breasts, on down to the core of her very being. She was glad to be wearing a long skirt, for she clamped her legs together in an attempt to quell the throbbing between her legs. She closed her eyes momentarily as she attempted to control her runaway pulse. The slight snickers from her class caught her full attention as Professor Bartholomew Lawrence Wainwright, III, stepped into her classroom. Tavia found out he had a Ph.D. in Mathematics and Physics and had won the Nobel Peace Prize for physics at the age of twenty-eight for the quantum theory of optical coherence—whatever that was.

His exceptional intelligence made her think about the movie A Beautiful Mind, only this professor wasn't Russell Crow cute, but she thought he was kinda cute in his black rimmed glasses with thick lenses, which made his round brown eyes seem larger than what she thought they were. To Tavia, he was the only black nerd she'd ever seen up close—he even had a pocket protector sticking out from his left breast pocket. Yet each time she thought about him, inexplicable heat crept up her body and set her on fire. She was afraid to wonder any further, for she couldn't understand the attraction. And then there was his voice—umph, umph! So deep, yet so soft and melodic it brought its own heat—enough to melt butter.

She looked at him and noticed that today he wore a pair of faded khaki Dockers, a blue shirt with a tie with mathematical equations scribbled across it and a pair of large Birkenstocks on his feet. She'd never noticed he had big feet. Yup, she thought, this brother is truly different in an oddly sexy way.

"Sure Professor Wainwright," she replied and pointed to the rear of the class. "Go ahead. I'm not going to be using it today."

Professor Wainwright tripped into the classroom, and the class broke out in raucous laughter as his body met the hard wooden floor. Tavia rose quickly to her feet and rushed over to him. She gave her class a disapproving glare as she assisted him to his feet, and then was taken aback at the solid feel of his bicep. She gasped lightly when her sights landed on the warm, honey-brown eyes staring into hers as he stood to his full height of what she guessed was at least six feet, three inches. As he stared, she felt the odd heat of them bore into the depths of her entire being. She shivered involuntarily, and then shook her head.

"My glasses," he whispered. Tavia tore her eyes away from his and looked up to see Devon standing with the glasses in his hand. She took them from him and held them out. She watched as he slipped the thick lenses over his face, adjusted the black frame onto the bridge of his nose, straightened his tie, and then proceeded to the rear of the room, taking the board from her class.

Tavia forced her attention back to her class. The heated look from the professor stayed fastened in her mind with her for the rest of the day—even as she walked across the campus and headed for home.

"What a dufus," Bartholomew said to himself as he stood looking down upon Tavia as she walked across the campus then disappeared from his sight. "She's so beautiful." He backed away from the window, then sat down at his desk. He rubbed his hand down his face as he shook his head. His eyes rested on the series of numbers and equations on a large piece of white butcher paper. He'd been working on solving the equation for nearly two weeks—trying to stump a fellow professor of mathematics, Richard Langston, who was also his friend and had talked him into going to Jamaica for Spring Break in place of a friend of a friend who had to back out at the last minute.

He raised his eyes and looked at the large map of the world situated on the wall. He had never considered going on a pleasure vacation to an island. His vacations always consisted of either visits to Alabama to see his mother and siblings or to conferences around the world to discuss math and physics. Never anything like what the all-inclusive brochure showed: white pristine beaches, people clad in bathing suits, couples lounging with drinks in their hand, folks daring to parasail over the sparking blue water.

Bartholomew, called Lawrence by close friends and family, stood and grabbed his London Fog overcoat and leather satchel, then shut off the lights to his office. As he walked across the campus, waving at a few of the students he recognized, his thoughts wandered to Tavia. He had always thought her beautiful—from the moment he laid eyes on her almost a year ago walking across campus. And when he got the opportunity to see her up close at a faculty event, he noted her smooth, rich, walnut brown skin, her slightly slanted dark eyes and her curvaceous physique. Even then he didn't have the nerve to ask her out.

And he had sat by and watched with a great amount of loathing, as she and that beat walker seemed to get close. But he had also noticed the Rent-A-Cop, who for weeks walked her to and from class every day, had suddenly, and much to his satisfaction, disappeared. Maybe, he hoped as his mind twirled around the possibilities, they were a thing of the past. He walked faster, his feet moving quickly as he made his way to his car, a 1965 Dodge Duster in mint condition. Starting it up, he put the car in gear and peeled from the staff parking lot.

After twenty minutes, Lawrence pulled up into the driveway of the large Georgian with the wrap around porch and massive wooden doors, he had lived in for all the years he'd been at the university—five total. He had found the house in an area that had yet to benefit from the surrounding gentrification. Once an eyesore, Lawrence had restored the exterior and interior of the house and found the four-bedroom home to be quite warm and inviting, especially the large stone fireplaces in the living room and his master bedroom.

Lawrence climbed the stairs to his house, unlocked the door and stepped inside. He shut the door, and then hung his coat on the hall coat tree. Slipping his feet from his shoes, he replaced them with black leather house slippers, a gift from his younger brother. He had to smile when he thought of his family. Lawrence was the forth of eight and the oldest boy. His mother had always said he and the baby of the family, his sister Jean, were geniuses and had them both tested when they were just two years old. Jean had a photographic memory, with a recall of letters and numbers with great clarity. Lawrence could do simple math at three and Algebra at seven. Both were reading by the age of two. Not to take anything away from the rest of his sisters and brothers, the family boasted an Ob/Gyn, a vet, two bank presidents, a contractor and a housing developer, who worked together designing and building homes all across the state of Alabama. But Lawrence's smartness had separated him from those outside of his home. The kids in his farm community teased him continually, especially when as a kid, he had to wear glasses because of his increasingly bad eyesight. By the time he reached high school, Lawrence was so introverted his cousin, Emma, accompanied him to prom. But when he got in front of a chalk board and began to solve the mathematical problems placed in front of him, he was in his own world, one that many would not or could not understand.

The one woman who had understood him was also the one who'd broken his heart. Karen Stephens was a fellow mathematician at the University of Alabama. When they met on campus and began to talking about math problems, Lawrence thought he'd finally found someone who understood him, would love him in spite of his quirky way of dressing, his thick glasses and often unruly hair. They had quickly become close, spending nearly everyday with each other. Karen had been the fifth woman Lawrence had slept with, but the only women he had fallen deeply in love with. Just when he was ready to propose marriage, Karen had said she didn't want to be tied down, resigned her position from the university, and then left the country to teach abroad, never once asking Lawrence's opinion or if he wanted to go with her. He'd loved her to near distraction, and he would have followed her to the ends of the earth if she would have wanted him to.

Up until a year ago, his mother had forwarded post cards to him from Karen. The last one he received informed him she had gotten married.

Lawrence had held onto the hope Karen would someday marry him, but when he finally thought with some clarity, he knew he had been holding onto a pipe dream. He knew she never intended on marrying him.

He looked at himself in the large mirror attached to the wall of the bathroom. He removed his glasses and tilted his head to the side. If he cut his hair, got rid of the glasses and wore different clothes, maybe Tavia would want to go out. At thirty-three, he was too young to say no to marriage and he wanted to marry. He had grown tired of dates of convenience or ones of sympathy. Those were the ones he hated the most—like he was a charity case, and they were doing him a great favor by being seen with him at all. He pictured Tavia in his mind.

The moment he read her work, before he'd lay eyes on her, he had become a fan of hers and began looking forward to reading more of her works, which appeared in the school's year-end book compiled by the English Department. He loved her poetry the most—the fluid words, full of soft sonnets that touched him deeply, and sang to his soul. And then there was her political commentaries that appeared weekly in the school's newspaper. Her words were always hard, clear and to the point—no room for ambiguity.

When he'd finally gotten the opportunity to meet her, to lay eyes on her, at the annual faculty luncheon where she'd been honored for her work, he had been too anxious to approach her and resolved to adore her from afar.

Lawrence sighed heavily at that thought as he removed his clothes, and then replaced them with his workout gear of shorts and a T-shirt, and then headed to his basement to workout. His mind wandered to Tavia, how she had rushed to him when he tripped in her class. If only, he mused, as his mind rewrote the ending to his embarrassing act. In his mind, she stood when he entered.

"What can I do for you, Lawrence?" she said as she rose from her seat.

"I need to speak with you, Tavia." He leaned on the desk and crossed his arms over his chest as he watched her turn her back to him and dismiss the class. He was pleased as she locked door behind the last student, then came and stood in front of him, so close he could smell the wicked fragrance of her perfume, the deep browns of her eyes.

"Again, Lawrence, what can I do for you?" she asked and tilted her head to one side. Lawrence pulled her to him, her middle rested along his groin and his arms wrapped around her before his hands trailed up and down her back, cupping her full behind in his large hands. Her body moved like a cat, slow and sleek, as she grinded her pelvis into him.

"You can take off your clothes for me, Tavia."

He watched as she stepped back and began to slowly unbutton her blouse. He sucked in a mouthful of air when he saw she wasn't wearing a bra. He reached out, touched one of her nipples, which were hard as pebbles and quite large. He played with her nipples, enjoying the way her eyes grew dark with desire for him. He pulled her close enough for him to lower his head, take one of the proffered nipples between his lips and began to suck and lave first her nipple, then her aerola.

"Oh, Lawrence, baby. Please." He heard her hiss between her teeth. He suckled her like a babe, pulling the nipple into his mouth, his tongue flicked the hardness over and over.

He pulled back. "Tell, me. What do you want me to do?"

"I want to feel you inside me Lawrence," she said as she wiggled out of her skirt, letting the garment fall to the floor. He shook his head and smiled at her, one eyebrow raised. She stood before him fully naked.

He watched her dark eyes as she moved closer, her warm body against his as her small hand made a trail down his chest, across his stomach, over the waistband of his trousers, past his boxer briefs and settled on his…

The jangling sound of the telephone broke him out of his sensuous daydream. He exhaled heavily and tried to right his erratic breathing as he walked over to the bar in his basement to pick up the phone. He had been so engrossed in the erotic daydream he hadn't even noticed he had been sitting on the floor near the weight bench. He picked up the cordless phone and cleared his throat before answering. "Hello."

"Hey, big brother," the voice sang. Lawrence nodded his head and forced his breathing to regulate. He then smiled as he sat down on the workout bench.

"Hey Jean, what a surprise. How's everything?"

"Great. I'm in Chicago. I'll be there tomorrow."

"What are you doing in Chicago?"

Lawrence listened as his baby sister, the other professor in the family, who at twenty-three had two masters, one in science and the other in anthropology, and was working on her Ph.D. at Stanford in Roman-Greco studies, told of an anthropology seminar to be held over the weekend at the university.

"You're staying here," Lawrence insisted as he rose from the weight bench and headed up the stairs to the main floor. He walked into the kitchen and began scribbling out a grocery list. All of the Wainwright children knew how to cook, clean and sew—their mother made sure of it. "And you can help me get ready for my trip."

"What trip?"

"To Jamaica," he said, then rested his hip against the edge of the Formica countertop. He glanced outside of his window and watched his neighbors as they sat cuddled up in a swing on their back deck. He thought of Tavia again, then shook his head. His breathing had regulated, but his body had yet to return to normal. The hardness of his penis made him ache inside with a need so great he thought he would loose his mind. He knew he had to get a grip. A woman like Tavia would never agree to go out with him, much less do anything else. Yeah, he mused to himself, that may be, but I can still dream.

"Lawrence? Are you listening to me? When are you leaving?"

He returned his attention to the phone call. "A week from tomorrow."

"We've got just enough time. I won't be leaving until Wednesday to head back to Stanford. Yup, that gives me just enough time."

"To do what, Jean?"

"You'll see. Hey, my group is here and ready to head out. I'll see you tomorrow afternoon. Where are you going to be?"

"Probably on campus. I need to finish up some papers before spring break begins."

"Good, I'll catch up with you there. See you tomorrow. Love you, Lawrence."

"Love you, too." He shut off the phone, finished his grocery list, then headed back to the basement to begin his workout. As he lifted the bar above his head, his mind drifted to the daydream he'd been having before the phone rang. He shook his head and began to bench press the 250 pound weights up and over his head. Lawrence tried to fight the erotic pull. The searing images floated in and out, and he gave up as the dream took over. He placed the weight bar on the bench and gave in to the sensations as he tried to pick the fantasy up where he'd left it. Oh, yeah, she reached out and stroked me, his mind whispered, his penis rock hard as she slid her body up and down his. He inhaled as she undressed him; her hands lit a fire on every inch she'd touched—until he could stand no more. He grabbed her by her shoulders, twirled her around and bent her over, her ample behind jutted high in the air. He steadied himself as he watched her behind slowly gyrate the closer his penis came to her vagina. He poised the head and then...He lost it!

Chapter 2

Tavia rose early. She wanted to get in a few laps in the university's Olympic size swimming pool before heading over to her office to finish grading mid-term papers. She didn't want to even look at them once she came back from Jamaica. As she walked to campus, her imagination conjured up images of sandy white beaches and deep blue water.

Stepping into the women's locker room and changing quickly into her one-piece blazing red bathing suit, Tavia headed out to the pool area, covered her eyes with goggles and positioned her body to dive head first into the deep end of the pool. Her body sluiced through the tepid water as she kicked her feet to bring her to the top. She rolled over to float on her back, looking up at the clear dome overhead. The blue sky and billowing clouds rolled lazily by. Tavia loved the water and hoped to get as much sun and water as she could for the entire week she'd be in Jamaica. After several backstroke laps, she began the front crawl, her body moving easily though the water as she began her regimen of laps. After the fifth lap, she began to slow her pace, easily cutting the water, her legs propelling her forward as her arms sliced though the water. Four more, she told her self as she touched the pool wall with the tip of her finger and headed to the other end.

Normally alone at this time of the morning, Tavia sensed someone watching her and looked up to see the young professor standing at the edge of the pool. Losing her momentum, Tavia went under the deep water and began to struggle to propel herself up so she could tread the water. Moments later, she felt strong arms about her as she was pulled upward, her face now above the water. She felt her body being dragged along the pool, then up and out.

"I didn't mean to startle you," he said as he patted her back. Tavia coughed several times, gagging on the chlorinated water that burned her throat. She was an excellent swimmer, so she didn't understand how his presence could have caused her to lose her train of thought to point of near-drowning.

"I'm okay," she sputtered and sat up. She looked at the professor, his face missing his glasses and his hair and clothing soaked. "I just lost it for a moment. I'm better."

"Are you sure?" he said as he rubbed her back, the heat of his hands bore through the light fabric. She shivered.

"Yes, thank you. I'm sure." She began to stand and watched as he quickly rose to his feet and effortlessly pulled her five-foot six frame upward. She was mere inches from him, the warmth of his body so close that her mind began to twirl, her legs twitched as she imagined his lips upon hers. She closed her eyes and leaned forward, her head rested on his chest, her arms held him by his large biceps. She inhaled deeply, the fresh scent of his laundered shirt, her mind taken aback by the strong arms which held her closely. *Wait! What am I doing?* Her mind screamed as she pulled back and looked up into his eyes.

"Ummm," she stepped back and wrapped her arms about her. "I'm okay. Really, I am."

He looked around, saw the towel lying near by, grabbed it and wrapped it around Tavia, pulling her closer as he rubbed the thick cloth across her arms. He noticed that her toned arms had goose bumps raised all over them and allowed her to slip from his embrace. He fought the urge to pull her back to him, to hold her in his arms and feel her close to him again. Instead, he let his hands fall to his side and settled on watching the droplets of water cascade from her curly short hair to her face.

"Are you sure you're okay? We can head over to Medical Services and have them check you out," he said as his eyes took in her form in the bathing suit, the mocha colored tops of her breasts peeked out at him, her long shapely legs spoke to him and her voluptuous behind made his hands itch to touch. He wanted to scream as his manhood stirred to life. He was glad to be wearing dark pants.

"I'm okay, Bartholomew, thank you."

He smiled. She knew his name. "Not a problem, Tavia."

They stood staring at each other for long moments. Tavia couldn't shake the feel of him as he'd held her, and she'd held onto him, his strength and masculinity shouted out to all that made her a woman, and if she didn't know any better, she'd swear that his touch had ignited a fire in her that could only be quenched by him. Ha! Likely story. That'd never happen in a million years.

"Hey, Professor Dennison, how's the water?"

Tavia turned her head to see one of her students enter the pool area. She watched as the student looked from her to Bartholomew and back. This would surely be in the school newspaper's gossip column—they had been spied by the editor.

"Well, I better get going. I've got to go get into some dry clothes." He looked at her and smiled wistfully.

"I feel bad. How can I make this up to you?" Tavia asked as she looked at his bare feet. She had seen enough men's feet to know that most didn't take good care of them, but his feet were nice for a man's, the nails trimmed low, no bunions or corns. She looked up to his face. His glasses were now perched on his broad nose.

He tilted his head to one side. He wanted to ask her to dinner, but thought better. A woman that gorgeous would never go out with someone as nerdy as him. "No need. Just glad I was here. You take care." He walked toward the other end of the pool, picked up his shoes and headed out the door.

"Wow. Was that Professor Weird?"

Tavia ignored the student's question and headed to the locker room. As she showered, she thought of the feel of the strong arms that wrapped around her and the long dormant sensations that had been awakened. Admittedly, it had been a long time, but she didn't think she was desperate, yet something about the professor was intriguing—and she found herself more than mildly attracted to him. Her thoughts tumbled each time she saw him and the twitching between her legs! She was at a loss to explain it. She shook her head and forced the image of the young professor standing in front of her with his clothes sticking to every inch of his magnificent body. Why, she mused, would he hide all that under those clothes? "Bad girl, Tavia," she chided herself. "Get a grip."

Once dressed, Tavia headed to her office to go over student papers. And even as she looked them over, she still couldn't shake the thought of the professor from her mind.

"Lawrence, what's wrong?" Jean asked. She came to stand next to her big brother as he looked out the window. She watched him as his eyes followed a woman across the campus. She smiled and thought that finally her big brother, in all his sweet shyness, had gotten over that Karen woman. She hadn't liked that woman and knew she was only looking for an opportunity—Lawrence was a Nobel Peace prize winner and anywhere he'd go he could command his own destiny, and Karen was just on for the ride. She also knew Karen would get tired of waiting for him to command the destiny she thought they should have.

"She's so beautiful," he whispered lowly as he placed his arm around his sister's shoulder and gently swayed her from the window.

"What did you say?" Jean asked as she moved to sit in the seat across from his desk.

"Nothing. How about we grill some steaks for dinner?" he asked in an attempt to change the subject.

"Can I bring my friend?"

"Sure, what's her name?"

"His name is Philip and he's a cop."

Lawrence looked at his sister. And though he realized she was a grown woman, he didn't quite like the idea of some man holding her like he wanted to hold Tavia that morning. He had happened upon Tavia, while taking a short cut through the athletic building. This time instead of cutting across the basketball court, he took an even shorter way that took him past the observation deck of the pool, and he spotted her.

"Can he come? He's staying at a hotel."

"Sure he can come. You know you're staying with me, though?"

"Umm, Lawrence, I don't want him to be here in this small town all alone."

"And I don't want you lying up under him and y'all aren't married." He stood up and headed back to the window. He frowned when he didn't spot Tavia walking across the campus. He looked at his watch. They had only been on campus for a few hours. Maybe he'd catch her view as she headed for home.

"We're engaged," she held out her left hand and showed off the diamond solitaire on her ring finger. "I brought Philip here to meet you—to get your blessing."

Lawrence turned and faced his baby sister, so much a woman. He missed the fact she wasn't his Pee Wee any longer. He shrugged his shoulders and inhaled deeply.

"Okay, have him check out of the hotel. You'll both stay with me. That will give us an opportunity to get to know each other. Has he met the rest of the family?"

She shook her head "no" and he laughed. Lawrence knew she was using him as the litmus test, and if this Philip character passed his muster, then the rest of the family would be cake walk. "Okay, Jean. Call him up and tell him to be ready in a few hours." He returned to gazing out of the window. His body attempted to betray him as he thought about Tavia in his arms.

"Who is she, Lawrence?" Jean asked.

"Tavia Dennison, professor in the English Department, a writer, a poet. A woman whose words flow effortlessly, lyrically. You should read her work. She's edited a book of poems written by several students here on campus. She even put in a poem called the 'Perfect Storm.' "

"Have you asked her out, yet?"

He shook his head.

"Why not? You're good looking. Young. In shape. What's not to love about you?"

"Jean, look at me." He faced her and swept his hands down his Dockers. "I don't dress in the latest fashions, you know? I don't even know how to begin to approach a woman like that. She's out of my league, Pee Wee."

"No, you just need to update your look. Let me take you shopping for your trip to Jamaica. All that money you make!" She waved her hand up in the air. "It's time you spent a little of it on yourself. Stop being so dog-gone frugal, Lawrence." She rose to stand next to him and removed his glasses. "And you mustn't take these. We're going to get you some contacts and sun glasses. You're going to be the hit in Jamaica. "

"I don't want to be the hit. I don't want a new look. I just want to ask her out."

"Aww, Lawrence." She stomped her foot. "Come on. You're a young, good looking brother who's hiding. Let me and Philip hip you up a bit."

"Hip me up?" He brushed past her and sat down behind his desk. "I don't want to be hipped up!"

"Why not?" Jean sat on the edge of his desk. "Give me one good reason why."

He rolled his eyes upward and breathed out loud. What difference would it make to Tavia whether he had on the latest "hip" gear or what he found as practical wear, the end would still be the same: she wouldn't be interested in going out with him.

"No, Jean. Let it go."

Jean folded her arms across her chest and poked out her bottom lip. "You are as stubborn as a pack mule, Bartholomew Lawrence Wainwright." She stormed over to the window and looked down just as Tavia appeared escorted by a muscular male who took her bag from her. "And your princess is about to be charmed by another king if you don't do something, Lawrence." She pointed downward just as he came to look out of the window.

"Devon, you don't have to carry my bag." She reached out for her leather briefcase.

"No, my pleasure. Besides, I need to ask you a question. Sort of personal."

"Oh." She looked at him.

"It's about Laurina." Her name came from him in a loud huff. "No matter what I do, she ignores me, acts like I get on her nerves." His large shoulders drooped. "I like her, Professor Dennison—a lot! And I know she works with you on the student paper. If you put in a good word for me, you know, maybe say something nice about me..." He looked at her, his eyes clouded with desperation. Tavia wanted to laugh. Not at him, but at the feelings he was grappling with—the intense emotions he was feeling at such a young age. She had watched them interact in her class and knew Laurina was just as crazy about him as he was her, but what Devon didn't know was Laurina was different from most of the young women on campus. The flashy clothes he wore and the bling-bling jewelry didn't impress her. The only time she had truly been impressed by Devon was when he'd read his essay about what he thought a man should be. His voice had been full of passion as he read the words; his eyes had met and held Laurina's as he did.

"Devon, if you really like her, really want to get to know Laurina, then you may want to get rid of some of the jewelry." Tavia pointed to the large diamond like studs in his ears. "And skip some of the Pelle-Pelle." She nodded at his oversized sweatshirt emblazoned with the designer's name. "You may have a chance." She looked in his eyes and noted the warm brown orbs were full of hope.

"You think so?" He looked down at his attire. "I thought she'd like all this glitz and glamour."

"What made you think that, Devon?"

"I saw her walking the yard with this dude all blinged out. They like twins. You see one, you see the other. He might as well be attached to her hip."

Tavia laughed. "He's her twin."

"No shit? Ooops, my bad. I'm sorry. I mean...for real?"

Tavia nodded her head, and then laughed again when Devon enveloped her in his arms, lifting her off her feet and swung her around. "Thanks, Professor Dennison. Thanks a bunch."

"You're welcome, Devon. Now, please, put me down."

"Oh, my bad again. I done lost my head." He smiled brightly as he removed the large studs from his ear. Tavia was surprised to find he actually had only one ear pierced. The other stud seemed to be glued on. "I'm going to go call her and ask her out. Wish me luck, Professor Dennison." He turned and headed across the campus.

"Devon," Tavia called out. "You've got my bag." She smiled as Devon rushed back to her and handed over the bag.

"Here. Thank you." He kissed her on the cheek and ran across the grass, heading toward the dorms.

Tavia waved to Devon's back and watched as he ran much like he did on the playing field—with purpose. She smiled, thinking of the first time she had fallen in love with Jonetta's father, Keith, and how she had felt each time they were together. In the beginning their love, much like Devon and Laurina, had been tested by each other, one trying to be sure, the other hoping their feelings weren't some game and each wondering if the other meant every word whispered at night.

Back then she had loved hard and had tried to make everything alright for Keith—had played crazy to make him sane, had shuttered her own intelligence as to not to overshadow his. And when he walked out, she hadn't shed a tear, for the truth is harder than a lie, and the truth was that she had been a pack mule, always piling his and Jonetta's needs upon her back.

Ten years into the marriage, when he asked for a divorce, she didn't fight it and was glad to unload the burden of being it all: wife, mother to two—birth to one—lover, therapist, analyst and cheerleader. She wouldn't have minded it had she had the same when she needed it. And in the years since, love to Tavia didn't exist. She hadn't met the man who made her pulse race, her palms itch, or that special spot ache to be touch, teased and pleasantly tortured.

She inhaled deeply and started walking slowly as her thoughts tumbled. No, there was no fairy tale—no dark knight to ride in and ravish her. She snickered at that thought. Umph, someone built like a brick, swinging at least eight and a face to put Morris Chestnut to shame. Hahmercy! She giggled just as her mind conjured up the image of the young professor.

From what she felt though his clothes, he was built like a brick. She was afraid to know if he was swinging eight, but she found herself attracted to him—found his nerdy-ness kind of cute and sexy. She wondered if she'd go out with him if he asked her. In the next breath she answered "yes." Yet, he didn't seem interested in her the few times she'd been in his presence. And Tavia wasn't about to ask him out. That was something she just didn't do—couldn't get used to the new ways of doing things. Nope, if Professor Wainwright didn't ask her out, then she guessed they'd never go out.

She slowed to a complete stop, turned and looked upward toward the English building. She saw him standing in the window, his hand raised in a wave. She returned the gesture, then continued across the campus and headed toward home.

Tavia climbed the stairs to her third floor loft, opened the door, then shut it behind her. She flipped through her mail and smiled at the "welcome" package from the all-inclusive resort in Jamaica. Slipping off her mules, Tavia padded barefoot across the Pergo flooring to sit in her overstuffed armchair, the one piece of furniture she had saved from her married days. Quickly opening the large white envelope with the gold embossed emblem of the resort, Tavia was in awe as she turned through page after page of the enclosed brochure, which outlined all the amenities Royal Plantation had to offer. She had asked Joanne how much the package cost and had been summarily chided to "keep quite and enjoy." Tavia smiled wide as she read the description of the two-bedroom, two-bath with Jacuzzi, private villa she would be staying in for an entire week.

"Too bad I don't have a date," she mused as she flipped a page to reveal the offering of a spa, which came with the private villa. As she continued to flip the pages, an image of the professor and herself lounging in the Jacuzzi sipping champagne seeped into her mind. She sat up quickly and looked around the room, then shook her head. She'd be on the island, and he'd be who knows where.

"Anyway, who needs a date when there are plenty of men on the island?" she asked herself out loud then thought about how Stella had found her groove. Tavia frowned—Stella's groove ended up with a hitch in the hips.

She stood suddenly. She needed to go shopping. There was no way she was going to pack anything in her closet in any suitcase she owned. No way. Besides, she reasoned with herself, she never splurged—had always been mindful of how she'd spent her money. But Tavia knew that new clothes were in order for this trip.

Walking to her bedroom, she opened the doors to her walk-in closet and shook her head at each article, including the shoe boxes neatly arranged on the floor.

"This will not do," Tavia mumbled, then headed to where she had left her purse and keys. "Spend just a little," she added as she climbed into her 1995 Jeep, tapping the accelerator and patting the dashboard, hoping "Betsy" would start up. Upon the third try, the vehicle finally kicked over and Tavia was on her way to indulge in a shopping spree.

Chapter 3

"I don't know how I let you two talk me into this," Lawrence said as he climbed out of the back seat of the SUV his sister and her fiancé had rented and headed into the mall as Jean dragged him by his hand. "This is crazy, Jean."

"No, your clothes are. Come on. Stop being such a big baby."

"I am not." He pulled his hand from her grip and folded them across his chest. Jean laughed as she gently took his hand in hers.

"You are going to be a hit in Jamaica. I promise. And I won't make you look odd or too hip, just add a little flavor to you."

"Flavor?" he barked, his eyes wide behind his glasses.

"No, Jean," Phillip spoke up. "Flavor is too drastic, sweetheart. Let's try to just update his attire a little."

"I like this man, Jean. He makes sense." Lawrence patted his future brother-in-law heartily on the back. Earlier when Phillip arrived, he had stood next to the man, sizing him up and noted Philip stood a few inches shorter and weighed maybe fifty pounds less, but he also noted that when Phillip looked at his sister, he did so with love and adoration.

"All right, Jean. Let's do this. But I don't want to be here all night. We still have those steaks to grill, and I need to get some rest."

"You sound like an old man. Let's go."

For nearly three hours, Jean and Phillip dragged Lawrence from one store to the next.

Lawrence watched as his sister held up a pair of linen slacks and a matching collar-less, button down shirt. He couldn't help but laugh as she tilted her head from one side to the next as she attempted to imagine her big brother dressed in the chosen attire.

"Now, that's hot. You wear that the first full day in Jamaica and you'll have more than one date, I guarantee you."

Phillip chuckled at Jean as she continued her shopping. She had chosen several pairs of slacks, in addition to the casual linen 2-piece, three pairs of walking shorts, a couple of knit, short sleeve shirts, two pull over T's, one pair of walking shoes and two pairs of sandals, two packages of boxer briefs in varying colors, two pairs of swim trunks and two bottles of cologne. Lawrence balked as he watched the bill roll well past seven hundred dollars.

"Next is the optometrist. You have got to stop hiding those beautiful eyes."

Lawrence shook his head and shrugged his shoulders. He glanced over at Phillip.

"Sorry, my brother." He held up his hands in mock surrender. "I can't help you. You know how your sister is. I suggest you go along with the program."

Lawrence chuckled and imitated Phillip when he held up his own hands.

After two hours of having his eyes checked, then measured for contacts, he sat through another hour of his sister choosing a pair of sunglasses, along with a pair of Dolce and Gabanna frames with prescription lenses.

"Okay, Jean, you've spent enough of my money." He stopped when his sister attempted to pull him into yet another store. "I'm tired and hungry, and this place is about to close." And though he was pleased with the purchases, he had never been big on shopping and what little patience he owned he had actually exhausted on the ride out to the mall.

"Okay, you're right on both accounts. How about we go to Pappadeaux's across from here?" she asked as she looked innocently from Lawrence to Phillip. Lawrence smiled at his baby sister. He looked at his wrist watch.

"Well, it's too late to cook." He looked at Philip. "I'm game—how about you?"

"I'm with her." He pointed to Jean, who beamed up at Phillip.

"Fine, then lets head over there before the rest of the folks in this mall get the same idea and we'll have to wait over an hour just to see the inside of the place."

After placing all of the purchases in the sheltered cargo area of the SUV, the trio walked across the parking lot to the restaurant. Jean chatted about his need to do something to his hair as they walked.

"Now, what's wrong with my hair?" He looked incredulously at her. "It's an Afro, Jean. And I've been seeing the kids on campus sporting them. Seems to me it's in now."

Jean sucked her teeth and rolled her eyes as they reached the restaurant. "And yours makes you look like Fredric Douglas. You should try some twists or maybe even go dread. This makes you look too old, Lawrence."

As they neared the glass doors, Lawrence stole a glance at his reflection. He hadn't really taken notice. Sure he got a cut on a regular, but he'd paid little to no attention to how it made him look. He had heard the snickers and had even once overheard a student refer to him as Professor Weird, but he didn't care about what they thought—he was a tenured professor of a prestigious university, a Noble Peace prize winner and all alone. He sobered at that final thought. He may have not cared what others thought, but he certainly didn't like being alone. He had to agree with Jean—Karen was history, it was time to move forward. Time to ask Tavia out on a date, and he knew once he returned from Jamaica he'd do just that.

Lawrence stepped forward to give his name and was told that there would be at least an hour's wait for a table.

"If you don't mind the company, you can sit with me. I'm about to sit at a table for four."

He looked over his shoulder. His eyes met the deep, slightly slanted eyes of Tavia Dennison.

"Ummm…Hi," he stammered as she stood next to the wait staff.

"Hi, yourself. You and your guests want to join me?"

Lawrence just stood there. He felt the tug on his arm, and then heard his sister's voice. "If you don't mind, we'd love to. I'm Jean, Lawrence's sister."

"Lawrence?"

"Oh, you probably call him Bartholomew. Family and friends call him Lawrence."

"Gotcha." Tavia extended her hand. "Nice to meet you. I'm Tavia Dennison. I teach over at the same university Bartholomew does."

Jean stepped on his foot, and Lawrence found his voice. "You can call me Lawrence, Tavia."

Tavia smiled up at him and looked into the somewhat sleepy eyes that met hers.

"I think they are waiting on us," Jean said as she grabbed Phillip's hand, stepped around the couple and followed the waiter. She paused to see Lawrence and Tavia standing there. She wanted to whistle out to them, but she also found their mutual attraction sweet—happy that maybe her big brother had finally found someone to shower some attention on him. Finally, Lawrence looked up and pointed to where Jean was leading.

As they made their way to the table, with Tavia walking in front of him, Lawrence took the opportunity to size up this woman who'd accidentally lain in his arms just a few hours earlier. He took in the silky-like smoothness of her curly hair and the way her shoulders seemed to sway with her slightly full hips. He forced his eyes upward to rest on her head full of curls. He wanted to touch them, twirl the curls gently around his fingers, and then pull her to him to rest on his chest as he met her lips with his.

He shook his head. What in the world was he thinking? A woman like Tavia wasn't to be mauled.

Tavia tried to contain the jiggle in her walk, but knew that the loose khaki material did little to hold it all together. She was tempted to turn around, to look up into his face, and see the serious softness in the beautiful eyes of the only black man she'd ever known as a Geek. Instead, she kept her head straight as she followed Jean and the greeter to their table.

How could this be happening? She mused. Earlier she had been shopping so much that her feet began to protest, but in spite of that she had continued onward until her stomach began to protest louder than her aching feet. A taste for seafood brought her to the restaurant. All she wanted was to sit, order a drink, eat some crab legs or tilapia and provide her feet and stomach with a little respite. She had just gotten word from the wait staff that they had a table only for large groups when she heard the sound of his deep, baritone voice as it reverberated across her skin, skimming and skipping, making her senses overload—it was both unmistakable and sensuous.

Lawrence held out the chair and waited for Tavia to sit. He bent slightly, inhaling the fragrance of coconut oil wafting up from her hair before he sat to her right. He barely noticed Jean and Phillip as they sat in chairs opposite them. He wanted to drop to his knees right then and there and thank whatever god had smiled on him and brought them together—he wasn't a man who believed in happenstance. Didn't believe in coincidences either—all equations added up to something. Dare he wonder?

"Do you come here often?" Jean asked Tavia.

"Yes, they have great seafood. But the service can get a little slow on really crowded nights," she turned her head to scan the patrons seated around them and came within inches of Lawrence's face. She was so close she could see the slight stubble on his smooth cheek, the specks of deep green in his eyes, feel the heat from his body, smell the wicked cologne he wore—an intoxicating mixture of bergamot, citrus and honey with a hint of coriander. Tavia thought he smelled good enough to eat!

"Excuse me," she said as she pulled back. Tavia sat up straight in her seat and cast her eyes down to the menu resting on the table in front of her. She flipped the pages quickly, her hands making busy work, but the words blurred as she thought of the heightened awareness of him each time she'd been in his presence.

Having ordered drinks, Tavia and Lawrence fell into an easy conversation that started with issues at the university, to the state of Black

America. Yeah, Tavia thought, this brother may be a nerd, but he definitely was well-rounded.

By the time their meals arrived, the two couples enjoyed a light banter, with Tavia hearing all about Lawrence and Jean's childhood.

At the end of the meal, Tavia passed on desert and informed Lawrence, Jean and Philip that she needed to be getting home. As Tavia reached inside her purse to pay her portion of the meal, her hand was covered by Lawrence's. She looked down at his large hand over hers and felt the warmth of it snake up her arm, then across her chest. She wondered what they would feel like touching her…

She pulled her hand from under his. "No, I can't let you do that." She glanced up into his eyes.

"Please allow me. My treat." He smiled at her.

"Thank you, Lawrence."

Tavia rose. Lawrence followed suit. "Allow me to walk you to your car, Tavia."

She nodded, bid goodnight to Jean and Philip and headed to the exit, Lawrence's hand rested at the small of her back.

Once they arrived at Tavia's Jeep, Lawrence removed the keys from her hand and opened the door. He gave the keys back and watched as she rolled down the window.

"Lawrence, thank you for joining me," she said as she leaned closer to the door. "I had a great time with you and your sister. She's really sweet."

Lawrence smiled. "Well, thank you for allowing us to intrude," he responded, his eyes cast down to the paved parking lot.

"I guess I better get going."

"Ahh, umm—yeah, I guess you better." He looked up at Tavia, then away. He wanted to ask her, wanted to see her again, cook for her, rub her feet. Cook for her and rub her feet? His mind asked. Where did that come from?

"Well, good night Lawrence. See you on campus." Tavia started up the vehicle and threw the car into drive. She wanted to kick herself. Why didn't she at least suggest he allow her to pay him back? Oh well, she thought, he's not interested—just being friendly.

Her mind tumbled and tossed over images and things she should have said, but didn't. Even as she readied herself for bed, she couldn't help but think about Lawrence, his beautiful eyes and his deep, smooth mellifluous voice. Heat pooled across her cheeks, down her chest and settled in the core of her body, the throbbing near maddening as her body responded, once again, to the mere thought of Lawrence.

Tavia took a cool shower in an attempt to quell the heat. After her shower she dressed in her favorite pajamas, a silk top and short set, then lay down in her bed. She settled on her left side as she pulled the body pillow close to her, her leg wrapped over one side. She pushed the pillow from her. She imagined holding Lawrence. Tavia shook her head, lay on her back and closed her eyes. Her eyes opened instantly as an image of Lawrence's smiling face popped behind her lids. She groaned and flipped over to her right side. She closed her eyes again, only to have the image of a naked, well-built Lawrence pop into her mind. She gave up and allowed the image of him, well formed and much endowed play out until she was panting, her body ached and center wet and throbbing.

Tavia hadn't felt this type of heat—hadn't ever wanted to feel the touch of a man across her body and in her body this bad in her life. Yet, here she was, her fingers trailing down to circle her clit, her hips rotated slowly as she thought about the man with the sensuous eyes and deep voice coming to her, in her, whispering how good she felt in her ear, filling her up. The more she thought about him, the faster her hips met her fingers until tears sprung from her eyes as the orgasm peaked, and then shattered around her.

She was breathing hard, the silk pajamas stuck to her chest. The release had brought some relief, but had no where near satisfied the growing ache she felt. She knew that there was only one person who could tame this fire, put out the heat that consumed her and soothe that ache just inside her core. And that person was Lawrence.

The following week, Tavia saw Lawrence at least ten times—and each time he smiled and waved, but didn't come talk to her. As a matter of fact, she thought he was avoiding her. Heck, she wasn't trying to have his babies, her tubes were tied, she just wanted to repay him for his kindness.

Her thoughts switched to the main topic that had been dueling for space in her mind along side Lawrence: Jamaica.

One day—one more day, she thought as her final class of the day wrapped up, and Tavia would be lounging on the pristine, white sandy beaches of Jamaica! Her early morning flight would end in Montego Bay and find her heading to the five-star, amenity heavy, Royal Plantation, in Ocho Rios, with their all ocean-view suites. Forget Lawrence! Jamaica men here I come!

Chapter 4

Lawrence stepped from the airplane, which had just landed at the Sangster International Airport in Montego Bay. He settled the sunglasses on his face, inhaled deeply and walked quickly into the terminal. During the nearly four-hour, non-stop flight, several women who were a part of a tour of seven, had engaged him in one idle conversation after another. Their conversations had been livened with innuendoes and sexual come-ones. Lawrence didn't know women could be so forward—on one hand he liked it—liked the lively back and forward volley of words and the images they conjured up in his mind. But on the other hand he wanted to be the one to choose, not be the chosen one.

He tried to escape the female crew and their blatant come-ons by excusing himself and heading to the plane's washroom. One of the women, who had been the boldest of the seven women, had allowed her hand to wisp across his butt as he headed to the rear of the jumbo jet. He had jumped, and she had only smiled and licked the tips of her fingers one by one before darting her long, pink tongue out at him. By the time the flight had landed, Lawrence had all but run from the plane.

As he searched for the complimentary limo that would take him from the airport to the resort, one women after another shot him bold glances, their smiles wide as they eyed him from head to toe, with one stating flat out that if he'd come over for dinner, she'd be his desert!

He became self-conscious, especially after one woman's eyes seem to settle on his crotch area, her mouth slightly agape. He looked down and wondered what on earth was she looking there for? He knew at that moment he shouldn't have worn the linen pants and matching shirt, nor should he have let Jean talk him into the twists. Ever since he'd gotten them, the day before he left Urbana for Jamaica, women had been doing a double take—something he'd never experienced before.

"You know, what goes on in Jamaica, stays in Jamaica," the crotch-watcher whispered in his ear as she passed so close that he felt the tips of her nipples brush his arm. Lawrence's eyes widened.

"Brother, we gonna hang out with you," Lawrence heard a deep voice say nearby. "You're a babe magnet." The man walked up to him and extended his right hand. "Donald. Donald Moultrie. And this is my cousin, Tommy, same last name."

Lawrence took the extended hand and shook it. "Are the women always this forward?"

Donald laughed. "Always. That's why I like it here. I mean, I pretend I live here, cause them the only brothers getting any."

"Getting any? Any what?" Lawrence's eyes were wide. He may not have gotten out much, but if this guy was saying what he thought he was, hell, he was ready to get back on that plane and head home. He wasn't trying to be no woman's sex toy. He thought about Tavia. No, he didn't want to be her toy, but he sure would like to see her again, take her out, get to know her better, have her lay her head against his chest as she did the day at the pool. He looked at the two men standing next to him.

"Aww, that's the game." Donald tapped Lawrence lightly on the shoulder. "Act like you stupid. No wonder the women on you. Tommy, we gotta get dumb."

"Look. I'm just here to relax," Lawrence began. "I'm not here to score, get any, or sleep with a bunch of women I don't know."

Donald and his cousin looked at each other, their eyes narrowed. Donald stepped back. "You ain't one-na them are you?" He flipped his wrist downward.

"One of what?" Lawrence asked as his annoyance level rose higher. He'd just about had enough. First the women, now this brother. "Brother, what are you talking about?"

"Gay," Tommy spat out so loud the nearby women turned in their direction and stared.

"No, I'm not gay, but I..." Lawrence shut his mouth, held up his right hand, shook his head, and then turned and headed into the terminal to retrieve his luggage. All he wanted to do on this day was rest.

He'd had a hell of a time getting to O'Hare Airport; his car had a flat on the way. Once he arrived, the flight was delayed by three hours. To add to it all, the women and their continued hints that he should sleep with one of them, if not all of them. Even though the woman who had touched his rear end was quite attractive he had thought of inviting her out to dinner once they arrived, but quickly changed his mind after she'd copped the free feel, and then wickedly suckled her fingers.

At the luggage turnstile, Lawrence spotted a tall, reed thin man, the color of rich coffee, as he stood nearby holding a sign with Lawrence's name on it.

"I'm Bartholomew Wainwright," he said as he approached the older gentleman. Lawrence noted the man's clear, brown eyes sparkled as he took the sign in one hand and shook Lawrence's hand with his free one.

"And I'm Abraham, Mr. Wainwright. I'll be your driver and valet during your stay at Royal Plantation. Let's get your luggage and get started. We've about a forty minute ride to the resort."

"Nice meeting you Mr. Abraham. And please call me Lawrence." He had said to the valet, noting the man looked old enough to be his father, and he would grant him the respect of such.

They nodded at each other and made small talk as they waited for Lawrence's luggage. Once they found the two pieces, Lawrence followed his valet out of the airport to the curb where a black, stretch limousine sat. He watched as Mr. Abraham clicked the remote and the trunk rose. Lawrence stepped to the door and was waved away as Mr. Abraham rushed over and opened the door. Just as Lawrence was about to enter the vehicle, he looked over to his right and noted that the group from the airplane was climbing into a min van. He guessed the group was staying at another hotel. He wasn't quite sure if he should be overly relieved by that fact. He had hoped to meet other black folks like himself; so far he'd only attracted what amounted to crazy people.

Lawrence settled into the rear of the cool, roomy interior, laying his head back against the soft leather of the seats. He closed his eyes and wasn't surprised at the face that appeared. Her face had been appearing with more and more frequency since he'd seen her at the pool. And the impromptu dinner didn't help matters. Each time he thought about her, he got warm all over and he became hard as granite. He felt like a randy teen and not a grown man, but he couldn't deny how he felt and knew that he was more than mildly attracted to her. He was crazy about Tavia. He'd made up his mind. Once he returned, he was going to ask her out.

His body began to sink further into the seats as he felt the vehicle pull from the curb. He opened his eyes and watched through the smoke-colored window as the scenery turned from what he considered rural to pristine. He gasped loudly at the beautifully shoreline that rolled past them. He asked questions about the weather and people, and listened intently as Mr. Abraham responded in his smooth native patois, ending by telling Lawrence that he was the first non-celebrity to come to the resort in some time.

"How do you know I'm not some celebrity?" Lawrence chuckled. "I could be a famous football player. Or one of those rap guys."

"No." Mr. Abraham looked up into the rear view mirror. "Your whole aura speaks different. You are self-assured, not arrogant. There is a difference."

Lawrence nodded.

"Mr. Wainwright,"

"Lawrence," he corrected.

"Lawrence, will you be dining in your room? Or may I make a suggestion?"

"You're my valet. You suggest."

"Great. We will get you settled, and then I will set up your meal on the veranda."

The pair continued to talk, and then became silent when Lawrence saw the resort come into view. All the stress and trepidation Lawrence had felt eased out of his body, and he smiled warmly at the large yellow building, its white columns and marble fountain out front belied the jewel that lay ahead.

"Lawrence, welcome to Royal Plantation."

Chapter 5

Miss Dennison?" the man standing nearby asked as he held a card in front of him with her name spelled in black block letters.

Tavia looked up from her place on the floor, where her garment bag had exploded, her clothes hanging out of the sides. She nodded her head and stood.

"Yes, I'm Tavia Dennison."

"I am Jonathan. I will be your driver and valet during your stay at Royal Plantation," he said as he stooped and began picking up her clothing. "No, please let me. I've a garment bag in the trunk. I'll be right back."

She watched as Jonathan walked away and returned moments later with a plastic garment bag. He carefully placed the items from her destroyed one into the plastic one. She was truly grateful. The trip had started out as promising, then quickly turned into one mishap after another once she arrived at O'Hare International Airport. She had been bumped from her flight, had waited five hours to get another one, and then got to the airport in Jamaica only to find her luggage looking as if it'd been eaten by hungry lions, the seams and ends torn and ragged.

"Thank you, Jonathan," she exhaled. "I'm sure glad to see you."

"So am I. I was beginning to think you were lost. The earlier flight had arrived, and I didn't see you."

"Thank you for waiting. I'd be totally lost."

"Well, you are in Jamaica now, and I will take care of you," he assured Tavia as he placed the last of her clothing into the garment bag. Zipping it up and then pulling her suitcase by the handle, Jonathan led Tavia out of the airport and to the waiting white Lincoln Town car, the windows tinted.

Jonathan held the door and waited as Tavia dropped her body onto the seat. After several moments, whereby Jonathan deposited her luggage into the truck, he slid into the driver's seat. He turned to face her.

"Here," he handed her a glass of champagne. "We'll be arriving at the resort in a little under an hour. Sip this and unwind."

Tavia smiled as she sipped the sparkling wine. She had slipped off her high-heeled sandals the moment Jonathan shut the rear door and inhaled deeply. Finally, her mind sang, she was in Jamaica and heading toward one of the most exclusive resorts in all of Jamaica. Tavia became giddy and thought back to the last time her toes tingled like this. Umph, it was when Lawrence had held her after pulling her from the pool. She could still see the beauty of his eyes. She wondered how he was spending his spring break as she drained her glass, and then laid her head back against the cool leather seats.

Tavia jumped at the hand that had reached out to lightly shake her. She looked around her, and her mouth fell open as she took in the majestic view standing before her. Slowly she stepped from the Town car, her bare feet on the cool white and tan colored stones that lined the path to the large, pristine plantation house, painted a cool yellow and supported by four white columns. She followed him inside, her bare feet loving the feel of the smooth, marble-like bricks. She knew it looked country, but she didn't care. As a matter of fact, she wanted to be barefoot as much as possible during her week stay, and she knew her first order of business was to sink her body into the ocean.

Tavia was in love—everything looked perfect and so far had been. While she checked in, Jonathan had taken her belongings to her villa and then came back to lead her through the garden, stopping to show her the short cut to the ocean before opening the pale peach door that lead to the villa which would home for the next five days.

Her eyes widened as she stepped on the cool white tiles of the living room, floor to ceiling windows gave a spectacular view of the ocean below. She walked further inside, noting the butter colored interior decorated with wicker chairs, with floral overstuffed cushions. She looked up to see Jonathan smiling at her as she walked slowly behind him, taking in the beauty of the exterior. Her villa was situated near the end of a row of private villas, each separated by rows of fresh, green vegetation. Up several flights of stairs, Tavia watched as Jonathan opened the white double doors. She stifled the urge to squeal—the large poster bed with mosquito netting was the focal point of the bed, a matching nightstand, armoire and dresser sat tastefully around the room. Tavia wanted to climb onto the bed but changed her mind as she looked over to the sitting area. She stepped down into the area and opened the large French doors, which led to a private veranda where she could see and hear the ocean. This was it! An image of Lawrence popped into her head. She could only wish.

"Jonathan this is so beautiful. I think I'm in heaven."

He smiled, placed her luggage on a rack and opened them. He began to arrange her clothes on hangers and hung them in the armoire followed by placing her things in the drawers and her toiletries in the bathroom. Tavia was still standing near the opening to the veranda when she heard Jonathan call out to her.

"Would you care for a light meal after your swim?"

"Oh, that would be great. I'm going to change. I'll be back and ready in two hours. Thank you." She smiled at him and watched as he nodded his understanding.

"If you need me." He handed her a cell phone. "Just hit the number two, and I'll be where ever you are." He stepped back. "Enjoy your swim."

"Thank you. I will."

Lawrence sat on the chaise lounge at the far end of the veranda and sipped the rum punch Mr. Abraham had brought for him. After finishing his meal of chicken salad with raisins and nuts on sweet black bread, with a side of waffle fries, he settled back and listened to the sounds of the ocean. The sun was setting, and to Lawrence it was the most magnificent thing he'd ever seen. He took another sip, and then watched as a woman, dressed in a white two-piece swimsuit, the bottom barely covered her ample derrier, came into his view. He smiled when she began to skip, twisting and turning her body around and around. Laughing to himself, he knew the feeling—he had been tempted to do the same thing but settled on non-activity for his first day on the island. As the woman got closer to the water, he continued to watch her and felt there was something familiar about her.

He became fascinated as the woman waded out into the water a few feet before diving head first under the water. Lawrence stood up, having lost sight of her. His eyes remained where she'd dived, but she had yet to resurface. He pulled his shirt from his body and had turned to rush out of his villa when he looked back and saw the form of her head break the surface. He righted his shirt, sat back down and watched in rapt attention as the women smoothly backstroked across the crystal blue water. To say he was hypnotized was putting it mildly—Lawrence found the figure slicing through the water, her legs lifted slightly above the water, rather appetizing. He could make out the outline of a full bust line, a small tummy pouch and toned thighs. He shook his head. *What am I doing?* He felt a bit perverted, sitting on his veranda watching the obvious outline of a feminine body, but he also found the view oddly erotic and the pull to watch her overly stimulating. He then noticed the form disappear under the water and resurface moments later as she began the forward stroke toward the shore. He continued to watch as she walked up the beach and headed toward the entrance just ten feet from his own. He thought she'd looked his way, and he raised his hand in a wave, but quickly put it down to his side and knew she hadn't even noticed him.

Lawrence took another sip of his drink and refocused his eyes on the warm setting sun slowly dipping below the horizon.

Tavia felt the eyes watching her every movement—had felt it when she first stepped out of her villa and onto the beach. Jonathan, her valet, had said that she and another American, a black male, were the only two on this side of the beach. The ten villas were normally full, but the beginning of the season hadn't really started yet. With that in mind, she had half hoped she'd see her neighbor, and half hoped not to. She really wanted some quiet time, snatch a bit of solitude before being bombarded with the normal touristy questions: Where are you from? You came by yourself? Tavia was accustomed to the questions, seeing has how she'd been traveling alone for several years.

She could see the figure from the corner of her eye. She didn't dare look directly at him—he could just be sitting there napping, he seemed to sit so still. And when she dove into the water, she felt free as the warm tropical water covered her body, and then buoyed her effortlessly to the surface, where she floated on her back before beginning a backstroke. After a half hour of swimming, she'd gotten out of the ocean and headed to her villa and that's when she saw him, his dark complexion and hair. She couldn't see the rest of him, but she knew he was there and had been watching her. She rushed to her villa, an electric excitement skittered up and down her body, settling in the core of body. Never in her forty-five years of life had she ever been so turned on by such a simple and common practice; but it was something about the eyes watching her.

Tavia closed the door to her villa and rested her back on it. Her breathing came in short pants and slight beads of perspiration dotted her forehead and the valley between her breasts. She knew she was just on the verge of menopause, but she had never felt a flash like this.

"I'm tripping," Tavia said aloud in an attempt to get her act together. She looked around the villa and rushed to her bedroom. A nice shower and then some dinner, followed by a good book out on the veranda would do her some good. "Yeah, that's what I need—a nice cool off." She rushed to her bedroom and began taking off her swimsuit. She stilled and looked out of the doors leading to the veranda. Her mind was playing tricks on her, for she thought she'd seen his eyes staring into her own. She shut her eyes tightly, shook her head ,then opened them. The image was gone.

"Umm, I need to get a drink or something. I'm imaging things." The veranda was at least ten feet above ground.

After her shower, Tavia dressed in a floral print, spaghetti strap sundress she'd purchased the day she bumped into Bartholomew. Or did he prefer Lawrence? She heard his sister, Jean, call him Lawrence. Actually, she liked both names. One gave him an air of old-world sophistication, while the other was common but seemed to fit him well. Tavia picked up the phone near the large mahogany poster bed. She stood near the bed covered in a beautiful cream-colored spread with sheers above and surrounding the posters as she dialed Jonathan's number.

"Yes, Ms. Dennison?"

"Jonathan, what's the special tonight at the Bayside restaurant?"

Tavia listened as he rattled off several mouth-watering dishes. She had flipped through the room-service menu earlier and though she'd found some appetizing items, she wanted to know what the restaurant featured. After Jonathan finished, she said, "Sounds too tempting. I think I'll dine in the restaurant."

"Excellent choice. I'll turn down your bed while you are dining. Will you require any thing else?"

"No, I'm fine. I'll speak with you tomorrow."

"Please do not hesitate to contact me if needed."

"Thank you, Jonathan. I will." She replaced the phone, grabbed her white, lace-like shawl, slipped her feet into three-inch sandals with a strap around the ankle and headed out of the villa to the path that would take her to the restaurant. Tavia inhaled the sweet fragrance of the flowers that lined the path, which was lit by flaming torches. She looked up into the dark sky and noticed the bright moon and stars. She felt as if she were truly in paradise.

For the umpteenth time since their impromptu dinner date, she thought of Lawrence. She shook her head and continued on her way, as her stomach growled loudly.

"Welcome to the Bayside Restaurant. You must be Ms. Dennison," the waitress said in a smooth voice, her patois slight and barely noticeable. "Jonathan asked me to take care of you, and I have taken the liberty to select what I think will be a perfect seat for you. Please follow me."

Tavia smiled as she followed the waitress through the restaurant and out to a large out-door dining area. Several couples sat among the tables set for two or four, each covered by pristine white cloths topped with decorative hurricane lamps; the candle inside was lit and dancing. Tavia followed the waitress and nodded enthusiastically when the waitress stopped at a table for two next to the railing, which was the only obstruction between her and the ocean.

"This is great. Thank you."

"I'm glad you approve," the waitress said. "I'll bring you a glass of wine and you take your time perusing the menu. I'll be back shortly."

Tavia leaned on the highly polished wood rail and peered over the side. Lights lit up the bottom of the ocean floor as tropical fish swam lazily about. She closed her eyes and inhaled the clean smell of the ocean breeze. She was truly happy to be in Jamaica. And to think, just scant hours before she had been in the hustle of O'Hare airport, now she was in paradise.

"Excuse me?" the voice behind her said. She turned slightly in her chair and noted the brown hands resting on the chair directly behind her. Her eyes traveled up the hand to the sleeve of the white gauze-type shirt. "Umm," Tavia began. Her eyes widened as she took in the form standing near her. She knew him. Knew she had seen this dark, chocolate god standing before her somewhere before. Had to have been in her dreams, though, for she would never forget a brother that fine if she'da met him in person.

"Tavia?" she heard the brother call her by her name.

"Tavia, it's me. Lawrence." She blinked and then squinted her eyes. "You know, Bartholomew Wainwright from Urbana."

Shut up, her mind screamed. Not the geek. She looked him up and down. Gone were the glasses, the ill-fitting pants and the wild afro. In its placed stood a brother who exuded sexuality, the off-white tunic and pants complimented his deep complexion, his eyes twinkled in the light of the candles and twists were arranged neatly about his round head. Tavia inhaled the musky fragrance of his cologne and swallowed hard. She crossed her legs—that funny sensation was back with a vengeance. And she didn't want to say a word, for fear something stupid would come out.

No way! This can't be Professor Weird.

"Tavia, you okay?

She nodded her head and knew she'd have to say something or else he'd think she had gone and gotten daft on him. "Wow!" was the only word that came out. She shook her head again and tore her eyes away from the too-fine brother standing over her. "Umm, you, can…umm, feel me. Oh, umm, no. I mean, you can sit down."

Lawrence chuckled and did as she requested. He was surprised when he noticed her sitting near the rail. He called out her name to make sure he wasn't hallucinating since he'd been thinking of her almost nonstop since the dinner. He looked into her face and watched as the light from the candle danced in her eyes. He smiled at her.

"Okay, since I don't believe in coincidences, how did you come to be in Jamaica the same time as me?" Lawrence asked, crossed his arms over his massive chest, and then leaned back in his chair.

Tavia inhaled deeply and watched as he reared back and stretched out his long legs, his sandal clad feet brushed up against her ankles. She noted the way the light fabric strained against his arms, and as her eyes took a leisurely tour upward, they came to rest on his smile, warmingly wicked, followed by his eyes, bedroom brown. Wait! she mused. *What am I thinking?*

She blew her breath out slowly through partly opened lips. "A friend of mine had booked this trip month's ago with a man she was dating, and they recently broke up, so she gave the room to me as a belated birthday gift. What about you?"

"Same here, but it was a friend of a friend."

They exchanged names of their respective friends and found that the only connect was that they were all professors at the university.

"Just the same, I'm glad you're here." He looked at her, the woman who had tormented his dreams and occupied many of his waking moments. His eyes took her in, from the top of her curly hair to the smooth color of her skin to the small hands, her nails painted a wicked red, that wrapped themselves around the glass of wine the waitress had brought just moments ago. He realized at that moment that the woman he was watching swim was Tavia. Just the same, he wanted to make sure. "Were you swimming earlier?"

"Yup," she responded, nodding her head up and down. "Was that you I felt watching me?" she asked as her eyes narrowed and her mouth turned into a playful pout. For some inexplicable reason, she felt giddy, almost like a schoolgirl as she looked at this brother across from her.

He nodded his head. "I'm guilty. I didn't mean to intrude."

She smiled at his politeness. It was so endearing. They fell into small talk as the waitress appeared, took their orders, left and returned. They both ordered steaks, his medium and hers well-done. They topped the meal with dessert—key lime pie. After the meal, Lawrence suggested they take a walk. Tavia agreed and allowed him to assist her from her seat.

Lawrence threaded her hand into the crook of his arm as they strolled lazily along the beach, their conversation peppered with laughter.

Tavia thought she detected a hint of a southern accent as she listened to him talk about his life, his family and how he felt being an "egg head" and a "geek" as he had heard many say behind his back. A few bold ones stated it directly to his face. She sensed that at one time those things had hurt him, but now, as one of the highest paid professors at the university and a Noble Prize winner on top of that, he was surely having the last laugh.

"I've been talking for hours." He paused and looked down at Tavia. "Tell me about you."

Tavia laughed and complied, told him about her daughter, her love of the written word and how long she'd been a professor.

As they continued to walk, their conversation flowed so naturally that Tavia felt as if she'd known Lawrence forever. Now she wished she had gone up to him the day she saw him lecturing at the conference—she hadn't had a clue that he was interested.

She didn't say a word as Lawrence took her hand in his—swinging gently back and forward as they continued to walk further down the beach.

Tavia looked around—the lights from the hotel were barely discernable, and there wasn't a soul in sight. In the distance ahead of them, she spotted an oblong form that she couldn't quite make out. They continued until they could make out the oblong form: a white chaise lounger, its legs sunk into the sand, water lapped at its base. Lawrence stopped.

"I've been crazy about you from the moment I laid eyes on you months ago," he spoke quickly, then without warning, lowered his head and captured Tavia's lips with his, his arms snaked around her body and pulled her close. He couldn't control what they both felt bulging from the thin material of his linen pants. Lawrence pulled his lips from hers and heard the heavy breathing from them both. "I'm sorry. I…I—" His apology was interrupted when Tavia rose to the tips of her toes and kissed him back. Her lips parted his as her tongue darted in and out of his mouth, insinuating the wicked, sensuous, heady, throbbing sensations of just what he wanted to do to her. Her hands raked across his head, pulling him closer. He felt the hard pebbles of her nipples, and he ground the knowing bulge of his penis into her heat. He wanted to scream when she began grinding against him, her hands stroking his back before making their way down to his ass.

Reluctantly, he broke the kiss, but knew, felt deep within him that if he didn't this moment would be lost, and he couldn't allow that.

"Please," he breathed as he led her to the lounger nearby.

Lawrence sat down, his legs on either side. Tavia straddled his lap, took his face in her hands and began kissing his face, starting at his flat forehead, moving down his broad nose, the dimple in his chin, then finally his lips, nipping and suckling them into her own. She groaned loudly as Lawrence's thumbs rubbed the tips of her nipples through the fabric and she pressed her heat into his groin. She thought that if what she felt was real, she was in trouble. She had never had anything this large.

Her mind scrambled as he continued to play with her nipples. She reared backward, giving him access to her breasts as he slid the straps down her shoulders, the fabric across her bodice. He unhooked the strapless bra, freeing her breasts to the warm breeze and the bright moon overhead.

"You are so beautiful. May I suck your titties, please?" he asked, a wicked glint in his eyes as he licked his lips salaciously. Tavia knew she wanted to feel those same lips on hers, and she didn't mean the lips on her face.

"Do you know how?" she brazenly asked.

He answered by flicking his tongue across one nipple, his forefinger traced lazy circles around the other. He switched several times before he pushed her breasts together and feasted on them as if starving. Tavia wanted to cry, the pure carnal pleasure of it all caused her entire body to ache with need.

"Baby, stand up for me," he ordered and watched as she pulled herself slowly from his lap. "Take off your dress."

She did as he ordered and pushed the fabric down her hips. She was pleased when she heard the sharp intake of breath—the thong worked its own magic.

"Take that off," he pointed to her thong. "And then hand it to me."

His deep voice had hypnotized her, and she followed his orders, sliding the flimsy material from her and passed it to him. She wanted to fall to her knees as he brought the crotch of the thong up to his nose and inhaled, his eyes fluttered close. When he opened them, she was startled. In all of her years, she had never seen desire and lust mixed with such raw passion.

"Come here," he said as he rose from the chaise. "Lay down."

She complied. Covering the short distance slowly, she turned her back to him and crawled onto the chaise, her ass jutting upward, before rolling over and lying on her back. Once on her back, she allowed her fingers to twirl in the long tufts of her pubic hair.

This man was making her brazen—wanton. And she had never felt this way in her life. She wondered who this man was that one day he looked like a geek, acting all shy and reserved, and the next he looked good enough to eat, giving her orders that she aptly followed without question.

Lawrence pulled off his shirt, then dropped to his knees. He removed her sandals with his teeth, pulling the straps loose before removing the shoes from her feet. He licked each toe, suckling and licking before he kissed his way up her thighs. Tavia grabbed his head as he blew, then nipped at the hidden bud between her legs.

"Tavia, am I teasing you?" he asked as he sucked, then nipped, then sucked, then nipped at her clit. "Can I have you? Can I slide all of me inside of you?"

She couldn't talk, the sensations he had awakened and set out to conquer had her mindless. All she could think of was the orgasm that hung on the precipice. She shut her eyes tightly and thrust her hips into his face as he began to suck on her clit in earnest, grabbing her ass and holding her captive as his tongue and lips made love to her. She tensed, then cried out as the first orgasm grabbed her at the same time that she grabbed his head. Shamelessly, she ground her pelvis into his face and rode out the wonderful sensations his oral assault elicited.

When she felt his finger outline the area around her vagina, she opened her eyes in time to see Lawrence lick his lips then insert a finger in his mouth before inserting it into her vagina, slowly intimating intercourse.

"Tell me, my love, what do you want me to do next?"

Without thinking, Tavia replied, "Take off your pants."

Smiling, he removed his finger from her, licked it, then rose to his feet. He untied the drawstring that held the trousers up and slid them from his hips, followed by the white boxer-briefs. Tavia wanted to run. She wasn't that great at math, but her mind calculated at least eight inches in length and five around. She was in trouble. It had been years, and she wasn't sure she could handle a magnificent masterpiece that large. But on the other hand, she had to admit, the length and girth rose curiosity in her. She motioned him closer with a crook of her finger. He obliged until he and his penis were mere inches from her face.

Taking the offered gift in her hand, she tried to enclose it in the palm of her hand and found she couldn't. She kissed the tip of his penis and suckled the head.

"Tavia, I won't last if you keep that up. I need you. NOW!" He picked her up from the chaise. She wrapped her legs around his waist as he sat down. She grinded her clit up and down his penis as her vagina made strange sucking noises, like it had a mind of its own.

"Baby, you must be ready?" he asked as he reached out to his discarded pants and retrieved the condom. He quickly opened the package and rolled the sheath over his throbbing penis. He then laid back, lifted her above him and slowly lowered her vagina onto his thick penis.

"Damn," he hissed as her tightness enveloped him centimeter by centimeter, until she had sheathed him completely. He held her hips to keep her from moving. "Oh, my goodness, baby, you feel so good. I could love you forever. Don't move. Please, don't move."

But Tavia couldn't grant that one request, as her hips began an up and down rhythm, clinching on the down stroke, barely releasing on the upstroke. She fit him like a glove and the added sensation of feeling full only drove her further as her hips danced wildly.

"Lawrence. Give it to me. Give it all to me." She leaned over him and whispered in his ear, her entire body ground into his, her nipples flattened on his hairy, muscular chest. When she felt his hands roam up and down her sides, rubbing the sides of her breasts, she raised her body slightly and watched as he suckled her nipples, pulling the hardened pebbles into his mouth, biting them gently, then sucking them, letting his tongue snake out around the dark areola. She wanted to scream as her body ground into his urgently.

"That's it, baby. Take me. Take it all," he said as she began to ride him harder; her breasts bounced to her movements. He watched and listened as her vagina spoke to him, the suckling noise made him harder. He'd had a few women before, but he'd never had one as passionate as Tavia. He was gone. He was in love.

Picking her up, he switched their position. Holding her close, he gently laid her on her back, with his ass near the edge of the chaise and her thighs resting over his. He had accomplished this without allowing his penis to leave the tightness of her vagina.

"Come for me again, Tavia."

He began to stroke her—both with his penis sliding in and out of her and his thumb gently circling her clit. He knew she was close by the way her vagina grabbed and squeezed him. He wanted to come so bad, but knew he wanted to see her face, the way it contorted as her eyes rolled into the back of her head, her bottom lip bitten down on.

"Come for me, my love. Come for me." He ordered as he began to pump into her, his thumb frantically circling her clit. And when she screamed out his name, he continued his sensual assault, allowing her hips to slam into his. He was captivated as he watched his penis slide in and out of her vagina. When he felt her muscles give a little, he pulled from her with a smooth pop and rolled her over on her stomach, sliding back inside of her, pulling her hips to back up to his pelvis. He placed his hands around the front of her and began plying and lightly tweaking her nipples between his thumb and forefinger.

His motions were fluid, as he pumped in and out of Tavia. Lawrence heard her tell him what to do and how to do it. They were words he'd only heard in a porno movie, but unlike the porno movie, her words were turning him on to the point of no return. He slid in and out of her faster, wanted to cry when she rose up and her full, luscious ass began to continuously and melodically hit his pelvic bone. The ecstasy of it all was in itself an undoing, and he pumped into her viciously as her words filled the air.

He pulled from her again, turned her, and lifted her above him as she wrapped her legs and arms around him. Her slickness allowed him to ease into her and he sighed loudly as she tightened her vaginal walls around him and she whispered, "Baby, you cum for me. You are so good. And so big." He lost it, pumping furiously into her tightness—his penis throbbed uncontrollably as he reached his orgasm.

He gently laid her back onto the chaise, and then covered her with his body, supporting his weight on his side. He kissed and stroked her face as the moon overhead cast a sensuous glow across their bodies.

"Are you okay?" he asked.

"Yes, Lawrence, I'm okay. How about you?"

"I've never been better." He pulled her into his arms and kissed her deeply.

Tavia snuggled into his massive chest. They lay in each other's arms for what seemed like hours, touching and talking and feeling each other until their bodies were awakened again.

"I think we need to take this back to the villa," Lawrence said as he dressed Tavia, pulled the condom from his semi-hard erection before putting on his own clothes. He held up her thong.

"You won't need these," he waved the thong around his finger, then placed the garment into his right pocket and the used latex in the nearby trashcan. "Come on, I'll give you a piggy back ride back." He squatted down and waited for Tavia to climb onto his back. They passed two couples, both under blankets, outlines of bodies moving, sounds of loud moans. Lawrence smiled when she heard Tavia giggle close to his ear. He almost dropped her when she began to kiss his neck, trailing her tongue down the side of it.

"Baby, that's gonna get you in more trouble."

She ignored him and stretched her hands downward until she reached his nipples where she circled, and then gently pinched them between her fingers. His breath hitched, and she knew that tonight, her first night in Jamaica, wouldn't be one she'd ever forget.

Chapter 6

Tavia awoke and smiled. She was lying next to the man she had wondered about many a day. The sound of the waves rolling to and from shore could be overheard as she took the opportunity to examine this enigma asleep in her bed. She lightly traced the outline of his full lips slightly apart—a soft snore escaped between them. Her mind replayed the wicked things those lips had done to her body over and over again. She hadn't had many men, but she didn't think many had the stamina Lawrence had. Tavia then thought about his body and remembered the hard planes of muscle when she'd held on to him. She wanted to see all of him—especially that part of him that had her saying things and doing things she'd never thought she'd do.

She slowly peeled the sheet from his massive chest, the hairs on it curled all across his chest. She continued, as the unveiling exposed the beautiful body of this dark, sexy god, inch by engrossing inch, until she had the sheet pooled around his lower legs. Her eyes traveled down to his penis. Even flaccid he was big.

"Do you like what you see?" a deep sleepy voice said. He lifted her to lie on top of him. "'Cause I sure like what I see," he nipped on her bottom lip as his hands traveled lazily up and down her body.

Tavia knew this man had awakened a sleeping lioness. She had never been this sexually satisfied, and she found it both intriguing and scary, for each time she'd allow him to enter her he left something behind, a piece of him that she would carry for life. No, she wasn't thinking of pregnancy, they had used condoms, she was thinking about the way their hearts beat and how they fit perfectly into the close spaces of each other. She had never believed in love at first sight, had always believed in the slow-burn of love, yet as he entered her, slowly, methodically, her mind and body grabbed him, held him tight and wrapped itself around him. If she had to believe in love at first sight, then Lawrence was it and she'd have to deal with the "how come" of it all later. Right now she had a man with a rather large bone to deal with.

For the rest of the week, Tavia and Lawrence were inseparable. He had moved out of his villa and into hers—telling their respective valets that both wouldn't be needed, and they flipped a coin to see which one's services they would utilize for the rest of the week. Jonathan had won, and Tavia felt she had to explain to him how long she'd known Lawrence, for he had been lying in her bed when Jonathan came to check on her.

On the second day of their Spring Break, they had lounged lazily around the villa, ordering room service, talking and making love in each of the rooms when the notion hit either of them. They were like elixir to each other.

On the third day, they had decided to go to a privately owned beach. Tavia whistled at Lawrence when he stepped out of their villa wearing stark white swimming trunks, his thighs peeked out from under them. She was glad he wore long trunks and not Speedos—she didn't want another woman to see what she was getting. His eyes appraised her, looking her up and down, admiring the banana yellow, thigh high one-piece that dipped low, resting just at the top of her full behind. A green sheer sarong was wrapped around her waist.

They held hands as they made their way to the waiting limo that would take them from Royal Plantation to the beach where they'd spend the day. Lawrence waved away Jonathan as they approached the limo. He held open the door for Tavia, then climbed in behind her. She looked at the basket sitting on the floor.

"I took the liberty of having Jonathan pack us a picnic. I thought we'd stay at the beach all day, lounge, do a few water sports, shop, have a little dinner." He moved closer. "And maybe dance into the night with me in you."

Tavia chuckled, the spot he had touched, felt, licked, invaded just hours earlier began to tingle.

He wrapped his arms around her shoulder, and she leaned her head on his as they watched the lush green scenery roll lazily by.

After about forty minutes, the limo came to a stop and Lawrence stepped out, assisting Tavia from the vehicle. He took the basket, tote bag and beach blanket from Jonathan.

"We'll call you when we're ready to return." They waved at Jonathan as he climbed back into the vehicle. Tavia took the tote and blanket from Lawrence's arms, and then followed him to the concession stand near the boardwalk that led to the private beach. He removed his wallet from the tote, purchased two tickets to enter, then paid an additional fare to rent jet skis.

He took Tavia's hand in his, and they walked onto the beach, both looking for a good spot to lay out the blanket. They continued until Tavia spotted an area where rocks jutted up from the water. She motioned for them to walk to the rocks. Lawrence assisted Tavia as they climbed over the rocks and found a private spot further down the beach. She laid out the large blanket—big enough for both of them to lay on, then opened the tote, pulling out the small, compact, CD player, her book and a bottle of tanning lotion for her and sun block for Lawrence. She shielded her eyes as Lawrence stood nearby, his eyes hidden behind a pair of dark Ray Bans.

"I've got to be dreaming," she heard him say as he finally sat down next to her on the blanket. He picked up her hand and kissed it. "Pinch me, baby. Cause there is just no way that this geeky country boy is here with you, Ms. Dennison."

"You aren't geeky."

He chuckled. "You wouldn't give me the time of day."

She looked out onto the blue-green water; the waves rolled in and out, the horizon seemed blurred by the heat. He was wrong. She'd wanted to go out with him. She just didn't think he was interested and she told him so. "You're kidding, right?"

He looked at her, his eyebrows raised.

Tavia shook her head. "Every time I saw you I spoke and tried to come up with conversation, but it never happened. I just thought you weren't interested or you had someone. I had no idea you were shy. With the exception of…" She smiled at him and raised her right eyebrow. She watched his deep color grow darker. He was blushing, and she found it charming.

Tavia turned on her CD player, and the sounds of George Benson seeped out of the small speakers. She rubbed tanning lotion on her arms. Lawrence took the bottle from her and began applying the thick liquid to her legs, slowly, kneading her until her breathing became hitched.

"I want you to know just what you do to me," he said as he continued, sliding his hands up the elastic around her thighs, barely missing her clit. "I've dreamed of you, Tavia. Of our being together," he said as he continued to rub her, removing his hand from the bottom of the suit and moving them up farther until he reached the sides of the suit. He slid his hand through the sides and began to massage her breasts. Tavia closed her eyes. She had to be dreaming herself. This brother was turning her out—turning her mind to mush whenever he came within an inch of her.

"And don't even think about us not continuing this relationship when we return to Illinois. Baby, you are mine." He lightly pinched her nipples as he nibbled the side of her neck. "This is just a sampler, baby. Wait until we get to dessert." He removed his hands from under the front of her suit, and then leaned over and kissed the back of her neck, causing an involuntary shiver to rise from Tavia. Smiling, he laid back, and then crossed his legs at the ankles.

Not! Tavia wasn't going to let him get off. He started it, and she was going to finish it, she thought as she reached for the sun-block lotion and began to apply it to Lawrence. Her hands stroked up and down his massive thighs, inching higher up under the trunks. Her fingers played in his pubic hair, and she pursed her lips when she noticed the large erection straining against the light fabric. The sides of her hands lightly touched his penis, never coming into full contact, as she traced his penis. Lawrence's eyes grew dark as he watched her. She licked her lips and noted the change in his demeanor, the blatant need that shone clearly in his eyes. She thought of the phrase she'd heard: fair exchange is no robbery. Lawrence grabbed at her hands, and she swatted them away as her hands rolled up to his chest. She massaged and kneaded his well formed pectorals, lightly pinching his nipples until they resembled small peaks. She took a bottle of water, rinsed the lotion from her hands, dried them on the towel they were lying on, and then put her hands inside his trunks. She stroked him, plying and gently pulling up and down on his penis. She smiled as she heard his own breath hitch and felt his penis throb in her hand. She increased the tempo and marveled as he seemed to grow larger in her small hand.

"And, baby, if I'm desert, you must be my midnight snack," Tavia said as she pulled her hand from his trunks and inhaled the male fragrance of his sensuality.

"Umm, I can't wait." He pulled her to lay next to him, kissing her fully, his tongue mingled with hers.

They lay on the blanket. Tavia read while he sang one song after another, his voice off-key and a little flat, but she didn't mind, for he was singing songs about hope, love and redemption.

After a short nap, they claimed the jet skis Lawrence had paid for. At first Tavia allowed him to ride behind her, but the feel of him pressed up against her was a little too erotic, and she wanted to try this without the distraction.

Lawrence gave a few more directions, then climbed on the other jet ski. They rode the waves, the jet bobbing and skipping along the crystal blue water. Tavia laughed loudly as he began to chase behind her as she maneuvered the ski, taking sudden turns.

When they finished, they returned the jets and headed back to their spot. They both napped before waking to hunger pains. Tavia set out the seafood salad and crackers, fresh fruit of kiwi, pineapple, cherries, and mango, cheese and wine. They ate and laughed as their conversations crossed several topics. Lawrence not only found her beautiful, but highly intelligent and witty. Oh yeah, he was in love.

Once they finished the light meal, Lawrence laid back and requested that Tavia read to him. He liked the sound of her voice and wanted to hear her melodic sound—whether she was giving him orders as she made love to him or just talking. He closed his eyes and listened as she read him one poem after another of black love and need.

When he awoke with her lying on her side next to him, the sun was beginning its nightly descent.

"Tavia, its time to head back to the hotel." He shook her and watched as her eyes opened and focused on him, her heavy lids surrounded by long lashes batted slowly. She smiled at him. Forever. Forever was what he wanted with this woman.

For the rest of the week they took long walks along the beach, ate breakfast in bed, had each other for desert and talked about life as if they had been in each other's lives forever. By the time they were ready to leave the island, both had become ingrained into the other. The only issue between them was the fact that at forty-five, Tavia was past childbearing years and Lawrence, at thirty-three, wanted to marry and have children, in that order.

Their last night on the island was spent with her legs wrapped around his waist and his penis deep inside of her—tomorrow would surely come, and they'd deal with it when it did.

"I want to see you tonight. I've got to have you," the note stated. Tavia read it again as she sat in the English class she was supposed to be teaching, and she smiled in spite of it all as she folded the note and placed it in the pocket of her jean skirt. They'd been back for a month, and her thoughts traveled back to Jamaica and all that had happened between them.

He had emphasized to her during their last night in Jamaica that under no uncertain terms would she be able to cast him to the side once they returned to Urbana and the university—he wasn't going to allow it.

After their return, it was Joanne who first noticed the change in Tavia, followed by her students and even her last date, Bruce. She ignored each of them and tried to contain the deep color her face turned each time they commented on the satisfied, peaceful look on her face. Oh, yes, she mused, Lawrence had become a great compliment to her life, and she enjoyed every inch of him!

For Lawrence it was all together different. Sure they noticed he seemed more relaxed, happier even, but they also noticed the transformation from geeky professor to handsome, unattached man on campus. Tavia had said she'd even heard more than her share of women's assessment of the former Professor Weird. But, she had a secret. Professor Weird was Doctor Feelgood in bed, and she'd be the one to enjoy all of the attention he laved onto her, both in and out of the bedroom.

Tavia's thoughts were interrupted by one of her students who asked about the upcoming final exam. They had two weeks before the end of the semester. Neither Lawrence nor Tavia had talked about what they were going to do for the summer.

"The final is a take-home exam. It's a five page essay on modern day literature versus literature from the early part of the century. Think about some of the author's we've studied over this semester. Edgar Allan Poe. Mark Twain. Dorothy West. Pearl Cleage." She went on to finish her lecture, and then dismissed the class.

Tavia finished her final class of the day and wasn't surprised when she spotted Laurina and Devon walking hand in hand from the English building. She'd called it—they were an item.

She returned to her office for several scheduled meetings, beginning with several of her students, followed by a staff meeting, then ending with a meeting with the dean of her department. The sun was setting by the time she headed down the hall to Lawrence's office.

He smiled as she walked inside and placed a kiss on his lips.

"I haven't seen you all day," he said as he pulled her to sit on his lap. He looked around her and noticed that his office door was open. He rose, placing her on her feet, then walked across the room and closed the door to his office, locking it behind him. He returned to his high-back leather office chair and smiled as Tavia returned to his lap.

"How's your day going?" she asked him as she nipped at his earlobe. She smiled to herself when she heard the low moan and felt the knowing hardness beneath her. "Any more female students propositioning you?"

"The only proposition I want is from you."

Tavia slipped her shoes from her feet and swung her legs around to rest on the arm of the chair. Lawrence rubbed her legs, pushing her denim skirt up as his hand went higher and higher until he was mere inches from the hair surrounding her clit and vagina.

"Woman, have you no shame?" He grinned salaciously. "Where are your panties?"

"I dunno." She shrugged her shoulders and smiled wickedly.

He chuckled and lightly flicked his finger across her clit several times.

"Ahh, you keep that up, Dr. Wainwright, and we won't make it out of here tonight."

He nodded his head while his fingers did exactly what she'd hoped they would. Tavia ground her ass against his penis as his fingers teased and strummed her clit, threatening to bring her to an orgasm. "Just cum for me and I promise to take you home and replace my fingers with my tongue."

Tavia shivered as his fingers worked their magic, just enough pressure to make her mindless while giving exquisite, torturous pleasure. Her hips bucked against his fingers, the juices flowed from her as the orgasm began. She tightened her thighs against his hand.

"Umm, baby, that's it." He coaxed her as she came down from the orgasm. "Wait until I get you home. I've cooked dinner, but, baby, you're going to be my desert," he teased as the ends of the orgasm washed over her, and her breathing began to normalize.

She shook her head as she watched him lick his fingers. "Umph, ump, ump," was all he murmured.

Moments later, Lawrence rested his head against her bosom as she stroked his face. He sighed heavily.

"What's the matter, sweetheart?"

He inhaled deeply. "Tavia, I want to marry you," he blurted out, then looked up into her eyes. He knew this wasn't how he wanted to ask her, but his heart just took over his mouth.

"Lawrence, you know I can't have children and my daughter is nearly twenty years old."

"I know and I'm okay with that. Do you have any objections to adoption?"

She looked at him. "No. You?"

"No." He kissed her lips gently.

"Then what do you say, Tavia Joelle Dennison? I'm in love with you woman. You've got me wound around your fingers. When you are not next to me, I'm cold and alone. You compliment me like no other." He kissed her deeply. "Besides, there ain't no way I'm going to allow another man to get this." He moved beneath her. "So what say you, woman of mine?"

Tavia looked at the warmth and sincerity in this man, her man's eyes. When she'd married before, she didn't have the sparks or the satisfaction, just the empty, vague promise of forever, which didn't last over ten years. But for some reason, Lawrence was different—she could feel it, down in her soul. Their age had never been an issue between them, and Tavia knew it was because Lawrence dealt from the truth, refused to play games and wasn't given to lies and ambiguity—what you saw was what you got, and Tavia sure loved what she got.

"I'll marry you, Lawrence. I will."

He kissed her again and rose with her in his arms. "How about we get out of here? I've got a surprise for you."

After he'd straightened his desk, placing needed papers in his briefcase, Lawrence took Tavia's hand in his as they strolled across campus to where his classic vehicle was parked. Several of their students passed them and smiled. One even shouted: "Go 'head Dr. Wainwright." Lawrence smiled at the compliment.

He held her hand as he drove them to his home and then had Tavia wait in the living room after their arrival. For nearly an hour, Tavia head the clanging of pots and pans accompanied by the occasional squeak of the kitchen door opening and closing. Finally, he appeared in the living room.

"Dinner is served," he announced as he held out his hand to her. Tavia had sampled his cooking and knew that his momma had taught him well. The brother was not only great in bed, but he was equally as passionate with his ability to cook.

The large dining room table for eight was covered by a cream eyelet tablecloth and was set for two with china place settings trimmed in gold with matching stemware sat at the head of the table and another to the right. Lawrence led Tavia to the head of the table, seated her, and then disappeared into the kitchen, returning moments later with two covered dishes. He placed them on the trivets, then went back to the kitchen several times before sitting directly at her right.

He uncovered several dishes, shrimp Etouffee, red beans and rice with heaps of spicy Andouille sausage, collard greens, corn, hot water cornbread and corn muffins. He served sweetened tea in crystal goblets.

"To us." He raised his glass and tapped hers lightly.

They talked, as they normally did, in soothing tones and easy words. They'd had one disagreement that as she thought about it, she couldn't remember what the disagreement was all about. But she found that they each fought fair, no shouting or yelling, just a disagreement that she acquiesced and allowed him to settle. She knew she was hooked. She'd never let a man make a decision for her.

She looked up into his warm, honey-brown eyes as he took her hand in his, slid from his seat and knelt before her.

"Tavia, one more time, will you marry me?" he asked again as he placed a platinum band with a diamond solitaire mount surrounded by ruby baguettes, his birthstone, on the ring finger of her left hand. "Say yes again."

She held the tears at bay as she nodded her head up and down. "Yes, Lawrence I'll marry you. I'll become Mrs. Wainwright."

They rose, and he pulled her into his arms, lowered his head and kissed her, at first lightly, then with urgency as the passion they unleashed in each other sprang to life. Lawrence had been warned by his sister Jean that older women could be a challenge, but he dismissed that, knowing he'd please Tavia both in and out of bed.

"Hey, wifey-to-be, how about a little dessert?" he said as he picked her up, rounded the table and sat her down on the other end. She nodded her head as he removed his glasses and placed them to the side, then untied his tie before removing the blue dress shirt. He pulled a condom from the breast pocket of his shirt and laid it nearby on the table. She watched as he looked at her—a burning, intense passion mixed with want and lust shone in his eyes just like it had their first time in Jamaica. She loved that look—knew that she would be one satisfied sister when he was finished with her.

She rubbed her fingers through his soft hair. After enduring a lot of stares, unwanted glares and blatant sexual comments from some of his female students, Lawrence had gone back to wearing the glasses and had decided to return to an Afro, albeit a smaller one.

"What do you want from me, love?" he asked as she kissed him, softly at first, her lips pecking his, then more urgently as her lips forced his apart to feast on his tongue. She had become a brazen woman, making love to Lawrence in places and on things she had never done before. She found him and their insatiable appetites to be a real turn on.

Tavia unbuttoned her blouse, removed her bra, and wiggled her hips, sliding her denim skirt from her hips. Fully naked, she leaned back on the table, her upper body resting on her elbows as her legs dangled over the table. She smiled wickedly as Lawrence removed his clothing, then pulled up a chair and sat down. He placed both of her feet on his thighs, slid his chair closer, bowed his head and began to suck her clit while his hands kneaded her nipples. She rolled her hips against his face.

She knew that come eternity, this man worshiping her, making her know she was not only all woman but his woman, she would love him without question and follow him where ever he led her. She felt deep in her soul that this man who loved her, physically and emotionally, would sustain her to her final breath.

She grabbed his head and quivered uncontrollably as the orgasm tore through her like a massive quake, leaving her spent yet wound tightly like a clock. She held him by his shoulders more for support and fought to steel the emotions that were bubbling to the surface. She inhaled deeply.

As she came down from the sexual high he provided, he stood and watched as Tavia picked up the condom, tore the package open with her teeth, tossed the empty plastic onto the floor, then slowly rolled the latex over his penis. She opened her legs and gently tugged him forward. The head of his penis rested at the entry of her vagina. She scooted closer to the edge of the table and gasped loudly as he entered her, his massive penis slid possessively inside of her, pulling her, drawing her in, taking her, branding her, filling her with his essence—making it hard for her to ever love another.

Tavia scooted closer and wrapped her legs around him, her pelvis flush with his.

"Umph, baby," she whispered. "Do it, baby. Do me. Don't stop." She grinded into him harder, and he felt the seed gather at the base of his scrotum, the threat to erupt near. But he hadn't made her cum a second time and knew just what to do. He pulled from her and smiled at her frown, then chuckled at the expression on her face when he sat back down in the chair and motioned for her to sit in his lap. Tavia straddled him and he held her close as she began to ride him.

"My baby, I love you so much. Thank you for loving me," he whispered close to her ear. That simple phrase turned out to be the one phrase to cause the tears she had been trying to hold inside come forth and roll down her cheeks unchecked. He kissed her and pulled her closer as her body quaked with emotion and need.

Tavia rode him so hard the chair began to squeak loudly. He lifted them and walked with Tavia held firmly in his arms up the stairs into his bedroom. He placed Tavia on the bed and moved over her, sliding inside her as he did. Lawrence slid in and out of her, his arms wrapped around her. He held her tightly, their hearts beat in unison as Tavia began to buck against him, her orgasm taking over. He pulled back and looked down into her face. He loved watching her face as she climaxed. And knew that when he watched her his own release wasn't far behind—like now, he could feel the flow at the tip of his penis. He pumped inside of her several times, and then came hard when Tavia bumped her pelvis against his.

He rolled them over and held her as their breathing began to regulate after the incredible high of their lovemaking. He rubbed her back as she settled into him, their bodies nearly fusing into one as they spoke in hushed tones about when they'd marry and where. They had decided to return to Royal Plantation in Jamaica.

Chapter 7

Two weeks before the start of another academic year, Tavia walked down the aisle dressed in an ivory, tea-length spaghetti strapped dressed covered by a sheer tunic. White gardenias and rose petals lined the path that led to the arch set up on the beach. She smiled at her daughter, Jonetta, as they walked arm in arm toward Lawrence. She looked to both sides of the aisle. Not only had her parents and brother made it, but Lawrence's entire family had flown in to watch him get married. She had met each of them during the summer break, when she'd decided to forego teaching summer school and instead opted for a sabbatical wherein she would write a book of poetry dedicated to women and women's issues. Lawrence had followed suit, and they ended up spending many hours lazily loving and lounging in the large hammock in Lawrence's backyard. Tavia had put her loft up for sale and moved in with Lawrence.

As she reached the arch, Jonetta gave her mother's hand over to Lawrence. "You better take good care of her." Jonetta kissed him on the cheek, and then hugged and kissed Tavia before taking her place next to her mother as the maid of honor.

After the minister read from the bible, and then had them recite their vows, Tavia and Lawrence faced each other and smiled as they heard the words they'd been waiting two months to hear: I now pronounce you man and wife.

Lawrence took Tavia's face gently between his hands and kissed her, his tongue sought and found its way past her lips as they lingered, their arms wrapped around each other.

They forced themselves to linger longer than either wanted to at the small, intimate reception. Lawrence had complained to Tavia that it lasted a bit long—he was anxious to get their honeymoon started.

Tavia excused them and laughed loudly as Lawrence swept her up in his arms and carried her to the villa they had shared during their first visit to Jamaica. Carrying her over the threshold, he went straight to the bedroom where he changed his mind and took his time removing her dress, carefully hanging it up, brushing his hand across it as if straightening out wrinkles. Tavia sighed loudly. She didn't care about the dress—she wanted to feel her husband. She tapped her foot impatiently as he came to stand in front of her and began to slowly remove her undergarments, pausing to admire the garter and thigh-high silk stockings she wore. She nodded her head as he took the panties and sniffed them before stuffing them the pocket of his trousers.

Finally he divested himself of his clothes, picked her up and carried her to the large poster bed, laying her in the middle. He joined her and started what they both knew would be the ultimate high of their love.

As he entered her, she cried out in sheer ecstasy, the fill of him inside of her, and the way he responded to her. Yeah, forever. This man was definitely hers forever.

Summer Lovin'

by

Sapphire Blue

Chapter 1

"She said it's still not ready and your continuous phone calls are a distraction," Madison replied as she sat in the chair across from Lance's desk.

Lance swore and dropped the pieces of mail his assistant had just handed him onto the desk. "What the hell does she mean it's not ready? She's had weeks to do the re-writes I requested."

Madison, since day one of working for Lance Radford and Sadiq Productions for the last seven years was now used to her boss's temper, crossed her legs and let her hands fall serenely into her lap. "She's had the re-write requests for three weeks. But that was after she'd furnished you with the completed screenplay within a month's deadline. She's having a rough time, Lance. I think you should cut her some slack."

"Cut her some slack?" Lance clamped his mouth shut and stood, pacing his office to keep from completely losing his cool. His new film, Fountain of Love, was scheduled to go into production the first of September. It was now the second week of July. He needed that screenplay like yesterday.

"I'm paying her damn good money to produce a product. I'm in no mood for whatever female issues she may have going on."

Madison quirked a brow. "Excuse me?"

Turning to face her, Lance sighed. He liked Madison. She was a great assistant and a loyal friend. In this line of work a man didn't have too many female friends. And for Lance females came in one or two categories: friend or lover. He didn't have girlfriends or fiancées. That wasn't his style. And as of late his style had him viewing females as something else entirely. "I just meant that her personal problems are not my business. We're on a tight schedule here and if we miss it—"

"Calm down, Lance. We still have six weeks. Meena Denison is a great writer, that's why you hired her in the first place. She produced a wonderful screenplay based on the ideas you scribbled on a napkin. She'll come through. I know she will." With that said, Madison stood, leaned over his desk and retrieved the mail he'd discarded. "I'll take care of these. You go to the gym or play some tennis or do something to take your mind off business. All work and no play makes Lance a really big meanie," she quipped on her way out.

"A really big meanie with a boatload of money," Lance whispered and turned to look out his office window. But was money enough?

His New York office was in the middle of Manhattan and as he looked out over the great New York city skyscape he thought about money and his business and all that was important to him. More money and more business.

This was his life. And he loved it. Being a movie producer was his life's dream. Seeing his ideas on the big screen gave him a rush he'd never felt from anything else. And Fountain of Love was his best one yet. The idea of a couple searching desperately for something that some said didn't exist and finding each other in the process was not new. But it was the journey to finding that love that held all the fresh and exciting events that would make it a box office hit. And he was depending on Meena Denison to make it happen.

With that he went to his desk, picked up the phone and cradled it between his shoulder and his ear. What he was about to do was undoubtedly an administrative assignment, one which he would normally give to Madison. But since his wonderful assistant was clearly on the other side in this matter, he would handle it himself.

"This is Lance Radford. I need the jet ready to leave in three hours and I need someone to do some packing for me," he said simply.

For the fifth straight hour Meena stared at the crisp white screen of her laptop, the white signifying how empty the current page was. She should have been re-working the scene where Caleb and Wendy first realize their attraction to each other. The boss—the magnificent Lance Radford—wanted it hotter, more intense. His words, jotted in the margins of the original screenplay, stated, I want their attraction to reach beyond the screen so that each and every couple in that audience can't wait to get home and have sex. Meena had first frowned when she'd read it but then realized this was an intense love story and that fact needed to be stated as early in the movie as possible. And she wanted desperately to convey that intensity on the page as well as the screen if she could just stop being interrupted.

A half hour ago she'd gotten the mail. Another letter from Chris. She'd wanted to throw it directly into the trash but had foolishly opened and read it instead. He was sorry, again. For the past three months he'd written to her telling her how sorry he was and how he loved and cared about her and wished her well. How many times could he say the same thing? How many times could he tell the same lies?

Instead of putting the letter in the trash she'd stood over the stove and watched it burn. Yeah, that was dramatic but she was damn tired of him invading her mind. She was trying to get on with her life but he wouldn't leave her be. He'd done enough and she'd told him that. Apparently he didn't feel the same way.

Her cell phone rang and Meena almost jumped out of the chair. Another freakin' distraction. This had better not be Lance Radford questioning her progress again. Correction, he never called himself but had always had his very nice assistant do it. Since she'd been working with Radford Productions she and Madison Carey had become quite close. How the woman worked for a man like Lance Radford was beyond her.

"Yes?" she said curtly when she pressed the phone to her ear.

"Hi," the timid voice sounded on the other end.

"Oh, hi, Corine," Meena said in a much nicer tone. Corine was her sister who last year had gone through a horrific divorce from her high school sweetheart. Six months ago, Corine's ex, Dan had moved and now lived happily in LA with his dentist and Corine had barricaded herself in her house until finally loosing her job two months ago. She lost her friends because she never called any of them back. And in Meena's estimation, she basically lost her mind.

"How are you?" Meena asked closing her laptop with a click.

"I'm tired. These headaches are killer and I'm having trouble getting refills on my medication."

Meena knew Corine had been taking Oxycodine for the extreme headaches she'd been having before Meena had finally convinced her to take a trip out of the country. Corine had been seeing a psychiatrist who also had her on anti-depressants. Meena was concerned about all the medication her sister was on and had suggested a trip to make her feel better. Of course, Meena had also funded the trip just as she'd been funding Corine's entire existence since her lunatic sister had refused alimony.

"Maybe you should try to get along without them, honey. I remember the doctor saying they could be very addictive."

"I just don't know, Meena. I'm trying," Corine said.

Meena rubbed her eyes. "Corine, you have to start living your life again. You've been like this long enough."

Silence filled the line.

"I know. I know. It's better here. I like it here," Corine said quietly.

Meena frowned. Sure she liked it there. Meena would like it herself if she was in a posh hotel in Paris instead of sitting at her desk with writer's block. "That's great, honey. Listen, I'm kind of busy. Can I call you back?"

"Oh, sure. Do your work. You always were so good a writing. Mom and Dad would be proud of you."

Corine was older by four years, but Meena had always taken care of her. Their parents had died in a car accident five years ago. Corine had begun her downfall then. Her marriage had died as a result of that. Still, Meena despised Dan for not sticking with his wife after all Corine had done for him.

"Thanks. I'll call you tomorrow, ok?"

"Ok. I love you, Meena."

"I love you too, Corine."

Meena Denison went out every afternoon at three o'clock exactly. Lance knew this because once Madison had tried to call her and received the answering machine. Because Madison and Meena were women and shared an unknown amount of useless information, Meena had told Madison of this ritual. Madison, one day had mentioned it to him. And for whatever reason, he remembered.

It was now quarter to seven and she'd been back from her walk for a while. He was on a tight schedule. The plane was waiting and he needed to get moving. Lance stepped out of the black Lincoln Navigator and crossed the sidewalk to the door of her apartment building that actually wasn't that far from his own place in Manhattan. He exited the elevator on the tenth floor and moved quickly to stand in front of her door. He knocked.

She answered, the door swinging open, and for a moment he was speechless.

Meena Denison wasn't beautiful by normal standards, meaning she wasn't statuesque with huge breasts and a flowing mane. She was instead, more on the average size in height, with a butter cream complexion, shoulder length honey colored hair and mystical hazel-gold eyes. Her body was definitely on a scale of its own, he noticed, in her jean shorts cuffed at mid-thigh and her blue tank top that fit closely over plump breasts.

Lance swallowed the lump of lust in his throat and straightened his tie. "Hello, Ms. Denison. I'm not sure if you remember me, but I'm—"

She folded her arms and leaned against the doorjamb. "You're Lance Radford. Was my answer not good enough? You had to come all the way over here in person to check on my progress."

He frowned at her tone but as her eyes twinkled at him he felt tiny spikes of desire tickling his spine. "You are correct. Your answer was not good enough. But I'm here to remedy that."

With a tilt of her head Meena raised a brow. "And how do you plan to do that? Are you going to write the screenplay for me?"

She was feisty, he noted. That wasn't on her resume, but didn't deter him. With a smile he stepped to the side and watched her shock as Andre, Lance's bodyguard, effortlessly scooped her up dropping her over his shoulder and proceeded towards the elevator.

"What the hell are you doing?" he heard her scream a second before he slipped into her apartment and searched for her laptop. Once he'd found it he packed it up and left, closing the door soundly behind him.

Andre was holding the elevator for him. Meena had ceased screaming and Lance wondered why. Andre sensed his question and turned just as the elevator doors were closing. Lance noted his bodyguard had taken the time that he was in the apartment to gag Meena and tie her hands. He was sure that hadn't been an easy feat, but couldn't help feeling relieved they wouldn't draw attention as they left the building.

Surely a six foot five, two hundred and forty pound black man carrying a sexy, if mouthy, black female, over his shoulder would alarm some but this was New York, and stranger things had happened.

"You are crazy and insane!" Meena screamed. Her lips were chapped and her jaws hurt from the thick scarf stuck in her mouth for the forty minute ride to the airport. "Kidnapping is a felony in New York. I'm sure you know that."

He didn't answer. Her heart hammered in her chest, and her head throbbed. The plane engines revved as Lance settled himself across from her in the deep-cushioned leather seat and fastened his seatbelt as if they were off for a friendly vacation.

"Where are we going," she asked, "and why are you taking me against my will?"

A ding sounded and the seatbelt light above the cabin door went on. The plane's engine grew louder and she cursed again. Her hands were still tied and now so were her feet, but the big guy who carried her had had the good sense to fasten her seatbelt.

"I know you hear me. The minute this plane lands and I get off I'm going to tell the first person I see that you're a sneaky kidnapper. Then I'm going to call the police and then I'm going to burn your screenplay!"

At that Lance turned to face her. "If you don't be quiet Andre will have to gag you again."

He was too calm. Too damn calm and conceited to walk this earth. Of course, the fact that he was drop-dead gorgeous probably validated his conceit. He was as tall as his companion but his weight was better distributed into thick muscular arms and toned abs. He looked good enough to eat in his black slacks and fitted black shirt. She frowned. Didn't he realize it was summer in New York? He was probably sweating bullets in that outfit.

"That won't change the fact that you've kidnapped me."

"I'm trying to help you."

"By manhandling me and kidnapping me?" she yelled. "Where are you taking me?"

He sighed wearily and steepled his hands at his chin. "We're going to my beach house in Miami. It'll be quiet and away from whatever is keeping you from writing. I need this screenplay in four weeks, not a day beyond."

Despite her anger Meena chuckled. "Are you serious? All this is about your screenplay?" She lay her head back against the seat and took a deep breath. "Look, I know I'm taking longer than usual, but I promise you'll have your project in four weeks. Just tell your pilot to turn around and take me home. I'll work nonstop until it's done."

He rubbed his chin. She watched, mesmerized as long fingers glided over tree bark brown skin, covered with a thin goatee. Her nipples tightened with the thought of those fingers touching her.

"You can work nonstop in Miami and it's prettier there," he said in a measured tone.

Meena licked her lips. "It's hotter there than it is in New York in the summer." Or was it hotter in the cabin of this plane, with him beside her?

"My house is on the beach. It's beautiful and it's relaxing. It's the perfect place for your creativity to flow. You'll thank me later."

He looked at her then and smiled. His lips were of a medium thickness, just right as far as she was concerned. His eyes were dark and seductive, his close cut hair well-groomed. Lance Radford was a very attractive man. If she weren't careful she would be thanking him, but not just for a free trip to Miami.

Chapter 2

For the next three hours Meena fumed. How dare he presume to know what the best writing conditions for her were? How dare he come into her house and drag her onto this plane to take her…did he say to his house?

She couldn't stay in his house. Not only because she didn't take kindly to being manhandled but now because she'd been up close to him. She'd been sitting only three or four feet away from him for the past few hours, smelling his cologne, feeling the undeniable heat of his presence. Her nipples had remained hard since that first moment he'd glanced at her.

Meena had always been a very sexual person. From her sixteenth birthday when Tyrone Candler had so elegantly taken her virginity on the tool table in his parents' garage, she'd had an insatiable appetite for men. As she'd grown up her promiscuity had been tamed—there were diseases out there that couldn't even be pronounced, let alone cured. Yet the desire was always there, ready to be sparked by the right man. And evidently, Lance Radford was the right man.

But she couldn't. Chris and his ultimate betrayal was still fresh in her mind. The fact that even though they'd broken up three months ago and he continued to call her and write letters to her were probably major contributors to that. But each time she remembered sex with Chris she was repulsed. Add that to being more than twelve weeks without sex and she was a basket case. Just another reason her writing was suffering.

The pilot announced they were landing and Meena shifted enough in her seat so she could see out the window. Water, a deep indigo glistening from the moonbeams above stretched for miles until it touched the tips of the sandy shore. It looked wonderful and refreshing. She had to admit, if there was a great place to relax and focus on her work, this would probably be it. Meena felt herself warming to the idea of being here although easily acquiescing was not the norm for her. She was a fighter, a rebel. She did not take direction well at all, which was why she'd chosen writing as a career as opposed to a traditional nine to five with a supervisor to report to.

"I don't like seeing you tied up that way and I'd rather Andre not have to carry you off this plane," Lance said tightly. She definitely would not be fully dressed. He'd purposely kept her tied while they were on the plane to suit his own fantasy while his mind toyed with the way he would like to tie her up.

His voice startled her out of her reverie. He hadn't spoken in such a long time she'd almost forgotten he was there. No, that was impossible. Even the sound of his voice had her nerves on end, but she held the outside façade. "I'm not going to scream down the airport or run away if that's what you're worried about." Although she probably should, instead she turned to see him watching her skeptically. "Look, I don't like your tactics. You could have just asked me to come down here."

"And you would have accepted?"

She had to smile at that one. "No."

He nodded and his lips tilted slightly as if he wanted to smile back but refrained.

"But I deserve some respect. I agreed to write a screenplay for you, not be your writing slave. I do have other work besides this screenplay."

Lance shrugged although her mention of the word 'slave' provoked sexual thoughts he'd been trying to fight. "I'm not concerned with your other work. I need this screenplay completed as soon as possible."

And because she knew she was behind on the project, she forced herself to remain calm. "I will work at your house until I finish the screenplay. And I will finish it in your time frame. Then I'm coming back to New York and I don't want you contacting me again."

The pay was good—but not enough to work for someone who would take such drastic measures to meet a deadline. Out of nowhere

Andre appeared. He undid the ties at her hands and feet and looked up at her skeptically as she'd finished speaking.

Lance frowned. "We shall see."

He had to get the hell out of this seat but the hard on that had grown steadily since he'd seen her ass up over Andre's shoulder, was prominent. Her shorts had ridden up so that the barest hint of butt cheek was viewable. It had taken Herculean strength to keep from smacking his palm over it.

Thoughts of spanking her, feeling her pliant flesh heat beneath his palm, caused an erection that nearly blinded him. While all his life Lance had wanted to be a movie producer there was another part of him no one knew existed. No one outside of the Lifestyle that is. And truth be told, he hadn't totally committed himself to the BDSM Lifestyle. He leaned more towards dibbling and dabbling which caused an uproar with the dedicated participant. But he didn't care. This was his life and he'd live it as he pleased.

If he happened to like spanking women or having his way with them while they were bound and gagged it was his business. And on other occasions when he leaned more towards catering to a woman's needs, loving her body in the most sensual and primal way possible, that too, had nothing to do with anyone but himself.

Lance hadn't played with a submissive in quite some time. Meena Denison's feisty attitude scraped against his raw need for control. But when she was dropped into the seat across from him her tank top stretched even tighter over her breasts until pert nipples pressed through the material, watching him, taunting him. He bit down on his urges and looked away.

For the duration of the flight he'd stared out his window, refusing to even look her way again for fear of seeing those nipples and lunging to take them into his mouth without further thought. Now, they were landing and he had no choice but to acknowledge her presence. Her hair was a little disheveled, as if she'd been tossing around on a bed, thrashing beneath him was more like it.

He jolted in his seat as the pilot made a not so smooth touch down. Clearing his throat he undid his seatbelt and was about to make a dash for the bathroom and the cold water faucet when she said his name. He took a deep, steadying breath and turned to her.

"My seatbelt is stuck," she said as she continued to jerk on the belt.

Her breasts jiggled with the motion and his erection stiffened against his thigh. With teeth clenched Lance walked over to her and knelt down to help. She moved her hands and he grabbed the clasp. He did not look up, her breasts would be at eye level, only about a foot away from his mouth. Way too much temptation.

His fingers brushed her lower stomach and the button of her shorts. Lance felt tiny beads of sweat tickle the back of his neck. She shifted, as if she were trying to squirm out of the seatbelt and his arms grazed her bare thighs.

"Dammit! You'd think with all the money you probably spent for this jet the seatbelts would have the decency to work."

You'd think a grown woman would know when she was driving a man insane, he thought and gave the belt one last tug. With a click it came undone and she lifted her hands and clapped.

"Yaaay. My hero," she said in a clearly mocking tone. .

Taking a chance he looked up and realized that he didn't want to be her hero, he wanted to be her Dominant. "You're welcome."

The cabin door opened and Lance heard Andre's deep voice, "The car's waiting."

"Good. I can't wait to get out of here," Lance grumbled as he quickly stood and walked away from where Meena still sat. What he was thinking was ridiculous. She was a writer, not a Submissive.

Behind his back Meena frowned.

Rising from her seat she vowed that if he were going to be an arrogant jerk, she would be one too. As she stepped off the plane she vowed to work all night long if need be, but that screenplay would be finished and she wouldn't have to stay the entire four weeks he required to get it done. The sooner she was away from Lance Radford, the better.

Meena was not easily impressed by any man but when the car stopped in front of an iron gate surrounded by trees, her heart thumped. He'd said he was taking her to his house. She knew from talking to Madison that he had homes in LA, Spain, New York and Miami. Come to think of it, she'd learned a lot about Lance Radford from his assistant, much more than she probably needed to know.

But none of her conversations with Madison prepared her for this. The gate opened slowly and the driver proceeded through. Meena thought it was like a scene out of a movie the way they moved up a winding driveway draped by color-rich trees. Entering a circle path with a fountain of—from what she could see—a Greek god in the center her attention was soon claimed by the house.

It was a progression of pearly white buildings jutting forward in an abstract manner. Two stories with what looked to be floor to ceiling windows. Again, the colors were rich, from the bright white building to the deep green grass and brilliant red brick walkway.

She'd walked slowly behind Lance as they made their way to the front door, looking around the estate. He obviously paid someone to take great care of this property because there was nothing out of place, it was actually picturesque. If she were shopping for a vacation home, this one would definitely pique her interest.

"Your things are already in your room. Sara will show you where it is," he said matter-of-factly and continued walking across the beautiful white marbled floor.

Not liking the feeling of being dismissed Meena didn't spare the short woman to her left a glance before following behind him. "What things are in my room? I didn't have time to pack remember."

He turned abruptly and she bumped into him, her face coming into very close contact with his thick pectoral muscles. His hands quickly came to her shoulders and heat spread with a steady rhythm throughout her body. He held her still and took a step back, then looked down at her as he spoke. "I had your clothes and personal belongings packed before we left."

Meena blinked in confusion. "And just how did you do that?"

"Let's be clear on one thing, Ms. Denison. I always get what I want. So when I ask someone to go to your house and pack your clothes, that's what they do."

She folded her arms over her chest, not sure she liked the way he admitted to always getting what he wanted. At the moment she was wanting some pretty enticing things. Things that involved him. Things that she knew were too damn dangerous to even contemplate.

"So because you're rich and famous, you're also above the law? Breaking into someone's apartment and stealing their belongings is against the law."

He let out an exasperated breath and Meena couldn't help wondering what was really going on in that mind of his. He was dressed in a sort of business casual way and all he'd said to her was related to that damn screenplay. Granted, that was the only reason the two of them had to communicate but it seemed to her like he was obsessed.

"Before we spend the next few weeks going back and forth about this let me just apologize now for having brought you here this way."

His words stunned her as they were in stark contrast to the arrogant—yet deliciously attractive—jerk she'd convinced herself he was.

"This project is very important to me and I didn't want to waste time trying to convince you this was the right thing to do. Madison mentioned that you had been going through some things, so I thought a change of scenery might do you some good. But I have no intention of holding you hostage or otherwise breaking the law as you so eloquently put it. If you'd like to check into a hotel, that's fine. I'll find you one and I'll pay the bill. Whatever you need to make completing this project a priority, I will do."

He was obsessed, she thought with an inward jolt. He was clearly only focused on getting this project done. That shouldn't have bothered her, but it did. Here she was sweating over his body, his voice, his touch and he couldn't give a rat's ass about her as a woman. All he wanted was his precious screenplay.

Well—and only because she wasn't about to pass up a free vacation in beautiful Miami—she had already agreed to work here to produce the screenplay he wanted so badly. But she wondered if in the meantime she could get the famous Lance Radford to loosen up a little. He ran a hand down his face and she watched those long fingers pass his lips. Her entire body quaked.

No, she would not be helping Lance loosen up or anything else. She would be keeping her distance because everything about him said sex, pure and simple. And sex with Lance was not an option. For one, he was her boss. And for two, she was fed up with men. For all she knew, he could be just like Chris.

"I'll stay here and work," she said simply and turned to go find Sara and her own room.

Chapter 3

Her nice round ass was up in the air as she bent over the chair. Her wrists were bound and tied to the chair's arms so she couldn't change position. He stood behind her watching in awe as plump cheeks glared back at him.

"Open up," he ordered and watched as she spread her legs further apart.

From the viewpoint he could see her puckered anus, the tight hole making his body ache with need. Her nether lips were also visible, thick and aroused, coated with her essence.

She stood spread eagle, offering him everything and yet he wanted more. Quickly undoing his pants he released his engorged sex watching as it wobbled free, drops of murky liquid covering its tip. He took one step towards her and smacked her left butt cheek. The sound resonated throughout the room.

She moaned.

His penis thrust forward, more pre-cum coating him.

He smacked the right cheek. His palm burned from the contact.

Again she moaned and stuck her bottom out further, giving him more. He slipped his palm between her legs and felt her hot essence leak into his hand. Pulling away he brought his hand to his face and licked the moisture then with the same hand smacked her bottom again. And again. And again.

Until her honey toned skin was now a fiery red, her inner thighs drenched with arousal.

His heart hammered in his chest, his sex bobbing steadily against his stomach, leaving a path of moisture. With both hands he grabbed her bottom, spreading her cheeks even wider, squeezing so hard he knew he was about to break her skin.

She did not scream, nor did she use their safe word to warn him to stop. Instead she braced herself, flexing her hips in invitation.

Her scent floated through his system in a heavy haze and he felt the skin of his penis stretching to accommodate its ever growing length. He was so hard it hurt. So needy he could probably beg. And yet he only stared.

She was perfection, from the smooth roundness of her ass, to her tight back entrance and down to the juicy sweet thickness of her center. He was lost in the beauty of her, so much so that he could not make another move.

"Take me, dammit!" she demanded, breaking him out of his trance.

Lance turned over onto his stomach and groaned as his protruding arousal pushed into the mattress. On a string of curses he jumped out of the bed before he'd reverted to his childhood years and wet the sheets.

He stepped out onto his balcony hoping the night air would cool his thoughts. The last few hours had been complete hell. Sara had prepared dinner and he was all set to eat his in his office when Sara scolded him for ignoring his houseguest. To keep the peace he'd agreed to eat in the kitchen with Meena. Meena, who had changed into a dress that was nothing more than two straps and a minimal amount of material.

This woman had a fantastic body and definitely wasn't afraid to show it. He didn't remember her looking like this when they'd met six months ago to sign the contracts for the screenplay. Actually, he'd only been in the meeting for about five minutes since he was leaving to look at location sites in Italy. He vaguely remembered she wore a pantsuit with a short jacket and…yes, delectably round breasts he'd wanted to squeeze even then.

Dinner had been excruciating. She talked and he tried to keep up ordinary conversation with her but his eyes kept falling to the ample cleavage she displayed and when he forced himself to look at her face he wondered how her lips would feel wrapped around his throbbing length. It was pitiful, he admitted to himself. He was a thirty-two year old man, used to having any woman, any time he wanted them. And because the need was growing desperately he even thought of a few unattached Submissives he knew in the South Beach area. One of them would love to come and play with him. Except, Lance was almost certain another woman would not do.

He'd made his way downstairs deciding on a drink to take the edge off when he heard noise coming from the kitchen. Another distraction, he thought as he walked in the opposite direction of the den to find out who else was up at this time of night.

The moment he entered the room he knew this distraction was going to be the death of him.

Meena was reaching into a cabinet above the counter, much too high for her to reach without the assistance of a step-stool or a chair, yet there she stood on her tiptoes, one arm bracing herself on the counter while the other reached over her head. The tiny wisp of satin she most likely called a nightgown rose high with her efforts so that once again Lance was faced with that mouthwatering ass of hers. And just like clockwork, his sex rose to the occasion.

This time there was no redirecting his thoughts. He crossed the floor in two long strides and grabbed her at her waist. With his palms at her sides he held her still, cradling his throbbing erection in the soft crevice of her backside.

"What do you think you're doing?" she asked in a voice too breathy to be outraged.

"I'm taking what you have been so blatantly offering," he said through gritted teeth. She was killing him.

She tried to squirm free but only managed to settle him more comfortably between her legs. Later, he would ask himself if she'd done it on purpose.

"I haven't offered you anything. You're the one who brought me here, remember?"

He did remember. It was a rash decision he'd made when he was focusing on business only. She was the key to his next box office hit. She was his employee. She was not his Submissive.

"And because I brought you here, you'll do as I say," he heard himself saying despite what he knew to be true.

She was silent for a moment then she said, "I don't hear you saying anything."

Again blood pumped hard and fast through his veins. What was she saying? Did she have any idea what her tightly spoken words were doing to him?

"Bend over," he directed.

To his surprise she did and his mouth watered. Earlier today she was argumentive and feisty. He would have never guessed she could be submissive, yet here she was doing what he told her…willingly.

He pushed her night gown up to her breasts and let his hand slide down her bare back. She wore a thong and his fingers trailed beneath its rim. Lance took a step back but didn't stop touching her. Just as he'd seen in his dream her golden ass glared back at him only marred by the thin line of the black thong. He wanted to smack that ass but instead grabbed it with both palms. He squeezed and let the flow of lustful power soar through him.

She lay over the counter letting him touch and look at her all he wanted, without saying a word. He loved it. Dropping to his knees Lance buried his face in her crease and inhaled. This was no dainty, feminine scent but a strong sexual odor that called to him like a beacon. He needed more. Pulling her butt cheeks apart he licked her crease and groaned when he heard her sigh.

With lightening quick movements he turned her around and lifted her onto the counter. "Spread your legs wide." He waited for her to do as he said and smiled inwardly as she did. With a finger he slid the wisp of her thong to the side and looked at her open center. Her nether lips were thick and coated with the beginnings of her arousal. With his thumb he touched the hood of her clit and looked into her eyes for a reaction.

She looked directly at him, her hazel eyes clouding with arousal. She didn't blink nor did she speak, just held her head high watching and waiting for his next move.

"I want to see you come," he told her.

She licked her lips. "Then make me come."

She still challenged him too much to be a Submissive, but she was alluring as hell. "I want to see you do it. You make yourself come all the time don't you, Meena? When you're alone in your apartment writing those steamy love scenes for the movies, you get aroused. And once you're aroused you have to slake that need." He knew because he had the same weakness and was feeling it now. "Show me how you get off, Meena."

Without another word she slid back on the counter until her back hit the tiled wall. She lifted her legs so that the heels of her feet rested on the corners and gaped her legs open wide. With her left hand she palmed her crotch with slow strokes. He was mesmerized. Her hand continued to cover her mound when one finger disappeared into her center. Her tongue stroked her bottom lip as Lance looked from between her legs to the gloriously erotic expression on her face.

She pumped herself slowly as if to draw out the pleasure for the both of them. Lance reached down and grabbed his erection pulling roughly on his length. He didn't wish to be inside her because watching was far more erotic then the actual act of fucking her. She would be in control of her own pleasure and thus lead to his. His body was tense with anticipation.

When her other hand joined between her legs and she began thrusting two fingers, one from each hand, in and out of her hole, Lance thought he would lose his mind. Spreading his own legs he pumped into his hand with quick strokes.

She was panting now, her head rolling around as she continued to work herself. Her essence coated her fingers and dripped onto the counter. He wanted to lick them up but refrained. Faster and faster her fingers began to move as did his hand. She was growing closer and he was right behind her.

Her hips lifted slightly as she pumped against her fingers moaning with the onslaught of her release. Lance jerked his erection until hot cum shot out of its tip creating a stream that landed on the counter just inches away from her dripping center.

And as he stood there still holding his sex in his hand she lifted her head and looked at him.

"I should get back to work," she said smartly then let her legs down and slipped off the counter. She walked out of the kitchen without saying another word and Lance could do nothing but watch her go.

What the hell had he just done?

Chapter 4

In the light of day Meena had no choice but to face herself and what she'd done last night. She'd made a graceful exit from the kitchen and when she was sure he hadn't followed her she'd bolted up the stairs and locked herself in her room.

She had no idea what had come over her. Why had she acted so wanton? So quick to do his bidding? That was totally against her character. While she was not even going to deny being attracted to Lance, she would never have propositioned him in the kitchen. Come to think of it, she hadn't propositioned him, he'd been the one making the demands and she'd been the one accommodating them.

Masturbating had never felt so good. The mere fact that he was gleaning some sort of satisfaction from watching her, had pushed her arousal to the limits. Even now her body hummed with expectation.

But that humming would have to quiet down. She hadn't forgotten she was here on business. Lance needed his screenplay, he'd made no qualms about that fact yesterday. And if a man was willing to risk kidnapping charges to ensure his screenplay was done on time then it must be damned important to him. Therefore, that would remain the priority.

Besides, Meena wasn't looking for a relationship, or an affair, for that matter. Chris and his antics were still fresh in her mind and she had no desire to travel that path again. She'd finally come to the conclusion that maybe a real relationship wasn't in the cards for her. Men just didn't seem to want to treat women right, just look at how messed up Corine was over Dan?

Meena took extra special care to cover up more of her body today which was a shame since it was a balmy eighty-nine degrees. She stepped out onto her balcony and enjoyed a few minutes of the unabashed sunshine and intense blue skies of Miami. Inhaling deeply she'd sucked in as much of the beachfront air as she could. All too soon she'd be back in her New York City apartment. And while she thoroughly enjoyed the city, this tropical setting was quickly growing on her.

Not one to hide from anyone or anything Meena left her room, taking the stairs in a leisurely stroll then heading straight for the kitchen. She'd wanted a snack last night but had found…so much more. Now, she was starving. But as she walked toward the kitchen she found herself thinking that she hoped someone had cleaned that counter.

The smell of bleach hit her the moment she entered the kitchen and she tried to smother a smile. There was nobody there to see it though so she walked to the refrigerator and grabbed a bottled water. On the table was a tray of bagels and muffins. Meena was ravenous. She helped herself to a cinnamon raisin bagel and a blueberry muffin then grabbed some napkins and headed to the office Lance had designated as her work space.

After devouring her bagel Meena slowly picked at the muffin as she read over the last couple of pages she'd written. She was at that love scene again, the one Lance wanted to be intense and invigorating. Her thoughts immediately went back to last night and she picked up a piece of paper and began to fan herself.

"Hot? Should I turn up the air conditioning?" the deep familiar voice asked from the doorway.

Meena spared him a glance. "Go away, I'm working."

Lance ignored her and entered the room, closing the door behind him. "I wouldn't want you to be uncomfortable while you work."

"Then you should definitely leave," she said as she watched him approach the desk and then take a seat on its side.

"Do I make you uncomfortable?" he asked.

She looked at him because she knew that he was used to women cowering beneath his candid questioning. "No. But you are distracting me. I thought your main purpose in bringing me down here was to avoid that."

He nodded. "You're absolutely right. Yesterday my focus was my screenplay."

He was looking at her hungrily and Meena was having a hard time ignoring the same need growing inside herself. "And today?"

"Today I'm torn. I don't like to be torn, Meena. I'm used to knowing my goal and heading directly for it."

"Then if your goal is no longer the screenplay I can return to New York to work." She stood only to have his hands on her shoulders stop her. Without much effort he pulled her until she was standing between his legs.

"I said yesterday my goal was the screenplay." He let his hands fall to her arms moving slowly up and down. "I'm torn today because I can't figure out what I want more, the screenplay completed or you naked."

She should have been shocked but after last night that would have been foolish. She was, however, determined to keep a sane head in this situation. "While I'm sure both are equally pressing in your mind, I have to keep my mind on my work. As you've stated I've taken longer than either of us anticipated and I'd like to remedy that situation." She pulled away from him and he grabbed her at the waist.

"It's not that easy."

She turned back to face him. "It is for me."

"I find that hard to believe," he said and knew he was telling the truth. She looked great this morning. He'd seen her when she'd come down the stairs in her white capris and teal t-shirt. She wore silly teal flip flops with white polka dots on them that for some reason seemed outrageously sexy. He'd awakened with one intention this morning, to get her in his bed as soon as possible.

He hadn't lied, the screenplay was important, but so was this overwhelming urge to experience everything he could sexually with her. Last night had proved she was open to lots of things whether she was aware of it or not he wasn't quite sure. Wouldn't that be something if he were the one to break her in?

The mere thought was an aphrodisiac.

"Look, at any other time this might be fun. But right now, at this point in my life, my career, I just don't have a lot of time to play."

Lance sensed something else behind those words but figured if she wanted him to know she would have just come right out and told him. Still, he didn't think the dominant approach was going to work with her, just yet, so he shifted gears. Meena definitely had a submissive nature, it was just going to take a moment for him to pull it out of her. "Then I'll help you work so you can have more time to play," he said and leaned over the desk to pick up the screenplay with his notations on it. "Where were you?" he asked ignoring the fact that she'd rolled her eyes at his suggestion.

"Act Three, Caleb and Wendy are in the library when they discover they're attracted to each other. You didn't like how the scene originally played out so I have to re-write it."

Lance nodded. "Right. I thought it was too tame, too safe. I want something more intense and pivotal."

"So should Caleb just jump her in the history section and get it over with?" she asked sarcastically and returned to her seat.

He looked at her and almost smiled. "No, not quite that intense. Something more like a slow build up." He took a step towards her. "They're in the library pouring over maps and books about Italian geography yet they can't stop thinking about this heat between them."

Again she used a sheet of paper to fan herself. "Yeah, the heat. Well, it is summertime," she whispered.

Lance did smile inwardly this time. He was getting to her. "I've got an idea. Why don't you and I act out some scenarios and see what works best."

She raised a brow.

"C'mon," he said, "it'll work. Let's get those creative juices flowing."

She squirmed in the chair and Lance knew she'd picked up his real meaning.

He stood behind her and leaned over her shoulder. "So I'm Caleb and you're Wendy. We're looking at these maps," he spoke his voice lowering as he moved in closer over her shoulder. "I can't really concentrate on what I'm reading because the scent of your hair is tickling my nose."

She moved to the side, away from him.

"Meena, really, I'm trying to help."

With a heavy sigh she returned to her position not believing for one second he wasn't enjoying toying with her or Wendy or whoever the hell she was supposed to be. "Fine. I'm Wendy and I'm nervous because what I'm feeling for you shouldn't be. We're supposed to be tracking the Fountain of Love together, colleagues, not lovers," she said with emphasis.

Lance only smiled. "But the connection between us is so strong, so potent. Like right now I can almost hear your heart beat and it's in sync with mine. Every time you move your fingers over those pages I get chills because I imagine them moving over me, wrapping around me."

He was so close his breath tickled her cheek. He smelled heavenly and looked even better. Meena closed her eyes. "I feel it to. It's a simmering kind of heat that starts at the pit of my stomach the moment you walk into a room. The closer you get to me the hotter it grows. I feel like I'm on the edge waiting for you to reach out to me, needing you to come soon."

Lance touched her shoulders and Meena tilted her head to the side. He kissed the spot just beneath her ear then blew his breath over the moistness. "And I'm telling you I'm here, I know you've been waiting and I've come to give you your release. Will you allow me that pleasure?"

His tongue made a heated path down her neck and Meena's hands gripped the arms of the chair. "I'm begging you to give me release."

Lance turned the chair around so that she was now facing him. Quickly he lifted her shirt to find her unbound breasts. With open mouth he leaned forward and took one dark brown nipple into his mouth while his hand squeezed its mate.

His teeth scraped over her sensitive skin and Meena's legs instinctively fell open. She was so hot for him, so ready for him to sink that long black penis she'd spied last night into her that she couldn't breathe. His mouth was working her into a heated frenzy and she couldn't stop her hands from moving to the back of his head, holding him in place. "We should stop," she whispered.

His head lifted quickly. "Don't sáy 'stop'," he said seriously.

She looked confused and he smiled leaning forward to take her mouth in a tender yet sensual kiss. Pulling away Lance stroked a finger over her cheek. "We need another word, a safe word that's not so jarring as 'stop'." In the Lifestyle sometimes Doms pushed their Submissives further than they wanted to go. So it was highly likely for a submissive to say stop but not really mean it. Using a safe word cleared all confusion.

Meena didn't have a clue what he was talking about but was torn between wanting him to just screw her and get it over with and wanting to catch the first plane smoking back to the Big Apple.

"Let's say 'tomatoes'. I hate tomatoes, so if you say it I'll know you really want me to stop."

"I don't understand," she heard herself saying as his tongue twirled lazy circles over her nipple and she couldn't think straight.

"It's okay. Just go with what you feel."

That was the problem, she was feeling way too much with him. She wanted him so badly her teeth were about to chatter, her legs were already shaking. "Caleb…Lance," she corrected.

"Lance," he repeated. "I am Lance and only I can do this to you. For the time that you are here you belong to me." It wasn't a traditional collaring but his declaration would have to suffice. He took one nipple into his mouth and bit down on it until she screamed. The sound of her scream was like music to his ears. .

Lance was just about to unbutton her pants when a chirping sound interrupted their interlude. Her body stilled and his hand paused at the waistband of her pants. The chirping persisted until she reached over onto the desk and grabbed her cell phone putting it to her ear and answering in an unsteady voice.

"Meena Denison."

Lance continued to kiss the underside of her breasts loving the weighty feel of each globe in his hands.

"Oh no, Corine, you're not disturbing me at all," she lied.

Lance groaned and nipped her skin. She jumped but didn't make a sound.

"So are you feeling better? Oh, you found a doctor there? Corine we really need to talk about all these drugs you're taking. I just don't think they're necessary."

The tone of her voice had changed from unsteady and aroused to concerned. He stopped kissing and continued listening.

"I know, honey, but it's been over a year since the divorce, you've got to move on. Maybe when you come back we can start looking for another job for you."

She sat up straighter in the chair tension emanating from her in waves. Lance pulled her shirt down, but did not move from between her legs, instead he rested his palms on her thighs trying to massage her into a calmer state. She rubbed her temples as she spoke.

"Well, you can't hide in Paris forever." Especially since I'm footing the bill, Meena thought. A few moments ago she'd been ready to sing a blissful tune of release. She'd wanted Lance inside of her so desperately and she knew it was coming, they were so close. Corine's call was definitely an unwanted interruption. Compounded with the fact she was getting more than a little tired of hearing her sister whining about not being happy and missing her life and feeling so desolate she could scream with frustration.

Now she was completely out of the mood as she suspected Lance realized by the way he'd abruptly stopped kissing her and fixed her clothes. But he hadn't left her as she'd half expected. In fact, his hands were working some nice magic on her legs. He'd started at her thighs and was now massaging her calves. It was a stark contrast to the growing frustration of speaking to Corine.

"I know. Yes, Corine. Yes, call me tomorrow. Ok, honey. I love you, too," she said then snapped the phone shut. Tossing it back onto the desk she let her head fall back and she groaned.

"Trouble in Paris?" Lance asked casually as his hands moved from her calves to massage one foot.

"That was my sister, Corine. She went to Paris a month ago as a part of her year long therapy."

"That's a lot of therapy. What's she being treated for?"

"Mmm," Meena moaned as he worked the ball of her foot. His hands were definitely heaven-sent. "She went through a messy divorce. Her husband left her for his dentist and moved to LA."

Lance nodded. That kind of thing happened everyday yet he could still see how it would jolt someone who wasn't prepared. Although he didn't know how one would go about being prepared for something like that especially since he barely took time away from business to have real relationships. That was another reason the Lifestyle hadn't worked one hundred percent for him. He just didn't have the time it would take to properly learn everything he needed to know to be a Master Dom. Yet he thoroughly enjoyed the bits and pieces he did know and practiced them when the opportunity arose.

"She's unemployed?"

"Mmhmm," Meena nodded.

"Then how is she paying to stay in Paris?"

"She's not. I am."

Lance's hands stilled and she looked up at him in protest. "You're paying for her to stay in Paris as some sort of recuperation?"

"I know it's crazy and I know I need to pull the plug. That's actually what I've been working on for the past few weeks, which has kept me from the screenplay. Well, one of the things that's kept me from working."

He looked up at her then, with what appeared to be concern on his face. "What else has been distracting you?"

With a wavering smile Meena slipped her foot from his grasp and attempted to stand. But he was still on his knees so that she was now looking down at him. He was eye level with her crotch and her entire body began to tingle. "Nothing," she stuttered. "I should get back to work."

Lance stood using a finger to tip her chin as he did. "I want you to tell me what else is bothering you. I can't fix it if I don't know what it is."

"I didn't ask you to fix it," she stated blandly.

"It's interfering with your work and that's not acceptable."

Meena blinked in confusion. "Well, you and this," she flailed her arms. "Whatever we were just doing was interfering with my work."

"No. It was putting you in the right mood to write the scene."

Meena opened her mouth to object but realized he was probably correct. Last night combined with these past few minutes with him had given her a line on where Caleb and Wendy could take their newfound attraction.

Lance rubbed a finger over her bottom lip. "Now, let me handle your distractions while you work. Corine is one and what's the other?"

Meena sighed, hating to reveal her personal dilemmas to a virtual stranger. But there was just something about this man. He had a charisma that was alluring. His good looks and arrogance were blatant but every now and then there was this spark of compassion that appealed to her as well. And that spark had her ready to reveal something she hadn't told anyone else. "I caught my boyfriend cheating on me."

Lance raised a brow as if to say 'is that all?' and she continued. "He was having sex with two other men. In my bed."

The look on Lance's face was priceless and Meena couldn't hold back her laughter. "You asked."

Lance cleared his throat. "Ah, yeah, I guess I did." He shook his head as if that action would make the words go away.

"Chris and I had been together for about nine months. I thought I knew him. I guess I was wrong. I mean I had no idea he was interested in those things, sexually, I mean."

"The two of you never discussed sex?"

"To the extent that we knew how to get each other off, yes."

He was toying with her hair now, seemingly recovered from his shock. "There's so much more to sex than just getting off."

She looked at him probably not believing he—a man—had just said that. "I know that. I'm just saying that Chris and I didn't talk about sex a lot. Come to think of it, we didn't talk a lot at all. But I never would have guessed…anyway, now he keeps calling me and writing me notes to apologize."

"And have you accepted his apology?"

"Yes. Well, no. I mean, I just can't get that vision out of my mind. Him naked with those men, in my bed, doing those things."

"What upset you most? That he was cheating in your bed or that he was cheating with men? Do you have something against bisexuals?"

Meena thought about the question for a moment. She wasn't quite sure what he was asking her but damn she hoped Lance didn't like men too, she couldn't take it happening to her twice. "I guess I don't have anything against someone who wants to live an alternative sexual lifestyle. It's their prerogative. But I do have a problem with dishonesty. If that's what you're into then you should just say so from the get go."

Lance considered her words. "I'll keep that in mind." He leaned forward quickly and brushed her lips with his. "In the meantime I'd like you to get to work on Scene Three."

"I should call Corine back, she didn't sound too good."

"No." Lance retrieved her phone from the desk and slipped it into his pocket. "No more phone calls. You," he said guiding her to her seat and pushing her down into it, "need to get to work. We're having dinner at seven. That gives you six uninterrupted hours."

Meena looked at her computer screen. "You're right. I need to get cracking. Okay, so just tell Corine I'll call her back and when Chris' name pops up just ignore it," she said then scooted her chair closer to the desk and set her fingers on the keyboard.

Lance left her alone with no intention of following either one of her directives.

Chapter 5

Control. Lance thrived on it. In business and in his personal life, what personal life he had. And with Meena, there would be no exception.

It only took a few calls to narrow down where Meena's sister was in Paris and to send over a therapist to get the woman out of the hotel room and on a plane back to New York. From there he was paying this therapist damn good money to get Corine Denison on the right track, without bothering Meena.

Now, Chris was another problem all together. He had no idea who this person was and was only minutely hesitant in contacting him. His number was programmed in her phone which meant he still meant something to her. But Lance would not let that deter him. After giving it an hour of thought he decided he'd simply wait until Chris called, which, if Meena were correct, he would. Lance couldn't help but wonder why the man was so intent on obtaining Meena's forgiveness for the life he chose to lead. Lance made it a rule never to apologize for who or what he was.

Meena made him want to further explore the sexual desires he had. Funny how he hadn't realized how much he'd neglected himself on a personal level, but it had been important for him to succeed in business, for him to succeed in everything. Now that he was here, spending time with Meena to get this screenplay completed he figured he could give himself a little personal attention as well.

In his office Lance pulled out some of the books he'd acquired on the BDSM Lifestyle. Some things he remembered, others were new, he absorbed it all in preparation for tonight.

Meena felt rejuvenated. She'd written non-stop for four of the six hours Lance had given her alone. After she completed Scene Three and the following two scenes as well, she'd gone for a swim. Lance's house was gorgeous and the pool that encompassed two levels in his back yard had been too tempting to pass up. So beneath the intense rays of the Miami sun she'd swam until her arms ached, loving the feel of the cool water against her warm skin.

It was the same warmth that had surfaced the moment Lance walked into the office and radiated just beneath the surface when he was away. Lance Radford was a gorgeous man, a rich and successful man, a dominating man Meena wouldn't ordinarily be attracted to. She liked her men relatively cute, employed and just a tad on the thuggish side. Lance surpassed all of that. Yet he didn't strike her as a relationship man, else why would he be single? Actually, she didn't know for a fact if he was single. She'd never asked and she probably should have considering the things she'd done with him already.

But there was only the attraction between them, an attraction she'd decided to act on and deal with the consequences later. If her thoughts were correct and Lance was not a relationship type of man then there would be no consequences. She'd enjoy him just as she was enjoying his house and the time to write without interruption. Oh, who was she kidding? It wasn't even about all that. At this point it was about the throbbing in her center every time she thought about him. It was about the intensity of the climax she'd experienced last night by her own hands as he'd watched her. It was about sex and she was going to have herself a healthy helping of it with Lance Radford before all was said and done.

That's why she took extra special care in dressing for the evening. She'd taken out a lovely silk peach sundress that just skimmed her knees, laying it on the bed before heading into the shower. But after scrubbing her body with the delicious smelling peach soap she'd returned to the bedroom to find another dress on the bed. It was black. She lifted it by the thin straps and held it in front of her. A slip dress with slits up each side, not bad. Beside the dress was a note: 7:30. Don't be late.

Yep, Lance Radford was arrogant and dominating. Her nipples tightened with the thought. She slipped into the dress loving the feel of the satiny material against her skin. Deciding to leave her hair hanging straight, she applied her makeup and sprayed herself with perfume. At seven twenty-eight she walked down the stairs.

He stood at the door like a Greek God for the twenty-first century wearing all black. Slacks, a ribbed shirt that perfectly sculpted his pecs and abs and a blazer gave him an aristocratic air. Black was definitely his color. His goatee was tight, trimmed to perfection, his dark eyes bearing into her as she moved. She was entranced, unable to take her eyes from him as she grew closer. There was this magnetic pull between them so that words were not necessary.

"Right on time," he said smugly. "You will be rewarded for your obedience."

For a split second Meena wanted to argue with his choice of words but the level of attraction heightened between them as he spoke, her heart actually hammering at the sound of his voice. "I like rewards," she said simply and allowed him to escort her through the door.

If Meena thought Lance's house was impressive, his yacht was unbelievable. It was a Silhouette 540 Pilothouse Motoryacht, he'd told her, whatever that was. All Meena knew was that it was big and shiny and beautiful. In the waning sunlight boats were docked all along the pier, but the swirling black letters that spelled out Ecstasy seemed to sparkle.

With the help of a man she assumed was the Captain, Meena boarded the boat after Lance. The interior was decorated with cherry wood and a luxurious beige carpet that her four inch heels sank blissfully into. Seconds after they were aboard, the engine started and they pulled out of the dock.

Lance immediately went to the bar and poured two glasses of champagne. Turning to face her with both glasses in hand he gave her a slight smile. "Sit down, Meena. I have something I want to talk to you about."

Meena sat because the caramel colored leather sofa was very inviting. She reached for the other glass of champagne and was puzzled when he didn't offer it to her.

"What I have to say might be different from what you've ever experienced." He took a sip from one of the glasses. "But I have a feeling you're more open to it than you would like to believe."

Meena let her hand fall in her lap and stared at him quizzically. "What are you talking about?"

"In essence I'm talking about sex."

She smiled. "Then you're correct. I'm definitely interested in sex."

Lance smiled as well and finally offered the glass of champagne to her. "I know that part." He took a seat beside her and watched as her lips touched the rim of the glass and she sipped. His gut tightened as he thought of those lips on him.

"I'm not the man you think I am," he said finally.

"Really?" She sat back against the sofa and looked at him with an amused expression. "And who exactly are you?"

"I have these fantasies I guess you would call them. I think of them more as cravings, deep desires that I like to act out."

Okay, she was intrigued. "And what are some of your fantasies, Lance?" If he wanted her to be his fantasy lover she could most likely oblige. She had a naturally adventurous spirit coupled with a healthy sex drive. This evening should be interesting.

"Are you familiar with BDSM?"

Meena had been in the process of taking another sip of champagne and almost choked on his question. With slow, deliberate movements Lance rubbed her back and took the glass from her placing it on the coffee table in front of them.

"Excuse me," she coughed.

"Bondage and Discipline. Dominance and Submission. Sadomasochism."

She licked her lips and swallowed deeply. Of course she'd heard of it and while she didn't quite understand it, she admitted only to herself with some semblance of curiosity. "I've heard of it. Is that what you're into?"

Lance took both her hands rubbing his thumbs over their backs. "There are certain aspects of the Lifestyle that I am into. I wanted to tell you this up front so there would be no misconceptions between us."

Like there had been with her and Chris. Meena thought it incredibly sensitive of him to approach her this way. Three brownie points for Lance!

"What aspects are you into?" she asked quietly.

"I like the power," he stated simply. "The Submissive giving the Dominant complete control."

"Are you talking about whips and handcuffs? Is that what you want from me?" Her heart thumped at the thought. She was game for the handcuffs but wasn't entirely sure she was going to let Lance whip her for his sexual satisfaction.

"I'm talking about you trusting me, completely. About you allowing me to bring us both into the throes of pure primal ecstasy. BDSM is not about abuse, Meena. It is about the exploration of two people and their sexual limitations. I want to share that with you."

She tried to pull her hands away. She needed to stand, to walk and think about this for a minute, but he would not let her go.

"Above all else you must trust me. I won't hurt you."

His eyes bore into hers and Meena couldn't turn away. Something moved around them, as if they were caught in a sexually charged twister that wouldn't let either of them go. She didn't know what to say or do for that matter. She'd resigned herself to sleeping with him but she had no idea the extent of that decision.

"I don't think you would hurt me, Lance. I'm just not sure where this BDSM will lead or if I'm even ready for it."

Lance lifted a hand to cup her cheek and smiled. "You are more ready than you think." His thumb traced her bottom lip and he watched as she trembled. "You're very responsive and very eager to learn. You just have to let down your guard. Trust and enjoy."

Lance led her up a winding staircase into the bedroom where a king sized bed was against one wall and a long dresser against the other. The dress he'd had Sara take to her was perfect. It's plunging, or should he say non-existing back left it impossible for her to wear any underwear which had been driving him insane for the last hour. Unable to further resist he ran his fingers down her bare back and watched her shiver.

"You like when I touch you, don't you, Meena?"

"Yes," she whispered and turned to face him. Lifting her arms she attempted to pull him to her but he grabbed her wrists and held her away.

"You must be submissive to my will now. That means you do what I tell you, when I tell you."

Meena let her hands drop to her side. "Okay."

"Most Submissives call their Dominant Master, but you don't have to. I like the sound of my name on your lips." He removed his jacket. "But you will obey as I am now your Dominant."

Meena nodded not sure how in depth this dominant and submissive thing was but in for a penny, in for a pound.

"Take your dress off."

Taking a step back Meena slipped each strap off her shoulder and let the dress fall to the floor. Her unclad nipples hardened instantly. She probably should have felt uncomfortable being all but naked in front of a man she'd really only met yesterday, but she didn't. It felt natural and erotic to have him watching her with such hunger. She could tell that it was a test of his strength to keep his distance. His dark eyes drank her in as if he wanted to retain this moment for future memories.

"Turn around," he said gruffly.

She did and he took a step toward her. Her skin was golden and his fingers itched to touch it. She was sheer perfection, her butt round and protruding. She had runner's legs, muscles stretching in her thighs and calves. He couldn't wait to sink into her. Although playing with a submissive did not have to actually involve penetration he definitely planned to go deep.

He slipped a finger beneath the band of her thong, rubbing his skin against hers. "Part of being a good submissive is knowing how to take direction. Knowing that whatever I do is for your enjoyment as well as my own. Knowing I will not hurt or berate you in any way." His hands spanned her hips and he pulled her back against him. She felt so good there, his penis throbbed pressing deeper into her back.

"Get on the bed, on your hands and knees."

Again, Meena did as she was told.

"Very good," Lance whispered and watched her butt cheeks spread until he could see the puffy lips of her center. He swallowed deeply and reached out both hands, palming her cheeks, pulling them further apart. His fingers dug into her, yet she did not make a sound. "Relax. I want to know how this makes you feel. What does my touching do to you?"

He squeezed her again and had the pleasure of seeing a line of essence dripping down her thigh. "You like this, don't you?"

"Yes. I do."

"How much?"

"Very much." It was a breathy whisper. "I like when you're rough," she added.

He squeezed her tighter and felt a trickle of sweat down his back.

"I've dreamt of punishing you for not having my screenplay completed."

Meena didn't know what the hell was going on. How had she gone from deciding to sleep with this man to agreeing to be his test submissive? What she did know was that with every command he gave, her need for him grew. With every touch desire built to a bursting temple inside of her. She clenched the coverlet between her fingers to keep from screaming out. He hadn't even touched her intimately—well he hadn't touched her dripping wet center—and she was ready to come.

Any longer and she was sure to explode. "Punish me, please!" She heard a voice say but couldn't distinguish if it was hers or not.

"Relax," Lance said and moved to the stand beside the bed. Reaching into the drawer he took out a fur covered paddle. Moving to stand behind her he brushed the back of his hand over her butt again. Meena arched her back and hissed.

"Do you trust me, Meena?"

"Yes," she answered softly.

Lance's mouth watered at the delectable sight before him. Her juices ran down her legs, staining his coverlet. She was waiting for him to do his will, she was waiting for him to punish her. Blood roared loudly in his head, his erection straining against his pants. He wanted to sink his erection deep inside of her, he wanted to feel the hood of her womb and find his release there.

Drawing back his arm he came down with a swoosh, letting the paddle smack against her right butt cheek.

She jolted then moaned.

He smacked the left butt cheek, his teeth gritted with restraint.

"More," she growled.

He gave her what she asked for until her butt turned a cherry red. Falling to his knees he licked the bruised flesh then blew cool air over it.

"Lance, please," she begged.

He moved with slower, more precise movements kissing her plump bottom while slipping his fingers between her crease. She was wet all over, from her anus to her slick folds. He craved her like an addict craved drugs. He wanted her like a child wanted toys on Christmas day. It was addictive, this lifestyle he dabbled in. So much so that he knew now he would take the time to learn all he could and to find the right submissive to share his newfound knowledge with.

"Turn around and touch me," he told her.

Meena stayed on her knees but turned so that her face was now lined up with his groin. Her center pulsated with need, her heart hammering in her chest. But more than her desire for him physically Meena felt an overwhelming desire to please him, to do whatever he asked in the hopes of making him happy. He had punished her for not having his screenplay completed. After tonight she would write like the wind to finish that screenplay in anticipation of what she might receive as a reward.

She unfastened his pants, released his thick erection and held it in her hand, staring indulgently. He was gorgeous. Last night she'd glimpsed him, but up close and personal there was no comparison. Thick and long she stroked his silky dark skin. Her tongue moistened her lips as she stared at the mushroom head, the murky fluid seeping from his slit.

"Taste me," he said in a voice that sounded tortured.

Meena dipped her head taking him into her mouth. In one, slow gulp she had his entire length ensconced, his bulbous head resting at her tonsils. He sighed but did not touch her. She hummed around him and he cursed.

Meena sucked him like she'd never sucked anyone before, taking his length in and out of her mouth with fluid precision. He tasted wonderful, masculine and musky, big and invigorating. God, she wanted to swallow him whole. He started pumping into her mouth and Meena knew he was about to come. Lance must have known it too because he quickly pulled out of her.

"Not yet. Take off my clothes."

With the back of her hand Meena wiped the spit that mingled with his pre-juices from her lips then proceeded to remove his shirt. Stepping from the bed she bent down to undo his shoes, discard his socks and push his pants and boxers down his strong legs. When she stood in front of him he cupped her face.

"Safe, sane, consensual," he said holding her gaze, "that's what this is about. You are here to please me. But I, too, am encouraged by your pleasure. Tell me now if you want this. If you don't, tell me so I can walk away now."

Biting on her bottom lip Meena tried to remember why she shouldn't be agreeing to virtually being his sex slave, why she should grab her clothes and get the hell off this boat. "Yes, I want this."

"Get up on the bed and show me your pussy."

While she climbed onto the bed Lance retrieved a condom from his nightstand drawer and sheathed his erection. She'd done exactly as he'd told her and he was more than pleased, now he would give her what she wanted. Climbing between her legs he looked down at her swollen labia, the folds glistening with her essence. Leaning close but not touching her Lance inhaled deeply. Her scent was intoxicating. He'd smelled it in the kitchen long after she'd left last night, which was why he'd been sure to ask Sara to clean with bleach this morning. He could smell her all day and all night, but he definitely did not want anyone else smelling her.

"Hold yourself open for me."

Slipping her hands down her torso Meena used her fingers to part her labia then tilted her hips.

Grabbing the base of his erection Lance guided his tip into her. Above all else he wanted to go slow, to savor every moment of this first penetration but he was too aroused. The combination of the paddling on her juicy buttocks and her hot mouth on his rigid cock had him overworked. The moment his tip touched her hole he plunged deep, pulled out and plunged deeper still, determined to stretch her until her walls were crafted just for him.

She took his thrusts, lifting her legs and clasping them around his waist. Her breasts jiggled and his thrusts went deeper, faster. He was losing control, he was in danger of coming before her and that was not allowed.

"Come for me, Meena. Now!"

Lance knew that he'd yelled. He saw the quick flash of fear as he spoke the words then felt her walls clamping tighter around him. So this is what she liked.

"I want you to come for me. Show me how much you want me, how much you want to please me. Now, Meena! Scream how much you want this!"

She thrashed beneath him and he covered her clit with his thumb, rubbing roughly over the tightened bud. Her hands moved to her breasts, squeezing them tightly.

"Lance!" she yelled. "This is too much! I can't! I can't!"

But she hadn't said the safe word he'd given her earlier today. She hadn't used the only out he'd given her. So Lance kept going, pumping into her and working her clit at the same time. When her breathing became erratic Lance moved his hand to her hip, then slipped around to squeeze her butt cheek and move further to her ass. Because she was already so wet the tip of his finger slipped into her tight sphincter without much effort. And Meena released the first of several screams as a prelude to the sweetest release he'd ever felt.

His erection slid in and out of her, gliding effortlessly on her release. "Good girl. Very good girl, Meena."

When she stopped writhing Lance pulled his finger from her anus and pumped her slowly once more before pulling out. He kissed her forehead, then her cheeks, then her lips before whispering, "Turn over. I want to come all over your beautiful ass."

When she was again positioned beneath him with her back to him Lance touched the ass he was sure would haunt his dreams for the rest of his life. He lifted her slightly so that her butt was in the air but she wasn't quite on her knees. She was still feeling her release and so her body was pliant and willing for him to do with what he pleased. And there was so much more he wanted to do to this gorgeous body yet his own was screaming for release.

So with the decision made for him he spread her ass cheeks and plunged inside pumping her so hard the globes jiggled against him. The deep penetration, the slickness of her walls, her scent filtrating through the room and the small moans now escaping her mouth made his efforts short-lived and well-deserved. Lance pulled out of her just as he felt his balls tightening. Slipping the condom off and tossing it aside he stroked the base of his erection until his release spurted in thick waves to land on her still red bottom, sliding down the rounded globes like icing on a cake.

Chapter 6

True to her word, in the next weeks Meena worked diligently on the screenplay feeling the sweet rush of accomplishment at the end of each re-written scene. It probably helped that Lance often worked with her and more often ended each writing session with another Lifestyle lesson.

Meena had been in Miami for almost a month and had learned more about herself and her sexual needs and desires than she had in her entire thirty-one years. For instance, she'd always had a really strong personality, part of her Taurean nature. But she now found that she secretly desired someone to take charge, to guide her, to dominate her. And Lance took pleasure in doing just that.

He was also true to his word; he never hurt her. Even the night he'd taken her into the basement and tied her to a platform then covered her in wax, he hadn't hurt her. The sensations were new and intense and she'd come like fireworks on the fourth of July, when Lance had finally given her permission. That was something else she thoroughly enjoyed. Orgasm depravation sounded painful and cruel but instead was intense and very rewarding. When—and some nights it took longer than others—Lance finally gave her permission to come it was like being reborn. She had no idea how she would ever go back to having regular sex after her time with Lance.

Or if she even wanted to do.

But Lance didn't speak of permanence. During aftercare, which was the time after playing or sex that the Dom took care of his Submissive, performing tasks like cuddling, cleansing and explaining the things that had just occurred, Lance had told her a lot about himself. She now knew that in addition to being arrogant and self-centered he was ambitious and controlling. These traits sounded bad, but they made him who he was and he was a man that she could quite possibly fall in love with.

That was a scary thought and each night when she lay in the huge bed in his room where she now slept, she pushed it to the back of her mind. While Lance had outdone Chris by telling her up front what he wanted and expected of her, she still was afraid of getting too close. The fact that Lance could dominate her body and her mind put her heart and her soul in grave danger.

It was late in the afternoon and Lance would be coming to visit her soon. Meena pushed thoughts of him and where this relationship was going out of her mind, moving her fingers over the keyboard instead. The screenplay was almost completed. She would make Lance's deadline with time to spare. For that he would be pleased.

What happened after that was anybody's guess.

"How's she doing with the therapy?" Lance asked Madison about Corine Denison. The therapist he'd hired had successfully gotten Corine out of Paris. The woman was now in an intensive session in which she was being forced to admit her innermost feelings, no matter how painful. This session required that she focus only on herself and her feelings so her contact with the outside world was minimal. Which for Meena and the screenplay, turned out to be a good thing.

Meena was working diligently, her changes were brilliant and Lance found himself growing more excited each day he checked on her progress. The screenplay was wonderful and the movie would be a definite hit. He would be forever grateful to Meena for that.

In return he felt like he was helping her by getting her dependent sister to a more independent status. Even without this deadline Meena didn't deserve to have to take care of a grown woman who couldn't accept that her husband had left her. Lance wasn't totally uncompassionate he just wished the woman didn't lean on Meena so hard. Perhaps this therapy would get her on the right track.

In the last weeks Meena had only asked about her cell phone and the calls, once. She'd seemed totally satisfied with his report that he'd spoken with Corine and she was doing well. She didn't ask at all if Chris had called. This made Lance feel good. It meant that his presence in her life was pushing the memory of Chris and his blunder out of her mind. But was that enough? Did Lance just want to be a mental block for her hurt or did he want to mean more to her?

"Lance?" Madison's voice jolted him from his thoughts.

"Yes?"

"I asked when you were coming back? Dale wants to talk about that screenplay he sent you last month and you need to sign off on some of this pre-production stuff."

"FedEx me the pre-production invoices and I'll look at them, sign them and send them back. Tell Dale to hold off. I want to get Fountain of Love off the ground first." Thinking about Meena had his body hard and tense. Glancing at his watch he realized it was past time he saw her today. They had breakfast together every morning, this was after their shower and a little play which usually left him sated and satisfied until early evening. It was almost five and he was desperate for her again.

"You still didn't say when you're coming back?" Madison pressed.

"When the screenplay is done," he said simply and disconnected the line. He knew that Madison was searching for something. In his daily calls to the office she'd repeatedly asked how he and Meena were getting along. Without him telling her anything Lance was sure that his assistant knew much more than he was comfortable with.

Lance was on his way to Meena's office when need prickled almost painfully against his skin. The cravings he had for her right now surpassed anything he'd ever felt. What he had in mind for her tonight would take some time, time he didn't have since dinner would be on the table in an hour. So with great restraint he turned and went into his office. Picking up the phone he dialed the number for the other room and waited for her to pick up.

"Hello?"

"I'll see you at dinner in an hour."

"Ah, okay," she said her tone more than a little confused.

"Wear the green dress," he commanded, "And nothing else."

After his phone call Meena looked at her watch and immediately wrapped up the scene she'd been writing. Turning the computer off and making sure her notes were in order for tomorrow she stood and went upstairs to get dressed, fully expecting to see him in the room as well. But she was wrong.

He wasn't there and she couldn't tell if he'd been there and dressed already. Instead of continuing to wonder Meena showered and slipped on the emerald green silk dress Lance had purchased for her on their shopping spree last week. This was one of the five outfits he'd selected that she could actually wear outside. The rest were harnesses and leather thongs and bustiers and corsets intended for private viewing only.

She liked the dress, Lance had great taste. However, she knew he liked seeing her naked even more. The dress clasped at the back of her neck. It had no sleeves and almost no back. It came to just above her ankles where it flared out like a ballroom dancer. She slipped her feet into silver strappy sandals with three and a half inch heels. Meena was tall and Lance was taller. The heels were sexy and exciting especially when he told her to walk along his back with them on. She'd been hesitant at first, for fear of hurting him but each spike print that dotted his back as she did solicited guttural moans from him that totally aroused her. And when he'd turned over and he'd had her take the shoes off and scrape the heels over his toned chest the jutting of his massive erection and the spurt of pre-cum convinced her that pleasure could come in the form of pain.

After pulling her hair into a loose knot at her nape Meena applied a light coating of lip gloss and heavy mascara on her eyes. That was the only makeup Lance liked to see on her. She clipped on earrings and sprayed herself with the Kenneth Cole perfume he'd also purchased for her and left the room. Lance liked her to be on time. If not, she'd surely be punished. With that thought she paused at the top of the stairs. Punishment from Lance was not necessarily a bad thing.

He was already seated in the dining room wearing a brown short sleeved shirt and brown slacks. He'd shaved so that his goatee was thin and precise. She remembered the rough feel of it scraping her inner thigh this morning in the shower and her knees buckled.

He didn't look up to greet her just continued eating. He'd started without her which was his privilege. She, however, as his submissive, had to wait for his permission to eat. She knew she wasn't late so she couldn't figure out why he was already eating but knew enough from her training not to question him.

Instead she stood beside him until he nodded and then took her seat. Sara bought her a plate of food and a glass of wine. With another nod Meena knew it was okay to eat. So this is how tonight would start. Lance was also true to what he'd told her that night on the boat. He did switch from being a normal man having a normal affair to a Dom using his Sub. She didn't really have a preference, each side to him was arousing and satisfying. She considered that her primary reason for participating.

So tonight would be the Dom/Sub night. That was fine with her, her skin tingled with the thought of what play he would introduce her to tonight. Nobody would ever believe Meena Denison liked to be tied up gagged and spanked. All of these things were tremendously arousing when done properly. Lance had taught her that.

They were half way through their meal, Meena deep into her fantasies of what lay in store for her tonight, when Lance finally spoke.

"Corine is doing well. I spoke with Madison today and she's entering the final stages of her therapy."

Meena had been reaching for her glass when her hand stilled. "Therapy? What therapy?"

After wiping his mouth with his napkin, Lance looked at her. "The therapy I put her in. Jayne McDougal is great with women's issues. I gave her a synopsis of what Corine had suffered in the last year and she was more than happy to go to Paris to help her."

Meena could see Lance was proud of what he'd done, however, she wasn't feeling that pleased. "You sent a therapist to my sister? You told her personal problems to a stranger?" She couldn't really fault him since she'd in essence done the same thing by telling him.

"I got your sister the help she needed," he said simply.

"Who told you to?" she asked vehemently.

Lance let his hands fall into his lap. "Nobody tells me to do anything."

"Obviously," she said on a hoarse chuckle. "You're the great Lance Radford. You can do whatever you damn well please."

"I don't understand why you're angry." And she was just that. In the instant he'd mentioned her sister and the therapist Lance had watched her calm, contemplative features turn heated. The change was immediately arousing.

"I'm angry because my sister is none of your business."

"She is when she distracts you from doing work I hired you to do."

"Bullshit! My life is my own." Meena stood, leaning over to face him. "Just because I signed a contract to write a screenplay for you doesn't give you permission to run my life."

"No," Lance stated calmly. "The moment you accepted yourself as my Submissive you gave me that permission."

"Sex has nothing to do with this."

Lance stood then grasping her by the wrists. "What we do is not just about sex."

She pulled out of his grasp. "Like I said, what we do has nothing to do with my sister."

Lance didn't touch her although his body screamed for the connection. In her anger she was sexier, more desirable than he'd ever seen her and when he'd grabbed her the nipples he loved to suck had hardened, poking through the thin material of her dress, admitting she felt the same way.

"Anything and anyone connected to you is my concern. Your total focus must be on me. There's no room for anyone else."

Meena looked appalled as she stepped back away from the table. "That's ridiculous. She's my sister."

"And I am your Master. You belong to me!" he yelled.

Meena continued to back away. She'd never seen him like this before. He was yelling at her as though she'd done something wrong when he had been the one to overstep his grounds. He looked broad and formidable and for the first time since she'd met him she was afraid. "No. This is not what I want," she said shaking her head trying to get away.

Lance was on her in a second. Using only his body he pushed her against the wall trapping her. He grabbed her wrists and pinned them to her sides. "You don't want this?" he asked then ground his mouth down on hers taking her in a rough kiss that included his teeth sinking into her lips and sucking her tongue forcefully into his mouth.

"Or is it this that you don't want?" He yanked her skirt up and plunged his fingers between her freshly shaved crotch.

Meena struggled for coherent thought but his kiss was only the prelude to his next assault. Her heart hammered with fear, her hands began to sweat from nervousness yet the moment his fingers entered her center she was lost in desire. All she could focus on was his touch. "Lance," she breathed.

"You don't want this? You don't want me? If you say 'no' I won't believe you." He thrust three fingers deeply into her core, scraping along her honey-coated walls. "Your body says differently."

"I…I don't…want you taking over…my life," she hissed while what felt like his entire hand pumped in and out of her. "My sister…is…my…concern."

"No!" he roared and pulled his hand out of her. "You and everything about you are my concern!"

With that he lifted her carrying her back to the other end of the table opposite where they were eating and sat her on the edge. He pushed the dress up until her breasts were also bared before him. Pushing her back on the table he kneaded them roughly. "I won't allow anybody to come between us. Your focus will remain on me."

Her eyes closed to the pleasure and he yelled again. "Open your eyes! Look at me when I touch you!"

She opened her eyes, saw the intense rage mixed with equally intense lust and felt her essence seeping onto the table. All she could think of at that moment was soothing him, giving him whatever he needed, whatever he wanted that would make him happy again.

Of her own accord Meena lifted her legs so her heels were on the edge of the table. "I am focused on you now," she said offering herself to him. Lifting a hand she touched his face when he didn't move but continued to squeeze her breasts.

With hurried motions Lance freed his erection from his pants and entered her. Deep, swift strokes seemed to slake his anger and Meena took it all, her body jerking on the table. When he pulled out of her and put his mouth where his erection had just been she screamed his name.

His mind was so full of her. He'd been trying to help her by helping her sister. Why couldn't she understand that? Her sister needed to become independent? He wanted to help Corine get to that point so that Meena would not have to dedicate so much of her time holding Corine's hand. He was only looking out for Meena, his mate, his submissive.

She had to trust him, to understand that everything he did to and for her was so that they could be together. His tongue entered her hole and he felt her walls tighten around him.

"Please, Lance, pleeease," she begged.

"No." He didn't yell this time, he didn't have the heart to. "Not here. Not yet." He moved from between her legs, lifting her into his arms and carried her upstairs.

In his bedroom Lance lay her on the bed and removed her dress. From under his bed he removed a black box and opened it. Picking up three items he closed the box and put it onto the floor.

"I told you this was about trust, Meena. I need you to trust me. Completely."

Her eyes darted from the toys in his hand to his face and back to the toys again. He climbed onto the bed with her. "Do you trust me?"

She licked her lips. "Yes."

With that he applied the first clip to her taut nipple. Meena hissed and looked to him for guidance. "Relax. Just breathe and everything will be okay."

She took a deep breath and he clipped the other nipple. She closed her eyes tightly and he glided his fingers over her stomach.

"In a minute you will feel only pleasure. Just breathe."

As she continued to breathe Lance lifted her legs and spread them wide. He knew he was pushing things with her but she had to trust him completely, she had to rely on him for everything. He opened the tube of lubricant and applied it generously to his fingers then rubbed up and down her crease, over her puckered rear hole. She was so pre-occupied with the new sensations of the nipple clips that she wasn't paying attention to what he was doing…until he inserted the first finger.

Meena's hips lifted from the bed and she yelled out his name. He pushed his finger deeper, past his knuckle. He had to close his eyes at the extreme pleasure he felt from her tightness. Pulling his finger out he pushed it back in again thrusting his hips with the motion. In his pants his erection throbbed, wanting desperately to be gripped by her inner walls as his finger was. Before he came all over her, Lance slipped the anal plug into her then put her legs down.

Reaching up he removed the nipple clips and licked each nipple, tenderly, lovingly.

"Lance,"

"It's okay. You're doing great," he whispered while releasing his hot sex from his pants. He slipped his arousal into her wet center once more. He didn't take her forcefully this time but instead moved in and out of her with slow torture. He knew the anal plug was causing foreign sensations just as the nipple clips had and he did not want to completely overwhelm her. His goal was to make her feel good, not to hurt her or scare her.

In moments her entire body was shaking and she chanted his name.

"Yes, Meena, come for me. Come hard for me."

And that she did. So hard Meena felt like she was having an out of body experience. Seriously, she felt like she'd stepped out of her skin and now hovered above looking down on him pleasuring her. When she thought she couldn't move another muscle she felt herself lifting up off the bed grabbing his erection in her hand then lowering her head to take it into her mouth. "Now I want you to come hard for me."

And when she sucked him while cupping his balls Lance knew he was going to do just that. Steadily Lance pumped into her mouth enjoying the feel of her hands on his balls when she shifted and he felt her small fingers at his anus. Instinctively his muscles tightened then she began licking his mushroomed head until pre-juices coated her lips. He looked down and saw her shining lips sliding down over his rigid length again and felt everything releasing. Her finger slid into his puckered hole just seconds before his cum shot into her throat. Tilting her head Meena swallowed every drop.

Licking her lips as his fingers whispered over her cheeks Meena wondered what she'd really gotten herself into.

Chapter 7

So she's into the Submissive thing, Meena thought while she soaked in a hot bath the next morning. What did that mean?

Lance explained more to her last night after their interlude in the dining room and then the bedroom. As her Dominant he would basically control her. Whatever he told her to do she would do and she would do it because she wanted to, not just because he told her to. Already she thought of what he would think of her hair, her dress, even how she walked before she did it. And the moment she saw him she was ready and willing to do whatever she could to please him. Did that make her a Submissive?

According to Lance it signaled she was definitely open to being collared. This meant that once he, her Dom, gave her a special collar, it would signify to the world that she belonged to him and him alone.

Could she be branded by a man? Wasn't that the equivalent to wearing a man's wedding ring after you married him?

Sinking down into the tub she acknowledged so many other questions, so many reasons for walking out of this house and never looking back and only one that said she should stay: Lance.

These past few weeks had been the most relaxing and fulfilling she'd ever experienced. Lance was more than a thoughtful lover. Because he demanded much more of her than opening her legs and coming after his performance, their sexual experience was so much more memorable. Some would probably say him spanking her was medieval or cruel but it turned her on, heightening her pleasure beyond belief. And the thing that really tripped her out was that he enjoyed every minute of her ecstasy as if he, too, were feeling it. The whole experience was mind blowing and she found it hard to imagine her life now without it.

What would her sister think?

Again Meena wondered about Corine. Lance told her that the therapist he hired for her was the best and Meena had to agree that having Corine on her feet again would take a lot of stress off her. It had been so long and so taxing trying to take care of Corine, to keep her from falling apart and for Meena to live her own life. She should probably be thankful to Lance.

Still, it was awfully presumptuous of him to do so. But as he'd said so many times to her last night. She was his only concern, as his Submissive he had to make sure that she was taken care of so that she could, in turn, take care of him.

Funny, Meena would have never considered Lance Radford as being a man who needed to be taken care of. But he was. He liked the sheets turned down in a specific way before they slept at night. Meena did this for him. He liked his bath and shower water at a certain temperature. Meena did this for him. He liked his back massaged and his feet rubbed. She did this, too.

And in return, Lance sexed her like crazy.

But was that all there was to this BDSM thing? Was that all there was between her and Lance?

In just a few short weeks his life had been completely turned around. No longer was his work his sole focus. It was still a top priority but now there was something else. While he'd peaked into the BDSM Lifestyle he'd never spared much time to really explore what it could be like. Now that he was with Meena he made the time. He'd contacted a reputable Master Dom by the name of O'Rourke, who would train him in the Lifestyle. He wanted to be the very best he could be, for her.

All his life Lance had done things that suited him only to please himself. Now, he was thinking of someone else. Yes, the premise of their relationship would be that she served him but he would also serve her. He would cater to whatever she needed to keep her focused solely on him. That didn't mean he would take away everything in her life as Meena wrongly assumed last night. He wasn't trying to remove her sister from her life, he was simply trying to keep the woman from depending on Meena for everything. He would be the only one to depend on Meena from now on. He would be the only one she owed something to.

This felt right, this new relationship between them was absolutely right. It was what he'd been searching for all his life. In this house, with her, he'd opened up a new door to happiness and contentment.

He still needed to tie up a few loose ends before they returned to New York, before he could dedicate the time needed to his training and in turn, Meena's training.

With that in mind he lifted the phone and dialed his office in New York.

"I'm going to give you a telephone number and I want you to find out all you can about this person and send me his info," Lance told Madison.

"Okay," she said after he'd recited the number. "Anything else?"

"Yes. I need you to do some shopping. Just preliminary stuff like underwear, casual clothes, shoes, things like that."

"A shopping spree for me? What did I do to deserve that?" Madison said sarcastically.

"You know it's not for you."

"Then who's it for?"

"Madison, you are my assistant. There really is no need for you to know about my personal life. Now, I'll give you the sizes and—"

"Why don't I just call Meena Denison and ask her what size she wears? She can tell me specifically what styles she likes, too."

Lance frowned. She knew too damn much. "Just get it done, Madison."

"Will do," Madison said in a cheerful voice. "Now, what about Fountain of Love? Is it done? Do I need to arrange location flights? The Casting Director called yesterday, too. What should I tell her?"

"Tell her that Fountain of Love will be done on time. My name is on the line and I'm not about to take a financial hit for being late. I'll make sure it's complete if it's the last thing I do," he said adamantly.

Meena had been on her way to see him, to surprise him with the new jasmine scented soap she'd bathed in—those were the types of things she'd been doing lately. Lance loved the smell of her skin before and after he'd played with her. She craved his attention, his touch, so much that she'd stopped writing early to prepare for her time with him.

His office door was ajar and she'd slipped inside then closed it quietly behind her. He was on the phone, sitting in his chair facing the window. She tiptoed across the room wanting to be the very next thing he saw when he turned to hang up the phone. And that's when she heard it...

"Tell her that Fountain of Love will be done on time. My name is on the line and I'm not about to take a financial hit for being late. I'll make sure it's complete if it's the last thing I do," he said adamantly.

"So that's what this has all been about?" she asked before she realized he hadn't even disconnected his call yet.

Lance whirled around in his chair and faced her. "I'll call you back," he mumbled then placed the phone in its cradle.

"Meena. I didn't hear you come in."

"I guess you didn't," she said clenching and releasing her fists at her side. "Tell me all this Dom/Submissive, Lifestyle, crap you've been feeding me for the last few weeks wasn't just for this screenplay? Tell me you didn't bring me down here with the express intent of getting me into bed so I could ultimately do your bidding and provide this screenplay when you wanted it?" Her voice was rising, her anger growing as he continued to sit back in his chair with a calm look on his face.

"You know the reason I bought you here," he said simply.

Meena shook her head. "You used me!"

"No. I did not."

"You took me away from my home, you took me away from my sister, just so you could have your way with me! Just so I could do nothing but work on your damned screenplay!" He was still sitting, staring at her with blank, dark eyes. Meena took a step forward and lifted the statue on his desk and hurled it across the room. "You bastard!"

"Pick that up, Meena."

"Go to hell!"

Lance steepled his hands and continued to glare at her. "I told you on the plane that I needed you to focus on completing the screenplay. I never deceived you about your reason for being here."

"The moment you put your mouth between my legs you deceived me."

"I gave you pleasure. I would hardly call that deceitful."

"I didn't ask for your pleasure and I didn't ask to be flown down here in the midst of the summer heat to work on that screenplay. I told you I could complete it just as well at my home, in New York."

"But you weren't doing that. You were taking too long and I have a deadline."

"So you slept with me to meet a deadline?"

"No. That's not what I said."

"You aren't saying much of anything! But that's just fine. I'm outta here!" Meena stormed across the room and opened the door. She was halfway down the hall when she heard him yelling for her. She kept right on walking until she was in the room he'd originally assigned to her. With a slam of the door she locked it and began packing.

How could she have been so stupid? Lance Radford didn't want her as his submissive, he wanted her as his writing slave!

Chapter 8

Lance sat in his office for what seemed like hours after she'd stormed out. He had never run after a woman in his life, and didn't plan to start now. She would come to her senses. He was sure of it. In the meantime, Madison had emailed him the info on Chris Johnson, the man who had called Meena's phone at almost two A.M. this morning.

Meena had been fast asleep and her cell phone was in Lance's bottom dresser drawer. He probably should have just turned it off, but truth be told he was waiting for the man to call. Meena seemed to still harbor some feelings for this guy although Lance was sure they weren't feelings of love. She was confused and hurt by what he'd done. Lance didn't care who the guy slept with, he only wanted him to stop badgering Meena about his choice.

By the time he'd gotten to the phone it had stopped ringing, but the name illuminated on the caller ID screen bothered him all night long. He couldn't wait for the moment he was alone to talk to Madison. And as expected, his assistant had done a thorough job. On his computer, Lance viewed Chris Johnson's vital statistics, home address and work history for the last five years. He was about to pick up the phone to call the man and give him his final instructions when there was a soft knock on the door.

Sitting back in his chair Lance allowed a smile to tickle his lips. He'd known Meena would come to her senses. Her quick temper was something he admired but admitted would need to be tamed if they were to truly be together in the Lifestyle.

The knock sounded again. He'd let her wait a few more minutes before allowing her entrance. And when she came in he'd accept her apology, after she'd proven her trust and loyalty to him.

Again the knock sounded but the door opened before he could give permission. Lance frowned and stood prepared to discipline her once again for her rudeness.

"Mr. Radford," Sara began speaking immediately upon entering.

With a tightness in his gut he didn't want to address, Lance answered his housekeeper tersely, "Yes, Sara."

"She's gone."

"Who's gone?"

"Ms. Denison, sir. She's packed her bags and called a cab. They just pulled off."

"Dammit!" Lance slammed his fist down onto the desk. "Why didn't you come get me when the cab first got here? Why would you wait until she'd left?"

Sara simply shook her head. "She was crying, sir. I heard her crying for almost an hour before I got her to let me into her room. I know it's none of my business but she seemed so miserable, so pathetic. I just had to do what she asked me."

"You work for me, Sara! I pay you and I put a roof over your head. I won't tolerate you putting someone else over your loyalty to me."

"Yes, Mr. Radford. You're right. That's why I came to tell you as soon as they left."

Lance ran a hand over his face and was about to yell at the housekeeper again but caught himself. Sara was every bit of sixty years old. She'd worked for him ever since he bought this house ten years ago. She was good at her job. She took care of this house while he was away and did everything he asked when he was here. She was more like his family and he loved her. Thus, he reined in his temper and looked at her with a more mellow heart. "Thank you, Sara. You were right to inform me that Ms. Denison has left." Sara, who was still wringing her hands as she stood in front of his desk asked, "Would you like me to pack your suitcase and call the airport?"

"No, thank you, Sara," Lance said simply and picked up the phone.

"Oh, you're going to call yourself? I'll get your things ready."

Lance held up a hand. "There's no need, Sara. I'm not leaving."

Sara blinked in confusion. "You're not?"

"No," he answered then frowned when Sara continued to stare blankly at him. "Is there some problem with me staying in my own home?"

"No," Sara said hastily, shaking her head again. "No, Mr. Radford. There's no problem at all. I just thought…well, I figured since the two of you had grown so close…that maybe you just had a fight and you would want to go and square things with her as soon as possible."

For a moment Lance considered the woman's words. That's probably what Meena figured as well. But she would have to learn obedience and restraint. She couldn't go running off like a child every time things didn't go her way. "I am not following her. She will come back when she realizes how wrong she was to leave." And with those words Sara was dismissed.

Lance resumed the phone call he was about to make before he was interrupted. The rest would work itself out.

The next morning Lance received another shock. Not only had Meena left but she hadn't completed the screenplay and from the note she'd scrawled with the smeared ink, she had no intentions of doing so.

Blind with fury Lance boarded his plane for New York, not sure what he was going to do about his wayward submissive but certain that his screenwriter was going to abide by the terms of her contract or face the consequences.

Meena slammed her door shut and ripped the envelope open. This was the third letter she'd received from Lance's attorneys. The third threat to sue her for breaching her contract.

She crumpled the paper and tossed it on the floor behind her as she walked back into her bedroom. With a depleted sigh she sank onto the unmade bed dropping an arm over her eyes.

She hadn't been out of her apartment in the two weeks since she'd been back in New York. She hadn't answered her phone nor responded to any of the messages. None of them were from Corine which was a blessing and a hindrance. She wondered about her sister but didn't have the strength to deal with her and her problems at the moment.

No, Meena's mind was more focused on her latest debacle. After catching Chris in the act hadn't she sworn not to trust a man again? Hadn't she resigned herself to meaningless sexual affairs instead of committed relationships in which trust was a key factor? Yes, she had.

But then Lance had appeared.

Out of the blue he'd come into her life on a level that she'd never considered before. He'd taken her away from her home against her will and she'd forgiven him. He'd disconnected her from her sister and life as she'd known it and she'd allowed it. He'd used her to get what he wanted and for that she despised him.

And she despised herself.

Despite the term Dominant, Lance hadn't put a gun to her head to make her do the things she did with him. He hadn't used blackmail or any other manipulative ways to get her to submit to him. A few days ago she'd faced the fact that she'd done all those things on her own. She'd submitted to his will and his ways because there was a part of her that longed for that type of man. For a man who cared enough and wanted her enough to take control from her. All her life she'd been the independent one, the self-assured and self-sufficient one. With Lance, she was allowed to follow and obey for a change. And as strange as it sounded, she liked that.

She liked all the things he'd showed her how to do from running his bath and massaging his shoulders, to cutting his food and sometimes feeding him. All of these actions had given her a pleasure she'd never known before. And the way they were so sexually tuned to each other was unspeakable. Whatever he did excited her, even the infamous whipping that they'd eventually tried.

Her body shivered as she recalled the stinging sensations of the tip of the whip slicing across her back. Lance only allowed the tip to touch her skin, never had he hit her full force with the entire whip, that would have flayed her tender flesh and caused scaring, he'd told her. That would hurt her and he'd promised to never do that.

And yet he had.

His words on the phone that day had hurt her more than Meena thought any whipping he could ever inflict would. He'd spoken as if the screenplay had been his number one focus all along and that she had just been a pawn for him to move about as he wished. She knew she was bound by a contract and yes, he had told her this was the reason for him bringing her to Miami, but the personal bond between them had changed all that.

She no longer felt like his employee. She'd begun to totally embrace the fact she was his Submissive, he her Dominant. Should being his Submissive have included doing his will regarding the screenplay? Probably. But Meena felt the sting of betrayal anyway. And that was what she couldn't handle. That was the same reason she hadn't officially forgiven Chris.

How did one deal with betrayal? Should she dole out a punishment and be done with it? Or should she just cut them both completely out of her life? The problem with the latter were the feelings involved. Where Chris was concerned, she'd cared about him and enjoyed the time they'd spent together. Finding out he was bisexual was a blow to her ego and her emotions. She thought she'd known him and been wrong.

Lance was a different story all together. She knew who and what he was. What she hadn't known was the extent he'd go to get what he wanted. Her feelings for Lance went way beyond just caring. A few weeks ago she feared she was falling in love with him. The moment she heard him say those words she knew her fears to be true.

But Lance did not love her.

She was a means to an end and that hurt her more than anything else.

Chapter 9

How long are you going to stay angry with her?" Madison sat on the end of Lance's desk, one stocking clad leg dangling over the other.

With a lift of his brow Lance questioned her seating preference but she did not move. "You know nothing about it," he said, but for a fleeting moment thought he may be wrong. Meena confided in Madison so there was a chance she'd told his assistant something about what was going on between them.

"I know you pissed her off. And because of whatever you did, the screenplay is now a week late."

"I don't care about the screenplay," Lance admitted before he could stop himself.

Madison only smiled. "Then you care about her."

That simple statement should have angered him. Madison was stepping way beyond her boundaries as his assistant. His personal life was none of her business. Yet he feared she'd hit the nail right on the head.

He'd been back in town for five days now having returned after finding that Meena had not completed the screenplay. He was so pissed with her when he'd boarded his plane in Miami he couldn't see past the numbers he dialed on his cell phone to reach his attorney. The paperwork was already completed and signed. With another phone call Sadiq Productions would be suing Meena Denison for 2.5 million dollars. Money which he knew she did not have. Money he did not need.

It was the principle he'd told himself. She'd signed a contract and he expected her to honor it. It was business.

At least it had started out that way.

"Whether I do or not, it's not enough."

"I think it'll be enough if you just tell her how you feel," Madison offered.

Propping his elbows up on his desk Lance stared straight ahead. "I told her the rules and she purposely broke them."

To that Madison chuckled. "She's not a student, Lance."

Oh, but she was. She was learning to be his Submissive and as such she should not have left him. Although they weren't collared, there was an understanding between them, a bond he hadn't expected her to break.

He'd held up his end of the bargain. Her sister was on the road to recovery and he'd even contacted the infamous Chris letting him know in no uncertain terms that further contact with Meena would end badly for him. It was a thinly veiled threat but Lance was sure the man had gotten his point.

So he'd done all of that and allowed her the time and space to work uninterrupted. He'd given her everything and she'd still left him. He couldn't quite grasp that fact.

"She made a commitment. I take commitments very seriously."

"And women take the way a man treats them very seriously," Madison said. When Lance didn't respond she slipped off the desk and stood beside him. "I could call her, make up some reason she needs to come to the office, or I could send flowers to her apartment and sign your name. I could actually call her and apologize for whatever you did to her." Lance looked up at her impatiently so she held up a hand to keep him quiet.

"But none of that would mean a thing to you or her. I've known you for years, Lance and in that time I've seen how controlling and unyielding you can be with your staff as well as people you call friends. It's not attractive. And at this point in your life you should be working to change those bad habits. You like Meena Denison. Hell, you probably love her. But you'll never know for sure if you stay cooped up in this office scowling at the walls forever. Go to her and tell her how you feel." She put a hand on his shoulder as she spoke the last words.

"I don't know how I feel," he said with resignation.

"I think you do. And I think it's the first time you've felt this way and it scares you. Whatever rules you set for her and whatever commitment she made were both done out of caring and respect for each other. Don't throw it all away because of stubborn pride.

Madison walked quietly out of the office leaving Lance totally alone.

Alone, he thought cynically. He always ended up alone.

And for once in his life he was tired of that.

"Damn, it's hot!" Meena sighed as she stood in front of her window air conditioner absorbing all the cool air she could. One look out onto the street and she saw that the sweltering end-of-summer heat didn't stop New York city residents from going on about their business.

She was in a better mood today and thus had showered and dressed—in minimal clothing of course. Her thought was to resume her daily walks in the park and hopefully ending up at Sadiq Productions, but the weather reports boasting ninety-six degrees and eighty-five percent humidity had quickly detoured that plan. So instead she would stay in, order some food and watch the old movies she loved.

Meena was proud of the conclusions she'd come to about herself. Somewhere around noon yesterday when she received her mail and the thank you card from Corine—who was now in her own apartment in Brooklyn and looking for another teaching job—and when her agent had called her with another offer to write a screenplay, she'd had an epiphany.

Lance Radford had given her the greatest chance of her life. He'd hired her to write his screenplay, a story which she really loved, and he'd introduced her to her sexual self. Immediately she'd known what she needed to do. But first she poured a huge glass of iced water and sat down with her lap top. Her apartment was quiet except for the buzz of the air conditioner as she'd finally finished Fountain of Love. All of the re-writes Lance had originally requested, she completed, as well as adding some new scenes.

A cool shower and a tuna sandwich later she felt rejuvenated enough to leave her apartment and board the subway. Where was she headed? To the nearest adult book store. An hour later she had a bag full of resource books on BDSM, sexual toys and the old faithful, Kama Sutra. The clerk who rang her up had been all smiles as she whipped out her credit card to make payment. Meena laughed to herself as she couldn't figure out if he was smiling about her selections or the obscene amount of money she'd spent.

Neither bothered her as she left the store anxious to get home and start reading. Deep into the night Meena had sat in her bed reading and researching. Some things she already knew from Lance's lessons and others were totally new. So she'd awakened this morning energized and ready to begin her new life, except it was too damn hot to go outside and do anything.

So after the fed ex guy—who was sexy as hell, or was she just horny as hell?—had picked up the screenplay she'd resigned herself to an afternoon of total laziness. Yes, her mind still wandered back to Lance as it had persistently done since the moment she'd returned from Miami. She'd decided how she would handle Lance. The first step had been to finish the screenplay. The next would come when the incessant heat wave broke.

Meena had just plopped down onto the couch, the opening credits to The Philadelphia Story just appearing on the television screen when a knock sounded at her door. Padding barefoot across the room she pulled the door open not at all prepared for who waited on the other side.

"Hello, Meena," he said in that smooth, melodious voice that gracefully grazed her nerve endings.

"Lance," she breathed his name as it had been replaying in her mind for the last two weeks. "What are you doing here? I sent you your screenplay."

He nodded. "I received it. Madison sent it straight to the casting director."

"You didn't read it?" she asked incredulously.

"No."

Meena couldn't believe it. After all his talk and pestering about that screenplay and he hadn't even taken a moment to read it. She was about to go off when he took a step closer to her and she caught a whiff of his cologne.

It was another in her long line of mistakes with Lance. She'd read the books on how to be a good Submissive and knew arguing with her Dom was not appropriate. But as far as she knew Lance was no longer her Dom. She would endeavor to change that.

"Come in," she said and stepped to the side to allow him past.

He walked, no he sauntered into her apartment. His broad body dressed in his expensive shoes, slacks and dress shirt that the heat had forced him to roll the sleeves up to his elbows on. She watched his butt as he moved into the living room, her mouth watering to take a bite out of the dimpled cheeks she remembered so clearly.

God, he was sexy and she had been lucky to have him for the time she did. One of Meena's revelations last night was that she wanted desperately to please Lance. Completing the screenplay had been the first step in doing so. Today she'd planned to implement the next step but the weather had axed that idea.

Now, here he was, standing in her living room as fine as ever. She wasn't about to let another moment slip away.

"Lance," she said when he'd taken a seat on her couch. "Can I get you something to drink?" she offered wishing like hell her landlord would hurry up and install the central air units. It was stifling in here or was that her personal body heat soaring?

For a moment he only stared at her then he nodded. "Yes. Water."

She went to the kitchen and retrieved the tallest glass she had, filled it with ice cubes and then water and returned to the living room.

"Thank you," he said accepting the glass.

Meena rubbed her sweating palms against her bare thighs then took a deep breath and sank to her knees in front of him.

Lance almost choked on the water. He'd planned to come over and say his peace. He'd thank her for the completed screenplay and make sure she was doing okay and then he would leave. Okay, maybe he'd tell her that he couldn't stop thinking about her, that he…needed her. That was the part that parched his throat. He'd never admitted to needing anyone before. Meena would be the first.

But once again she'd answered the door dressed in the shortest shorts ever to be made and a half shirt that barely covered her heavy breasts. His penis had instantly recognized her, standing at attention the moment she opened the door. And just like that he wanted her.

Now she was kneeling in front of him, her long cocoa colored legs bending down, her hands going to his knees pushing his legs apart as she moved between them. He gulped down the water and set the glass on the table to his right.

"I need to apologize," Meena began.

Her hair was pulled into a messy ponytail that appealed to him in the basest way. A fine sheen of sweat covered her face, her neck and the part of her stomach that the shirt did not cover. His fingers ached to touch her.

"For what?" he finally managed to speak.

"I was wrong to get angry with you. I was even more wrong to leave Miami when you had gone through so much trouble to take me there."

Lance's heart began a slow dance at her words. Her voice was steady, her eyes focused on his. She looked like the sex goddess who had blown his mind in Miami yet she was different.

"You should have talked to me instead of running away. I told you I would never hurt you."

"I know. I should have trusted you. But when I heard you talking on the phone I just jumped to conclusions. I thought you were using me."

Lance reached out a hand, cupping her chin. "Only for pleasure, Meena. I would never use you to write a screenplay for me. That you should have done because you were contracted to do so."

Meena nodded. "You're right. And as far as the pleasure," she said then lifted his hand to her lips and kissed its back. "You can use me for pleasure anytime you want. I am submitting myself to you."

Lance nearly bolted off the chair when her tongue laved his knuckles then she took one finger, sucking it deeply into her mouth. His erection pressed tightly against his zipper and he had to take deep breaths to keep from passing out.

"Are you sure this is what you want?" he asked praying to all that was holy that she was.

She circled her tongue around the tip of his finger then smiled. "I'm positive. And to prove myself I'll prepare for my punishment."

Meena stood and went into her room. While she was gone Lance ripped his tie off and unbuttoned his shirt completely. It was burning up in here.

When she came back he stripped the damn shirt off. She was naked carrying a whip and handcuffs. With measured steps she brought the items to him, then bowed her head in offering. He took them from her.

Meena then turned and went to her dining room table, moving a chair to the side she planted both hands on the top of the table and leaned forward, spreading her legs. "Punish me, Master. I have been disobedient."

Lance almost creamed in his pants. The sight of Meena so totally submissive was almost overwhelming. His arousal had peaked and he walked slowly into the other room where she stood waiting for him. She was beautiful, her butt plump and inviting, her muscled legs braced and eager for him to do his will.

With a sway of his arm he brought the whip down to tap against her plump flesh. She jumped slightly but otherwise remained still.

"I was so disobedient, Master."

"Yes, you were." He brought the whip down again watching in delight as it shook the left side of her plump ass.

"You will never disobey me again," he said licking his lips and bringing the whip over her legs.

"No!" she screamed. "Never!"

With continuous strokes Lance whipped her across her back, her ass, her legs until Meena's sweet nectar was running down the inside of her thighs. With his chest heaving Lance fell to his knees thrusting his head between her legs to lick it off She tasted heavenly and his body yearned for more.

Standing abruptly Lance took the handcuffs he'd tucked in his back pocket and pulled her up. "Consider yourself collared, Meena. You now belong to me."

She fell limply into his arms. "Yes. Yes, I belong to you."

With that admission Lance pushed her into the chair pulling her arms behind her and cuffing her there. He grabbed her knees and pushed them roughly apart then thrust three fingers into her sopping cunt. Deftly he stroked her G-spot until she dripped onto the chair. Her head fell back and she moaned.

Lance wanted nothing more than to sink his rigid length inside her. But this was her punishment so that would wait. "Do not come, Meena. Not until I tell you."

She panted. "Yes."

"No. You will wait until I say so." Lance moved his fingers, pressing deeper into her honeyed cove. Her walls were tight around his fingers and sweat dotted his forehead with the restraint he exercised.

Spreading her legs until her feet were tucked around the legs of the chair Lance used his other hand to roughly knead her breasts, pulling the nipples away from her chest then letting them drop, loving the sight of her heavy breasts bouncing. Then he pulled his hand out of her, replacing it with his mouth, devouring her nether lips, stroking his tongue over every crevice until she was moaning loudly and squirming in the chair.

"No," he murmured when he felt her thighs stiffening around his head. "Not yet."

"Please," she begged.

Lance stood yanking at the button of his pants so hard it flew across the room. Pushing his pants down he freed his length and opened his legs until he was straddling the chair, his arousal in line with her mouth.

"Show me how sorry you are for being disobedient. Show me how much you want to please me from this moment on."

With lust filled eyes Meena dropped her gaze from him and watched as he guided his length into her mouth. He teased her lips, rubbing the head over them then pulling away. She extended her tongue and he obliged by placing the tip onto its moistness. She laved him until his manhood shone with her saliva.

Placing his hands on either side of her face Lance thrust his dick into her mouth. She took him in hallowing out her cheeks so that he felt like she would suck the cum right out of him.

When he couldn't take it another moment, Lance pulled out of her mouth, reaching behind her he undid the handcuffs. Switching positions he sat down on the chair and brought her over him, sitting her squarely on his lap.

It was giving her control he knew but he couldn't resist. He wanted to watch her ride him, to see the pleasure overtaking her and to know that it was all because of him. So when she slid down onto his length, her walls clenching him as tightly as her mouth had, he couldn't help but moan.

Meena rotated her hips, loving the depth of him inside her, the width of him that stretched her to the limits. Her back and butt still tingled from the whip, while her center dripped its abundant nectar onto his groin. She loved this man, there was no doubt in her mind now. And she would do whatever she could to make him happy. If it meant serving him, then that's what she'd do. If it meant writing every one of his screenplays from here on out, she'd do that as well. As long as this exquisite pleasure never ended.

His hands gripped her waist as she bounced up and down on his dick. Her breasts bounced just inches from his face and every now and then he'd extend his tongue to trap her erect nipple. Damn she loved his tongue.

Emotions and sensations tore through her ferociously and she opened her mouth to scream. His name came out repeatedly as her nails dug into the skin of his strong shoulders.

"Mine. All mine," Lance said over and over again. "Come for me, baby."

"Yes. I'm all yours," Meena answered just as her climax ripped through her body. She stiffened over him feeling the gush of her release slipping out alongside his penis.

But Lance was not finished yet. Finding his pants he retrieved a condom packet from his wallet and quickly sheathed himself. Then he stood her up and pushed her face down on the dining room table. With both hands he spread her butt wide then slipped his wet cock into her waiting heat loving the sound of her juices rubbing against him. He thrust hard, once then twice, until he'd created a forceful rhythm, tearing into her with all the need and desire he had inside.

And when his release came like a stream of fire he groaned. "Meeeeennnaaa." With a couple more strokes he emptied every drop into the condom then leaned over her deciding to admit what he could no longer deny. "I love you."

It was a raspy moan said between heavy breathing, insufferable heat and the weight of a two hundred pound man on her back, but Meena knew she'd never heard anything as sweet.

"And I love you, too, Master."

Falling Into You

by

Maureen Smith

Chapter One

"Looks like tonight is your lucky night, Edmonds."

Rebecca Edmonds glanced up from setting a tray filled with empty glasses onto a crowded countertop to look at her coworker through the slits of a black lace mask. "Lucky?" she echoed as if the word was foreign to her. "How's that?"

Stacey Brenner leaned in the doorway of the kitchen with one hand propped on a shapely hip as she gazed out into the smoke-filled nightclub. Onstage, a trio of topless dancers slid up and down long silver poles as they performed to Donna Summers's "Love to Love You Baby."

"The sexiest man in Baltimore—hell, the state of Maryland—just walked through the door," Stacey explained. "And guess whose table he was seated at?"

"Lucky me," Rebecca muttered, unimpressed. As far as she was concerned, there was nothing remotely sexy about a man who got off on watching women strip in public. Although The Sultan's was known to be one of the city's classiest gentlemen's clubs—with hefty cover charges to show for it—the place still drew enough of the kind of patrons that made Rebecca's skin crawl.

"You'd better get out there," Stacey told her. "You know how Bruno feels about keeping customers waiting."

Bruno Rossi, the owner of The Sultan's Gentlemen's Club, had built his reputation on taking excellent care of his customers, starting from the moment they stepped through the doors until they departed several hours later—at least five hundred dollars poorer. He prided himself on having the best exotic dancers and waitresses in Maryland. If any of his employees failed to deliver on this promise, he had no qualms about firing her on the spot. He'd been known to dock the paychecks of waitresses who kept customers waiting too long to be served, or cooks who prepared less than satisfactory meals, or dancers who stumbled once or twice onstage. When it came to his establishment, Bruno Rossi had little patience for imperfection.

These thoughts ran through Rebecca's mind as she left the kitchen and made her way across the crowded nightclub. The plush décor evoked the decadence of ancient Rome, complete with faux marble columns and expensively reproduced Pompeian wall paintings. A thick cloud of cigar smoke hovered above the tables, all of which were occupied with men—and more than a few women—sipping drinks and watching the naked acrobatics onstage. Because it was Halloween, many customers wore costumes. While some of the getups were creative enough to warrant a second glance, none were elaborate enough to compete with the main attraction—the exotic dancers.

Rebecca passed a waitress balancing a tray laden with food and drinks. She smiled encouragingly at the young brunette, Nina, who'd been a victim of Bruno's displeasure last week when she showed up fifteen minutes late to work. Nina knew, as did everyone else, that she was just one misstep away from being fired.

Mentally praying that the girl wouldn't drop her tray, Rebecca kept walking until she reached a table in a private corner of the club where a lone man sat, idly perusing the menu.

"Welcome to The Sultan's," Rebecca began cheerfully. "My name is Rebecca and I'll be your—"

The rest of her spiel died on her lips as the stranger's head slowly lifted, and she found herself staring into the most arresting pair of eyes she'd ever seen. Black as coal, with the power to zero in on a woman's face and leave her utterly breathless. Those piercing eyes were set in a face that was equally compelling. Deep brown skin was stretched taut over hard cheekbones, a slightly crooked nose and a square jaw. A neatly trimmed goatee framed full, sensuous lips that made Rebecca wonder—shockingly—what they'd feel like against her own, and on other parts of her body.

She fought to regain her composure. "My name is Rebecca, and I'll be your servant—I mean, server, tonight," she quickly corrected herself, blushing as that sensuous mouth curved into a knowing, irreverent smile.

She cleared her throat, grateful for the mask that partially concealed her face. "Is this your first time at The Sultan's?"

"Yes, it is," he answered in a deep, husky voice that was black magic and liquid sex rolled into one. Never before had Rebecca felt more exposed as his dark gaze raked over her body, taking in her black leather bustier, matching micro-mini shorts and stiletto heels. But rather than repelling her, his slow, deliberate perusal left her feeling hot and tingly in unspeakable places.

She tapped her pen against her notepad. "What can I get for you this evening?"

His gaze returned slowly to her face. "What do you recommend?" he murmured, a hint of that wolfish smile lingering on his lips.

"Depends on what you're in the mood for," Rebecca said.

In the background, Donna Summers sighed and moaned her way through a simulated orgasm. Rebecca's face heated as the stranger's smile turned downright wicked. Before he could respond, she quickly recited the house specials, mortified by the breathlessness she heard in her own voice.

"Tell you what, Rebecca," he drawled when she'd finished speaking. "Why don't you just start me off with a glass of whiskey? We can work our way slowly to the main course."

Rebecca nodded jerkily. "Coming right up." As she turned and headed toward the bar, she felt the man's searing gaze on her back, burning away what scraps of clothing she wore. She shivered convulsively and walked faster.

"I need a whiskey," she told one of the bartenders working busily behind the counter.

"Sure thing, beautiful."

While Rebecca waited on the order, Stacey sidled up alongside her, a knowing grin on her face. "What'd I tell you? Isn't he a hottie?"

Rebecca feigned ignorance. "Who?"

Stacey laughed, tucking a strand of auburn hair behind one ear. "Nice try, Edmonds. You know very well I'm talking about that gorgeous specimen at your table, the one who couldn't keep his eyes off your ass as you walked away."

Rebecca flushed. "Him? Sure, he's attractive."

"Attractive?" Stacey snorted in disbelief. "Sweetheart, you need to get your eyes checked."

"Whatever you say," Rebecca quipped as the bartender produced her drink. She scooped her tray off the counter and started away from the bar.

She prayed for steady hands as she served the glass of whiskey to her sexy customer. "Is there anything else I can get for you?"

"Your phone number would be nice," he said lazily.

Rebecca laughed, surprising herself. "Sorry. I never mix business with pleasure."

His eyes glinted with mischief. "Never say never," he told her, his voice a silky promise she would remember long after she left the table.

A constant flow of customers over the next two hours kept Rebecca too busy to dwell on thoughts of the seductive stranger. But as she bustled from table to table, refilling drinks and taking orders, she was keenly aware of a pair of smoldering dark eyes that followed her, wreaking havoc on her nerve endings. He seemed more interested in watching Rebecca than the topless dancers onstage. Once when she braved a look in his direction, she saw him being treated to a lap dance by Giselle, a stunning, voluptuous blonde who could have starred as a Playboy centerfold. The dancer seemed to be enjoying herself immensely as she gyrated against the man's groin and fondled her large breasts to the tune of Sheena Easton's "Sugar Walls."

As Rebecca watched the performance, her mind wandered, creating a fantasy in which she, not Giselle, was giving the lap dance.

As her hips slowly and provocatively undulated in his lap, she could hear his breath quicken, becoming a shallow rasp in her ear. She could feel the bulge of his erection through his trousers. Long, thick and magnificently hard. It excited her, sent a rush of liquid heat pouring through her veins.

As his hand lifted to touch her, she sent him a warning look over her shoulder. "Uh-uh-uh," she scolded. "You know the rules. No touching."

His dark eyes simmered with desire and frustration. "Let me touch you," he whispered raggedly. "Just once. Please."

She shook her head, her lips curving into a naughty smile as she continued gyrating on him. It thrilled her to know she could have this power over him, a man who was probably used to having any woman he wanted, whenever he wanted.

A crisp fifty-dollar bill materialized between his long, lean fingers. "Can I give this to you?"

She hesitated, pretending to deliberate as she eyed the money. After another moment, she nodded.

As he slid the bill into the strap of her G-string, warm, callused fingers grazed the skin at her hip. Rebecca shivered at the brief contact, her nipples hardening as if he'd tongued them.

Her reaction didn't go unnoticed.

"Did you like that, Rebecca?" he murmured, his breath a hot, silky caress against her ear. "Do you want me to touch you again?"

God, yes! Aloud she mumbled, "Of course not."

"Are you sure?" he whispered wickedly. "Because when I touched you just now, I could've sworn your body said something different. Here, let me show you." This time his hand brushed against her thigh, and sure enough, Rebecca shivered again. Heat pooled between her legs.

"Mmmm. See what I mean?" he purred. "I bet if I touch you here—"

Rebecca's breath caught as she watched his hand curve around her thigh, trailing a hot path toward her moist center. He moved slowly, deliberately, drawing out the torture of anticipation. And then, just when she thought she would straight lose her mind, he slipped his finger beneath the lace crotch of her thong and touched her. She gasped sharply, then moaned as he began to stroke the slick nub of her clitoris, slowly and seductively. She arched her back as a wave of need tore through her, setting her body on fire. As his finger teased and caressed the soft folds of her flesh, she braced her palms on his muscled thighs and spread her legs wide, desperate for more. She wanted him, wanted him like no other man she'd ever wanted before. She didn't care where they were, or that other people were watching them.

She nearly sobbed with disappointment when he suddenly stopped rubbing her. "Looks like I was right again," he murmured triumphantly in her ear. "You do want me to touch you, Rebecca. Say it."

She could feel her blood roaring through her veins. She licked her lips and rocked her hips against him, silently begging him not to stop, to keep going until she couldn't take any more.

Soft, sensuous lips nuzzled her ear, then the nape of her neck, sending frissons of sensation down her spine. "Say it, Rebecca," he urged a second time, his voice a low, husky command.

"I want you to touch me," she whimpered helplessly.

She felt, rather than saw him smile. "With pleasure."

She nearly came as one thick finger slipped deep inside her. A sharp cry erupted from her throat, and she flung back her head. But she wasn't the only one affected. She could feel the stranger's erect penis throbbing against her ass, straining for release.

And she fully intended to give it to him.

A loud crash intruded upon Rebecca's erotic fantasy, jerking her back to the present. Shaken, she glanced around the club and saw that the young waitress, Nina, had dropped a tray full of glasses on her way to the kitchen.

As Rebecca stood there, debating whether to go help the girl or run to the restroom to wipe her damp crotch, she caught the stranger's hot, bold gaze. His mouth curved in the barest hint of a smile, as if he knew she'd been watching him and fantasizing about him.

Mortified, she hurried away to help clean up Nina's mess, before she made one of her own.

Sometime after midnight, Bruno Rossi found Rebecca in the kitchen waiting on a platter of appetizers.

"Edmonds," he said without preamble, interrupting her conversation with the cook. "I need to pull you off the floor for a little while."

Rebecca arched a quizzical brow at her boss. Despite the late hour, he looked crisp and commanding in an impeccably tailored Armani suit with Italian leather loafers that were polished to a high gleam. The scent of his expensive cologne mingled with the odors of cigar smoke, sweat and assorted foods that permeated the air.

At thirty-seven years old, Bruno Rossi had amassed a considerable fortune as a successful businessman. In addition to The Sultan's, he owned principal interests in two Atlantic City casinos and a thriving chain of delicatessens in New Jersey. Although there had been rumors over the years that he had ties to organized crime, he'd never received so much as a speeding ticket, and the IRS had all but given up on auditing him.

"What's up, Bruno?" Rebecca asked curiously. "Why are you pulling me off the floor?"

Bruno scratched his ear, and for the first time since Rebecca had known him, he looked slightly sheepish. "I need you in the Platinum Suite. A customer has requested the honor of your presence, and I accepted on your behalf."

Rebecca's eyes narrowed sharply on his handsome, olive-toned face. "Excuse me?"

"Come on, Rebecca, don't give me attitude. I'm only asking for a few minutes of your time—"

Her temper flared. "If you think I'm giving some creep a lap dance, think again!"

Bruno scowled. "Did I ask you to give anyone a lap dance? You think that's what I pay you for?" So as not to attract the attention of the other occupants of the kitchen, he lowered his voice. "Look, Edmonds, the guy's not expecting a lap dance or anything like that. He just wants to talk to you, get to know you a little better. You must have really made an impression on him."

"How much?" Rebecca demanded.

Bruno frowned, nonplussed. "How much what?"

"How much did he pay you for the 'honor' of my presence? Whatever it was, I'll double it."

"Aw, come on, Rebecca, don't be like that. You're making this harder than it has to be! Look, I told the guy you're one of my best waitresses, so I really can't spare you more than twenty minutes. That's all I'm asking of you—twenty minutes to make meaningless small talk with him, then you can be on your merry way. And you don't have to worry about him trying nothing funny—Paulie will be posted outside the door the entire time, I swear."

Rebecca hesitated. Bruno's willingness to loan her his own personal bodyguard was not lost on her, nor did it escape her notice that he was requesting her cooperation, when he could just as easily order her to comply.

Still, his eagerness to sell her to the highest bidder rankled. She understood wanting to please a customer, but this was going too far.

Seeing the adamant refusal in her eyes, Bruno tried another tack. "Do this for me," he said, looking her straight in the eye, "and I won't fire that clumsy little waitress you feel so sorry for."

Rebecca frowned. "That's not fair, Bruno. Nina's a college student—she needs the money."

His dark eyes flashed with triumph. He knew he had her. "That's the deal, Edmonds. Take it or leave it."

"You play dirty," she accused.

He merely grinned.

"Fine," she snapped, yanking off her apron and tossing it aside. "Twenty minutes, Bruno, and not a second more, you understand?"

He spread his hands wide in a conciliatory gesture. "That's all I ask."

The Platinum Suite was located on the second floor of the nightclub, next to the VIP Lounge. The room was reserved for customers who wanted more privacy to receive lap dances or to entertain business clients. As the name suggested, admission to the Platinum Suite was outrageously expensive, limiting its use to the club's most affluent patrons. Dancers who were invited to join customers in the exclusive room considered it an honor, a symbol of their elevated status in the food chain.

Rebecca wasn't a dancer. And she was anything but honored by the invitation.

"I'll be right outside the door," said Paul Colangelo, the tall, burly bodyguard who'd escorted Rebecca upstairs.

She nodded, giving him a brief smile. "Thanks, Paulie."

He held the door open for her as she stepped into a lavishly appointed suite boasting baccarat crystal chandeliers and gleaming black marble floors. The lights were dimmed low, creating a soft, romantic glow throughout the room. There was a private bar in one corner, and a small seating area occupied by a plush white sectional that curved into a semicircle. The facing wall was dominated by a large glass aquarium stocked with a brilliant variety of tropical fish.

But it was the tall, broad-shouldered man standing before the aquarium who caught and held Rebecca's attention.

As he turned slowly to face her, she felt a jolt of recognition, and her lips parted in surprise.

She couldn't believe it.

The customer who'd summoned her to the Platinum Suite was none other than the sexy stranger with the bedroom eyes, the very same man she'd been fantasizing about an hour ago.

Chapter Two

Seeing her shocked expression, the stranger smiled, a slow, sexy smile that made Rebecca's toes curl. "Expecting someone else?" he drawled.

Rebecca shook her head, stepping further into the room. The door closed behind her, sealing her fate. She swallowed, shoving aside the unsettling thought. "I wasn't expecting anyone," she answered coolly, "because I'm not in the habit of meeting strange men alone in this room—or anywhere else, for that matter."

He chuckled softly. "Like I said earlier. Never say never, Rebecca."

She didn't care for the familiarity in his tone. Her chin lifted. "In case you hadn't noticed, Mr.—"

"Gray," he supplied. "Vince Gray."

"In case you hadn't noticed, Mr. Gray, I'm not a dancer at this club. If you wanted private entertainment, any one of the girls would have been happy to accommodate you. Giselle, for example, is quite popular with—"

Vince shook his head slowly. "I didn't want Giselle," he said huskily. "I wanted you."

His words sent a shaft of heat coursing through her. Before she could regain the power of speech, he continued, "And I'm not interested in a lap dance, Rebecca. I've had my fill for one night." He walked toward her with a controlled stride, a cross between a strut and a prowl. It was only when he'd reached her that Rebecca realized just how tall he was. He was at least six three, towering over her even in the four-inch stiletto heels she wore. He looked darkly handsome in a well-cut blazer, pleated charcoal trousers and a snowy white shirt open to the strong column of his throat. But despite the tastefulness of his clothing, Rebecca had the feeling Vince Gray would be equally arresting in a pair of battered blue jeans and a sweatshirt with the sleeves torn off. He exuded the sort of raw animal magnetism that made him nearly impossible to resist.

Rebecca took an unconscious step backward, her pulse hammering. Hard as it might be, she would resist. "What do you want, Mr. Gray?"

His eyes searched her face from beneath incredibly long, sooty lashes. "For starters," he murmured, "I want you to call me Vince. And what I also want, Rebecca, is for you to have a drink with me."

She shook her head. "We're not supposed to drink on the job."

"You've worked hard all night. You deserve to relax, unwind a little." When she hesitated, he added with a conspiratorial wink, "I won't tell anyone if you don't."

Rebecca couldn't help but chuckle. "I'm okay, really. But if you'd like, I'd be more than happy to fix you a drink. Another whiskey?" she asked as she started toward the bar, as much to be hospitable as to place some much-needed distance between them.

He caught her arm to halt her retreat. His hand was warm, big and strong, his touch sending electrical currents through her body. "Thanks for the offer, but I'm fine. Why don't we sit down?" he suggested, gently redirecting her toward the seating area with a hand on her back that made her bones turn to liquid.

As they sat down on the plush sectional, Rebecca wondered how on earth she was supposed to spend the next twenty minutes with a complete stranger who wreaked such havoc on her senses. It wasn't fair. There ought to be laws against unleashing men like Vince Gray on the female populace.

He'd sat too close to her, so close she could smell him, soap and an intoxicating scent that was uniquely male. She could feel his heat and his vitality, and it shook her. She resisted the temptation to scoot a few inches away from him. No point in letting him know how much he affected her.

She strove for aloofness. "So tell me, Vince. Do you make a habit of cruising strip joints to pick up waitresses?"

He laughed, and damn if it wasn't the sexiest sound she'd ever heard in her life. His dark, bold gaze met hers. "Just the ones who take my breath away," he drawled.

His words sent a thrill of pleasure through her, which she squelched at once. The man was obviously a shameless womanizer. If she wasn't careful, she'd end up doing something really stupid.

"I was hoping you would come," Vince said huskily.

Rebecca felt a shiver of warmth puddle in her groin. She knew what he was referring to. But when spoken in that deep, dark voice of his, anything he said took on a sexual connotation. And when the speaker was as sinfully gorgeous as Vince Gray, it was only natural for the listener's mind to wander to forbidden territory. God, but he had the most penetrating eyes she'd ever seen. And those lips. They looked like the lips of a man who knew his way around a woman's—

Dragging her mind back to the conversation, Rebecca murmured, "I didn't really have much of a choice about meeting you here."

Vince looked vaguely amused. "I find that hard to believe. Something tells me you're a woman who makes her own choices and dares anyone to defy her." Those black eyes narrowed on hers with an intuitiveness that unnerved her. "What are you hiding behind that mask, Rebecca?"

She frowned. "I'm not hiding anything. I wore it for Halloween—all of the waitresses are wearing masks, in case you hadn't noticed. It's an annual tradition."

He flicked his wrist to glance at the watch peeking from beneath the white cuff of his shirt. "It's after midnight. Halloween is officially over."

"I'm aware of that."

"So take off the mask." When she hesitated, he softly cajoled, "I want to see you. All of you."

Heat rushed into her belly as a mental image of herself standing naked and quivering before him flashed through her mind. Remembering her erotic fantasy, she blushed, and was glad he couldn't detect it. No way was she parting with the mask.

"I'll take it off when my shift ends," she told him firmly.

He smiled indolently. "Ah, a woman of mystery. I love a good mystery."

Rebecca cleared her throat and crossed her legs, then wished she hadn't as Vince's dark, heavy-lidded gaze followed the gesture and lingered on the curve of her thighs. She tugged discreetly at the abbreviated length of her shorts. She would have given anything for a pair of pants, or a floor-length muumuu.

"What do you do for a living, Vince?" she blurted, eager to divert his attention from her exposed body parts.

He leaned back, spreading his arms over the back of the overstuffed cushions behind him, a man at his leisure. "I'm an investment broker."

"Really?" That surprised her. A man like Vince Gray seemed too edgy, too dangerous, to be confined to such a tame profession. But then again, what did she really know about him? Zilch, obviously.

"Do you enjoy your work?"

"Sure. It pays the bills."

She grinned wryly. "Pays for a few extras, too," she pointed out, gesturing around the luxurious room. "Only high-rollers can afford the Platinum Suite."

Vince chuckled, idly stroking his chin between his thumb and forefinger as he gazed at her. "So what about you, Rebecca? Is this your full-time gig?"

"Not exactly. I'm also a student at the University of Maryland."

"Is that right? What are you majoring in?"

"Women's studies."

That sensuous mouth curved in a lazy grin. "We have something in common, then. I enjoy studying women as well."

Rebecca felt the whisper of a smile tugging at the corners of her lips. "Ah, but somehow I suspect my studies are a bit more, shall we say, research-driven."

"I assure you," Vince said, with a wicked glint in his eyes, "I conduct plenty of research on my subjects. But what I enjoy even more than the research is actually testing my theories in a real environment. On willing participants, of course."

"Of course."

"For instance, I like to explore chemistry between men and women, to find out what attracts members of the opposite sex to one another." The slow, wolfish smile he gave Rebecca made her think of a predator intent on cornering its prey.

Her pulse thudded. "Researchers have performed a vast number of studies on that topic," she managed weakly.

"I know." His hooded gaze drifted to her mouth. "But I'm one who likes to test-drive my own vehicles."

At that, Rebecca uncrossed her legs and stood. She didn't need to see sharp, bared fangs to recognize imminent danger. "It's time for me to get back to work. If you'll excuse me—"

Vince unfolded his long body from the sofa with the fluid grace of a panther. Before she could take another step, he was in front of her, blocking her path to the door. His coal-black eyes smoldered in the soft glow of the room.

"I want to kiss you, Rebecca," he said huskily. "It's all I've thought about since you showed up at my table to take my order. You have the most incredible mouth I've ever seen, and I've been driving myself crazy wondering what it would feel like against my own."

Her knees almost gave out. The look in his eyes and the provocative things he said were nearly her undoing.

Shaken, she stared up at him. "This isn't a good idea. We're not supposed to get…intimate with customers."

"No one has to know." He leaned closer, his warm breath fanning her cheek and making her shiver. "Just one kiss," he whispered against her mouth. "A short one, no longer than ten seconds, I promise."

Rebecca gave a tiny nod as the last of her resistance melted away, and then his lips touched hers. She went still, holding her breath, her temperature spiking under a sudden onslaught of sensation. His mouth was soft and warm, gliding silkily over hers as his hand lifted and sank deep into her hair. Then he touched her bottom lip with the tip of his tongue, a polite request for entry, and she responded by opening her mouth.

His tongue slid inside, hot and tantalizing, and desire shot like a lightning bolt through her body. His fingers tightened in her hair, tilting her head backward as he deepened the kiss. His mouth moved over hers, his tongue tangling with hers in an erotic little mating dance. He drew her bottom lip between his teeth and suckled, making her shudder with need. She pressed against the muscled hardness of his chest, wanting to get as close as possible. He smelled so good, and tasted so damn good, that she couldn't get enough. It was like her fantasy, only better.

When his hand eased to her mask and slowly began to remove it, sanity returned like a bucketful of ice water to her face. Rebecca pushed her hand between them and broke free, breathing hard.

Vince gazed at her through heavy-lidded eyes. "I'm sorry," he murmured lazily. "That was a little longer than ten seconds. Math was never my strong suit."

"I have to go," Rebecca said in a breathless rush.

Before he could utter another word, she turned and fled from the room, hurrying past the startled bodyguard posted outside the door. Paulie followed on her heels as she flew down the stairs and headed straight for the locker room to retrieve her belongings. Thankfully, no other waitresses were around to question her disheveled appearance, and when she reemerged a few minutes later, Paulie was nowhere to be found.

On her way out, she encountered Bruno Rossi coming from his office located in the rear of the building. He smiled when he saw her. "Hey, Edmonds—"

"I'm leaving, Bruno," she told him without breaking stride.

He frowned. "But your shift doesn't end for another—"

"Good night, Bruno." She pushed open a glass door and exited the building without so much as a backward glance.

Chapter Three

Vince McCall stood in the shadows of a deserted parking lot on the other side of town and smoked his first cigarette in six years. With each toke of nicotine, his frustration grew until it simmered like the tiny embers bristling at his feet. He had no business smoking. His father had chain-smoked himself into an early grave, dying of lung cancer at the age of forty-seven. After that, Vince had sworn to himself, and to everyone else—God, mother and priest—that he wouldn't end up like his old man.

At the rate he was going, he'd be on his third pack by dawn.

Shaking his head in disgust, Vince took a long pull on his cigarette and sent a puff of smoke into the wind. The chilly night air had done nothing to cool his raging body temperature, which hadn't returned to normal since he left The Sultan's Gentlemen's Club thirty minutes earlier. But an exotic dancer wasn't responsible for the lust pounding through his body and boiling his blood. No, he could thank Rebecca No-Last-Name for that.

With a surly grin, Vince let his mind wander back to the moment when he'd first laid eyes on the sexy, mysterious waitress. He'd noticed her even before she came to his table, as she was waiting on other customers. The sight of her sweet, curvy body poured into scraps of black leather had made him instantly hard. When she leaned down to hear a customer over the loud music, Vince got an eyeful of a deliciously round ass that nearly sent him into cardiac arrest. Her leather shorts barely covered the ripe swell of her rump, and the stiletto pumps she wore accentuated long, shapely legs with killer calves. His mind was instantly filled with carnal images of those long legs wrapped around his waist as he thrust into her tight, wet heat.

When she walked over to his table and introduced herself as his waitress, he thought the Fates were smiling down on him—or playing a cruel joke designed to drive him completely out of his mind.

Even with the lace mask concealing most of her face, he could tell she was beautiful. Her mouth, slicked with red lipstick, was lush and incredibly sexy, curving in a smile that took his breath away. Her high, round breasts—though not as large as he usually preferred—spilled just enough from the top of her bustier to make his mouth water. Her jet-black hair was cut in long, silky layers that skimmed bare shoulders the color of melted chocolate.

From that moment on, his single-minded focus had been finding a way to get her alone and naked. If not naked, then at least unmasked.

The fact that her identity remained a mystery to him made her all the more alluring, and made him more impatient—hell, desperate—to see her again. And the next time he saw her, he wouldn't let her get away so easily. He fully intended to finish what they'd started tonight.

A brisk breeze, carrying the crisp scent of fall leaves, penetrated the cotton fabric of his shirt to reach his heated skin. He closed his eyes and turned his face up to the starry night, welcoming the chill. If the natural elements didn't cool his libido, his next resort was a cold shower.

A damn cold shower.

He opened his eyes as a pair of approaching headlights cut through the darkness. He straightened slowly from his Durango as a black SUV pulled up beside his. The door opened, and Detective Frank Sciorra aka Paul Colangelo stepped out and walked around to where Vince stood waiting.

Without a word, the burly Italian passed him the nine-millimeter Glock he'd "confiscated" from him earlier that evening when Vince arrived at the club.

"Thanks," Vince muttered, the cigarette dangling from the corner of his mouth as he cocked open the magazine to check the ammo.

Frank gave a derisive snort. "What? You think I put a cap in someone on my way over here?"

"With you, Frankie, anything's possible." Satisfied that no bullets were missing from the weapon, Vince returned the Glock to his hip holster, then drew a deep lungful of nicotine. He watched Frank through twin curls of smoke released through his nostrils. "No problems getting away?"

"None whatsoever. Told him I was taking one of the girls home to make sure she didn't get hassled by her prick of a boyfriend." He nodded toward the half-smoked cigarette in Vince's hand. "Rough night?"

Vince chuckled humorlessly. "You wouldn't believe."

Everyone in the Baltimore Police Department knew Detective Vince McCall's long and bitter history with nicotine. Every year, he commemorated the anniversary of his father's death by buying a pack of Marlboros—the brand his father had smoked religiously—then lighting a match to the cigarettes and watching them slowly burn. It was a private ritual no one questioned or interfered with. Cops, like anyone else, had demons that needed exorcising. Vince's comrades respected his right to exorcise his demons any damn way he saw fit.

Unfortunately, he hadn't gotten around to torching the last pack of Marlboros yet, hence the cigarettes were readily available when temptation came calling. Who knew that a scantily clad waitress in a strip club would be the catalyst that finally pushed him over the edge?

Frank frowned. "By the way, what'd you do to Edmonds?"

Vince gave him a blank look. "Edmonds?"

"Rebecca, the waitress. What'd you do to her, man? She came flying out of the room like a bat out of hell. By the time I went back up there to ask you what had happened, you'd already left."

Rebecca Edmonds. Vince silently mulled over the name, even as he answered, "I didn't do anything to her." Not yet, anyway.

"Well, you'd better not," Frank advised. "That's Rossi's favorite waitress. He's got a thing for her."

That piqued Vince's interest. "Did he tell you that?"

"He doesn't have to. I can tell by the way he looks at her when he thinks no one else is watching. He lets her get away with stuff that no one else can. Not that she pulls any crap, mind you, but if she wanted to, she could. The point is, if you wanna get in good with Rossi, leave his woman alone."

Vince shook his head, taking a slow drag on his cigarette. "If that was my woman, there's no way in hell I would've left her alone in that room with another man. But when I asked for her, Rossi didn't seem to mind."

"He's a businessman. You're a paying customer. He's not gonna mess with that. Money talks. And speaking of money, why'd you have to blow half a grand on the Platinum Suite? That wasn't in the budget, man. The brass ain't gonna be too happy about that."

"I know," Vince blithely agreed. "But it was worth every damn cent."

Frank groaned. "Just because you can have any woman you want doesn't mean you should, McCall. And I'm telling you again—stay away from Edmonds. She's a sweet girl, and really smart. She's even working on her Ph.D."

Vince grinned. "Definitely too good for me."

"Damn straight she is. If you insist on getting laid, pick any of the other girls. They were checking you out the minute you walked through the door. Any one of 'em would do you in a heartbeat, and you know it. I've heard that Giselle gives the best head— "

Vince chuckled dryly. "That's the second time someone's tried to push Giselle off on me. Poor girl—they must keep her mighty busy. No, thanks. I'm sure she's a very talented woman, but I like my meat a little fresher."

Frank heaved a resigned sigh. "And it doesn't get any 'fresher' than Rebecca. She's a beautiful woman. You know, she gets hit on all the time, but she's never let it get to her before." He glared pointedly at Vince. "Until tonight."

"I told you, man, I didn't do anything to her." Not as much as he would've liked to, anyway. He wondered how far things would have gone if he hadn't tried to remove her mask. He grew hard just thinking about it.

"Look," he said gruffly, "if I'm supposed to be some high-rolling investment broker with cash to burn, I have to play the part convincingly. Dropping half a grand on the Platinum Suite was expected of me. How am I supposed to convince Rossi to go into business with me if I'm tight-fisted with my money?"

"Yeah, I hear what you're saying," Frank grumbled. "Just don't get carried away, that's all. They've got us on a tight budget, and I'd hate to get yanked off this case just because you blew taxpayer dollars on the Platinum Suite. Next time you're at the club, do us both a favor and settle for one or two lap dances. At twenty-five bucks a pop, that shouldn't break the bank."

"Yes sir," Vince said with a mock salute.

Despite his cavalier tone, Vince knew better than anyone how important it was for them to play by the book on this case. The Baltimore Police Department, in conjunction with the local FBI division, had assembled a task force to investigate the financial dealings of Bruno Rossi, who was suspected of masterminding a lucrative money laundering operation. But five years and nine investigations later, the authorities still hadn't been able to prove Rossi's guilt. Sending two Baltimore police detectives undercover to infiltrate the club owner's organization was the government's latest—and perhaps final—attempt to snare the man who'd become, in many ways, as elusive as John Gotti had once been. In fact, some members of the local law enforcement community had already dubbed Rossi the new "Teflon Don."

Vince didn't like being thwarted by criminals who thought they were untouchable. He was determined to succeed where others had failed in taking down Rossi. But he couldn't afford any distractions, and Rebecca Edmonds, with her luscious lips and sexy-ass body, was the grand dame of distractions. The sooner he could have her, the sooner he could get her out of his system.

Or so he told himself.

"Look, I gotta head back before Rossi starts getting suspicious," Frank announced, backing toward his truck with his shoulders hunched against the chill. For such a big tough guy, Frank Sciorra had always been a punk where cold weather was concerned.

"See you tomorrow night, Frankie," Vince said.

He watched as the black SUV rolled out of the parking lot and disappeared down the street before starting toward his Durango. Pausing at the door, he took a long pull on his cigarette and gazed at the lights from the Inner Harbor twinkling in the distance.

All he needed was one night alone with Rebecca Edmonds. One night to bury himself deep inside her wet heat, to experience her luscious body writhing beneath his, to feel her nails digging into his back as they rocked through one mind-blowing orgasm after another.

One night, he told himself, and then he could turn his attention to other, more pressing matters.

Like taking down her boss, Bruno Rossi.

Rebecca lifted a cardboard box from the floor and hoisted it onto the Formica countertop of her new kitchen. Wiping a sheen of sweat from her forehead, she stood back, lips pursed, and swept a look around the sunlit room. It was smaller than the kitchen in the condo she'd just moved from, and she wasn't too crazy about the beige linoleum floor, but at least the room had a center island and modern oak cabinets. The rest of the two-bedroom apartment wasn't bad either, and at $1,300 a month, it was just what she needed at this point in her life.

Not that she wouldn't miss her condo in Annapolis with its lakefront views and manicured lawns. But when she'd made the decision to take a year off from teaching in order to focus on completing her dissertation, she knew she would have to make some drastic lifestyle changes. And if all went according to plan, by the same time next year, she'd be applying for a tenure-track faculty position at Johns Hopkins University, where she'd dreamed of teaching for as long as she could remember.

As Rebecca reached for a box-cutter, twenty-two-year-old Rasheed Edmonds entered the apartment carrying a large cardboard box labeled "Textbooks." He glanced over at her through the alcove in the kitchen. "Where do you want this?" he asked.

"Anywhere in the living room is fine." Rebecca smiled as her younger brother lowered the heavy box to the floor and made an exaggerated show of slumping over it in a fit of exhaustion.

"That was the last box," he panted breathlessly. "We're done. Finished. Finito."

"Are you sure?" Rebecca teased, walking out of the kitchen. "Did you check every crack and crevice of the U-Haul to make sure you guys got everything?"

Rasheed lifted his head to give his approaching sister a wry look. "Take my word for it. The truck's empty. Chris is locking it up right now."

Rebecca leaned down and planted a big wet kiss on his forehead, grinning as he groaned in embarrassment. "Thank you, baby boy."

At six feet tall, Rasheed Edmonds wasn't quite a "baby" anymore. The chubby face he'd sported most of his life had been replaced by lean, masculine features when Rebecca wasn't looking. Four years of working out in the campus weight center with his college buddies had given him a toned, muscular physique that drew plenty of admiring female gazes wherever he went. His caramel-brown skin was still sun-toasted from his summer trip to Costa Rica, which had been his college graduation gift from Rebecca.

Eight years apart, the siblings had always been close, a bond that had been further strengthened by the untimely death of their parents. Rebecca had just started on her master's degree when tragedy struck, claiming the lives of Frederick and Valeria Edmonds in a boating accident while they were vacationing overseas. Rebecca had immediately dropped out of school and taken on a part-time job, in addition to her full-time one, in order to help raise her orphaned fifteen-year-old brother. At her insistence, money from the insurance settlement was set aside for Rasheed's college education—no exceptions. Although they'd received occasional assistance from distant relatives, for the most part, Rebecca and Rasheed had been on their own. Money had been tight, but somehow they'd survived, learning to depend on each other through the good and bad times.

And in those dark, depressing years while they'd both struggled to cope with the devastating loss of their parents, there had been more bad times than good.

When Rasheed graduated from college with honors, Rebecca was so proud of him she'd wept like a fool at the ceremony. Out of the many job offers he'd received, he had accepted a position with a top executive firm in D.C. and was now thinking about pursuing an MBA.

Lost in her reverie, Rebecca didn't notice that her brother had risen from the floor and was walking through the apartment, carefully inspecting each room.

"Are you sure you had to move out of your apartment in Annapolis?" he asked as he returned to the living room, thick dark brows furrowed together in a frown. "This place ain't as big or nice as the other one."

Rebecca laughed. "Who says I need big or nice?"

His frown deepened. "It's not about what you need. It's about what you deserve."

"Aww, that's so sweet of you, Sheed." Reaching up, she gave his cheek an affectionate pat. "Seriously though, don't worry about me. This apartment suits my needs just fine. The rent is more affordable, and it's within easy walking distance of the Inner Harbor and Lexington Market, where I can buy fresh fruit every day. If you really think about it, for what I'm paying a month, this place is a steal."

"Yeah, I guess so."

Rebecca winked playfully at him. "Hey, if it doesn't work out, I'll just move into your bachelor pad."

"Works for me," chimed Rasheed's best friend and roommate, Chris Douglas, who had just strolled into the apartment. Short, stocky and good-looking, he flashed a megawatt grin at Rebecca. "You know you're more than welcome to move in with us, Rebecca. Any sister of Sheed's is a sister of mine."

Rasheed rolled his eyes toward the ceiling. "On that note, we'd better get this truck back to U-Haul before I end up using it to shovel up all this bullshit I'm hearing."

Rebecca grinned. "Now, now, Rasheed. Be nice. It was very kind of Chris to give up his Saturday to help me move. Thank you, Chris. I really appreciate it."

He sketched a gallant bow. "The pleasure's all mine."

As the boys were leaving, Rebecca heard Chris exclaim to Rasheed, "Man, your sister's fine as hell."

Smiling at Rasheed's growled warning, Rebecca closed the door behind them and surveyed the clutter before her. How could one person accumulate so much junk? she wondered, shaking her head at all the moving boxes. She definitely had her work cut out for her. But for now she was tired, thirsty and craving a hot shower. She would tackle the unpacking in the morning after a good night's rest.

If she got a good night's rest.

Rebecca frowned, remembering the way she'd spent the previous night tossing and turning, her mind filled with vivid images of Vince Gray. Two days later, she still couldn't believe she'd let a complete stranger kiss her. He'd kissed her, and worse, she'd kissed him back, and had enjoyed every last moment of it. The memory of that scorching kiss and the fantasy that had preceded it were seared on her brain, to the point where she'd been unable to think of little else since then. During the night, she'd awakened from a steamy dream to find herself moaning as she masturbated herself senseless.

She, who'd been too consumed with her doctoral studies over the past two years to give sex a second thought, had actually masturbated.

It's a sign, girl, a voice chided. *You've deprived yourself long enough. You need to get laid. And what better person to end your drought than that fine, scrumptious man?*

Just thinking about Vince Gray's deep, sexy voice and heat-seeking tongue made Rebecca's nipples get tight and tingly. She had no doubt that the man knew how to pleasure a woman, and that making love with him would be an unforgettable experience. But that was part of the problem. A man like Vince Gray would never be satisfied with just one partner. For all Rebecca knew, he'd probably spent the following evening at another nightclub picking up women. She was willing to bet he rarely—if ever—went home alone.

Why do you care? You're not interested in marrying him or bearing his children. You just need him to scratch an itch for you, and then you can both go about your business.

Rebecca frowned and shook her head at herself. Why was she entertaining these crazy thoughts about a man she'd met only once, and might never see again? Assuming Vince did return to The Sultan's, she wasn't scheduled to work again until Tuesday. He probably wouldn't even remember her or recognize her without her mask. By kissing her, he'd satisfied his curiosity about the mysterious woman in disguise, and that was the end of it.

Recalling that she'd left her car unlocked while they unloaded her belongings, Rebecca headed downstairs to the parking lot. She locked the doors to her Toyota Avalon, then checked the trunk to make sure she hadn't forgotten anything else. She found a medium-size box labeled Personal Items and lifted it out of the car, then closed the door and made her way back toward the high-rise apartment tower.

As she neared the building entrance, a couple dressed for a night out on the town emerged and held the door open for her.

"Thank you," Rebecca told them, flashing a grateful smile.

She crossed the lobby and rounded the corner to the service elevator, which the building manager had given her permission to use while she moved in. The thing was as old as the building and was so slow Rebecca could climb the stairs to her ninth-floor apartment in less time than it would take the service elevator to get her there. She'd fare much better in the regular elevator used by everyone else. But she was tired and sweaty, and not in the mood to stop on every floor with a heavy box in her arms.

As she was about to push the button to summon the elevator, a deep, unmistakably familiar voice asked, "Need some help?"

Rebecca whirled around, and was stunned to find herself staring into the darkly sensual face of Vince Gray.

Chapter Four

At the sight of Rebecca, those piercing onyx eyes that had filled her every waking thought since Halloween night widened slightly in recognition.

Her heart thumped. Oh God, she thought in a moment of sheer panic. He recognizes me. How can that be? And why did he have to catch me at my worst, wearing no makeup and a sweaty old T-shirt?

She tried to school her features into an impassive mask, hoping that if she played dumb, he might actually think she was someone else. "No, thanks," she said politely, responding to his previous question. "I'm fine. But thanks for asking."

"No problem," he murmured, his expression giving nothing away. She felt a glimmer of hope. Maybe he didn't recognize her after all. Just because he had an unforgettable face didn't mean the whole world did. "Moving in?"

She nodded wordlessly, realizing that the less she said, the less the likelihood of him recognizing her voice. Balancing the box on one hip, she turned away from him to push the elevator button, expecting the doors to open right away since she was the only one who'd used the elevator that day. It should have been waiting right there for her on the lobby level.

It wasn't.

She stabbed the button again, more impatiently this time. Where was the damn thing?

"Why don't you use the other one?" Vince suggested, standing close enough to make her pulse accelerate. "It would probably be much faster."

"It's all right," Rebecca muttered, keeping her profile to him. "I've been using this all day. It's my last run anyway."

To her surprise, Vince reached out, taking her chin between his thumb and forefinger and gently turning her face toward his. A hint of a smile played about the corners of his mouth as he gazed down at her. "How long are you going to pretend we've never met, Rebecca?" he asked huskily.

Her knees went weak. "I was hoping you wouldn't recognize me," she admitted sheepishly.

"Not recognize you?" Shaking his head slowly, he brushed the pad of his thumb across her bottom lip, making her shiver. "In a million years, I could never forget this incredible mouth."

Just like that, Rebecca got wet between her legs.

His eyes roamed across her face, as if he were trying to commit her features to memory. Self-conscious, she smoothed a hand over her makeshift ponytail and moistened her lips. She shouldn't look too bad, she reassured herself. Rasheed and Chris had done all the hard work. She'd mostly supervised.

"You're even more beautiful than I thought," Vince said softly, devouring her with those bedroom eyes.

Oh God. She set the box down on the floor and sat on it before her knees gave out. This was too much. He was too much, looking finer than any man had a right to in a black turtleneck that molded broad shoulders and a wide, muscular chest. Low-rise blue jeans clung to the corded muscles of his thighs, and he wore a pair of black Timberland boots that looked enormous.

You know what they say about men with big feet...

Rebecca swallowed hard and drew her gaze back up to his face. It was a long journey, he was so tall. "What are you doing here?" she asked. "Do you live in this building?"

He shook his head. "Just visiting someone."

"Oh?" An image of him clasped between some lucky woman's legs flashed through her mind, and without realizing it she frowned. It was only after six p.m.—too early for a booty call.

Wasn't it?

She'd been out of the game too long.

"Did you have a good time with your friend?" she asked casually.

His mouth twitched at her not-so-subtle attempt to learn the sex of the person he was visiting. "Not yet," he drawled. "I just arrived."

"Oh. Well, don't let me keep you, then."

His lips curved in a slow, lazy grin. "Believe me, Rebecca, I don't mind being kept."

She found herself smiling up at him. He was a shameless flirt, but he was so damn sexy and irresistible, she couldn't help herself.

So that she wouldn't have to keep stretching her neck to look up at him, he dropped to his haunches beside her. "You should do that more often," he told her.

"Do what?" Rebecca asked, trying not to stare at the way his jeans molded his powerful thighs. But anywhere her gaze landed was dangerous territory. From his mesmerizing dark eyes to his full, sensuous lips, Vince Gray was a minefield of throbbing, virile maleness.

"Smile," he answered. "You should smile more often. It takes my breath away."

Ignoring the way her belly quivered, she gave him a look of mock severity. "Do you talk this way to every strange female you encounter, Mr. Gray?"

"Depends."

Her brow arched. "On what?"

"Your definition of strange."

Rebecca laughed. He was sexy, charming and funny—a lethal combination. Hold on, my heart.

"You ought to be illegal, Mr. Gray."

"Said the pot to the kettle," he said silkily. There he went again, eating her up with those eyes of his. He leaned closer. "And whatever happened to being on a first-name basis?"

"We hardly know each other."

"That can easily be rectified," he said, his voice low and deep.

Their gazes locked. Suddenly, all Rebecca could think about was the lap dance she'd given him in her erotic fantasy, and the things he'd done to her afterward. Her blood heated at the tantalizing memory, and her body thrummed with a fresh wave of desire. Nothing had changed. She wanted him just as much now, as she'd wanted him then. If not more.

Without warning, the missing service elevator arrived on the lobby floor with a rusty chime. As the metal doors clanged open, Rebecca rose to her feet. Vince followed more slowly, never taking his eyes off hers.

"I don't work until Tuesday," she heard herself telling him.

His eyes darkened dangerously. "I can't wait that long to see you again."

Her mouth went dry. As she bent to pick up the box, Vince beat her to it, lifting it easily into his arms and stepping into the waiting elevator. Rebecca didn't ask any questions, just followed him inside and pushed the ninth-floor button.

As the ancient elevator began its sluggish ascent, they stared at each other from opposite corners of the freight-capacity cab. Keeping her trapped in the smoldering heat of his gaze, Vince lowered the box to the floor. Rebecca watched, with a heightened sense of anticipation, as he came toward her slowly. Without a word, he cupped her face in his large hands and slanted his mouth over hers. She responded at once, curving her arms around his neck and kissing him back as if her very life depended on it. With a muffled groan, he matched the feverish urgency of her kiss, plunging his tongue into her mouth, then retreating in a blatantly carnal rhythm that made her nipples harden against his chest.

Tearing his mouth from hers, Vince reached over and hit the emergency-stop button, and the elevator came to a shuddering halt. Since the building manager had disabled the alarm while Rebecca was moving in, it didn't go off.

Without missing a beat, Vince cupped her buttocks and lifted her from the floor, and Rebecca wrapped her legs tightly around his waist as he pinned her back against the wall. She could feel the engorged length of his penis pressed against her, and it was unbearably arousing. She was on fire, beyond the point of no return. All she wanted was to have him buried deep inside her, consequences be damned.

She didn't utter a word of protest as he tugged off her T-shirt and tossed it aside. As she watched, chest heaving, he lowered his head and brushed his mouth over the plump mound of her breast. She gasped, her back arching sharply. He unclasped the front hook of her lace bra, groaning softly as her breasts sprang free.

"I knew you'd be beautiful," he whispered huskily, meeting her heavy-lidded gaze.

She trembled as his hand covered one breast and his warm, silky mouth enveloped the other. He licked the left nipple, circling the tight point with his tongue before catching it between his lips and hungrily suckling. At the same time, his right hand tweaked and tugged at her other nipple until she cried out from the double onslaught of pleasure. She'd never known that her breasts could be so sensitive, or that her body could burn with this kind of mindless, uncontrolled lust.

She gripped the back of his head and urged his lips back to hers for a hot, openmouthed kiss that left them both panting hard. She unhooked her legs from his waist and lowered her feet to the floor. Hooded dark eyes followed her as she knelt before him and unzipped his jeans, reaching inside his boxers with a boldness she didn't think to question. Vince groaned as her fingers closed around his throbbing dick and gently squeezed. The feel of him in her hand made her grow wetter than she already was. He was the living embodiment of her fantasies. Long, thick and magnificently hard.

She rubbed her thumb over the swollen tip, drawing a bead of pre-cum fluid, then slid her hand up and down the smooth length of him as he moaned and grasped the back of her head. Watching his face, she took his penis inside the hot, moist cave of her mouth.

"Damn, baby," he groaned, low and guttural. His fingers bit into her scalp as she deep-throated him in a way she hadn't done to a man since she was an undergrad. Vince was big, even bigger than she'd first imagined, and his skin was hot and marble-smooth in her mouth. She sucked him hard and hungrily, using her hand to squeeze his balls at the same time. He threw back his head and moaned with pleasure, rocking his hips as he thrust back and forth into her mouth.

She wanted him to come inside her, could already anticipate the salty-sweet taste of him. But suddenly he pulled her to her feet and braced her against the wall. Crouching down, he quickly removed her cotton shorts, then slid her lace panties down her legs more slowly and deliberately, watching her face as he did so.

Rebecca expected to feel shy and vulnerable as she stood naked before him, but instead she found herself deliciously aroused, her breasts jutting forward, her nipples painfully erect. He devoured her with his eyes, then with his mouth, trailing a searing path from her navel to the triangle of black curls at the juncture of her thighs.

At the first touch of his tongue on her clitoris, she cried out sharply and flung back her head. Need pounded furiously through her. Her legs parted of their own accord, allowing him greater access to her pulsing center. She clung to his broad shoulders as his hot, wet tongue delved deep inside her. Her moans of ecstasy escalated, bouncing off the insulated walls. Vince's expert tongue glided over her slippery feminine folds, back and forth, in and out of her, until her body began to quake uncontrollably in the grip of an intense orgasm.

As her knees buckled beneath her, Vince swept her into his arms and backed her against the wall, crushing his mouth to hers. She tasted herself on his lips, and the raw carnality of it drove her crazy.

Breaking the kiss after several moments, he reached inside his jeans pocket and withdrew a condom from his wallet. He sheathed himself so quickly and effortlessly that Rebecca knew he'd had plenty of practice. But she didn't care. She wanted him inside her, and she couldn't wait much longer.

Vince lifted her from the floor and drew her legs around his waist. She cried out hoarsely as he drove into her with one deep, penetrating thrust. She wrapped her arms around his neck and threw back her head as he thrust into her again, burying himself to the root. With a groan that sounded as if it were ripped from his throat, he began to pump in and out of her, hard and fast, until their breathless moans filled the air.

Grasping her buttocks, Vince stepped away from the wall and freestyled it, holding her high in the air as he pounded into her relentlessly. Arching against him, Rebecca pushed her aching breasts out to meet his face. Greedily he took a taut nipple in his mouth, and with each suckle drove her closer to the edge. Their coupling was fevered and urgent, and unlike anything she'd ever imagined or experienced before.

"I'm about to come," she whimpered, squeezing her eyes shut as if to brace herself for the pending explosion.

Barely a second after the words left her mouth, she felt another earth-shattering orgasm rip through her, wracking her body with waves of ecstasy. She sobbed Vince's name as he rocked against her once more, then stiffened and groaned with his own powerful release, his dick throbbing palpably inside her.

Moments later, panting and trembling, Rebecca dropped her head onto his shoulder, and he held her tightly in his arms, running his hands over her slick back as her body began to relax. For a long time they remained locked in that position, her legs wrapped around his waist, neither making a move to end the embrace.

When their racing heartbeats finally returned to normal, Vince drew back and angled his head to gaze down into her face. "Where have you been all my life?" he murmured huskily.

Rebecca licked her lips into a sultry smile. "You've been looking in all the wrong places."

He chuckled, and her belly bottomed out at the low, sexy rumble. He brushed a kiss over her damp forehead, then across her mouth. She opened for him, seeking his tongue, and they kissed deeply and provocatively.

After a while he raised his head, and Rebecca unwrapped her legs from his waist as he eased her down and stepped back. He bent to retrieve her discarded clothing, and she dressed quickly, stuffing her underwear inside her pocket and sliding her feet into her flip-flops.

Vince zipped up his jeans, then pushed the emergency-stop button, and the elevator lurched back into motion. They stared at each other in supercharged silence as the cab climbed to the ninth floor. Without a word, Vince picked up the box, then followed Rebecca down the empty corridor to her apartment. Inside, he set it down on the floor, and before she could finish locking the door, he pulled her roughly into his arms and seized her mouth in a fiercely possessive kiss.

She tore at his clothes with desperate hands and he helped her, tugging his turtleneck off over his head as she reached for his belt buckle. In no time at all they were both naked, and Rebecca's hungry gaze drank in the sight of him. He was even more magnificent than she'd imagined, broad shoulders and a wide chest planed with hard, sinewy muscle over a tight six-pack. She ran her hands over his torso and sucked on the dark, flat button of his nipple, delighting in the tremor that shook his body.

He quickly sheathed himself with another condom, then they sank to the carpeted floor, surrounded by moving boxes. Her heart was pounding violently against her ribs, her body caught in a fever of need. Vince pulled her on top of him, and as she straddled him, she guided his long, thick penis into her body.

They groaned in mutual pleasure as she took him to the hilt and settled fully astride him, skin to skin. Vince swore softly as she began to gyrate on him, slowly and seductively, closing her eyes as she gave herself over to the exquisite sensations. He reached up and fondled her breasts, teasing and caressing her nipples until they ached. Heat poured through her body, drawing her backward like a bow. With her head thrown back, she braced her hands on his upper thighs and rode him like a thoroughbred as he began thrusting hard, fast, deeper with every stroke.

"Oh my God…Oh my God," she cried over and over again as their bodies slapped noisily together. She could feel another climax building, just as powerful as the first two had been. "Vince…Vince!"

Her back arched tautly as her inner muscles began to convulse around his throbbing dick, milking an orgasm from him at the same time that she came with a wild cry of ecstasy.

When her spasms eased, she collapsed against him in boneless exhaustion, and he gave a low, husky laugh. As she snuggled against him, he stroked lazy hands down her back and over the curve of her ass, whispering to her in that deep, hypnotic voice of his. Lulled by the sound, she drifted off to sleep.

Chapter Five

She awakened to the most sublimely erotic sensation between her legs. It was like velvet dipped in sun-warmed honey, lapping against the aroused, swollen folds of her sex. She moaned and writhed in mindless pleasure, convinced she was still dreaming.

But as she slowly opened her eyes, she saw Vince's dark head buried between her legs, which he'd thrown over his broad, powerful shoulders. He was eating her out, slow and deep, like she was a hot fudge sundae he wanted to savor.

As Rebecca watched, he lifted his eyes to hers. The scorching heat of his gaze melted her from the inside out. She clutched a handful of bedsheets as he licked and nibbled her pulsing clit. Then he did something incredible with his tongue that sent shock waves through her whole body. She called out his name hoarsely as her back arched off the bed. She climaxed so hard she thought she'd pass out.

Weak and exhausted, she could do no more than roll onto her side and close her eyes. Vince curled up behind her, fitting his hard, muscled body along the length of hers and draping an arm across her waist. The soft fabric of his jeans rubbed against the back of her legs, and his warm breath tickled the nape of her neck. She'd never been more deliciously sated in all her life.

Drowsily she opened her eyes and looked around the large bedroom. Night had fallen, and a Tiffany floor lamp glowed softly from the only corner of the room that wasn't cluttered with moving boxes. She realized that Vince must have carried her to bed after they made love. Good thing she'd taken the time to unpack her linens and make up the bed while her brother and Chris unloaded her stuff from the truck.

What a fabulous way to christen your new bedroom, she thought with a naughty smile.

"What're you thinking about?" Vince asked, the deep timbre of his voice vibrating through her body. Her flesh tingled as if he'd physically caressed her.

"I was thinking about how much I like my new apartment," Rebecca answered.

Vince chuckled softly. "Funny. I was just thinking the same thing."

She threw him a teasing look over her shoulder. "Don't you get any crazy ideas about moving in with me. I've never done well with roommates."

"That's too bad," he drawled, making her shiver as he kissed her shoulder. "I'd make a damned good roommate. I'd always pay my half of the rent, I'd keep the place pretty clean, and I wouldn't play loud music at all hours of the night while you're trying to study."

"Mmm. Sounds too good to be true. Would you also do backrubs?"

"Sweetheart," he murmured in her ear, "I'd do anything you wanted me to."

Rebecca's toes curled. He was so damn sexy she almost asked him to move in with her right then and there. But she couldn't even imagine coming home every day to a man like Vince Gray. With him around, she wouldn't get a single thing done. She'd spend too much time on her back, or on her knees.

"Where do you live, Vince?" she asked curiously.

He kissed the nape of her neck. "If I told you I was homeless, would you let me move in with you?"

She laughed. "No, I'd refer you to a friend of mine who's a social worker for the city. She'd help you find a job and obtain subsidized housing."

"Hmm. Nice friends you have."

"I like to think so. So what about you, Vince? Do you have a lot of nice friends?"

"Why? Are you tired of me already?"

As if! "Do you always answer questions with questions?" she teased.

"Is that what I was doing?"

"Yes," she said with a muffled laugh. "And you just did it again!"

He chuckled. "Sorry. It's your fault though."

"My fault?"

"Yeah. I can't think straight while holding the most beautiful woman I've ever seen in my arms."

If any other man had spoken those words to her, Rebecca probably would have rolled her eyes in disbelief. But Vince…well, Vince was somehow different. So when he called her beautiful, she didn't mock his sincerity; she melted.

"I've rendered you speechless," Vince said softly.

Rebecca smiled. "Maybe a little. It's becoming a rather bad habit of yours."

He laughed quietly. "Well, speaking of habits," he murmured, snuggling closer, "I could get very used to this."

"I was just thinking the same thing," Rebecca admitted, surprising herself. Vince Gray was a virtual stranger to her, yet she could think of no place else she'd rather be at that moment, lying in his arms, their bodies spooned together like two halves of a whole.

Who was this man? she wondered. And where had he come from?

The doorbell rang, jerking her out of her thoughts.

"That's the deliveryman," Vince said, rolling away from her and swinging his legs over the side of the bed. "I ordered Chinese for dinner."

Rebecca warmed with pleasure as she turned around to face him. "You thought of dinner?"

"Of course. We worked up one hell of an appetite, don't you think?"

She smiled demurely. "You could say that."

"Besides, I have to feed you."

"Oh, really? Why's that?"

He leaned down to nibble on her bottom lip. "Because I haven't had my fill of you," he said huskily, gazing into her eyes. "And by the time this night is over, beautiful one, you're going to need all the strength you can get."

Oh, God. If Rebecca had been standing, her knees would have given out on her. All she could do was lie there and watch as Vince winked at her, then rose from the bed and sauntered out of the room.

It was only when the fragrant aroma of Chinese food reached her nostrils that she finally climbed out of bed and padded to the adjoining bathroom. After emptying her bladder, she rummaged around in a cardboard box labeled TOWELS AND LINENS. Locating a thick terry wash cloth, she soaked it with hot water and poured a small amount of mango-scented body wash into the center. As she cleaned herself, she gazed at her reflection in the vanity mirror. Her long black hair was tousled, her dark eyes were heavy-lidded and hazy, and her lips appeared slightly swollen. She looked like a woman who'd been screwed out of her mind for the past three hours.

As Rebecca washed herself, the friction of the warm, wet towel both soothed and aroused her. She imagined Vince kneeling in front of her, slowly guiding the wash cloth over the plump, slick folds of her sex, then replacing the towel with his fingers. Her body throbbed in response. She could almost feel him massaging soap into the soft triangle of curls at the juncture of her thighs, then slipping beyond to caress her engorged clitoris.

Closing her eyes, she set aside the wash cloth, then reached between her legs and touched herself. Pretending she was with Vince, she teased and stroked herself as the pressure built inside her. She scraped a fingernail against the hood of her clit and shivered at the resulting sensation. Her breasts throbbed, and her nipples hardened. She slipped a finger deep inside her body and heard her own ragged moan as if from a great distance. Imagining Vince's long, thick penis filling her, she pushed a second finger inside herself, then cried out as she began climaxing, her hips pumping wildly.

When she opened her eyes moments later and looked in the mirror, her reflection was joined by Vince's, standing a few feet behind her. He was watching her quietly, his lids at half-mast, his nostrils slightly flared. Instead of feeling embarrassed that she'd been caught masturbating, Rebecca found herself more aroused than before. Especially when she lowered her gaze and saw the bulge of Vince's erection straining against the fly of his jeans. The knowledge that she could turn him on so easily sent a thrill of wicked pleasure through her.

Without a word, Vince closed the distance between them and reached around her body to cup her aching breasts in his hands. Rebecca moaned as he kneaded them, brushing the pad of his thumbs across her erect nipples. She gyrated her hips, rubbing her backside against the rigid, protruding length of his dick. With a low groan, he slapped her right butt cheek. Rebecca gasped as a melting warmth spread through her belly and settled heavily in her loins.

"You like that?" Vince whispered huskily against her ear.

She nodded quickly, and his hand rose and fell again, lightly at first, then with increasing pressure as she panted and writhed against him, on the verge of climax.

"Vince," she moaned. "I want you inside me."

The words were barely out of her mouth before he was unzipping his jeans and sheathing himself with a condom he'd retrieved from the back pocket.

She parted her legs, braced her hands on the countertop and leaned over the sink as the slick head of his penis probed at her swollen opening.

"Now, Vince," she half-commanded, half-begged.

He thrust inside her, so high and deep she felt him in her womb. She cried out and arched backward, her feminine muscles clenching tightly around him. With one hand he massaged her breast, while with the other he continued slapping her buttock to the beat of his hard, voracious strokes. Rebecca watched their joined images in the mirror, unbearably aroused by the sight of this gorgeous black man having his way with her.

As he pumped harder and faster, she felt the tension rising within her, felt herself approaching release. She reached behind her and squeezed Vince's naked butt, and he shuddered and began thrusting faster, his balls slamming heavily against her bottom. A moment later, she felt the blinding pleasure of an orgasm overtake her, wrenching loud, helpless cries from her throat.

As her body spasmed, Vince slid halfway out of her, then plunged deep and hard, one last tremendous thrust, locking their bodies together. He called her name hoarsely as he came, an orgasm so strong and violent it shook her own body.

They remained clamped together, his hands gripping her waist, her palms flattened against the countertop, until the tremors subsided and their breathing gradually returned to normal.

There was a wet suctioning sound as Vince eased out of the slick clasp of her body. With an economy of motion, he turned her around and lifted her onto the counter, then stepped between her legs. His onyx eyes smoldered with desire as he cradled her face in his hands, leaned down and captured her lips in a deep, provocative kiss.

"Are you hungry yet?" he whispered against her mouth.

Smiling sultrily, Rebecca curved her arms around his neck and licked the seam of his lips. "Yes, but not for food."

That was all Vince needed to hear. He lifted her into his arms and started purposefully from the bathroom. Before they even made it past the doorway, her legs were locked around his waist and he was thrusting inside her.

An hour later, the two lay spent in each other's arms, Vince's shaft cozily sandwiched between their bellies, his hands lazily stroking the lush curve of her ass. He couldn't remember the last time he'd felt so thoroughly satiated.

"We definitely couldn't be roommates," Rebecca drowsily declared, her warm breath tickling his neck.

Vince chuckled softly. "Why not?"

"Well, for starters, we'd both starve to death."

"Food is overrated."

She laughed. "Speak for yourself. I happen to enjoy eating."

"Hey, don't blame me. I asked you an hour ago if you were hungry."

She sighed. "I know. What can I say? I found a better way to satisfy my, uh, appetite." She fell silent and he waited, sensing she wanted to say more. Moments later she did, her voice soft and subdued. "I don't sleep around, Vince. Especially not with men I've just met."

"I know," he murmured. "I knew that the moment I laid eyes on you."

She angled her head back to give him a dubious look. “How could you have known that?”

He smiled into her eyes. “I have a sixth sense about these things.”

“Must come from a lot of experience.”

“Maybe.” He studied her expression. “Would that bother you?”

She hesitated, then shook her head and snuggled closer to him. Her exotic scent, combined with the musk of their lovemaking, filled his nostrils. His body stirred. “Whatever happened to your friend?” she asked.

“My friend?”

“The one you came here to visit.”

“Oh.” He wondered what she’d say if he told her the truth, that he actually lived there. But he couldn’t risk blowing his cover. It was bad enough that of all the places in Baltimore Rebecca Edmonds could have chosen from, she’d moved into his apartment building.

Seeing that she was still awaiting his reply, Vince said, “He wasn’t home.”

“He?” Rebecca asked casually. “The friend you were visiting was a male?”

“Yeah, an old buddy from college. We must have gotten our times mixed up. I’ll call him tomorrow and reschedule.”

If Rebecca doubted his story, she didn’t let on. “By the way, what did you order for dinner?”

“A little of a lot. I wanted to make sure I got something you liked.”

She chuckled. “You mean your sixth sense didn’t tell you what my favorite Chinese dish is?”

“If I could read your mind,” he drawled, “where would be the fun in getting to know you?”

“So you plan on getting to know me, huh?”

“Most definitely. It’s all I’ve thought about since we met.”

She slid one long silken leg up and down the length of his, sending heat through his veins. “I honestly didn’t expect to see you again after Thursday night.”

"Are you kidding? I had every intention of hanging out at the club until you agreed to go out with me."

There was a hint of pleasure in the teasing smile she gave him. "I've never really liked pushy men."

"That's because you'd never met me."

She gave a husky little laugh that made his pulse quicken. "Make that pushy, cocky men I've never really liked."

"Hmm. Interesting that you should use the word 'cocky.' " As he spoke, his dick thickened and hardened between their bellies.

"Oh my," Rebecca breathed, gazing at him.

Vince reached down and fitted his hand against the vee of her thighs, covering her mound with his palm, his fingers tapering downward and into her moist, silky heat. She moaned softly and closed her eyes as he rolled her gently onto her back.

"I know we're supposed to be taking a dinner break," he said as he settled between her legs, "but I can't get enough of you, baby."

She closed her thighs around his hips, holding him tighter. Removing his fingers from her wet sex, he slid them into his mouth and sucked off her nectar while she watched, her eyes turning smoky with desire. He reached for his wallet on the nightstand and quickly removed a condom, hoping he wouldn't run out of his supply that night.

"Let me," Rebecca murmured.

With an effort, he held himself still as her warm fingers slowly rolled the sheath down his engorged length.

The moment she finished, he cupped her buttocks, and she raised her hips to meet him as he plunged into her, then withdrew and thrust again.

As they began moving together, she whispered, "You're right. Food is overrated."

Chapter Six

When they finally emerged from the bedroom, it was after midnight.

Rebecca was delighted to find that Vince had set the dining room table earlier and lit scented candles, which, hours later, were still burning softly. While she warmed the food in the microwave, he dimmed the lights and built a cozy fire.

Seated across the candlelit table from each other and framed against the backdrop of the glittering night skyline visible through the living room window, they could have been dining at a romantic restaurant downtown, instead of Rebecca's cluttered apartment.

As they began eating, she forgot about the unpacked boxes that surrounded them, forgot about the fact that she was wearing a silk robe, instead of a silk cocktail dress. All that mattered was the sexy man sitting across from her, gazing at her in a way that made her feel as if she were the only woman alive.

"What're you smiling about?" Vince asked lazily.

"I was just thinking what a small world it is. What are the odds that I now live in the same apartment building as your old college friend, and on the day I moved in, you'd be here paying him a visit?"

"It was meant to be," Vince said huskily.

Rebecca had to agree, although she knew it was dangerous to do so. It was one thing to have mind-blowing sex with a complete stranger, but if she started attributing terms like 'serendipity' and 'kismet' to their chance encounter that afternoon, she'd find herself in deep trouble.

Just enjoy the experience, Edmonds, she told herself. For once in your life, don't overanalyze it. Just enjoy it.

"Where did you live before you moved here?" Vince asked conversationally.

"Annapolis. I wanted to be closer to the university where I teach, but now it doesn't matter because I took the year off from teaching to concentrate on completing my doctorate." She hesitated for a moment, waiting for him to get that guarded look on his face, as other men had when they learned about her academic accomplishments. But then she remembered that Vince Gray was a successful investment broker; he wouldn't be threatened by an educated black woman.

Sure enough, he smiled easily at her, his dark eyes alight with interest. "Women's studies, right?"

"That's right." She smiled, pleased that he'd remembered. "I've always been interested in women's studies, in learning how we've overcome social and political challenges throughout history. I guess you could say a part of me has always been something of a feminist." Her mouth curved wryly as she looked at Vince. "Does that scare you a little?"

"Not at all." His voice deepened. "There's nothing sexier than a strong, beautiful female who's in touch with her womanhood."

Rebecca grinned wickedly. "Well, as you witnessed earlier in the bathroom, I'm very much 'in touch' with my womanhood."

Vince made a sound that was half groan, half chuckle. "Damn, baby. That was one of the hottest things I've ever seen in my life."

Her belly quivered. "And here I thought maybe I should have been a little embarrassed," she confessed.

"Hell, no. Believe me, I enjoyed every damn minute of watching you."

"And I enjoyed every minute of what came next," she purred.

Vince's gaze darkened as he looked at her. "Eat your food, woman, before I change my mind about this whole 'dinner break' idea."

Rebecca laughed, but obediently picked up her fork again and cut into her sesame chicken. "Have you always wanted to be an investment broker, Vince?"

"Not exactly." He hesitated, then added, "I majored in criminal justice in college."

"Really?"

He nodded. "My father was a cop. While I won't say I always wanted to follow in his footsteps, I definitely entertained the idea of going into law enforcement—whether as a police officer, or an FBI or DEA agent. I even thought about going to law school and becoming a prosecutor."

Rebecca tilted her head thoughtfully to one side and studied him. "Funny you should say that, because I can see you more in one of those occupations than the one you're currently in."

"Why do you say that?"

"I don't know. You just don't seem like the investment-broker type."

Vince gave her an amused look over the rim of his glass. "How many have you known?"

"Not many," she admitted sheepishly. "In fact, I don't think I know any at all. Point taken, I guess."

Vince chuckled. "It's all right. I get that reaction all the time, especially from new clients."

"Oh, no. That's terrible."

"Not really. It makes it that much sweeter when I dazzle them with my investment knowledge and instincts. More water?" he offered, lifting a large glass pitcher.

"No, thanks. I'm fine." Rebecca grinned, eyeing the crystal wineglasses Vince had removed from a box labeled "FRAGILE." "Sorry all I have is water. I didn't plan to go shopping for groceries until tomorrow."

"Why are you apologizing? You just moved in. Besides," Vince said with a mischievous wink, "water's the best thing for the body. Water—and great sex."

Rebecca arched a brow. "Great?"

Vince gave her a slow, sexy smile. "Mind-blowing."

"That's much better." She grinned, taking a sip of her drink. "I'm looking forward to hitting Lexington Market in the morning. I promised my brother I'd bake him a peach cobbler as payment for helping me move today."

"You have a brother?"

She nodded. "His name's Rasheed. He's eight years younger than me, but we've always been close. Anyway, he joneses for my peach cobbler, so I promised to make him one in exchange for his services."

Vince chuckled. "I'm sure he would've helped you move without being bribed."

"I know," Rebecca said with a soft smile, "but he hardly ever lets me spoil him anymore. So I take every opportunity I can to do it on the sly."

Vince smiled at her. "I hope Rasheed knows how lucky he is to have such a wonderful big sister."

"Oh, we're lucky to have each other." She paused, then quietly confided, "We lost our parents to a boating accident eight years ago, so we've pretty much had to depend on each other for everything. I honestly don't know how I would have gotten through those tough times without Rasheed."

Vince's expression was full of gentle compassion in the flickering candlelight. "I'm sorry to hear about your parents. That must have been devastating for both of you."

"It was, but somehow we survived. Thank God for siblings." Smiling a little, Rebecca ran her finger around the rim of her wineglass. "What about you, Vince? Do you have any brothers or sisters?"

He nodded. "An older sister named Venetta. She lives in Los Angeles."

"Are you two close?"

"Yeah, we're pretty tight. We talk on the phone at least once a week."

"That's good," Rebecca said warmly. "What does she do?"

"She runs her own hair salon."

"Really? Well, the next time I'm in L.A., I'll have to look her up and get my hair done."

Vince smiled. "Sounds like a plan."

"And what about your parents?" Rebecca inquired, wanting to know as much as possible about her new lover. "Do they live in L.A. as well?"

"No," Vince said quietly. "They passed away several years ago."

"I'm sorry," Rebecca murmured. "I shouldn't have assumed—"

"That's all right. It was a long time ago." Vince gazed at her across the table. "It seems we both know what it's like to be orphans."

"It seems so," Rebecca agreed, as the words *kindred souls* whispered through her mind. She reached for her glass and took another sip of water.

They fell silent for a few moments, listening to the crackle and hiss of the logs in the fireplace. Although the Chinese food was delicious, Rebecca found she wasn't as hungry as she should have been, considering the lovemaking marathon she and Vince had just completed.

"You said earlier that you don't do well with roommates," he said, breaking the silence between them.

Rebecca glanced up from her plate with a teasing smile. "Still trying to figure out a way to move in with me?"

His dark eyes glinted with mischief. "Maybe. So which is it? Have you had lousy roommates in the past, or are you a lousy roommate?"

She laughed. "For your information, I'm a very good roommate."

"Yeah? In what ways?"

"Help me clear the dishes," Rebecca drawled, her lips curving naughtily as she rose from the table, "and I'll show you."

Chapter Seven

"Okay, it's not as bad as I thought it would be."

Rebecca glanced up from unpacking a box of glasses to smile at the tall, caramel-skinned woman who stood at the living room window that overlooked a view of downtown Baltimore. "What were you expecting, Cherelle?"

Cherelle Hagans turned from the window to flash a dimpled grin at her. "When you told me you were downsizing to a cheap apartment in Baltimore, I was afraid I'd find you living in some roach-infested tenement in the projects."

Rebecca arched a brow at her. "Do you realize what a snob you sound like?"

"Uh-huh. Now ask me if I care?"

Rebecca laughed, shaking her head. "Girl, you are a mess. Get over here and help me unpack these damn dishes like you're supposed to be doing."

With one last glance out the ninth-story window, Cherelle started across the room. She was a beautiful, statuesque woman with large, heavy breasts and wide, ample hips that swung as easily as a well-oiled door as she walked. Her long dark hair was stylishly braided, and she wore a burgundy cowl-neck sweater and a pair of rhinestone-studded designer jeans that hugged her thick, shapely legs like a second skin. The spiky heels of her black leather boots added another three inches to her height, so that when she stood beside Rebecca—who was five-six—she practically towered over her.

The two women met as freshmen at Morgan State University in Baltimore. Paired together on a sociology project, they'd discovered a mutual affinity for African art, conspiracy theories, and anything written by Audre Lorde. In no time at all, they became so close that some of their peers began speculating that they were lesbians. They'd laughed at the rumors, and every so often when they were feeling particularly mischievous, they'd strolled across campus with their hands in each other's back pockets—much to the amusement of friends who knew they were anything but lovers.

They'd always been there for each other, through bad break-ups with boyfriends to the tragic passing of Rebecca's parents. While Cherelle was studying feverishly for the bar exam, Rebecca had furnished her with meals and an endless supply of Starbucks coffee, a favor Cherelle returned as Rebecca worked toward her doctorate degree. As far as she was concerned, Cherelle Hagans was the sister she'd never had.

"How are things going at The Sultan's?" Cherelle asked, reaching for another box on the counter, this one filled with plates. "Are you making any progress on your research?"

"Some," Rebecca said, lining a cabinet with glasses. "Not all of the girls like being the subject of my dissertation."

Cherelle snorted. "Who can blame them? You're doing a study on how society exploits strippers."

"Well, not exactly. My dissertation explores gender differences in societal reaction and conventional support among exotic dancers in a large metropolitan area. In other words, what I'm trying to establish is that female dancers are less likely than male dancers to receive community support for dancing as a way to earn a living."

"Maybe you shouldn't have told the girls what you were working on," Cherelle said simply. "People get nervous when they're asked to speak on record, especially about their private lives. Maybe there's a way you could have interviewed them without them knowing they were being interviewed."

This time it was Rebecca who snorted. "Do you really think I could have asked these women a bunch of personal questions without arousing their suspicions? They would've thought I was a reporter or an undercover cop, and either way they wouldn't have talked to me. Besides, you know very well it would have been unethical of me to gather information on those women without their knowledge or consent."

Cherelle grinned. "I'm a lawyer. What do I know about ethics?"

"I see your point," Rebecca said dryly. "Anyway, I just need a little more time to gain everyone's trust. I've only been waitressing at the club for three months, and some of the girls have already given me plenty of empirical data."

Cherelle's light-brown eyes twinkled with mischief. "So when are you going to start working at a club with male strippers? That's when I'll start dropping by to meet you for lunch."

Rebecca laughed, tossing a wad of newspaper at her friend. "Girl, you are such a freak!"

Cherelle laughed. "Don't front. You know you'd much rather be watching a group of buff, gorgeous men strip down to G-strings than a bunch of chicks with sagging titties and nasty stretch marks."

"First of all, I'm too busy serving customers to be watching anyone on stage. And just for the record, The Sultan's has some of the most attractive dancers in Baltimore. Bruno pays those girls to keep their bodies in shape and maintain healthy eating habits. He even pays for their membership to Gold's Gym, and don't think he doesn't periodically check in with the manager to keep tabs on who's showing up to work out and who's not."

Cherelle frowned. "Sounds like a dictator to me. Or an obsessive pimp."

Rebecca shrugged, slicing open a new box. "He's a businessman, and a very savvy one at that. He's built his reputation on having the best exotic dancers around, and whether or not you agree with his methods, he delivers on that promise."

Cherelle paused in the middle of unwrapping a plate to study her through narrowed eyes. "Are you absolutely sure there's nothing going on between you and Signor Rossi? He's very good-looking, if I recall. And—perhaps more importantly—he's rich. That is, if you don't mind wondering where all his money comes from."

Rebecca shook her head. "You sound just like those feds who kept auditing him to find discrepancies in his financial records. If Bruno Rossi is a criminal, then I'm a long-lost heiress to an African dynasty."

"You might be. Remember how our history professor used to tell you that you carried yourself like a queen?"

Rebecca made a face. "He was also eighty years old and half blind."

Cherelle snickered. "Seriously though, Beck. What makes you so sure Bruno Rossi is on the up-and-up?"

"What makes you so sure he isn't? The fact that he's an independently wealthy Italian-American? Does that automatically mean he has ties to the Mafia or some other criminal enterprise?"

"Of course not. Girl, you know I'm not that narrow-minded."

"A lot of people are though." Lips pursed, Rebecca tipped her head thoughtfully to one side as she looked at her best friend. "You want to know why I'm convinced of Bruno's innocence? Because he told me. Seriously," she added when Cherelle shot her a cynical look. "I know it's hard for you to believe I'd be that trusting or naïve. You make a living defending corporate executives you know damned well are guilty as sin. Your cases have made you jaded, and I understand that. But I'm not jaded—or I try not to be.

"On a slow night when I was working late at the club, Bruno and I got into a conversation about our families. He told me how his relatives migrated to this country from Sicily with nothing more than the clothes on their backs. He talked about his grandfather working night and day at a factory to feed his large family and resisting pressure to get involved with organized crime, as many of his friends had done. The Rossis were dirt poor, and they never quite realized the American dream. But Bruno's grandfather died knowing he didn't have any man's blood on his hands, and that he'd led a life of integrity and honor that would impact future generations. Bruno Rossi's success today can be attributed to his grandfather's legacy, as well as the good head for business he was blessed with."

When she'd finished speaking, Cherelle began to clap. "That's one of the best oral summations I've ever heard."

Rebecca laughed. "Girl, hush. All I'm saying is that Bruno is a self-made millionaire who got where he is through hard work and determination. He took business courses at the local community college, saved up his money and made some smart investments along the way, including the purchase of a failing nightclub he breathed new life into. I don't know what kind of so-called evidence the government has on him, but obviously it hasn't been enough to bring him down. My gut tells me they'll never produce the kind of evidence they need to indict him, because it simply isn't there."

Cherelle looked vaguely amused. "Your gut tells you?"

"Yeah." A soft smile curved Rebecca's mouth as she remembered Vince's words. "I have a sixth sense about these things."

"All right. I'll take your word for it. However, if Signor Rossi ever needs legal counsel, be sure to drop my name. Landing a client like that would put me on the fast-track to making partner at the firm, and you know I need all the advantages I can get, being the youngest attorney and the only black female."

"Girl, you don't need any advantages. Those people are lucky to have someone of your talent and ability on their side. If they don't realize it, there are a hundred other law firms that would snatch you up in a second."

Cherelle gave her a grateful smile. "Can I take you to the office with me every day?"

"You could," Rebecca said with a grin, "but I don't think that would go over too well with the senior partners."

"Probably not." Cherelle turned away to stack plates in the cabinet. "By the way, you never answered my question. When are you going to start moonlighting at a male strip club?"

Rebecca laughed. "You just don't give up, do you? Like I told you before, the bulk of my research comes from survey responses provided by male and female exotic dancers at several different clubs around the city. But, yes, to present a more balanced study, I do plan to spend at least a month waitressing at the Spectrum to get the male dancers' perspective.

Bruno has already spoken to the owner, who's a good friend of his, and set it up for me."

"Uh-huh, I bet he has. And you say there's nothing going on between the two of you."

"There isn't. I'm not interested in Bruno that way." Rebecca paused for a moment. "Besides, I met someone."

Cherelle whirled around so fast she nearly dropped a plate. "What did you say?"

"I met someone. At the club." Rebecca grinned wryly at her friend's wide-eyed expression. "Damn, girl. You don't have to look so surprised. It's not like I've never dated before."

"Yeah, but you know it's been a long time."

Which would probably explain how insatiable she'd been with Vince, Rebecca mused. She still couldn't believe how many times they'd made love yesterday. She'd stopped counting after the fourth or fifth mind-blowing orgasm he'd given her.

"So tell me about this someone," Cherelle urged, abandoning her task to give Rebecca her undivided attention. "You say you met him at The Sultan's?"

Rebecca nodded. "Now, you know how I feel about men who get off on watching women strip in public. I generally think they're borderline perverts. But something about this guy was different. I got the feeling he doesn't visit strip clubs very often."

"What's his name?"

"Vince," Rebecca answered, remembering the way she'd moaned and screamed his name into the wee hours of the night. "He's an investment broker, and girl, he is beyond fine. Tall, dark as Godiva chocolate, and too sexy for his own damned good. Picture the buffest male stripper you've ever seen—big shoulders, rippling muscles, a six-pack you could bounce quarters off. Well, Vince's body is all that and then some."

Cherelle raised a finely sculpted brow. "How do you know so much about that man's body?"

Rebecca grinned. "Let's just say I had an up-close-and-personal encounter."

Cherelle's eyes widened in shock. "You little hussy! No, you didn't!"

"I did. Over, and over, and over again."

With a squeal of delight, Cherelle grabbed her hand and practically dragged her over to the small oak table in the sunny breakfast nook. "Details. I want details!"

Feeling like a naughty schoolgirl, Rebecca told her friend everything that had happened from the moment she met Vince Gray, starting from the unexpected summons to the Platinum Suite that had led to their first kiss, and ending with an account of the way he'd taken her roughly against the refrigerator when they finally emerged from the bedroom to have dinner, which had been more like a midnight snack. The memory of each erotic encounter was enough to make her body throb with renewed desire.

"Dayuum!" Cherelle exclaimed when she'd finished speaking. Grinning broadly, she fanned herself with her hand and shook her head at Rebecca. "Girl, you never cease to amaze me. Just when I think I've got you all figured out, you go and do something crazy like this."

Rebecca grinned. "Believe me, I shocked the hell out of myself. I hardly even know this man, but that didn't matter to me the moment I saw him again. All I could think about was how damned fine he was, and how his deep, sexy voice was making me weak in the knees. Before we even stepped onto the elevator, I knew I was a goner."

Cherelle laughed. "Girl, not even I have had sex on an elevator, and you know I've done some wild shit in my time!"

Rebecca flushed, curling her bare toes over the bottom rung of the chair. "I can't explain what came over me, Cherelle. It's like I was someone else. A woman with no inhibitions, no fears." She frowned. "No morals."

Cherelle snorted. "Morals have nothing to do with this. I don't care if you were named after someone in the Bible or not. There's a freak in all of us, Rebecca. It just took you thirty years to find yours." She grinned lasciviously. "Better late than never, I always say."

Rebecca chuckled. "I guess you're right."

"I know I'm right. And based on your description of Vince Gray, you chose the right man to unleash your inner freak upon. So when are you going to see him again?"

"I don't know." Rebecca bit her lower lip. "When he left early this morning, I was still in bed and kinda out of it. We didn't really discuss any future plans."

Cherelle smiled gently at her. "I'm sure he wants to see you again, if that's what you're worried about."

"I'm not worried," Rebecca said quickly. Hearing the glimmer of uncertainty in her own voice, she added, "I'm not looking for a serious relationship. If what Vince and I shared was just a one-night stand, then I'll just chalk it up to the best one-night stand I've ever had, and leave it at that."

Cherelle stared at her for a moment, then shook her head. "You haven't seen the last of him. If you rocked his world as much as he rocked yours, trust me, he'll be back for more."

Rebecca didn't want to admit, even to herself, how much she wanted Cherelle to be right. She told herself it was because the sex had been so phenomenal, but she knew there was a little more to the story than that. She'd felt a connection to Vince that she'd never experienced with any other man. Beyond his physical attributes—and there were plenty—he was warm, smart, funny and thoughtful. He'd ordered enough Chinese food to feed an NFL football team just to make sure he got something she liked, when it would have been more practical for him to wake her up and ask her what she wanted. Instead he'd chosen to surprise her with dinner. And she would never, ever forget the deliciously erotic way he'd awakened her.

Have mercy.

Cherelle rose from the table. "Maybe I need to start hanging out at The Sultan's, if Vince represents the kind of customers you're getting in that place."

Rebecca smiled, but something told her Vince Gray was one in a million.

Chapter Eight

"See anything interesting yet?"

Vince glanced up from the video monitor he'd been watching on and off as Frank Sciorra grabbed the chair beside him and sat down with a soft grunt. "Not yet," said Vince. "All he's been doing for the last two hours is paperwork. Not exactly must-see-TV. What'd you get us?"

"What else? Crab cake sandwiches and French fries from Mulligan's." Frank reached inside a grease-stained paper bag and pulled out his food before sliding the bag across the table to Vince, who eagerly helped himself.

He hadn't eaten since his midnight meal with Rebecca, and even then he'd been too distracted by her beauty to swallow more than a few bites of sesame chicken before he set out to devour her again. She'd risen slowly from the table, a naughty little smile on her lips as he backed her into the kitchen. Once he cornered her against the refrigerator, she'd wrapped those long, luscious legs around his waist and welcomed him inside her tight, silky heat as if it was the first time. Just thinking about the way he'd drilled into her like a jackhammer got him so hard he ached.

With a mental shake of his head, Vince bit into his crab cake sandwich and returned his attention to the video screen, which was filled with a live image of Bruno Rossi's large, opulent office at The Sultan's. The club owner sat behind a gleaming mahogany desk, his dark head bent over a mound of paperwork, oblivious to the hidden video camera that enabled two undercover cops to spy on him from a nondescript police trailer parked on the other side of town.

"I don't understand this guy," Frank muttered, shoveling a thick French fry into his mouth. "He's rich enough to hire a whole team of people to do his filing and bookkeeping, yet he insists on handling those responsibilities himself."

"Maybe he doesn't trust anyone else to do the job right," Vince suggested. "You said yourself he's a major control freak."

"Yeah. And maybe he knows he can't trust anyone with confidential information about his business dealings. The fact that one of his very own 'bouncers' is running surveillance on him is proof that he shouldn't trust anybody."

"Must be a damned lonely existence."

Frank snorted. "Small price to pay for being filthy rich."

"Yeah," Vince muttered. "It's the 'filthy' part I'm worried about."

Frank gave him a long, appraising look. "Have you ever considered the possibility that Rossi's clean?"

"No."

"Come on, man. Not even once?"

Vince hesitated, then gruffly admitted, "Maybe once."

"Yeah, me, too. I mean, I just find it a little hard to believe that after five years of investigating this guy, the feds haven't been able to build a case against him."

"That's not unusual. It happens more often than we'd like to think."

"I know, but after all the time and money that's been spent on investigating Rossi, the only 'evidence' we've come up with are a few questionable transactions to an account in the Cayman Islands and his long-ago connection to the leader of another money laundering enterprise, who Rossi hasn't been in touch with for years. Even after the guy served his time and got out a couple of years ago, Rossi made no attempt to contact him, and vice versa." Bemused, Frank shook his head. "If you ask me, Rossi pissed off the wrong person at the top of the food chain, and now he's doing penance for it."

Vince said nothing, though the same thoughts had occurred to him on more than one occasion. Frank was right. They had very little evidence on Bruno Rossi. His phone records were cleaner than the

Pope's, his financial holdings had held up under intense scrutiny by the IRS and FBI, and hours of surveillance tapes had failed to reveal any clandestine meetings with shady "business associates." But Vince had learned from his own father that nothing was ever as it seemed.

Vincent McCall, Sr. had been a vice cop with the Chicago Police Department for nineteen years. Frustrated with the systematic racism that denied him promotional opportunities year after year, he'd yielded to temptation and joined his partner in a money laundering operation that netted them over $200,000 before they were eventually caught.

Were it not for their slick-tongued, high-priced attorney who'd played the race card during the trial, Vince's father may have spent his remaining days on earth behind bars, instead of in a cold hospital bed at Northwestern Memorial, his body ravaged by lung cancer. He'd died without benefit of a stately police funeral, leaving a legacy of shame and corruption that tainted the lives of his surviving wife and children. Three years later, Vince's mother succumbed to depression and quietly wasted away. After that, Vince and his older sister dispersed—she to Los Angeles, he to Baltimore, both desperately in pursuit of new lives.

Oh, yeah. Vince definitely knew a thing or two about not judging a book by its pretty cover. If anyone had told him that his father—devoted family man and pillar of the community—was a common criminal, Vince would have knocked the unlucky person's lights out.

Now he knew better.

If Bruno Rossi was engaged in illegal activity, Vince considered it his personal duty to uncover the truth and bring him to justice.

Nothing less would do.

"I'm not just defending Rossi because he's a fellow Italian," Frank was saying around a mouthful of food. "I really think—" He broke off, distracted by something he'd seen on the video monitor.

Vince turned to look, and in silence they watched as a tall, voluptuous blonde in a tight T-shirt and leather miniskirt entered Rossi's office and sashayed over to his desk. As she leaned over the edge, the short hem of her skirt lifted to reveal her bare, milky-white ass.

"It's Giselle," Vince and Frank said in unison. They glanced at each other and grinned before returning their attention to the video screen, where the dancer had slowly rounded the desk to sit on Rossi's lap. Smiling coquettishly, she slid her fingers through his thick hair and lowered her face to his for an openmouthed kiss.

"Well, well, well," Vince intoned, polishing off his sandwich and settling back in his chair. "Now we know why she's the most popular dancer at the club."

Frank shook his head in disbelief. "I had no idea those two had a thing going. Rossi always seemed above crossing the line with his employees. I'll be damned."

Vince chuckled dryly. "And you wanted to push her off on me."

Frank grinned. "You'll find out why in a minute."

Sure enough, as they watched, Giselle knelt between Rossi's legs and unzipped his pants. They had a brief glimpse of the club owner's penis before most of it disappeared into the blonde's wide, willing mouth.

"Dayuum," Vince exclaimed under his breath.

Frank said, "Didn't I tell you I heard that Giselle gives the best head? Check out that technique."

Vince grinned. "She's not bad," he allowed, remembering the way Rebecca had deep-throated him in the freight elevator. He'd been so aroused he nearly came in her mouth. It was, by far, the best blow job he'd ever received.

Remembering the erotic elevator encounter only made him think about the rest of the time they'd spent together.

One night.

He'd promised himself one night with her, and no more. He couldn't afford to be distracted by thoughts of Rebecca Edmonds. He needed to concentrate on ensnaring the mark, not becoming a mark himself. Because there was no doubt in his mind that his desire for Rebecca could quickly turn into obsession, the kind that left a man too dazed and confused to know up from down. He'd already spent way too much time thinking about her, wondering if she'd slept in that morning or gotten up early to walk to Lexington Market to buy fresh peaches, as she'd mentioned last night. And try as he might to deny it, he wanted to be with her, not holed up in this damp, chilly trailer that reeked of mildew and stale coffee. On this crisp fall day, he wanted to stroll to the outdoor market with Rebecca and hold her basket as she poked and squeezed her way through a colorful array of fresh, plump fruit. He wanted to return to her apartment, share a laugh over steaming mugs of hot chocolate, then slowly peel away her clothes and make love to her by the crackling fireplace.

The bottom line was that he enjoyed her company. Not only was she beautiful, but she was smart, caring, had a great sense of humor, and appealed to him on more levels than a man could ever hope for. He enjoyed being with her, spending time with her.

He wanted more than one night.

"Hey, where are you going?" Frank demanded as Vince abruptly rose from his chair.

"I just remembered something important I have to do," he said, shrugging into his battered leather bomber.

"Right now?"

"It can't wait any longer." Vince paused, then clapped a hand to his partner's shoulder. "Go home to your girlfriend, Frankie. It's a beautiful day. Who wants to spend it cooped up inside a damn trailer watching Rossi get a blow job, when you could be getting one of your own?" Flashing a wicked grin, Vince turned and strode from the trailer without a backward glance.

"You know, when you showed up at my apartment and asked me to go out on a date with you," Rebecca said to Vince two hours later, "this isn't exactly what I had in mind."

Vince, seated beside her in the back of a covered wagon filled with hay and pulled by a tractor, gave her a lazy smile. "What did you have in mind?"

Rebecca laughed. "I'm not sure. Maybe something indoors and a little more, uh, stationary."

"Stationary's boring," Vince drawled, a wolfish glint in his dark eyes. "I like movement. And the more, the better."

Rebecca's belly quivered at the unmistakable implication. She moistened her lips and watched his gaze follow the path of her tongue. "Nothing wrong with movement," she murmured. Especially not the kind of movement he did inside her body.

Pushing aside the tantalizing thought, she smiled. "Seriously though, Vince. I've never been on a hayride before, so this was a wonderful surprise." As she spoke, she gazed through the wide opening of the covered wagon, which offered breathtaking views of the scenic countryside. Fall was in full bloom. A brilliant profusion of yellow, orange, red and gold leaves covered the giant trees that flanked the hillside trail they were following. The hayride concluded with hot apple cider and fresh-baked pumpkin pie served at a privately-owned farmhouse nestled on ten acres in northern Baltimore County.

"It's absolutely beautiful out here," Rebecca said appreciatively.

"You should see the view from where I'm sitting," Vince murmured, gazing at her in that way that turned her insides to mush.

"I was talking about the scenery," she said with a teasing smile. "And stop looking at me like that."

"Like what?"

"You know. Like a hayride isn't the only kind of ride you have in mind."

He gave a low, sexy chuckle. "Well, now that you mention it…"

Rebecca laughed, easing away as he leaned toward her. Not even her inner freak was adventurous enough to have sex out in the open like this, where they could be discovered by their tour guide at any moment.

"Spoilsport," Vince grumbled good-naturedly.

Again Rebecca laughed. She had been thrilled to answer her door that afternoon and find him standing there, putting to rest her secret fears about never seeing him again. When he asked her out on a date, she couldn't get dressed fast enough. Good thing he'd told her to wear something warm and casual. The low-rise jeans and red cashmere sweater she'd chosen were more appropriate for a fall hayride than a little black dress and high heels.

She reached out and took his warm hand, lacing her fingers through his as the wagon gently jostled them along. The late afternoon air was crisp and cool, but inside the covered carriage, they were mostly insulated from the chill.

"Are you originally from Baltimore, Vince?" Rebecca asked conversationally.

He shook his head. "Chicago. I applied for a job here a few years after college."

She nodded. "Why Baltimore?"

"One of my college buddies was from Baltimore. He always spoke of being homesick, so I came here to find out what all the fuss was about."

"And what's your verdict?"

"I like it here. But quite honestly, once you've lived in one big city, you feel like you've lived in them all." Holding her gaze, he brought her hand to his lips. "What about you, Rebecca? Where are you from?"

"I grew up in Upper Marlboro, forty minutes down the beltway. But I attended college in Baltimore, so it feels very much like home." She was having a hard time concentrating with his soft, warm lips on her skin. She wanted to feel his mouth on hers, and on her breasts and between her thighs.

She drew a shaky breath. "When I complete my doctorate next year, I plan to apply for a faculty position at Johns Hopkins right here in the city."

"Mmm, very impressive." Vince was now trailing hot little kisses down the center of her palm, making her nerve endings tingle. "I like a woman who knows what she wants out of life."

Oh, she definitely knew what she wanted. And right now, it had nothing to do with her career.

When Vince curved a hand around the nape of her neck and drew her close, she didn't protest. He slanted his head over hers and kissed her, sliding the tip of his tongue across the seam of her lips. She opened readily and touched her tongue to his, inviting him inside. He accepted, exploring her mouth, thrusting and retreating in a carnally familiar rhythm that made her moan softly.

Arousal was a low ache in her body, a weakness in her knees. She reached down, sliding her hand across the front of his jeans and molding her palm to the thick bulge of his erection.

With a husky groan of pleasure, he lifted his head from her mouth and pressed his pelvis against her hand. "Damn, baby. See what you do to me?"

A shiver of desire rippled through her. Holding his dark gaze, she unzipped his jeans and reached inside his boxers. His breath hissed out as her fingers closed around his hard, throbbing erection. The feel of him in her hand made her nipples harden and heat pool between her legs.

Vince groaned as she slowly caressed him, running her hand up and down his engorged shaft. Leaning back on his arms, he raised and lowered his hips in a sensual thrusting motion, urging her to stroke him harder and faster, which she happily did.

She rubbed her thumb over the swollen tip until she felt the first trickle of cum. As Vince watched her through heavy-lidded eyes, she smeared the salty-sweet juice across her parted lips, then slowly, provocatively, licked it off.

"Mmmm," she throatily purred. "I love the way you taste."

Vince swore under his breath, low and guttural, his eyes burning with raw hunger. Before Rebecca could lower her head to take him into her mouth, he sat up, gripping her shoulders and pressing her back until she was lying on the soft pile of hay.

He unbuckled her belt, unsnapped her jeans and slid them down her legs, her silk panties and ankle boots quickly following. He pressed his palm against the curve of her body, then stroked her moist, pulsing clit with one finger. She arched upward as a breathless moan escaped from her throat.

Suddenly she didn't give a damn whether the tour guide knew what they were back there doing. All she knew was that she wanted Vince, wanted him like no other man she'd ever wanted before. It was amazing how he'd stripped away all her inhibitions in such a short amount of time.

He covered her with his body and crushed his mouth to hers. Their tongues fused for a moment, an erotic glide of wet and heat.

Breaking the kiss, he fished out a condom from his wallet, then shoved down his jeans and boxers. Breathlessly she watched as he smoothed the latex over his thick erection and settled between her thighs. She felt the exquisite length of his penis against her throbbing wetness and spread her legs wide to welcome him, so aroused she was already on the verge of coming apart.

Their gazes locked as he rose above her. Grasping her hips, he lifted her slightly and filled her with one deep, mind-numbing thrust. Rebecca bit her lip to hold back the sharp cry that rose in her throat—just in case the driver could hear above the clatter of the wagon wheels.

They quickly found their rhythm, the gentle rocking of the wagon fueling their passion. Vince reached between their bodies and fingered her swollen clit, and she gasped into his mouth. Her body clenched for a suspended moment, then began to spasm and throb around him. As she climaxed, her head went back and her voice rang out with a rapturous moan she couldn't contain.

Vince groaned and thrust wildly, harder and deeper inside her, driving her to another blinding orgasm as he came, his powerful body bucking against hers. This time they cried out together.

For long moments afterward they clung to each other, Rebecca's face buried against his neck as their ragged pants filled the air.

At length Vince lifted his head and smiled down at her. "Wow. That was...something."

"Mmmm," Rebecca purred, idly stroking his firm, delectable butt. "How long did you say this hayride is?"

"One hour. It's only been thirty minutes." His eyes glinted wickedly. "Are you ready for round two?"

"More than ready."

As he rolled over, pulling her on top, she quickly straddled his hips, prepared to show him just how ready she was.

Chapter Nine

Two days later, Rebecca was walking on air as she boarded the elevator at her apartment building. Since meeting Vince last week, she'd had the most amazing sex of her life, not to mention some incredibly romantic interludes. After their steamy hayride on Sunday, Vince had taken her to dinner at a cozy little restaurant with a waterfront view of the Inner Harbor. Afterward they'd strolled along the pier, holding hands and talking as if they'd known each other for years, instead of a few days. After another explosive night of lovemaking, they'd risen early and strolled to Lexington Market, where they shopped for fresh fruit like an old, blissfully married couple.

On the way back to Rebecca's apartment, they'd cut through a park and stumbled upon a fresh pile of autumn leaves that had their names written all over it. Setting aside their purchases, they'd soon found themselves grabbing fistfuls of leaves and tossing them at each other like frolicking children.

At one point, Vince had stood beside the scattered pile of leaves and said, "Fall into me. I'll catch you."

Rebecca had hesitated only a moment before allowing herself to fall backward, into his waiting arms.

And now, as she absently watched the electronic panel above the elevator doors, she knew she wasn't just playing a game anymore.

She was falling in love with Vince.

The cab stopped on the fifth floor, and she was joined by an attractive, middle-aged black man she soon recognized as the night security guard, Marvin Holmes. According to what he'd told her the day she moved in, he received a discount on his rent because the building manager liked the idea of security personnel living on the premises.

Marvin smiled easily at Rebecca. "How are you enjoying your new apartment?"

"I love it." The company ain't too bad either.

As if reading her mind, Marvin grinned. "I see McCall wasted no time welcoming you to the neighborhood."

Rebecca gave him a blank look. "McCall?"

He nodded. "Vince McCall. I saw the two of you returning from the market yesterday."

"Oh, you mean Vince Gray?"

Marvin frowned. "Gray? Don't know anyone by that name. The fella you were with is Vince McCall."

The blood was roaring in Rebecca's ears. Maybe that's why she hadn't heard right. "You must be mistaken."

"I don't think so. He's lived here for some time now, though he mostly keeps to himself. I guess it's understandable why he keeps such a low-profile, him being a cop and all."

"A cop?"

"Why, yes." Marvin stared at her for a moment, then scratched his whiskered chin, looking sheepish. "I guess you didn't know. I'm sorry. I shouldn't have opened my big mouth. If McCall didn't tell you himself what he does for a living, I imagine he had a good reason."

Just then the elevator doors slid open, and the security guard seemed relieved to part company with Rebecca, who made her way out of the building and to the parking lot as if in a trance.

He's a cop, her mind echoed in shock. A cop. And he lied about it. Why?

A barrage of questions raced through her mind. Men lied all the time about their professions, usually to impress women. Maybe Vince thought she'd find him more attractive as a wealthy investment broker than a lowly police officer. But that explanation made no sense whatsoever. Vince was a sexy, virile man who could have any woman he wanted, regardless of how much money he had in the bank. He didn't need to resort to telling fibs to get a woman into bed. She knew it, and no doubt he did too.

So why had he lied to her?

And if he'd lied about his profession, what else had he been untruthful about?

If the security guard was right, Vince had also lied about living in the same building. He'd left her apartment early in the morning, then snuck to his own place—which could very well be right down the hall from her.

Why?

Because he played you for a fool, an inner voice mocked. He'd seen something he liked and gone after it. But his pursuit of her had been nothing more than a game to him, a challenge to see how quickly and easily he could get her on her back. And she'd put up very little resistance, not only falling into bed with him, but then falling in love with him.

Rebecca groaned as she headed uptown toward The Sultan's, where she was scheduled to work that evening.

How could she have been such a fool? How could she have allowed herself to fall so hard and fast for a perfect stranger? While she'd shared personal details about herself—her career aspirations, the tragic loss of her parents, her hopes and dreams for her younger brother—everything Vince told her about himself had probably been a lie. Was he really from Chicago? Had he, too, lost his parents?

How could she trust a man willing to build their relationship on lies?

She couldn't.

When Rebecca arrived at the club twenty minutes later, Stacey Brenner took one look at her and said, "Uh-oh. Must be a man."

Rebecca ignored her and went about getting ready for her shift. Over the next two hours, she was so busy serving customers that she almost forgot about Vince—that is, until he showed up. Ironically, he was seated at the same table in the corner he'd occupied on Halloween night, where it all began.

Rebecca considered asking Stacey or one of the other waitresses to take his order, but she knew that would be the coward's way out. Her only hope of getting over him was to look him straight in the eye and tell him she never wanted to see him again.

Schooling her features into an impassive mask, she made her way over to the table. He looked up from the menu with that sexy, irreverent smile that had seduced her from the very first moment they met. Even now, knowing that he'd betrayed her trust, she wasn't entirely immune to the potency of that smile.

"Hey beautiful," he said huskily. "What time do you get off tonight?"

Ignoring the question, she said sweetly, "Would you like to hear today's specials? Or should I just make a recommendation? You might enjoy the swordfish—it's very popular with all the cops who come here."

The smile disappeared. Regret filled his dark eyes. "Rebecca—"

"Yeah, that's my real name," she said coldly. "What about yours?"

He reached for her arm, but she snatched herself away. "Baby—" he tried again.

"I'm not your baby," she said in a voice that vibrated with fury above the pulsing music. "From now on, you're nothing more to me than a customer. If you're not interested in ordering anything, please stop wasting my time."

He gazed at her for a moment, a muscle clenching in his jaw. "Give me a few minutes."

"Fine." Rebecca spun on her heel and started toward the kitchen, tears burning her eyes, blurring everything around her—the flashing strobe lights, the writhing dancers onstage, the flurry of passing waitresses balancing drink trays.

Knowing she couldn't face her coworkers or other customers in her current condition, Rebecca made a quick detour and headed to the employee restroom.

She'd never been more relieved to find the bathroom empty. She hurried into the nearest stall and slammed the door shut behind her, then leaned against it and closed her eyes as the tears fell, fast and bitter.

She should have known that Vince Gray—or whatever he called himself—was too good to be true.

When she emerged from the bathroom fifteen minutes later, she saw no signs of Vince. She didn't know whether to be relieved or disappointed that he'd given up so easily and left.

On her way down the hall toward the kitchen, she was detained by Bruno. "There's someone waiting to see you in the Platinum Suite," he said quietly.

Rebecca's heart lurched. This was how it had all started. If Vince hadn't summoned her to the Platinum Suite in the first place, they would have remained strangers.

And your heart would still be in one piece.

"Rebecca?"

She took a step back from Bruno, shaking her head emphatically. "I have customers waiting on me."

"I've already asked Stacey to cover your tables."

"That won't be necessary. I—"

"I think you should hear what he has to say, Rebecca. He really seems like he needs to unburden himself."

"That's not my problem."

"I think it is." Bruno's smile was gentle. "Go hear him out. After that, if you still want nothing to do with him, I'll have him thrown out on his ass."

Rebecca hesitated, imagining herself doing the honors. "Promise?"

Bruno grinned. "Something tells me I'd enjoy throwing him out almost as much as you would."

"Don't count on it," Rebecca muttered as she walked away.

When she reached the Platinum Suite on the second floor, Vince stood in front of the large glass aquarium, his hands thrust casually into his pockets. She couldn't help the way her breath caught in her throat at the sight of him there, in that spot. It was like déjà vu.

He turned slowly as she stepped into the room and stood near the door, letting him know he didn't have much time.

"Thank you for coming, Rebecca." His husky voice caressed her name, and she hated the way her body reacted.

She folded her arms across her chest to hide her distended nipples. "You should know that Bruno plans to throw you out of his establishment the moment we're done here."

Vince gave a humorless chuckle. "Can't say I'd blame him, not if he finds out what I'm about to tell you."

Rebecca felt a sliver of unease. "What's going on, Vince?" She paused, her eyes narrowed suspiciously on his handsome face. "Is that even your real name?"

"Yes, it is," he said quietly. "My name is Vince McCall, and I'm a detective with the Baltimore Police Department."

"Why did you lie about that?"

He hesitated, his dark gaze flicking past her to the open doorway. "Would you mind if we closed the door?"

She started to say yes, then changed her mind, deciding he couldn't pose too much of a threat to her, being a member of Baltimore's finest.

She turned and closed the door, but remained right where she was. The look in her eyes dared him to come anywhere near her.

His mouth twitched wryly. "I guess I brought that upon myself."

"Damn right you did."

He hesitated, then turned and crossed to the plush white sectional that dominated the seating area. He sat down and leaned forward, bracing his elbows on his muscled thighs as he began speaking. "The reason I didn't tell you my real name is because I'm working undercover. Or at least I was until four o'clock this afternoon."

Rebecca frowned. "I don't understand."

"For the last two months, Bruno Rossi has been under investigation by the BPD and FBI. He is—was—suspected of money laundering. I've been working undercover as an investment broker to gather incriminating evidence on him."

Rebecca felt lightheaded. "And have you?" she whispered.

Vince gave her a grim smile of apology. "I'm not at liberty to discuss the specifics of the case. However, I can tell you that as of today, the government has dropped the investigation, and no charges will be brought against Bruno, now or in the future."

"What happened?"

"Rebecca—"

"I think you owe me at least that much, don't you think?" Of course he didn't, but she wasn't above pulling the guilt card.

Vince knew it, too. "This is what I'll tell you," he said evenly. "The order to cease and desist came from the top of the food chain, both within the BPD and FBI. I was called into my boss's office this afternoon and given the official rundown, then reassigned a new case and sent on my merry way. End of story."

Rebecca knew it wasn't that cut and dried, but she realized he wasn't going to provide any more information, no matter how much she pried.

"I had no choice but to lie to you, Rebecca," Vince said. "You work for Bruno Rossi, the man I was supposed to be investigating. I couldn't take a chance on you blowing my cover."

Rebecca said nothing. He was only doing his job, one side of her rationalized. Whether or not she agreed with his reasons for going undercover, she couldn't fault the man for doing his job. On the other hand…

"You lied to me," she murmured. "You entered my life under false pretenses."

Vince shook his head. "There was nothing false about the way I felt when I saw you for the first time." His gaze roamed across her body, clad in a soft white blouse and a short black skirt—the regular waitress uniform now that Halloween was over.

"You were wearing less than you are now," Vince said huskily, "and I wanted you. Wanted you so damn bad it was all I thought about for days. Believe me, Rebecca, there was nothing 'false' about that."

Her belly quivered traitorously. "I never disputed the fact that you wanted me, Vince. You made that very clear from the beginning."

"And you wanted me, too, Rebecca."

"We're not talking about me!"

"Yes, we are. We're talking about the fact that you now question everything we've shared over the last four days."

" 'Everything we shared' was based on a lie," she said accusingly. "Nothing you told me about yourself was true!"

"That's not true," Vince said, rising from the sectional and starting toward her. "I'll admit that there were some details, some embellishments, that had to remain consistent with my undercover identity. But those intimate things I shared with you, like the way my parents died and what it did to me and my sister. Those things came from my heart, Rebecca."

Without realizing it, she found herself drifting toward him, like a moth to a flame. "How can you talk about speaking from your heart when you looked me in the eye every day and lied to me?"

"I had no choice! Believe me, Rebecca, if I'd met you anywhere else, I would have told you my real name, where I worked and where I lived. Hell, yesterday when we returned from the park, I would have carried you to my apartment on the third floor, because I wanted to make love to you so bad it was pure torture having to wait and ride the elevator all the way up to the damned ninth floor!"

By now they were standing toe to toe, and both were fuming. "Is that all I am to you? A warm, readily available body to sleep with?"

Vince scowled. "No—"

"Because if that's all you're looking for—"

"No, damn it!" His chest rose and fell rapidly as he stared down at her, his nostrils slightly flared. And then, without warning, he cupped her face in his large hands and crushed his mouth to hers. Rebecca resisted for only a moment before melting against him, wrapping her arms around his neck and reaching on tiptoe to press herself tightly against his body.

"I love you," they whispered at the same time. Drawing back, they gazed at each other in quiet wonder for several moments.

"I know we've only known each other less than a week..." Rebecca began.

He didn't let her finish, slanting his lips over hers in a deep, intoxicating kiss that fanned the flames of desire licking through her.

"Vince," Rebecca panted into his mouth. "I want you."

"I want you, too, baby. And I intend to have you."

"But...right here?"

"Hell, yeah," he growled, lifting her into his arms and striding purposefully toward the sectional. "I paid for this suite out of my own pocket tonight. You'd better believe I'm going to make full use of it."

Rebecca watched through heavy-lidded eyes as he sat down and settled her astride his hard, muscular thighs. His thick erection pressed against the damp crotch of her panties. "Maybe one of these days we'll try out the Champagne Suite," she breathed as he stroked her swollen folds through the silk barrier. She ground herself against him in mindless need, then, impatient for the feel of him inside her, went for his zipper.

"The Champagne Suite?" Vince murmured distractedly.

"Mm hmm. There's a vibrating massage chair in there that's supposed to be really stimulating."

"Baby," Vince groaned as she reached inside his pants and freed his throbbing shaft, then rose up and impaled herself on him, "you're all the stimulation I'll ever need."

The Snowflake Seduction

by

A.C. Arthur

Chapter 1

Sydney Mills dropped her bags and slammed her palm down on the chrome bell. It dinged loudly, but she didn't care. She'd been on an airplane for about ten hours, her feet hurt, she was hungry…oh and she'd just left her fiancé standing at the altar.

There was no concierge in sight, so she hit the bell again. Then she groaned at the loudness and buried her head in her palms. Closing her eyes called up the scene she was sure she'd never forget in this lifetime.

It was her wedding day, and she'd been in the tiny room next to the church office waiting for her sister or her coordinator to come and claim her so she could walk down the aisle and marry the man she'd loved for five years.

She heard the door open and turned expectantly with a huge grin on her face. She was sure she'd never been happier in her life then she was at that moment. Unfortunately, this was only three seconds before the bottom fell out from beneath her.

"My name's Rachel," the strange woman who had entered her room said.

Sydney raised a brow at the female standing across from her. She gathered up her dress and took a cautious step forward. "Am I supposed to know you, Rachel?"

The woman named Rachel reached into her bag and pulled out an envelope. Sydney watched as long fingernails maneuvered effortlessly over the black leather purse. She was tall and slim, her hair braided into thick coils that hung past her shoulders. Sydney eyed her cautiously.

"No, you don't know me. I'm a frie…ah…I'm an acquaintance of your fiancé," she began.

Sydney relaxed just a bit. "Oh, you're here for the wedding. The sanctuary is down the stairs and to your left."

Rachel gave a bleak smile. "I doubt I was included on the guest list."

"Excuse me?"

Without another word, Rachel moved toward Sydney, thrusting the envelope in her direction. "This will explain."

Sydney looked from the woman to the envelope she now held, back to the woman again. Reluctantly she opened it, sliding her own just manicured nails under the flap, removing the envelope's contents. Tension filled the air as she unfolded the paper. Before reading she glanced up at the woman named Rachel again. She was watching her intently, as if the words on that paper were somehow detrimental to her life.

Sydney's eyes returned to the paper she now recognized as some sort of report. The header read Precise Laboratories. Her heart made one loud thump as her eyes roamed further down the page.

Subject No. 1: Rachel Ann Johnson, Subject No. 2: Diamond LaShae Winters and Subject No. 3: Derek Jonathan Winters.

The next thump of her heart seemed to echo off the walls as she continued.

99.7% probability that Subject No. 3 is the father of Subject No. 2.

There were no more thumps because she was certain her heart had ceased beating. Her fingers gripped the paper tighter as the words seemed to blend together. The letters spelling Derek's name and the numbers 99.7 stood out amongst everything else. "What is this?" she asked. Sydney possessed a college degree in marketing and worked at one of Chicago's biggest telecommunications companies. She was intelligent enough to know the answer for herself. Still, she wanted to hear the woman say it.

"Derek and I met almost two years ago in Tampa, after one of his games. We went back to his hotel room and—"

"And you got pregnant," Sydney finished her sentence. Groupies were her worst nightmare.

Rachel rolled her eyes. "No, we went back to his hotel room and made love."

"Oh, is that what they're calling sleeping with another woman's man these days?" Sydney moved the hand holding the letter to her hip.

Rachel folded her arms across her chest, lightly tapping her foot on the carpeted floor. "No, that's what you call consensual sex between two adults," she continued when Sydney rolled her eyes. "Derek and I were involved for about six months before I found out I was pregnant."

Sydney froze. "Six months?" Six months wasn't a groupie. That was a girlfriend.

"When I found out I was pregnant I immediately called Derek. He doubted that the baby was his. I knew it was. He agreed to a paternity test, and here it is." She motioned toward the letter still clutched in Sydney's hand. "The lab sent me a copy of the results, and I sent a copy to Derek."

Sydney looked at the paper again, hoping desperately that this was all a big mistake. Yet 99.7% still glared at her. "How old is this child?"

"My daughter is four months old now."

"Has Derek ever seen her?" Sydney wasn't sure why she even wanted to know. Why should she care if Derek had seen this woman's daughter or not? Then reality set in. This woman's child—Subject No. 2: Diamond LaShae Winters—was Derek's daughter. That fact was 99.7% true.

"He came to the hospital when she was born. That's when we took the paternity test. He's been to my apartment a couple of times since then."

Sydney laughed, an eerie sound that vibrated through the room. "So is he supporting you and his child?"

"Yes," Rachel answered.

"And your purpose for being here now? You've had plenty of time to tell me this. The letter is dated over six weeks ago. Why wait until my wedding day?" This was her wedding day, Sydney thought dismally. She glanced at the clock on the wall. In a very few minutes her coordinator/cousin, Ebony, would come in and tell her it was time. And she was supposed to make her way down the steps to the sanctuary to walk into Derek's waiting arms. Fat chance of that happening today or any other day for that matter!

"I told Derek he should tell you about us. He said he would, when the time was right. I figured that was after he'd married you."

Derek was a professional football player, a wide receiver to be exact. So you would think it would be common knowledge that he was involved with someone and had been for the last five years. But because Derek was in the public eye alot, he wanted his personal life kept quiet. Or at least that was the reason he'd given Sydney. Their engagement hadn't exactly been a secret but it wasn't known to the press. Derek said it was to protect her and their life together. In actuality it seemed like it was to protect him and his shady dealings. "So you plan to stop the wedding?"

"Look, don't take this personally, but I have to look out for myself and my child. I've invested a lot of time in this relationship with Derek, and now I've had his baby. I'm not thrilled about him marrying you, giving you that great big house and your kids going to private schools. But I'm not trying to stop you from getting those things. I just believe I deserve the same things!"

Had she said "her relationship" with Derek? Since when did she and Derek have a relationship? She had to know Derek already had a girlfriend. Regardless, Sydney had heard enough. "I'm not even going to get into what you deserve at the moment. Nor am I concerned with how you take care of your child. This is my wedding day, and you've caused enough damage. I'd appreciate it if you would go now."

As she finished speaking Sadie, Sydney's oldest sister, came in. "Syd, they're almost ready. The bridesmaid's are starting to walk down." Sadie was the maid of honor, so she would walk down just before Sydney. She was probably coming to get her because Ebony was tied up making sure everybody walked down correctly. Sadie looked from her sister to the stranger across from her. "What's going on?"

Sydney stuffed the paper back into its envelope. "Nothing. She's just leaving."

Rachel inclined her head, staring at Sydney a moment longer. "Fine, but this is not over." She strode out of the room before Sydney could say another word.

Rachel brushed past Sadie without a word. "Who the hell was that, and what's stuck up her butt?"

Sydney swore loudly. "Apparently, my fiancé was!"

Sadie's eyes grew larger, and she hurried to close the door behind her. "What are you talking about?"

Sydney gathered the folds of her dress in her arms again and walked to where Sadie stood. "Here, read this!" She stuffed the envelope into Sadie's hand, then moved to the small closet where Ebony had thrown her bag earlier.

"Oh my God! That bastard!" Sadie yelled.

Sydney was backing out of the closet, bag in one hand, an armful of her dress in the other. "My sentiments exactly."

Sadie was stuffing the paper back into the envelope. "I hope you gave her a piece of your mind."

"Her?" Sydney paused between clearing her makeup from the table and ripping the veil from her head. "Why would I have words for her?"

Sadie quickly came to her side, helping her with the tiara-ensconced veil before Sydney pulled all her hair out. "She slept with your man, got knocked up and brought this information to you five minutes before you walked down the aisle."

The veil was free, and Sydney quickly balled it up tossing it across the room.

"Does that mean you're not walking down the aisle?" Sadie asked.

"Look, I know she knew Derek had a girlfriend, but I don't fault her. I fault him. He's the one I trusted, he's the one I respected." Her voice hitched and tears threatened to fall. She grabbed her bag and headed for the door.

"Wait, Syd. Where are you going? You're not exactly fit to travel." Sadie eyed her up and down.

"I'm leaving. I don't want to see him, and I damn sure don't want to face Mama and the family." Sydney made her way through the door, turning sideways to keep the material from getting caught.

Sydney was out of the church and in the back seat of the limo in record time. Initially, she told the driver to take her home, but on the way she'd reached into her bag to find a tissue when those pesky tears had threatened to fall again and found their honeymoon tickets instead. They had planned to spend the week in Aspen, preferring a secluded winter wonderland over the more traditional tropical getaways.

Derek would surely come to the home they'd shared for the last two years as soon as Sadie told him she was gone. Assuming Sadie didn't try to kill him first. At this point, Sydney didn't really care what happened to him. All she could think about was getting way.

She'd changed into one of the outfits in her suitcase when she arrived at the airport and finessed an earlier flight out of Chicago to Denver. Still, it was late when she arrived at the resort. She was bone tired and her temples throbbed with all the stress she'd gone through today. Visions of Derek and Rachel popped into her head. On the plane she'd had a chance to think about her situation again.

She'd given Derek Winters five years of her life. They'd met just after she'd graduated from college. He'd just signed his first professional football contract and was new to the Chicago area. They were introduced by mutual friends. After the first date, Derek had told her she was his soul mate. It had taken her a little longer to fall for him, but when she did, she fell hard. He was everything to her.

The first three years of the relationship were perfect. Derek traveled a lot, but then so did she. This made their time spent together even more special. In their third year together, Derek's team won the Superbowl. They were ecstatic. The team, Sydney, their family—everybody was in a celebratory mood. Sydney had gone to the game. She had her own hotel room a floor below Derek's. That night after the game, she saw first hand all the fans, groupies and scantily dressed women flocked around the hotel and headed toward the floors where the teammates were staying. When she called him on the phone, Derek had come down to her room and stayed until she'd fallen asleep. She wondered now if he'd gone up to join the party afterwards.

The very next Christmas Derek proposed. By that time she'd begun to feel some reluctance. The stress of being involved with a professional athlete was beginning to take its toll on her. But she loved Derek and honestly couldn't see her life without him. So she accepted and began planning a really big and formal wedding. A wedding that his baby mama had ruined with a sheet of paper and news that Sydney couldn't ignore.

Hours later and thousands of miles away from Derek and his betrayal, she rested against the counter, emotionally run down. All she wanted at this point was a nice warm bed and a stiff drink.

"You're checking into the honeymoon suite alone?" a tall, very-built honey-toned man asked.

Sydney stared at him because he looked too good not to and because he wore a burgundy and gold vest with nothing beneath. Standing on tiptoe, she tried to peer over the counter to see if his bottom attire was as skimpy as the top, but she was still too short to see. "Uh, yes. I've had reservations for some time now, but my hus…I mean my boyfrie…I mean my partner wasn't able to come."

The man shrugged and continued punching her information into the computer. His arms were cut and glossed, and he reminded Sydney of one of those strippers Sadie had hired to perform at her bachelorette party. His attire still baffled her. It was February, Valentine's Day weekend to be exact. Derek had suggested the date for their wedding, and Sydney had thought it awfully romantic of him. The lying bastard!

Again her thoughts reverted to Derek, to what she thought they'd shared. Their friends and family had been supportive of their relationship all the way. Their blessing was a given making the expectations higher. By this time they were supposed to be married, to be on their way to happily ever after.

Instead she was standing in this resort. Alone. Pain swelled in her heart and she willed it away. Derek didn't deserve her hurt or the tears that threatened to fall. He didn't deserve a damned thing from her. She'd given him all she intended to give, from now on she'd be looking out for number one. And she started with offering the partially clad clerk—who she now dubbed Gorgeous Guy—a beaming smile.

"Shall I sign you up for morning or evening classes?" he asked.

Now this was a clever distraction. Although she hadn't thought of it herself, she figured it could work to her advantage. Looking at a man like this for the next week should wash Derek Winters right out of her mind.

"Classes? Oh, you mean ski classes. No, I don't need any. I doubt if I'll be doing much skiing this week." She adjusted her purse on her shoulder and bent over to pick up one of her bags and declared that looking was all she intended to do.

She was not an overtly sexual person, but in the years since she'd been with Derek, she'd learned to enjoy sex more often than not. Derek still had some complaints about her performance, but she was eager to learn. Maybe his complaints were what turned him to another woman. Whatever, cheating was cheating in her book.

Gorgeous Guy with the great biceps laughed. "No. I mean the pleasure classes. We have sessions that start at eleven in the morning, and then again at eight in the evening. We like to space them apart to give couples, and ah…singles, a chance to try out the lessons in between classes."

"Pleasure classes?" Sydney frowned. Was it hot in here? It was certainly dark enough. Outside of the fact that it was near three in the morning, there were virtually no lamps turned on, which was strange for the lobby of a resort. The huge fireplace in the center of the floor was ablaze, casting shadows over the walls, but other than that there was just the small lamp on the counter the Gorgeous Guy used to work on the computer.

He handed her a pamphlet. Sydney put her suitcase down again and opened it. For the second time in as many days, she was shocked by what she read. Apparently The Magical Moments Ski Resort was a front for some sort of sexual education class. There was a schedule of classes ranging from The Art of Kissing to Bringing Yourself Cataclysmic Orgasms.

She gasped and looked around, the darkness now making perfect sense. Her gaze flowed back to Gorgeous Guy who now sported a huge grin. His hands were on his hips, his vest opening to give an unfettered view of perfectly defined pectorals with small hardened nipples. She gulped, and her fingers clenched the brochure tighter.

"There must be some mistake," she whispered.

"There's no mistake. You and your, ah, partner had reservations for this week. You're in the Sensual Snowflakes suite on the third floor. There's only one other suite on that floor." As if it were possible, his smile broadened. "We like to offer our guests the utmost in privacy, unless they ask for other arrangements."

Sydney couldn't help but gape in wonder. Was this guy for real? Why would Derek have booked them in this resort? Probably because he thought she was less than proficient in bed. "Other arrangements? So I can get another room in maybe, the normal part of the resort."

Gorgeous Guy must have been feeling the way she was looking at him because one hand moved over his double six pack, rubbing the oiled skin until Sydney wanted to jump over that counter and take over the task for him. Her mind screamed as she wondered what the hell was going on with her.

"No. Other arrangements mean groups. We can accommodate up to three males per woman or three women and three men or—"

Syndey raised her hand. "I get the picture," she said, still struggling to grasp all this. "Okay, but my suite is secluded right? And I don't have to participate in any classes if I don't want to?"

"The other suite on your floor is occupied for the week. The tenant just checked in, but he's alone too, so I venture to say that your floor will be fairly quiet. However, I would advise you partake of at least one class." He smiled, his thick tongue moving slowly over plump lips. Sydney's gaze automatically fell to his mouth, her own nipples tightening.

"I teach a class every night at eight. It's called Make Me Wet."

Sydney almost swooned.

Kyle Jackson had checked in an hour ago. He'd gone to his condo and unpacked. After unpacking was completed, he'd set out to stock his refrigerator. He would be skiing as much as possible this week, which meant he'd be eating twice as much as he normally did.

As it grew later and he was unable to sleep, he fixed a snack and sat staring out his patio door at the snow-capped mountains that looked like smoky gray tents in the dark evening. His mind was filled with thoughts, starting with his failed attempt at marriage and ending with the new ownership of the resort where he'd purchased a condo for purposes of relaxation only.

Less than twelve hours ago he'd called his fiancée, Chantell Davis, into a small room of the hotel where they were to be married and told her that the wedding was off. Chantell had been cool. Her gorgeous model looks hadn't faltered as she called him every name in the dirty girl's vocabulary. He'd deserved it, so he didn't argue.

Their relationship had been perfect for the first year, and after he proposed, the second year had been blissful. Chantell had planned a lavish wedding. Along with his sister and mother, they had managed to use more of his trust fund than he'd used in the twenty years it had been in his possession.

Kyle's father and grandfather had made millions in oil and the family's brokerage firm, so he'd been born with the proverbial silver spoon in his mouth. But money didn't matter all that much to him growing up. As long as he had a basketball in one hand and a football in the other, he was content. At his mother's insistence, he'd gone to college and received a degree in journalism. The only thing he loved more than sports was writing, hence the reason he was the senior sports writer for the Boston Globe and author of "Grip the Ball," his tribute to his two favorite sports.

His decision not to marry Chantell had been quick and unchangeable. He didn't love her and now wondered if he ever had. Sure she'd been a pretty arm piece, and as a supermodel and popular sport's writer they were a great tabloid couple, but besides that there wasn't much else. He probably could have spent the next thirty or forty years attending celebrity parties and traveling the world with her, but then when would he ever find happiness.

So he'd come to his favorite retreat with his mind set on skiing and writing his book, the one that Chantell thought was a foolish dream. Upon arriving at the Magical Moments Resort, he'd seen a couple wrapped in towels. He assumed they were on their way to the Jacuzzi. But by the time he'd climbed out of the elevator—which held two women tongue wrestling in the corner—he'd known something was wrong.

He didn't have to go through any registration since he owned his the condo. But when he stepped inside and was about to call the front desk to complain, he noticed the brochures. He remembered receiving a letter stating that the resort had been sold and that the new owners would be making some changes but with the wedding plans and his deadlines he'd put the letter down without a second thought. With a chuckle he considered the irony of the situation. He'd averted marriage, but then he'd checked into a horny haven.

Dragging a hand down his face, Kyle decided to let it be. If couples came here to learn more about pleasing each other, then who was he to stop them. In fact, some of the classes sounded quite interesting. But right now he wanted a drink, and while he'd stacked the refrigerator, he hadn't stacked the bar.

He'd just stepped out of the elevator and was on his way to the front desk to ask if the bar was still open when he spotted a woman who looked as if she'd had one too many drinks already. Without hesitating, he grabbed her at the waist, letting her small frame lean into his chest.

She relaxed against him, and he let his arms enfold her, moving around her until his fingers rested just beneath her breasts. He inhaled and let her sweet feminine smell wash over him. She felt so good, so right in his arms.

"Ahhhh, maybe I can interest you both in my class," Gorgeous Guy said.

Syndey closed her eyes to the solid strength behind her. She'd been reeling from the information the attendant had given her, not to mention his god-like good looks. She'd thought she was going to faint, but then something had stopped her fall. For another minute, she rested against that something until it came alive. Or rather a specific part of him came alive.

For what seemed like the billionth time tonight, she gasped and tried to move away. He held her tightly until she turned enough to face him.

"If you don't mind," she said in a testy voice.

"Excuse me," Kyle said, then released her. "I thought you were fainting."

Sydney tilted her chin up. "I don't faint." She turned to Gorgeous Guy who was still smiling. "Can I have my room key now?"

"Certainly," he said, passing her the key card.

Sydney extended her hand to take it from him and their fingers touched, their gazes holding. His touch was warm, his gaze alluring. She stood in a trance until another hand closed around her wrist.

"I'll show the lady to her room," Kyle said, unusually concerned about the woman's solitary presence in this of all resorts.

Gorgeous Guy immediately released his hold and nodded at Kyle. "I was just asking if she'd like to attend my class tomorrow night. You are welcome to attend as well, Mr. Jackson. Maybe you and the lady can come together."

Kyle looked down at the woman. She was pretty and had one curvy body, but she looked at him with something less than admiration. Her body, which was once soft and accommodating in his arms, was now rigid and defensive. He knew without a doubt she hadn't come to Magical Moments to learn how to improve on her sex life.

"I'll let the lady decide," Kyle said simply and bent to pick up her bags.

"I can speak for myself," she said, then moved her bag just out of his reach. Sydney didn't know what had come over her, but she was in no mood for men at this moment. Not even the tall, dark, specimen that had caught her, then so openly displayed his arousal. He looked like your proverbial hero—handsome, kind and chivalrous. All the more reason for her to get the hell away from him. She didn't need a hero.

"Would you like some help with your bags?" Kyle asked.

"No, thank you. My room's on the third floor, so I don't have that far to go." She picked up one bag. Her purse slipped off her arm as she attempted to pick up the other one.

"Oh?" Kyle easily grabbed the other bag before her. "We're floor mates. All the more reason for me to carry your bags." He held his hand out for the other one and she pulled her arm back. It was a childish gesture but it told him a lot about this woman and why she was here.

"Or you can carry one and I can carry the other," he said politely, then turned to walk toward the elevators.

Sydney had no choice but to follow him since he had her other bag.

They rode the elevator in silence. Sydney refused to look at him. He didn't say another word to her, which was just fine. Now that she knew what really went on in this resort, she couldn't help but feeling like she was the odd man out. She was not sexual, had never been, or at least had never been bold enough to act on the dreams she had. Staying here for the entire week would be a test, and she prayed nobody would notice how out of place she really was.

They stepped off the elevators, and she immediately walked to the door with her number and a huge snowflake on it. "I'm right here."

"And I'm down the hall." Kyle jerked his thumb in the direction of his door. He noted her eyes were no longer glazed but were now giving him something akin to an evil glare. Amused and a little put off, he gave her a half smile and placed her bag on the floor next to her. She didn't have to tell him twice. He walked away.

Sydney frowned, grumbling, "That went nicely." Dropping her bag, she used the key card to gain access to the room. She didn't know why, but before she entered, she looked back down the hall. He was really tall, she thought absently and damned good looking.

Chapter 2

Hello?" Kyle's sleep filled voice croaked when he answered the phone.

"You owe me bigtime!" Malcolm's deep voice came through the line loud and clear.

A little too loudly and too clearly for—Kyle peeked at the clock on the nightstand—seven in the morning. He'd planned on sleeping in, waking to brunch and hitting the slopes by noon. But once he was awake, he couldn't go back to sleep. Rolling over onto his back, he pinched the bridge of his nose. "What are you talking about, and why are you talking about it so early in the morning?" Since it was seven o'clock in Colorado, it was five o'clock in Boston.

"I just came in. Mom was so upset about your wedding fiasco she got one of her headaches and had to be taken home immediately. Dad took her home under the presumption of giving her a migraine pill and putting her to bed. But the old coot gave her Percocet instead, and half an hour later she was throwing up everywhere. He got scared and called me. We got her over to the hospital where they finally figured out what the problem was. By that time her pressure was up, and we had to sit and wait for that to go down."

Kyle's eyes were wide open now as he listened to his brother's recitation of the events that had taken place after he'd left the church yesterday. "Is she alright now?" Little pangs of guilt stabbed at him.

"She's fine. Resting in her own bed with the proper medication. Now let's talk repayment."

Kyle grinned. He knew exactly what Malcolm had in mind as repayment. "What do you want this time? Basketball or, if you wait a couple of weeks, baseball?"

Malcolm chuckled. "Both. And for not telling Chantell where you'd gone, the use of that condo when you've vacated it."

Kyle rubbed his eyes. If anybody would enjoy staying at the revamped Magical Moments Resort, it was his older brother. There was no doubt that the once quiet, picturesque ski resort had shifted into something just shy of dangerously erotic. "I don't know why you won't just buy your own place."

"There's no need when you have one and you constantly owe me favors."

"You've got a point there." Kyle gave in easily. He could be on the slopes earlier now and beat the crowds. "If that's all, I'd like to get moving so I can hit the slopes."

"Yeah, that's all. Give Mom a call later. I told her you would."

"I will." He'd planned on it anyway, but was sure his mother had needed Malcolm's words to calm her down.

"Alright, I'll talk to you later."

Kyle replaced the receiver in its holder, then fell back onto his pillows.

What now? He'd broken up with his fiancée, caused his mother a night in the hospital and gotten a supreme hard on from helping a pretty woman. He smiled at the memory.

She was pretty. Her black hair was pinned up in some kind of bun with a few straggling curls at her ears. She'd had a small, round face with perky lips. Her eyes, although they'd flashed angrily at him, held hints of passion he'd found intriguing. In addition to all that, she was curvy just like he liked his women.

It was funny how he'd put his own wants to the side for the sake of his mother and Chantell. They'd both been excited by the wedding and all the plans it entailed, so much so that they rarely paid him any attention at all. Ultimately, that suited Kyle just fine giving him the opportunity to think about what it was he really wanted out of life. Luckily, he'd made the decision to back out in time. Marrying Chantell would have been a mistake. He was convinced of that and so had no regrets about what he'd done.

But now, the vision in his mind was of a shorter woman with a nice round bottom. His groin tightened again at the memory. He'd put his arms around her waist and held her close. For a minute he'd considered bending her over and entering her from behind. That thought had him rubbing his length. She would be wet, very wet. The way she readily leaned into him told of her passion and her responsiveness to his touch. He could just imagine sliding his engorged sex in and out of her moist depths.

In no time he was jerking his hardened shaft, moaning into the still dark room. He didn't even know her name, yet she'd made his blood run hot. She had nice breasts. He'd glimpsed that when she pulled away from him. They were full and so round that the chocolate covered mounds swelled over the rim of her shirt. He'd been overly thankful that the leather jacket she wore was unzipped. He jerked harder, his breathing accelerating.

His mind roamed to her face. Her pert kissable lips would look even more enticing wrapped around his penis. He spread his legs and pumped with the ministrations of his hands. She'd take him deep—he sighed—of course, she would be an expert deep-throater. Her eyes were the color of aged rum filled with heat and desire. His stomach clenched. Those very same eyes shifted from one hundred and fifty degrees to ten below zero in a split second.

Kyle's entire body stilled.

She spoke to him with the barest tolerance and he gritted his teeth. She had refused his innocent offer to help carry her bags. She was an angry black woman, the very type he'd managed to steer clear of most of his life. She was sexy but dangerous to his otherwise calm nature.

He released his erection, letting it thump against his stomach and brought his hands to his face. With a deep growl he covered his eyes and tried to clear all erotic thoughts of his new neighbor from his mind. The very last thing he needed was an involvement with another woman. Leaving Chantell had been a good decision, of that he was positive. Completing his book needed to be his first priority.

Even if he was staying in a glorified orgy haven.

Sydney had been up for the past hour, pacing the large suite. Pausing near the patio doors, she looked out to the snow covered mountains. She liked to ski. The idea of spending a week skiing with her new husband had been a good one. Now she didn't know if she even felt like enjoying the snow much less anything else. But, what was the alternative? Spending the week cooped up in this room thinking about the wrong turn her life had taken.

She took a hot shower and stepped out into the steam-filled bathroom. Staring at her reflection in the mirror, she decided to put all reminders of her almost wedding behind her. First order of business—getting rid of the wedding hairdo. Lifting her hands to her hair, she removed the pins and allowed the dark strands to fall about her shoulders. She picked up her brush from the vanity, dragging it through her hair.

Her thoughts drifted momentarily to the man down the hall and his fine self. He was built like he worked out on a regular. His smile was nice, his eyes even nicer. And when he'd touched her…her cheeks flamed with embarrassment at the memory. When he'd touched her she'd immediately felt aroused. She'd rested against his strong body as if she'd been sleeping with him for years. And he'd held her as if he felt that same comfort.

But then she remembered Gorgeous Guy's description of what type of resort this was, "sexual therapy for couples." That's what he'd said just before the hands had gone around her waist, and she'd almost fainted.

Sydney had lost her virginity at the tender age of nineteen, but hadn't achieved an orgasm until she was twenty-seven. And now, at thirty, she only needed both her hands to count how many times she'd seen the blissful abyss of pleasure since then. Activity in the bedroom with Derek had been pretty cut and dry, a fact that he'd always made sure she knew was her fault.

The turn of thoughts had her growing angry again, and she hurriedly dressed, anxious to get out of this room and start enjoying her new life. Whatever had happened between her and Derek was clearly out of her control at this point. And she wasn't about to sit here and blame herself for his indiscretions. He was a lying, cheating ass, and she was glad she hadn't married him.

A half-hour later Sydney was dressed in jeans, a turtleneck and snow boots. She decided she'd go shopping today and ski tomorrow. She wasn't really sure where the shops she wanted to visit were, and she needed to wait for confirmation of her rental car, so she sat in the lobby flipping through brochures.

Kyle saw her the moment he stepped off the elevator. Her hair was different this morning, but the quiet prettiness of her face still beckoned him. She turned the pages of a magazine, his gaze falling to her small, feminine hands and her white-tipped fingernails. Again, he thought of her touching him and had to swallow hard to keep from drooling.

She was dressed casually, looking content and relaxed. He was moving toward her before his mind even registered the motion. Sure he'd decided she wasn't a woman to bother with, especially since women had nothing to do with the book he was writing. Yet, his blood pumped at her close proximity. "Good morning," he said as he rounded the area where she sat.

Sydney hadn't heard anyone approach but instantly recognized the voice of the man taking a seat on the brick-style bench surrounding a huge fireplace. The lobby had been practically empty when she'd come down, but then Gorgeous Guy informed her that the first sessions of the day had just begun. Again, he'd given her a run-down of the classes. Today it was, Finding Pleasure With Touching and Role Playing In The Twenty-First Century. She'd refused to attend either, although she admitted to a small measure of curiosity.

He cleared his throat, and she craned her neck to see his face, again noticing his height and fantastic build. He wore dark-blue jeans and a jacket with a white shirt dividing the dark ensemble.

"Morning," she said, purposely omitting the "good" because she wasn't feeling that particular adjective at the moment.

"Are you heading for the shops?" He asked. She'd taken her gaze from him and resumed looking at the magazine after her brief greeting. Kyle experienced a sense of loss. The connection he felt with her was different and required more thought, more time to explore. Sydney shifted uncomfortably. Again, her body reacted strangely to this man's presence. Luckily, she was sitting down this time, so she wasn't in fear of swooning and him grabbing her intimately again. This weird attraction to him irritated her, and she didn't mind showing him how much. "No, I'm trying to read this magazine." She looked at him over the rim of the magazine. Just a quick glance because staring at him made her pulse quicken. But even a short look reminded her of how attractive he was, his skin the color of warm honey. She looked away before noticing anything else.

Kyle grinned. "I guess that means I'm disturbing you." Her lips turned up in a smirk, her eyes saying "you're damned right." He was again intrigued, wondering what or who made her so bitter.

"Unless you can tell me what this page says, yes, you're disturbing me." Her voice sounded abrupt to her own ears, but she really wasn't in the mood for small talk.

Damn, she was a tough one. In contrast to the women he normally dated, he admitted this feistiness was a turn on. However, he shouldn't be looking to be turned on. That thought almost made him chuckle, considering he'd just come from one of the meeting rooms where a class had started. Six couples dressed only in their underwear sat on the floor amidst an array of pillows. The instructor began the class telling them to get comfortable and to do whatever came to their mind as he said certain words. Kyle had left the room when the word was "masturbate" and uncomfortable memories from earlier this morning entered his mind.

She turned the pages with swift movements that made him think further conversation with her would be fruitless. There was definitely something going on between them, but he would have to figure it out on his own. He shrugged. "I'll leave you to your magazine then." Standing, he prepared to leave her alone. Unfortunately, his thoughts hadn't actually reached his feet, and he still stood in front of her. "But for the record, that's an area restaurant magazine you're reading. I could tell you what it says since I've probably frequented all the food spots in the area."

She didn't speak, just frowned in response.

Kyle suppressed a smile. Man, she was cute—even when she was ticked off. "Remember, I'm just down the hall if you want a personal referral."

"I know what room you're in," she said curtly. He smelled good, too, another fact that disturbed her.

Brrrr! He almost shivered. Instead, he wondered again who had upset her so badly that she was sounding off at him, a complete stranger, with such vengeance. Anyway, that was none of his concern. He had his own personal problems to deal with. His sassy neighbor would have to sort hers out on her own. "Right. Then I'll leave you to your reading."

She didn't respond, and he walked away without another word.

Sydney's shopping trip had been less than satisfactory. She'd found a few gifts for her mother—shot glasses, which Naomi had been collecting since forever. Whenever Sydney went out of town, she was sure to pick up one or two to enhance her collection. Selena and Sadie both had expensive tastes, but that was cool because so did she. Sadie was a year older than her and Selena a year younger. Naomi had been on a streak, the sisters liked to joke. All three of them were close in size and build so normally she'd get them a clothing article or shoes, something she could borrow later, if need be.

She'd stopped at a grocery store, sweets were imperative to her life. It was a good thing she worked out religiously or she'd be as big as a house. She was making her second trip to her car when she spotted her friendly neighbor at the front desk. He was laughing at something the young bubbly clerk had said. Gorgeous Guy had been replaced by a buxom babe with curly brown hair and huge breasts. He was probably inviting her to his room. Sydney frowned. Men were all sex-crazed jerks! Pushing the door open with exaggerated force, she admonished herself for the thought.

He'd probably signed up for all the classes offered by the resort. He looked like a man interested in the art of kissing. Actually, she sighed, he looked like he'd mastered that art a long time ago. Why she was thinking along these lines about a man she didn't know was a mystery. Her mind wandered back to her situation.

She'd assumed she and Derek were happy and they would build a great life together. Boy had she been wrong. From now on she had no intention of assuming anything. She also had no intention of settling down with another man. She was considering taking a page out of Sadie's book and simply have affairs. Another glance around the lobby and the hugged-up couples and scantily dressed staff had her thinking she was definitely in the right place for that.

She'd been standing near the elevators daydreaming when she looked toward the front desk again. Her neighbor was gone. Clenching her teeth barely kept her from wondering if he'd asked Buxom Babe out or not. She looked back and noticed the doors to the elevator were just closing. Great, now she'd have to wait for it to go all the way up and come back down. She rolled her eyes and struggled to get a better hold on her bags before they could fall to the floor.

"You getting in?"

His voice scared her, and she looked up to see her neighbor holding the elevator doors open. Oh Lord! Did she have to get in the elevator with him again? The look on his face seemed to say, "You could wait for the next one."

"Yeah. I'm getting in." She made her way into the small space. She stood against the side furthest from him, her eyes focused straight ahead.

Kyle noticed how she kept her distance and was tempted to let her stay hovered in the corner with all her bags. But when the doors opened, his breeding ultimately kicked in, and he reached for a bag after she'd stepped off ahead of him.

"I can manage myself," she told him matter-of-factly.

She was a bristly creature, he thought. The man had probably kicked her and her bad attitude to the curb. "Fine." He wasn't about to beg to be chivalrous again, no matter how much he wanted to get close to her.

She fiddled and made noise until she finally let herself into her room, just as he closed his door.

What was wrong with her? she asked herself as she began to unpack her bags. He wasn't Derek. And as bad as Derek had hurt her, she couldn't go around biting off the head of every man who tried to be nice to her forever. Her neighbor probably thought she was a bitch. She grinned, remembering the way she'd talked to him. She didn't blame him, she would have thought the same thing. Going into the bedroom to change her clothes, she noticed the message light on the phone blinking at the same time as she saw the champagne and strawberries on the nightstand.

She'd almost forgotten she was in the honeymoon suite. Making her way over to the small table, she decided to ignore the refreshments and listened to her message first. The second she heard Derek's voice she slammed the phone down. He'd obviously figured out where she was a little sooner than she'd anticipated. But she had no words for him or for what he'd done.

Unable to describe what she was feeling—a cross between anger and a need to retaliate—Sydney decided to take charge and go out to dinner. If she kept busy, she wouldn't have time to think of Derek or how big a fool he'd made of her.

She took special care dressing, why she had no idea. Dinner alone in one of the restaurants she read about was no cause to dress up. Out of the corner of her eye, she spied the champagne that was now floating in a bucket of water since the ice had long since melted. Unsure of what restaurant she would go to for dinner, she remembered her neighbor had offered a referral. She'd been so rude to him she wasn't too eager to ask him for help.

Buttoning her sky blue silk blouse and tucking it neatly into her black slacks, Sydney slipped her feet into her favorite leather boots and began applying her makeup. An apology was in order, she thought. She'd just have to march herself right over there and knock on his door. Her lips glossed, she puckered and smiled at her reflection. She wasn't bad looking, and she had a good job to support herself. So why had Derek wanted someone else?

Forget him. Forget Rachel and her daughter and the mistake she'd already made. They were no longer worth her thoughts. That bottle of champagne called to her before she had a chance to leave the room. Not so she could drown her troubles in liquor, because she'd never been a heavy drinker. Lifting the bottle, she dabbed it dry with the cloth napkin that had been left beside it on the table. She'd take it to her neighbor—a peace offering—that's what she'd call it.

Kyle had showered and changed out of his ski clothes. He'd plugged his laptop into the socket and set it up on the table in the dining area. While he waited for it to boot up, he walked to the big screen television and turned it on. He paid extra for satellite service so that when he was here he could keep abreast of what was going on in the sports world. Clicking the channel button, he found a college basketball game and set the remote down. He was just about to return to his computer when the phone rang.

"Hello?"

"You're the biggest jerk I've ever met! Do you have any idea how many men would kill for the opportunity to marry me?" A female voice screeched through the phone.

"Hi, Chantell," Kyle said calmly.

"It's in all the local papers how you dumped me at the altar. Do you know how embarrassing this is?"

Kyle took a deep breath, confused as to how Chantell had managed to find him. In the two years they'd been together, he'd never once brought her here nor had he shared his love of skiing with her. "Chantell, I've apologized already. But I really think I stopped both of us from making a really big mistake."

"A mistake? A mistake? We were together and happy for two years!"

"That didn't mean we should get married. It wasn't right for us. I care about you, but not enough to devote my life to you as your husband. You should be thanking me." He pinched the bridge of his nose, trying desperately not to get upset. Chantell had been so calm at the church; he'd almost felt as if she was relieved that he'd stopped the wedding. Now she was on the other end of the phone yelling hysterically.

"Thanking you?" she screeched. "Oh yeah, I'll thank you for all this negative publicity you've sent my way. I'll be lucky if I ever get another gig again. So thank you, Kyle. Thanks a lot!" Chantell hung up before he could respond.

He replaced the receiver and shook his head. She was a model, nobody cared about her personal life unless it affected her looks. He was about to go back to his computer when there was a knock at the door.

Kyle was still reeling from Chantell's accusations when he pulled the door open. The first thing he noticed was that she was smiling. He'd never seen her smile before.

The first thing Sydney noticed was that he looked good in whatever he wore. He was tall, but she'd already surmised that much. What she hadn't taken note of before was the way his strong jaw led to a deep dimple in his chin. Her stomach did a quick flip-flop before she got it in check and spoke. "Hi. Were you busy?"

Busy? If he was, she was a welcome interruption. "Ah, no. I was just about to start some work but hadn't gotten in to it yet."

"Oh? Then I'll be quick." She thrust the bottle in his direction. "A peace offering and an apology. I'm sorry for being such a jerk earlier and yesterday. I was having a really hard time, but I shouldn't have taken it out on you."

Her eyes were light brown. She was saying something but he barely recognized the words. She looked great in her fitted slacks and shimmering shirt. "Apology?"

He folded his arms and leaned against the doorjamb. His biceps bulged, drawing her attention to the steely mass. If she thought Gorgeous Guy had a great body, her friendly neighbor put his to shame. He'd changed into a beige sweater that melded to his physique and matched his Timberland boots. His eyes were dark brown, which only complimented his outfit more.

She swallowed deeply, thinking he was one scrumptious piece of eye candy. "Yes. Despite what you may have thought about me, I do have some home training. I was wrong and I'm apologizing."

He smiled. An attractive woman showing up at his door with a bottle of champagne didn't happen everyday. He wanted to savor the moment. "Apology accepted—on one condition." He took the bottle from her.

His eyes were alight with amusement, and she couldn't resist asking, "What's that?"

"That you come in and have a drink with me."

She should say no. He was a stranger. She didn't even know his name. "Fine, but I'd also like a restaurant referral, since you've been to most of the places around here." She didn't wait for his response but slipped past him, making her way into his room.

The contact was brief, but Kyle could have sworn sparks fizzled between them during the connection. By the time he closed the door and followed behind her, she was in the living area staring at the TV. "Fifty-nine, forty-nine, Terps up," she said, dropping her purse and jacket onto the chair.

"You know basketball?" he asked, intrigued by her quick assessment of the game.

"I know the Terps are a shoe-in for the final four." She sat down.

He took a seat less than a foot away from her. "I don't know about that, Duke's defense is looking kind of tight."

She shook her head, turning her lips up. "It's second half already. Too little, too late."

"Don't count 'em out just yet."

They both settled on the couch, exchanging sports banter until half an hour later when the game was over.

"I should have bet you. The Terps are going to the Final Four," Sydney chimed cheerfully.

"Yeah, you would have had me." He re-filled her glass and his. They had polished off over half the bottle as they'd watched the game. And he'd enjoyed it. He'd never watched a basketball game with a woman before. It occurred to him that he didn't even know her name. "This has been a nice experience, there's only one way it could be better."

Peeking at him from the side, Sydney swallowed the lukewarm liquid. "What's that?"

"I'd like to know your name. That way when I bet on the winner of the Final Four, I'll know who owes me money."

She laughed. A hearty chuckle that said he'd really tickled her. "It's so weird how we've been sitting here like homies and don't even know each other's names." She licked her lips and sat up straight. "I'm Sydney." And I was supposed to be a married woman at this time today. That thought hit her heavily, and she rubbed her palms nervously over her thighs.

He saw the quick change in her demeanor and feared she was about to bolt. "It's nice to meet you, Sydney. I'm Kyle." He held his hand out.

Reluctantly, she took his hand, shook it and smiled bleakly. "Same here."

"You mentioned you wanted a restaurant referral. You haven't had dinner yet?""

She should go. She could order room service or something. "Ah, no. Not yet."

"Great. Grab your coat and let's go." He was up before she could answer. "Steak or pasta?" he yelled from the closet where he pulled his leather jacket from a hanger.

Sydney tentatively poked her arms through her jacket sleeves, scooped up her purse and followed him to the door. "Steak. I haven't eaten since yesterday morning."

Kyle closed the door behind them, glad she hadn't declined his round about dinner offer. "Are you on some type of diet?" he asked when they were in the elevator.

"No, I've just been a little upset. I can't eat when I'm upset."

He nodded, wondering once again what had upset her and if he could do anything to make it better.

They were on the elevator again, but this time Sydney was hugging the far wall as if her life were in jeopardy. Kyle was almost positive part of the reason she wasn't was because they'd at least become friends in the time they'd watched the game together. The other part was there was another couple in the elevator with them, and they were pushed up against the wall.

At first Kyle had tried to ignore them, but the moans coming from the woman were affecting him, and he'd had no choice but to look their way. The man was about Kyle's height and build, the woman a little shorter than him and very curvy. This was easily noted due to the skintight mini dress she was wearing. Another thing that was apparent was the entrance of he and Sydney on this elevator wouldn't stop their progress.

Beside him Sydney gasped as the man slipped his hand between the woman's legs and the woman lifted one leg, wrapping it securely around the man's waist. It didn't take a rocket scientist to know that the man was now fingering her. The woman moaned, and Sydney turned her head. Kyle tried to stare ahead, but the soft sound of the woman's juices building as the man's fingers slipped in and out of her center made him more than a little hot.

Sydney could hear the sounds to and felt her own nipples tighten. The man had been kissing the woman, his tongue scraping boldly over hers as the woman's mouth opened wider to accommodate him. Sydney had never been kissed like that. A part of her envied the woman. Another part wanted them to take their sexual antics someplace else.

Kyle slipped his hands into his pants pockets, trying to privately stroke his growing length. Beside him was a warm, attractive woman. A woman he would gladly plaster against a wall and slip his finger inside of, but his erection had other ideas. He looked over at Sydney at the exact same time she glanced over at the couple.

Her eyes found his and held. For a moment they spoke silently, asking if the other would like to join in the fun. Kyle took a step closer to her, but Sydney backed away, her gaze falling to the floor.

As soon as the doors opened, Sydney hurried out of the elevator and headed toward the front desk.

"Where are you going?" Kyle asked, grabbing her arm to stop her retreat.

"I'm going to report them. That display was disgusting and rude. They knew we were on the elevator. The least they could have done was stop until they got to their own room."

Kyle did not release her arm, but tried to direct her to the door instead. "There's no use complaining. That type of behavior is allowed here. I'd venture to say it was encouraged."

"What?" Sydney sounded appalled.

"Didn't they tell you about the classes and the whole purpose of the resort when you arrived?"

Sydney remembered Gorgeous Guy inviting her to his class and the other classes they had daily. Closing her eyes she sighed. "Yeah, they told me. I guess I forgot. I can't believe I'm here."

"I wasn't going to pry, but why are you here, in this resort, alone?"

Sydney did not want to tell him what had to be the most embarrassing story of her life. "Let's just say it was booked as a couple but things changed," she said absently.

Kyle nodded, taking the hint that she didn't want to discuss this further. "Let me just clear up the fact that while I do own my condo here, the resort has recently changed owners. I had no idea what changes the new owners were going to make. I was just here last year and things were normal." He looked around the lobby at the five or six couples he saw going here and there. "But I presume it's profitable."

Sydney looked around and shrugged. "I guess everything eventually boils down to sex and money."

He frowned at the sad look in her eyes when she spoke, then pulled her along to the door. "I can drive my car and follow you to the restaurant," she offered.

Kyle grabbed her gloved hand. "That would be silly and a waste of gas. The place is only a couple of blocks down. It's a nice night, we can walk."

Sydney acknowledged his logic and let him lead her out of the parking lot.

The first two blocks they walked in companionable silence. Sydney wondered what exactly they were doing, while Kyle held her hand possessively. They were simply neighbors, she told herself. There was no reason they couldn't share a meal together. Besides, after tonight she'd go to her room, and he would go to his. She probably wouldn't even see him for the remainder of her trip.

"So how long are you going to be here?"

His question startled her since she'd just been thinking along those lines. "Saturday to Saturday," she told him.

"I'm leaving next weekend, too." Kyle tried to mask his pleasure that she'd be there all week. Walking through the brisk night air with Sydney seemed strangely comfortable. It was also strangely arousing. Coupled with the little show they'd witnessed in the elevator and his visions of her this morning, this romantic walk was playing to the tune of getting her into his bed tonight. Pushing those sexual thoughts aside, because he wasn't entirely sure he wanted that type of involvement with another woman this soon, Kyle tried to figure out this effect she seemed to have on him. He knew he probably shouldn't be thinking of another woman in the dating sense so soon after his failed nuptials, but something about Sydney got to him. When she was near, something settled inside him—warmly, smoothly, like fine wine. He figured he had a week to figure out exactly what that something was.

The Skiers Chalet Steak House was crowded when they arrived, but a gracious host approached them as soon as they entered and asked their seating preference.

"We'll take a booth downstairs," Kyle told the man dressed in all black.

They followed him through the upper level to the steps that led to the downstairs dining room. Red naugahide booths and chairs, roaring fireplaces and black and white vintage photos on the wall created a homey and authentic atmosphere.

Sydney unzipped her jacket, removing it before slipping into one side of the booth. Kyle did the same, sliding along the seat until his thigh brushed against hers.

Sydney tried to ignore the warmth spreading through her from the contact, but wasn't very successful. "So what's good on the menu?" she asked.

They were here to eat and that's all. The sooner they got this over with, the sooner she'd be back in her room alone.

"Steak." He passed her a menu and smiled.

"Really?" she suppressed a grin. "I would have never guessed."

"Good, you're still relaxed." He'd been afraid her quietness during their walk meant she was slipping back into that irritated mood she'd been in when he'd first bumped into her.

"What's that supposed to mean?" she questioned. Was he thinking of this as a date? She should explain to him right now that this was definitely not a date.

Uh-oh, he should have kept that thought to himself. "Nothing. I usually get the T-Bone, it's excellent, and a huge baked potato with lots of butter and a beer. How does that sound?"

Her stomach growled. "Like a heart attack on a plate." She looked at her menu another moment. "But I'll have the same, with green beans."

Kyle laughed. "You are hungry, aren't you?" He folded his menu and pushed it to the side. He was hungry, too, but looking at her he realized his hunger wasn't solely for food.

Chapter 3

Stuffed from their meal, they walked back to the resort at a much slower pace than before. Throughout dinner Kyle purposely kept the conversation light. Sydney had seemed to appreciate that. He'd been with her for almost three hours now and the connection he'd sensed earlier had only increased. It was a physical attraction, which initially he'd thought was weird—not weird in the sense that there was something wrong with her or anything—just weird because twenty-four hours ago he walked away from a gorgeous woman, a fairy tale wedding and a promising future. And now he could swear that what he was feeling toward Sydney was a growing romantic interest.

It was along those lines he was thinking when he asked, "So how come you're here alone?"

Sydney wasn't shocked at his question. She'd known he wasn't pleased with her half answer earlier and admitted to wondering the same thing about him. Still, she wasn't sure how to answer him. Humiliation was a bitter pill, even for a strong woman like herself, to swallow. She was not in the mood to air her dirty laundry, or Derek's for that matter, to this man. But she couldn't ignore him. He had bought her a wonderful dinner. "I was supposed to get married yesterday," she began as they crossed the street.

"Oh, really?" he asked.

"Mmmhmm. It was billed 'The Sport's World Wedding of the Century'."

The tagline rang a bell in Kyle's head. "Sport's World? Who were you marrying?"

She sighed. "I've been dating Derek Winters for five years, and yesterday we were supposed to be married."

"Derek Winters, the wide receiver?" Kyle asked incredulously. He'd just written an article about Winters and his successful career. What were the odds he'd be walking down the streets of Aspen with his fiancée? Or ex-fiancée, as it was.

"That's the one," she frowned. It figures she'd meet up with a fan of Derek's.

"So what happened? You get cold feet?"

"No, Derek got pregnant," she said dryly.

"Excuse me?"

Taking a deep breath, she gave him a wry look and launched into a synopsis of yesterday's events. Kyle was so shocked at her words he'd stopped walking to take it all in. "You have got to be joking. That type of stuff only happens on soap operas."

"Hmph! Then show me where to sign, because this is sure to boost ratings." She chuckled.

At the sound Kyle looked at her carefully. "Are you okay?" She looked fine. Except for the tip of her nose, that had reddened beneath the cool night breeze. But he was asking about the inside. He wanted to know how she was feeling emotionally.

"You know, it's weird, but I'm okay. I guess I should be upset and hurt." She shrugged and stuffed her hands into her pockets. "But I'm actually relieved. Does that make any sense?" This was the first time she'd admitted to being relieved to have not married Derek, and it felt a little strange but liberating.

Not at all, he thought. "It depends. Are you relieved you didn't have to go through with the wedding? Or are you relieved you found out about Derek's indiscretion?" He knew he should be asking himself that question in some round about way.

She shivered. "I'll be more relieved when I'm in front of a crackling fireplace." She'd told him enough. She did not want to explore her feelings, or lack thereof, for Derek with this man. No matter how his smile tugged at her insides, begging her to trust him.

He took a step toward her, wrapping his arms around her and the thick coat she wore. "Here let me share some body heat before we continue."

The way her temperature soared at his touch, Sydney would have bet he'd given her every ounce of heat he possessed. His masculine scent filled her nose as she turned her head sideways against his chest. Derek's hugs had never felt like this.

"There. That should hold you until we get inside." He kept one arm around her and began walking to the resort. He could have given her his coat. He was suddenly very warm himself.

Sydney was glad when they walked through the front doors of the resort, at least until she looked toward the lobby and realized they'd interrupted…something…

Kyle kept his arm around her, sharing sight she saw. The lobby consisted of a huge fireplace in the center of the floor with a bench winding around it. There were four deep cushioned couches placed in a square. The fire was blazing, and the lights were dim. But that wasn't what caught their attention. Pillows had been thrown on the floor and women, naked women, were laying on them. Above the women, between their legs to be exact, their partners knelt. Three of which were males and one female.

Sitting on the bench near the fireplace was the male concierge from last night. He didn't wear his vest this evening, only skintight gold pants that left nothing to the imagination. The man was speaking in a low voice, seemingly giving instructions to the couples.

"Making her wet is not as easy as it sounds," he said. "First you need to familiarize yourself with her private parts. Women spread your legs, partners take a close look. See her clit and its tiny hood. Move down to her plump nether lips and watch them part to reveal her deep heated center."

The smell of sex wafted through the air, and Sydney inhaled repeatedly, getting high on the level of excitement in the room. Her nipples had tightened again, her own personal parts swelling and throbbing. Kyle's arm around her shoulders suddenly felt even warmer.

Kyle cleared his throat. “I think this is the evening class,” he said in a hoarse voice.

Sydney nodded, unable to take her eyes from the couples. “I think so.”

Kyle’s fingers moved on her shoulder, his entire body responding to the scene before him and the woman beside him. He’d admitted to himself at the restaurant he would have her beneath him or on top of him or whatever way she’d prefer. Seeing these other couples about to enjoy themselves gave him ideas. “Would you like to join them?”

Sydney’s eyes flew to his. “What? In this class?” She was no exhibitionist. As aroused as she was feeling at the moment, the idea of shedding her clothes and laying spread eagle on the floor amongst them was tempting but not likely in her mind.

He turned to face her, effectively blocking her view of the other couples. “Okay. We don’t have to join the class, but we could take the lesson upstairs.”

One arm remained wrapped around her while his other hand brushed lightly over her cheek. She was more than hot all over and more than conflicted over what her answer should be.

“Don’t think about it anymore,” he said knowingly. “You came here to get away from all that was wrong in your life, and so did I. Let’s just enjoy the week. Let’s enjoy it together.”

He ducked his head and brushed his lips across hers. Syndey sighed into his mouth, then kissed him in return. She had no idea what she was agreeing to or even why she was agreeing to it. All she knew with certainty was she was tired of doing what was expected or what seemed like the right thing to do. For once she wanted to be impulsive, to just go with the flow without thinking. “Your room or mine?” she whispered against his mouth.

They were enclosed in the elevator again, this time Kyle pushing her up against the wall similar to the way the man had done the woman earlier. Sydney wore pants, so wrapping her leg around his waist wasn’t going to help re-enact the scene. Instead, Kyle unbuttoned her jacket and the first few buttons on her blouse. He’d glimpsed these magnificent globes last night and thought of tasting them this morning. He wouldn't wait a moment longer. Slipping the thin material of her bra to the side, he released the heavy mounds until they dropped into his palms. He groaned, then bent his head and captured one long, thick nipple into his mouth.

"Mmm, I love thick nipples. How did you know I loved thick nipples?"

Sydney let her head fall back against the wall. "I didn't. But I'm glad you do."

He stroked one with his tongue and then the other, growing ever more aroused by the turgid feel of them against his tongue. His palms squeezed her breasts until he almost expected milk to shoot from them. In which case he would gladly suckle like a baby.

The ding signaling they had arrived on their floor was the only thing that could tear Kyle away from her lovely breasts. He pulled her blouse closed, then scooped her up into his arms and headed for his apartment.

Sydney's mind whirled. Her body tingled from his touch, from his tongue. Flashes of those women so open and so exposed to the men, and woman, in their lives arousing her. Still, realistic thoughts battled for a chance to be heard.

She didn't know Kyle. She didn't even know his last name or where he was from. He was a virtual stranger. A stranger that loved thick nipples.

He lit his fireplace and tossed some pillows on the floor so it resembled the downstairs lobby. She stared down at the makeshift bed he'd made, wondering if she'd really be able to go through with this.

Kyle stood in front of her with an idea of what was possibly going through her mind and the mindset to push that aside. They'd only known each other for a day, and yet there was a bond, a connection that neither of them could deny. It most likely was not love at first sight but after what she'd told him tonight, he knew it was more than fate that had brought them together. They were both running and had managed to run right into each other's arms.

He took a step closer, cupped her face in his hands and kissed her softly. Deepening the kiss, Kyle mixed his confusion and longing with hers and let the sensations roam. They were in a sex palace, a resort that specialized in the erotic feelings of man and woman. But if they weren't he knew he'd still want her with the ferociousness he did now.

When he released her he saw her desire and the depths of passion in her hazel eyes. He knew without a doubt what he wanted and prayed she would continue to want the same thing. Taking a step back, he removed his shirt, keeping his eyes on her as he did.

Sydney's mouth went dry as she watched him. Beyond his physique she saw something else, something she wasn't sure she could hold on to. Here was this gorgeous man, and she did mean gorgeous. From his close cropped black hair, to his strong jaw and warm eyes to the now exposed chest that could have easily belonged to a male model, he was giving himself to her.

She did not want another man in her life. That's what she'd told herself, yet she wasn't sure she could resist him or that she even wanted to. The firelight cast him in a golden glow as his hands moved to his pants buckle. Her heart hammered in her chest, spiky pulses of heat soared through her body, pooling between her legs. She licked her lips and his eyes darkened. She'd removed her coat, yet she felt hot enough to burn something. She should leave this room. She should return to her own suite and think about her life and what her next step would be. She couldn't run from her problems and didn't know why she'd even tried.

"Make no mistake about the fact that I want you, Sydney. What happens in this room tonight will always be very special to me. I need you to know that."

Lifting her chin, Sydney cleared her throat and said, "I want you, too."

"Tell me how you want me," he told her with one hand on his hip, the other resting over his burgeoning arousal.

Never in her life had she been this aroused, this eager to be claimed by a man. Shaky fingers went to the remaining buttons on her blouse as she removed it. "I want you to kiss me, long and deep."

Kyle's chest tightened as he watched with unrestrained interest. Her breasts were gorgeous, he noted as she removed her bra. They were heavy, with the natural hang that confirmed they were all hers. Her mocha skin glowed in the firelight, the dark areolas puckered. The nipples he'd not so long ago sucked extended in invitation. He swallowed, hard. "Tell me more."

Sydney had never been good at sex talk. Truth be told, she'd never talked much during her sex life with Derek. Derek was a commanding lover, always calling the shots, always getting what he wanted and moving on. Never had she had the chance to tell him what she wanted him to do to her.

Noticing how Kyle's eyes rested on her breasts she had an idea. Bending down so that the heavy globes hung in front of her, she made a big production of removing her boots. She heard his intake of breath and felt empowered. Rising again, she was rewarded by the look of sheer torture on his face. With her hands on the button of her pants, she told him what she'd like done next. "I want you to kiss and fondle my breasts until I scream for mercy."

His hand tightened on his groin. The pain building there was exquisite, the thought of immediate release life saving. He watched her push her pants and panties past her hips, stepping completely out of them. He did the same, frowning when it became apparent that she'd had the foresight to remove her boots, while he had not. Leaning forward, hating to miss one moment of her bold display, he removed his boots and his pants hurriedly.

They were both completely naked. Two people illuminated by the golden flames in the fireplace, warmed by the sweet sense of desire between them. He moved closer, reached out and softly touched her right breast. She sucked in a breath, and his erection jutted forward, begging for attention.

"I need you to touch me, Sydney," he said in a strangled voice. "Now."

And so she did. With fingers that were no longer shaking she grasped his arousal, wrapping them around his hot length. If she had to guess, she'd put him at seven to eight inches. Nine was the standard for premium enjoyment according to Sadie, but Sydney had a feeling that Kyle knew just what to do with the equipment he possessed. He was thick, so much so that her fingers barely met as she stroked him. "Like this?" she whispered and was rewarded by his throaty groan.

"Yeah. Keep it up."

Her palm brushed the bulbous head, and she felt beads of moisture against her skin. Licking her lips, she stroked him again, harder.

Kyle squeezed her breasts so hard that tingles of pain mixed with the swamp of pleasure coursing through her body. He pinched her nipple, pulling it tightly away from her chest, then releasing it to watch her breast jiggle.

"I think the name of that class was Make Me Wet," she breathed heavily. "You could probably be the instructor."

He chuckled. "Are you wet for me, Sydney?"

Her head lolled forward and rested on his shoulder. Her mind drifting somewhere between sweet torture and explosive ecstasy. She felt like doing things she'd only seen on television or read about in books. Possibly, because after this week she knew she'd never see him again. Whatever the reason, she went back to her earlier vow to not think, but to just act. "Oh yes. Why don't you see for yourself?"

Kyle didn't need additional instruction. His hand moved from her breast down her torso, over her soft belly to cup her neatly shaved juncture. His fingers slipped inside her tight folds and cream coated him instantly. "Damn! You are wet."

Feeling bold and encouraged, Sydney backed out of his grasp and lay down on the pillows he'd prepared. Lifting her feet to rest on the floor, she let her knees fall. "I said see for yourself." Her hands moved between her legs, opening her moistened folds for his viewing pleasure.

Chapter 4

If he died right now, Kyle he'd go a very happy man. Nothing in his life had ever been this beautiful, this alluring before.

Falling to his knees, he watched as she stroked her center, evoking more glistening essence from her opening. Before his mind went completely blank to her charms, he reached for his pants and retrieved his wallet from the back pocket. Pulling out a strand of three condoms, he dropped them on the pillows beside him. Then he grabbed his arousal, stroking its length as he had this morning when he'd thought of her.

"I want to taste you," he groaned as he watched her hips rotate with the ministrations of her finger. "But I want to sink inside of you, too. I can't decide what to do first."

"Let me help you." Sydney sat up, picking up the condoms and tearing one pack open. With a skill she hadn't known she possessed, she smoothed the latex over his rigid sex, then slipped a finger between her legs again, delving deep into her core and rubbing thoroughly. , Surprised by how good she could actually make herself feel, she moaned with the action.

His hand went to her shoulder and squeezed. "Sydney," he groaned.

She pulled her hand from her core with a suckling sound and lifted it to his mouth. "Taste me," she instructed him.

Kyle opened his mouth, taking her finger deep. He licked her finger until it was clear of all her sweet nectar, then sighed. "Damn," was all he could muster before pushing her back on the pillows. "Tell me how you want it, baby. Fast and hot or slow and sweet?"

Sydney cupped her breasts as he lifted her legs, planting her ankles securely on his shoulders. "All of the above," she moaned anxious to feel all seven, eight or how ever many inches he had for her.

Shaking with anticipation, Kyle positioned his tip at her entrance. "Your wish is my command."

Her hole was tight so he took his time sinking inside. Inch by excruciating inch, he let her tight heat clutch him. He groaned and she hissed, their mutual pleasure engulfing the room. When he was buried to the hilt he stilled, his arms shaking as he leaned forward, planting his hands on the pillows on either side of her face.

For a minute, Sydney lay still adjusting herself to the feel of him implanted inside her. She'd known he was thick, and the stretching of her center to accommodate his girth proved her point. Beyond that initial stinging was deep-seated pleasure that spread like a virus through her already aroused body. She undulated her hips and felt that pleasure increase. She did it again and again and looked up to see Kyle's face contorting with her motions. "You like this, baby?" she asked wanting to make sure she was pleasing him.

Kyle could have screamed. Was she serious? What man in their right mind wouldn't like what she was doing? "Yes, baby. Keep moving."

She did as she was told, and Kyle matched her movements, taking them both deeper and deeper into this primal abyss. He deep stroked her until he felt she was made especially for him. He fit her perfectly. She took him willingly. He cringed with excitement.

His adrenaline flowing, Kyle changed from the slow and sweet. Staying completely embedded in her, he scooped her up from the pillows and shifted until she was straddling his lap. She gasped at the deeper penetration, and he kissed her long and lovingly. Yes, lovingly, because at some point from the time she'd almost swooned in his arms last night until she'd brought him champagne and watched the basketball game with him, he'd felt something well beyond a friendly attraction to this woman.

Sydney submerged herself in that kiss. The almost painful comfort of his thick shaft thrusting into her womb and the intense heat of his tongue fiercely dueling with hers made her head swim. She'd never considered herself sexual, had in fact, entertained the thought that her lack of sexual allure had contributed to Derek's infidelities. Yet, here, in this resort, with this man she was uninhibited. Touching herself, moaning on command and now riding his length, she couldn't believe how far she'd come. Or how good he made her feel.

And it wasn't just the physical. At dinner he'd talked and she been intrigued by his voice as well as what he was saying. She'd talked and he'd listened, attentively. He treated her like a lost treasure, catering to her every need. She was entranced by his chivalry and his compassion. Even now he touched her gently, cupping her buttocks, lifting her slightly off his lap, then settling her back down with a satisfied groan.

She bounced on his lap, her breasts rubbing against him. The kiss deepened and grew more erratic, more desperate. He licked her chin, her jaw, nipped her ear and came back to her mouth to devour again. Sydney was so wet she felt her juices dripping around his shaft. The sounds they made were erotic and exciting, encouraging her to move faster, to take him deeper.

Kyle moaned and grasped her hips tightly as she rode him, his teeth clenching with the extreme pleasure. When he couldn't take it anymore and knew his release was imminent, he slipped a finger between them and stroked her hardened clit.

Sydney's whimpering turned into low screams, and her nails sank into the skin of his shoulders. The movement of his fingers increased, and she felt her entire body go taut with expectation. He tongued her and thrust his shaft deeply inside of her while flattening his thumb over her tightened bud. She screamed as her body shivered and crashed, the sound caught successfully in his mouth.

She went limp in his arms and was breathing heavily when Kyle stood, holding her so that their connection was not severed. In a few swift steps he had her just where he'd envisioned her. Back against the wall, legs wrapped around his waist, breasts level with his lips. He pounded into her once, she screamed and his penis hardened to the point that he was sure his skin would break from the sheer force.

Pumping fiercely, he worked his own release until it spewed hotly inside the condom. Her head lolled back against the wall, then forward to his shoulder. He nipped her shoulder, then kissed the dampened skin until he'd completely emptied himself.

By the time Kyle had moved them back to the pillows, the fire had died down. Syndey shivered, and he cradled her in his arms.

"Kyle," she began, but he kissed her into silence.

"Shhh," he said. "I'll fix some cocoa and run you a warm bath." He dropped an innocent peck on her forehead and got up.

When she was alone, Sydney wrapped her arms around herself and hugged tightly, trying to keep this wonderful feeling for as long as possible. She'd never been this completely satisfied with Derek. She halted that thought. She wasn't with Derek. And wouldn't ever be again. She should stop reverting back to all the things he didn't do in their relationship.

She was living for the moment now. And the moment consisted of one very tall, very handsome man who had worked her so good her thighs were still quivering.

"Here, drink this," he said when he returned.

She sat up next to him and snuggled close. Holding the warm mug in both hands, she tentatively brought it to her lips and sipped. "Mmm. This is great. Is it homemade?"

"No. I got it from a friend of mine who really knows chocolate." Kyle watched as she took another sip. If she loved the cocoa, her bath was going to put her right over the top—where he would be anxiously awaiting for round two. He was sure he'd never been as effected by a woman as he was by Sydney. Something about her signaled forever.

She sighed. "You can tell your friend for me he's got himself one hell of a recipe here." She rested her head against his shoulder and closed her eyes. "The whole room smells like chocolate now. I love chocolate."

Absently, Kyle ran his fingers through her hair as he smiled to himself. "Oh really? What is it about chocolate that makes you love it so?"

Sydney thought for a moment. She was well aware of the theories of chocolate as an aphrodisiac and believed some to be true, but she wasn't about to tell Kyle that. Besides, she liked to think her love of chocolate went beyond the general adrenaline rush that was akin to a powerful orgasm—of which she had just sustained without the help of an aphrodisiac. "I love the smooth texture as it melts on my tongue. The sweet intoxicating smell when I first take it out of the wrapper or box. It's like a comfort food for me, except I eat it all the time. It's a wonder I don't weigh three hundred pounds by now." She giggled, very aware of the fact that they were sitting here totally naked.

With his free hand and his hot gaze, Kyle stroked her arm to her breast, cupping the small pouch of her stomach before moving on to her thigh. "You're body is perfect."

She remained quiet, and Kyle figured nobody had ever told her that before. This woman had a lot of past hurt, and he was determined to clear it all from her mind. "So what's your favorite type of chocolate?"

"Dark chocolate," she said without hesitation. "It's not too sweet and has a smooth taste that lingers in your mouth long after you swallow." Because her mouth was dry and she clearly remembered Kyle's tongue in her mouth and its lingering effect, she took another sip of her cocoa.

"Chocolate is a very passionate food." His fingers made small circles against the skin below her ear. "The release of Phenylethylamine into the brain evokes a rapid mood change." His fingers persisted as he inhaled the scent of chocolate permeating the air. "As the substance travels through your system, your heart rate increases…"

Sydney held her mug with shaky hands. "Much the same as when you're about to climax," she finished.

Silence fell over the room.

"Yes, much the same as when you climax. Did you enjoy your climax, Sydney?"

There was no hesitation, no discomfort and no dishonesty. "Yes. I did. Did you enjoy yours?"

"I most definitely did," he whispered in her ear.

Sydney sighed when his tongue stroked her lobe. She inhaled and was about to turn to him for a kiss, but then she sniffed. "This sure is some powerful coca. I've almost finished and the smell is still so fresh."

Her words jogged his memory and he tore his thoughts from sinking slowly into her again, to the matter at hand.

"You're bath is probably ready. I'll go and shut off the water."

She watched him walk away again and instantly felt the sting of separation. Standing on wobbly legs, she set the mug on the coffee table and began to fan herself. "Lord, that man is doing something to me."

"Second door on your left," he told her.

"Aren't you joining me?" she asked, still not ready for their connection to end.

As much as Kyle wanted to, he recognized what they'd just shared had caused some confusion in both their lives. He wanted to give her space, and he wanted to take a moment to get his thoughts together as well. He had two bathrooms, so he'd shower while she enjoyed her bath. "Not this time, baby. I want you to enjoy this for yourself."

She didn't dispute his words because he seemed so sincere. He led her to the bathroom and kissed her once more before closing the door, leaving her alone. The gray marble floor was cool to her skin as she reached for the buttons of her shirt. Her eyes surveyed the room, taking in the gray, black and burgundy décor. It was very manly, yet very chic. She spotted Kyle's razor and cologne on the double sink to her left. Lifting the glass bottle of cologne, she inhaled. Yes, that was exactly how he smelled. Sexy, manly, intoxicating.

While she was inhaling the cologne, she noticed the scent of chocolate still in the air. "Good grief, how much chocolate did he put in that cocoa?"

Finally, she turned her attention to the tub and the allure of hot water. It was brimming with bubbles and she almost squealed. She loved bubble baths almost as much as she loved chocolate.

Chocolate. The smell increased. She stepped into the almost too-hot-for-human water and slowly lowered herself in. Her heart pounded, her senses going haywire. She smacked her lips, wondering if the after-taste of the cocoa was still in her mouth. No, it was fading. Yet, she still felt overwhelmed with chocolate and those damned Phenylethylamines. She sank into the tub until the bubbles touched her earlobes, and it hit her.

These weren't regular bubbles. Moving her hands quickly from side to side she peered down into the tub and noticed the milky white water. A smile lit her face. He'd run her a cocoa bath. She sank back, resting her head against the back of the tub and closed her eyes. Her skin tingled from the warmth of the water as her nostrils flared and her middle region throbbed from the chocolate aphrodisiac.

Using the guest bathroom, Kyle took a cool shower. Hot water would have been more appropriate, but since his goal was to think clearly he needed the shock effect. He'd known he would sleep with her. As arrogant as it sounded, he'd selected her, and he'd gotten exactly what he wanted.

Only he hadn't realized it would happen so soon or it would be so intense. She'd been so close to him. His hands had felt the softness of her skin. He'd wanted her so badly, surely he would burst from overexcitement. It wasn't humanly possible for a man to grow so hard so quick. Yet buried deep inside her, his arousal had grown to new and higher heights.

Now that he'd had her, he should be sated. Sex with Sydney should have relieved his tension and made him feel rejuvenated and ready to face the world. Instead, he felt drained and incomplete.

Not because sex with her had been lacking in any way, shape or form, but because he still wanted her so desperately, so completely.

That posed an undeniable question, one he was hoping the chill of the water would summon an appeasable answer to.

What exactly did he want from Sydney? They lived in different states. Had lives of their own, problems of their own. One in particular—they'd both just barely escaped marriage. Was it probable for him to be considering anything more than sex with this woman so soon after declaring he couldn't marry Chantell?

But Sydney wasn't Chantell.

No, he'd certainly never wanted Chantell the way he wanted Sydney. Even that supermodel face and body hadn't appealed to him as much as the small cherub like facial features of Sydney or the bodacious body that continuously had his blood boiling.

With that in mind the question became more prominent, more insistent: what did he want from Sydney?

Sydney's hands moved slowly over her stomach as she imagined Kyle sharing the bath with her. Her usually low-key sexual demeanor had changed seemingly overnight. Now she craved the touch of a man, the feel of thick hands over her skin. Nobody had toyed with her breasts until she was in danger of climaxing from that act alone. Not until Kyle.

Her hands traveled north, cupping each heavy mound, gripping them strongly the same as Kylc had donc. It wasn't thc samc, but desire shot through her body instantly. Her nipples puckered, and she tried to lift her breasts as she extended her tongue, in an effort to suckle them for herself.

Sadly, it didn't work. She released her breasts and lay her head back against the tile. She'd never masturbated before, never touched herself in a sexual way. But in this hot chocolate scented water, her fingers became acquainted with her most personal parts. She'd stroked her nether lips, felt the stretched entrance where his large penis had penetrated, brushed over the nub that had brought her so much pleasure when he'd stroked it.

Now her body hummed with sexual energy. She felt anxious and on edge, like she needed another fix, now.

"Mmm," she moaned. Her legs fell apart, the heels of her feet touching beneath the water. She imagined herself his sex slave. He commanded she spread herself before him and she obliged. He looked at her bared sex, his face rigid with desire.

"Touch yourself," he ordered.

Again, her fingers slipped beneath the water, feeling her silken folds.

"Pump yourself the same way I did," his hoarse voice instructed.

She inserted four fingers, in an effort to match the thickness of his penis thrusting wildly against her now undulating hips.

"Touch your breasts. Touch my breasts."

With her free hand she gripped her right breast, squeezing it until her nipples stung with the pressure.

Water sloshed over the rim of the tub, hitting the floor with a sound that echoed throughout the bathroom. Sydney snapped out of her trance. Kyle was surely wondering why she'd taken so long.

After bathing, she stood in front of the mirror and toweled herself dry. Reality struck and her thoughts reverted to what had happened between her and Kyle and what had led to her coming to this resort in the first place. There were a lot of serious issues she needed to consider, a lot of soul searching she needed to do. But that wasn't going to happen tonight.

Tonight, she had other plans.

Stepping out of the bathroom, Sydney tightened the belt on the heavy white terrycloth robe that had hung on the back of the bathroom door. Heat engulfed her as she entered the living room, and she noticed Kyle had re-started the fire. He sat on the floor amongst the pillows, a matching terry cloth robe loosely tied at his waist. Through the opening she glanced his honey glazed abs and swallowed. Hard.

"Thanks for the bath," she said, coming to a stop next to him.

Kyle smiled and held out a hand to her. "Please join me."

When she was seated beside him, she crossed her legs Indian-style, giving him an unfettered view, if he so wished to take a peek. "Let me guess, you're friend who knows so much about chocolate helped you out again."

Kyle chuckled, glad she had apparently enjoyed the bath. "Yeah, he's an exec at Hershey."

"That was a very nice treat." She smiled, very interested in more treats offered by Kyle.

He lifted her hand and held it gently in his. "We'll have to see what you do to deserve more treats."

"What I do?" she said, amused.

"Yes. I'm feeling a little stressed. I think a massage would be good. Depending on how well you perform, I might let you have another chocolate treat."

His smile was devilish, his hold on her hand tighter, his eyes intent as they openly gazed over her body. She was beyond aroused and intended to massage him until he was in the same blissful state. "That sounds like a nice deal."

She smiled. He liked her smile. Hell, he'd come to realize he liked just about everything about her, including the bits of indecision he saw in her eyes. That meant this type of involvement was new to her, too. She had questions about what was happening between them, just as he did. But she was determined not to address them at the moment. He decided to do the same.

Removing her hand from his, she made like she was tightening her belt again and got to her knees. "Okay, lie down so I can begin." She threaded her fingers together and stretched her arms in front of her as she cracked her knuckles.

Kyle gave her a bemused look as he shrugged out of his robe, being careful to keep it wrapped around his waist and lay on his stomach. "Oh my, please don't hurt me." He pretended to whimper.

Sydney laughed. "Just lie still and relax." When he was still she straddled him, his tight buttocks firmly tucked beneath her throbbing sex. Damn, it is hot as hell up in here! she mused.

Taking a deep breath, she let her hands fall softly onto his shoulders. Taut skin over hardened muscles had her heart dancing to a new rhythm. She dug into his skin timidly at first, then with the sound of a low murmur from him, she increased the pressure and moved closer to his neck. Her thumbs gently massaged the back of his neck as she noted how tense his muscles were there. "You really need to relax," she told him.

"I know. This last year there's been so much going on. I simply haven't had any time for myself."

"I know what you mean."

He didn't ask about that remark, knowing that it involved Derek. A part of him wondered if he should tell her about Chantell. But then her hands moved further down his back along the line of his spine where she dropped hot, open mouthed kisses. Thoughts of any other woman quickly fled.

Reaching around him, Sydney undid the belt of his robe and pulled it completely off. His taut buttocks were exposed, and she began to massage. "I've been thinking about those classes they offer here," she talked slowly as her hands moved down to his thighs.

"Hmm," he groaned. "You have?"

Her fingers moved to his inner thighs, kneading the thick muscles, then moving to the back of his knees and his calves. "Yes. How about you? You aren't tempted to attend one session to see what you could learn?"

She moved off him, then pushed him until he turned over. His erection caught her gaze first, its length jutting forward, resting against his stomach.

Kyle enjoyed the way her eyes drank him in. His blood heated as he wondered what she'd do next. Folding his hands behind his head, he answered, "I'm not sure what they could teach me, but I'm willing to try any class you want."

Sydney arched a brow at his arrogance. "So you believe you know everything about pleasuring a woman?" She massaged the front of his thighs, then skirted around his arousal to run her fingers along his six pack.

"I believe I have enough knowledge in my repertoire and enough satisfied customers that I don't need further instruction."

Her hands hovered over his nipples. With her mouth open, she lowered her head. Then just before touching him, she said, "I'm sure there're some things even you haven't tried."

Her tongue flattened over his nipple, and he grunted. "You are probably right. But like I said, my current knowledge has proved more than successful."

"Well, mine hasn't. I'm thinking I might like to study the art of kissing. But right now I'd much rather sample all the ways you could make me wet."

Kyle reached up a hand and cupped her mound, slipping a finger inside her moist heat. "I can oblige."

Sydney rode his finger, gasping as he deepened his thrust. "So you don't want to go to the classes?"

With his free hand, Kyle grabbed hers and moved it to his throbbing erection. When her fingers clamped around him he sighed, saying, "No. I'd rather keep you here, all to myself."

She sighed and reached out with her free hand to grab a condom from the pillow beside them. Sheathing him, she raised her hips until his fingers slipped out of her, then she settled down over his length. "That can definitely be arranged."

Chapter 5

As weird as it sounded and after all that they'd shared, Sydney did not spend the entire night with Kyle. Around three a.m. she insisted on returning to her room. Reluctantly, Kyle had donned his robe and walked her to her door, leaving her with a kiss so heated she was loathe to change her mind and jump back into bed with him. But she needed to separate herself from this powerful attraction for a few hours at least.

She'd been in a blissful sleep when the blare of the telephone roused her. Squinting at the clock, she groaned as she rolled over and picked it up.

"So how are you?" Sadie asked.

Sydney sat upright in the bed, the phone clutched between her ear and her shoulder. "I'm good, I guess." She glanced toward the window. "It's snowing up here. The mountains are so pretty when it snows."

"Derek's been calling all over town trying to find you."

Sydney sighed. "He found me. I got a message from him yesterday."

"What did he say?"

"I don't know. As soon as I heard his voice, I hung up. I really don't want to hear anything he has to say. It's not like he can really deny it." Sydney hadn't been ready to start thinking about Derek and her home situation, but she knew she couldn't completely hide from it.

"That's what I told him at the church. He just looked at me funny and said it wasn't that big a deal because he loved you and not that other chick."

Sydney rolled her eyes heavenward. "Yeah, he picked a brilliant way to show me how much he loved me, sharing his sperm with someone else."

"That was so foul. You know he thinks you're going to take him back," Sadie announced.

"Please. He's already proven his thinking skills are impaired."

There was a knock at the door, and Sydney paused. It was only nine forty-five. It couldn't possibly be house keeping. The knock came again.

"Syd, did you hear me?" Sadie yelled through the phone.

Throwing the covers from her legs, Sydney got out of bed. "No, Sadie. There's someone at the door. I'll call you later."

"Who's at the door? You don't know anybody in Colorado?"

"I'll call you back," Sydney whispered before hanging up the phone. She slipped her feet into her slippers and made her way to the door. It probably was housekeeping dropping off fresh towels or something. That's what her mind had decided. So when she pulled the door open, shock was the least of what she felt. Standing in the doorway bundled up like he was ready for a blizzard, was Kyle.

"Hey, sleepy head. Go get dressed so we can hit the slopes." He ignored the exposed midriff and pushed past her into the room.

Closing the door, Sydney shook her head. "It's barely ten o'clock, and you're up and ready to go out. Plus it's snowing out there." She motioned toward the window.

He pulled off his hat and gloves, unzipped his jacket and took a seat on the couch. "Snow usually helps with the skiing." He grinned.

"Very funny," she chimed as she walked into the living area where Kyle sat, hands on her hips.

She wasn't wearing a bra. The tips of her high breasts made a tent in the short top to her pajamas. The pants covered her from just beneath her belly button down, but the silky red material molded seductively to her rounded hips and plump behind. He sucked in a quick breath. The one thing Chantell lacked was curves. But Sydney had enough for the both of them.

"Normally, I like to be able to see where I'm skiing," she said.

He looked at her with a dazed expression. Her nipples started to tingle, and she realized her state of dress. She probably shouldn't feel self-conscious in front of him after all they'd done last night, but she found it very hard to argue convincingly while she was half dressed.

"I'll go get dressed," she said awkwardly, then turned toward the bedroom. She'd taken a few steps before turning back to him. "The least you can do is make some coffee, since you barged in here at the crack of dawn."

He finally managed to drag his gaze from the pleasant curve and boldly stood without caring whether she saw the evidence of his arousal. "Coffee will be ready when you return. Dress warmly, its cold out."

Sydney wanted to roll her eyes or give another smart retort, but he'd been staring at her as if he'd like to have a sip of her instead of a cup of coffee. Her body warmed instantly, Kyle's apparent approving assessment turning her on. "I would have never guessed," she said with a lot less bite than was intended before disappearing into the bedroom.

Man, he had it bad, Kyle thought. He'd lain in his bed alone for as long as he could this morning. Which actually hadn't been very long at all. He'd felt lonely without her. After having her in his arms for so long last night, he'd wanted to wake up with her still there. If she'd stayed with him instead of coming back to her room, he had no doubt they'd still be in bed, skiing be damned.

While dressing this morning he wondered if he were completely out of his mind for seducing her. She'd walked away from her wedding on the same day he'd walked away from his. By all accounts, they should both be emotionally confused right about now. Funny thing was, he wasn't. And Sydney, once she'd calmed down, had seemed no more than irritated by the fact her wedding hadn't taken place. To him, that meant one thing—they were both available for a wintery fling.

Filling the coffeemaker with water and turning it on, he looked out the window to the huge flakes falling quickly to the ground and started to plan. First, they'd hit the slopes, then she'd be ready to come back in around one. They would have lunch by the fireplace. Good things happened when they were near the crackling fire, he thought with a smile. Quickly, he moved to the phone and ordered a lunch fit for kings.

He returned to the kitchen and found two mugs in the cabinet. Sydney looked like a cream and sugar type of woman—soft and sweet. Both of which he'd thoroughly explored last night.

There was a man in her suite, Sydney thought as she showered. She wasn't naïve enough to wonder why. Their sex had been mind blowing for her, and while she didn't for one minute believe it had broken any records for him, she was fairly certain he'd had a pleasurable time as well. However, she'd yet to decide how the day after would play out. Kyle seemed hell bent on making that decision for her.

He appeared casual enough, suggesting they go skiing. After all, they were at a ski resort. And he hadn't mentioned last night, although the heat still lingered between them. The way Sydney figured it, she had two choices: go along with his program—which seemed to lead toward a casual affair between them—or she could put a stop to this madness and begin the steps of getting her life back together. That meant deciding where she would live when she returned to Chicago, because she definitely was not returning to the house she and Derek had once shared. Other changes would also have to be made, changes she readily admitted weren't the most appealing things to her right now.

Procrastination had never been a trait that described her, but as she brushed her teeth Sydney realized last night had changed her. The scene just before her wedding had changed her. She was no longer the same woman who was so blindly in love a few days ago. She was different, and she wasn't totally against the changes.

But even that didn't mean she was looking to start something with a new man so soon. By the time she reached her bedroom and dressed in her warmest ski outfit, in her favorite shade of purple, she'd decided there was no harm skiing with the man. A few days of uncomplicated companionship would do her good. Besides, he was looking good this morning. For the billionth time since she'd left his room earlier this morning, Sydney wondered why he was here alone. Surely some woman must have her claws in him by now. She probably should have considered that before sleeping with him, but shrugged off the oversight, vowing to find out definitely today.

She smelled coffee as soon as she entered the kitchen. "Mmm, that smells heavenly," she said as she stood at the counter beside him.

Kyle lifted her mug, holding it in her direction. "I added cream and sugar. I hope that's okay."

Taking the cup from him, she sipped. "Oh yes, I love lots of cream and sugar."

She closed her eyes after taking another sip, but not before chancing a glance at his left hand. No wedding ring and no tanned line where a ring used to be. Good, because the last thing she wanted was to wreck some happy home. The way Derek and Rachel had so casually wrecked hers. Then again, how happy could her home have been? Was she really ready to live with the constant doubts of what Derek was doing and with whom?

Kyle watched her enjoying the coffee, wondering how she'd managed to slip herself so securely into his world so fast. Her hair looked soft, slicked back into a practical ponytail. He felt an overwhelming urge to pull her to him, to hold her closely forever. He shook his head vehemently. They both were leaving on Saturday. That was as long as their forever could be.

"Are you okay?"

Her sultry voice interrupted his thoughts. "Yeah, I'm fine. You ready to go?" He put his cup in the sink and held his hand out for hers.

"Not quite. What's your last name, Kyle?" It wasn't the foremost question on her mind, but it was a start.

He blinked in momentary confusion at the turn of conversation, then realized that while she'd shared something about her past last night, he really hadn't had the chance to tell her anything about his. "I'm Kyle Jackson, sports writer from Boston. I live alone, have no criminal record and am the youngest of two boys and one girl born to Mathias and Rebecca Jackson." He folded his arms across his chest. "Is that enough background for you to go skiing with me?"

A grin played on her lips at the impromptu bio. She took another sip from her cup as she leaned her hip against the counter. "Considering we've already surpassed the casual meeting, I say no, that's not enough. What are you doing here alone? I'm sure you have women at your beck and call in Boston. Besides, this is…for lack of a better description…a pretty romantic getaway spot."

He nodded in agreement. "Actually, I often come here alone. I own the condo down the hall. I like skiing, and this is a good place to come when I need to be alone. At least it was before the sexual revolution hit." He laughed.

"So if you need to be alone, why do you seem so content to be with me?"

Because he wasn't sure how much of that question she really wanted answered, he opted to tell her the main purpose. "As unbelievable as it may sound, I was supposed to get married on Saturday, as well."

Her cup shook in her hand. "Oh?" She quickly put it down before making a mess.

"I was engaged to a really nice model. We'd been together for two years and marriage seemed to be the next step in our relationship." He thought of Chantell's words from yesterday and cringed. The next step for their relationship had been the end. He knew now that he'd come to that conclusion at least three months before the wedding.

"So why aren't you married? I assume you're not because I don't see a ring or a wife."

He cleared his throat. "At the last minute I decided it wasn't what I wanted. I didn't love her enough to marry her," he told her honestly. Her eyes bore into his, and he knew she was comparing him to her ex. "No, there was…is no one else. I just believe you have to feel like your love can last forever when you marry someone. And I didn't feel that way about Chantell."

Sydney looked down at the floor. She tried to figure out how she'd come to be standing in an Aspen sexual education resort with a man who'd walked away from his wedding the same day she'd walked away from hers. There was one question burning in her mind. A question she wanted to ask Derek as well. "Did you ever love her?" Her gaze met his and held.

Kyle took a moment to think about the question. Then he moved closer to her until their hands almost touched on the counter. "In the beginning, she was fantastic. She was everything I needed her to be. But somewhere along the line my needs changed and hers didn't. I loved her then, and I care about her now, but I know she wasn't meant to be my wife. And I was not meant to be her husband."

His words were sincere and honest. Something she wished Derek had been with her. On impulse she reached out a hand and cupped his cheek. His face was shaved except for long sideburns that joined the thin beard and mustache. His dimpled chin strusk a cord in her heart. "She should be grateful you were so honest. Even though you could have spared her all the wedding hoopla by telling her before Saturday."

He smiled, relieved she'd taken his admission so lightly. "Are you kidding? Chantell loves to dress up, and she loves to be the center of attention, no matter what the reason."

Sydney giggled and moved away from him. Touching him had caused a stir in the pit of her stomach. One she didn't even want to address. "She sounds like my sister, Sadie."

Following her into the living room, Kyle picked up his jacket. "You have a sister?" he asked.

Grabbing her own jacket and slipping it on, she zipped it up, then pulled her hat down over her ears. "I'm Sydney Mills, middle daughter of Naomi Mills and Thomas Pierson, who went AWOL twenty years ago. I have an older sister, Sadie and a younger sister, Selena. We all live in Chicago, and we all love chocolate."

She slipped her gloves on and watched a slow grin spread across his face. "What?" she inquired. "Did I say something funny?"

"No, not at all. I'm just very pleased to meet you, Sydney Mills."

Sydney smiled in return. "You say that now. Just wait until I get you out on those slopes!"

She hadn't exaggerated, Kyle thought as they stepped off the elevator and headed toward her room. She'd been nothing short of spectacular out on the mountain. Her form was excellent as he recalled watching her tight little body maneuver the hills and curves like a pro. He'd thought he would have to slow down so she could keep up with him. Instead, he'd been the one panting behind her.

Still, it was a good run, and he'd enjoyed spending the last three and a half hours with her. "I'm ready for lunch," he said as they approached the door to his room.

"That sounds good." She looked over her shoulder, then opened the door. "But I'm treating this…" Her voice trailed off as she entered the living room. The fire was already ablaze and a thick cream-colored wool blanket was laid out on the floor in front of it.

Atop the blanket was an opened picnic basket, but she couldn't see what was inside from where she stood. There was an ice bucket with another bottle of champagne and a bowl full of fruit. Two plates were placed neatly across from one another with ivory napkins beside them.

"I hope you like seafood." Kyle had already removed his jacket. Now he walked up behind her, reaching around to undo the zipper on her coat. She stood perfectly still, staring at the picnic he'd arranged.

She lifted her arms so he could remove her coat, then turned to face him. "When did you do all this?" Her voice held a hint of amazement.

He carried her coat with his to the closet. "While you were in the shower this morning I got to thinking how convenient it would be to have lunch waiting for us when we returned."

Convenient and damned sexy, she thought. While Derek had always been free with his money, he'd never done anything this…romantic. Sydney sat on the sofa and removed her boots. "That was a good idea." She tried to sound unaffected by the gesture, but that he'd gone through all of this was touching and disconcerting.

Kyle joined her on the couch and quickly removed his boots. "C'mon." He stood in front of her, holding out his hand. "I'm starved."

She took his hand. "Me, too. For some reason I didn't have breakfast this morning." She cut him a sly look as they made their way to the blanket.

"My fault. I'll make sure you get breakfast tomorrow."

He's already planning for tomorrow. "What do we have?" She ignored her misgivings and concentrated on the food.

Kyle pulled out the first covered dish. "Crab dip."

"Mmmm," Sydney moaned.

"Shrimp Fettuccine Alfredo. Fresh bread sticks. And for dessert, chocolate cake." He'd called room service again when they were on the slopes and Sydney was busy trying to get her skis on. He had plans for her love of chocolate. Sweet, indulging plans.

"Sounds delicious," she told him. "Just think, I was going to take you out for a nice juicy hamburger," she laughed.

Kyle looked at her. Wisps of hair had escaped her ponytail as a result of pulling her hat off. Her cheeks were still a little flushed from the cold and her eyes danced happily. He felt a lightness in his chest and wondered what kind of fool would cheat on her. If she were his woman, he'd never let her go. There he went again, thinking of not letting her go. She wasn't his woman, and regardless what was going on between them now, come Saturday she would be on a plane back to Chicago. Back to the man who had betrayed her.

But he wouldn't think about any of that now. "We can have hamburgers for dinner."

"Kyle?"

He stopped scooping crab dip onto her plate to look at her. "Yes?"

"What are we doing? I mean, it's obvious we both came up here to get away from our emotional entanglements. But now it seems we've taken to each other like this was a planned rendezvous. What's up?" She looked at him questioningly.

He continued to serve the food, then sat back on the blanket. "I can't speak for you, Sydney. But I'm enjoying myself. I'm glad I didn't go through with the wedding. And I believe everything happens for a purpose." He poured champagne into each of their glasses. "Like fate.

Face it, what are the odds I would leave my bride at the altar and you would leave your groom on the same day. And that we'd both end up here, together?"

"Slim to none."

"Exactly. So I've got to assume we were meant to meet. That we were meant to spend this time together."

"And then what?" she lifted her glass to her lips and sipped.

He grinned. "I don't know. We'll just have to wait and see what fate has in store for us."

"While I don't normally subscribe to the philosophy of fate, I'm inclined to agree our meeting is more than coincidence. Still, I'd like us both to stay clear on what's going on."

He lifted his glass, holding it in the air and waited for her to do the same. "I'm having lunch with a very attractive woman. And you?"

Repeating his motions with her glass, she hunched her shoulders and smiled back at him. "I'm having lunch with a very attractive man."

Chapter 6

What made her so different? Was it the stubborn tilt of her chin? The keen glare she gave when she wanted a straight answer? Or, the disappointed light in her eyes she thought she hid well? Kyle wasn't sure.

But he lay in bed after their hamburger dinner in front of Sydney's television where Gone With the Wind had been the movie of the night. He grinned. He'd never wanted to watch Gone With The Wind before. Scarlet O'Hara and her pouting held no appeal to him.

That hadn't mattered tonight. And although she'd made it clear early in the day they would not be sleeping together tonight, he'd still wanted to be near her. It was ridiculous, he knew. He'd only met her two days ago. He'd known Chantell for two years. And he'd never lain awake at night thinking of her.

Things with Chantell had progressed so smoothly. He'd met her at a fashion show he'd gone to only because a retired basketball player had started his own clothing line. He'd seen her on the runway. Though she wasn't his usual type, he'd appreciated her beauty, and when the show was over, offered to buy her a drink.

They'd slept together that night and the following three nights until she'd left town on business. From that moment on, it had been a given that when she was in Boston, she'd be at his condo with him.

They got along great. He suspected it was because of the percentage of time they actually spent together. Less than fifty percent—and half of that was in bed. His parents liked her, he looked good standing beside her in the pictures captured in the magazines and newspapers, and the sex was nothing short of amazing.

But until he'd come to Aspen and met the sexy little spitfire across the hall, he'd never realized how empty his relationship with Chantell had been.

Damn, he was glad he'd stopped them from making a big mistake. Chantell was not meant to be his wife.

But who was?

He tucked his arms behind his head, letting out a whoosh of air.

Sydney Mills had a lot going on in her life. He suspected she was much more upset about Derek and his offspring than she was willing to admit. She didn't want to talk about it, which told him Derek had really hurt her. She tried to pretend it didn't matter, which told him she was strong and would get over this betrayal, eventually. She knew almost as much about sports as he did without sacrificing the mushy romantic that was revealed during their movie watching. And, if he wasn't mistaken, he was falling for her.

Falling for Sydney.

Now that was something. What did he really know about her? She lived in another state where she had a family and a life. He lived in another state where he had a family and a semblance of a life. They were at opposite sides of the spectrum, thrown together by abandoned nuptials. They were not ill-fated lovers waiting for their chance at happiness. Or were they?

Draping an arm over his forehead, he realized he didn't have any answers. He only had facts. He liked Sydney, fact. He was attracted to Sydney, fact. He and Sydney had been great together last night, fact. He wanted Sydney again, undeniable fact.

Closing his eyes he allowed her face to fill the darkness. Smooth mocha skin, full mouth coated with a light neutral lip gloss. Honey toned voice. Shoulder length hair, black, silky. Small frame, about five feet three inches. She smiled, laughed. He heard the melodious sound deep within. He could trace her lips with the tip of his finger—soft, smooth. The smile died, bringing to life a serious glare. Her eyes held him captive, drawing him toward her. His lips found hers, his tongue tasting the sweetness of her mouth. Her hand gripped his waist. His hands found the back of her head, pulling her closer as he deepened the kiss. She gasped, the sound rendering him too weak to speak.

He kissed her neck, her collarbone. His palms found the plump swells of her breasts. His thumb flicked over puckered nipples and her hands tightened around him. She whispered his name, and he felt himself hardening beyond belief. In seconds they were both naked and just as he was about to enter her, to spread her legs and sink into the waiting abyss of pleasure, his cell phone rang.

The sound jarred him, and he sat up abruptly in the bed. A long line of expletives left his mouth as he pulled the covers over his painful erection.

"Yeah?" he yelled when the phone was to his ear.

"Jackson?"

It was Randy, his boss. What the hell did he want at two o'clock in the morning?

"Yeah, man. What's up? Why are you calling me at this time of night?"

Randy cleared his throat. "We just got word that Derek Winters' wedding was crashed by an angry girlfriend with a pending paternity suit. You need to get your butt to Chicago and get on this story while it's hot!"

Kyle groaned. He already had an inside track to the story. One he was just thinking of exploring. "I'm on vacation, Randy," he explained.

"It'll be a permanent one if you don't get me this story."

Thoughts of Sydney and this ordeal spread out in the papers had him pausing. "Put somebody else on it," Kyle told him.

"You're my senior writer. I want you on it."

"I can't think about this right now, Randy. Damn, I'm supposed to be on my honeymoon."

"But you're not. Yeah, I heard you chickened out. But I don't care about that,"

That was for damned sure, Kyle thought.

"I want this story. And I want you to write it."

Kyle knew it was going to take a lot to convince him he couldn't write this story, especially since he was still struggling with the reasons himself. From the moment Sydney had told him of her escape from marriage and the man whom she'd left, he had known there would be a story. Known he'd be asked to write it. But he'd pushed those thoughts aside, refusing to give them any of his energy. Now, Randy confronted him and he really didn't know what to say as an excuse.

"I'll call you back, Randy."

The other man swore on the phone. "Jackson, when you call me back it better be from Chicago."

Kyle hung the phone up, falling back onto his pillows.

Closing his eyes again, he tried to recapture the picture of Sydney naked and waiting for his touch. Instead, he saw Sydney alone and broken, newspapers and magazines with headlines marking Derek's infidelity scattered at her feet. His heart sank in his chest and he fell into a fitful sleep.

Sydney awoke early in the morning, visions of a sexy stranger pulling her from the depths of slumber.

She'd dreamed of him. His deep intoxicating voice and his alluring smile. He'd touched her in her dream. Those long piano-playing fingers had stroked her skin while she whimpered and begged for more.

Now in the shower, she cursed herself for being too foolish to spend some intimate time with Kyle last night. He'd wanted to, she was sure of that in the way he kissed her goodnight. And a part of her wanted the same thing, but then she'd thought about it. Casual sex had never been her forte. She'd chalk their first night up to a mixture of hurt feelings and the sexually charged ambiance of the resort. But now she was more alert, more in control of her mind and her body.

She lifted the lathered wash cloth to her breasts and moaned. Her body was in desperate need of attention whether or not her mind wanted to accept that fact.

Quickly finishing with her shower, she wondered what Kyle would want to do today. She wanted to be dressed and ready when he arrived.

He might not want to be bothered with you today. Did you think about that? An annoying little voice that had become her best friend since she'd arrived in Aspen greeted her for the first time this morning.

Frigid air hit her as she stepped out of the shower. Her heart thumped in her chest at the thought of seeing him. She was actually looking forward to seeing Kyle. To seeing this man she'd only met two days ago. She shouldn't want the company of a man. After all, one had just betrayed her. But he wasn't Derek, she continuously reminded herself.

How do you know that? "Because I refuse to believe the good Lord would make more than one of those types of men and place them both in my path," she answered herself.

She brushed her teeth and left the bathroom. In the bedroom she changed her clothes twice, in an effort to find the perfect outfit. She didn't have a clue what they'd be doing today, but whatever it was, she planned to look her best. Deciding on the fitted tan pants and equally fitting tan and black turtleneck, she donned her boots and went to the kitchen to put on a pot of coffee.

After starting the coffee, she was about to go into the living area to look out at the snow topped slopes when the phone hotel rang. Her good mood kept her from being leery of answering and she picked it up saying a chipper good morning without thinking.

"Thank God, Sydney. I've been trying to get a hold of you. Are you okay?"

Her good spirits plummeted at the sound of his voice. She realized she still did not want to talk to Derek. Was she okay? What the hell did he think? "Hello, Derek. I'm fine. How's your daughter?" Getting angrier with each passing second, she tapped her booted foot on the carpeted floor.

He let out an exasperated breath. "There's no real proof she's mine, Syd. Please come home so we can talk about this."

At one time she would have done anything for him, saying please had never been a pre-requisite for her compliance. Now, all she wanted to do was hang the phone up and stay as far away from him as humanly possible. But you loved him up until a few days ago? She rolled her eyes toward the stark white walls in the empty room, getting damned tired of that pesky little voice. "I saw the DNA results from the lab. It seems you picked a pretty smart groupie to sleep with."

"Syd, I'm so sorry. I never meant for any of this to happen. I love you."

His voice sounded pitifully weak, but she didn't falter. "Look, Derek, I really don't feel like doing this right now. The least you can do is give me some time alone."

"How much time will you need? I really think we should talk about this now. You should come home. Or I could come there. We just need to be together right now. We need to show there's no truth to the rumors that we've broken up."

Sydney narrowed her eyes. Was he serious? Did he really think she was still going to be with him after this? "I don't give a flying fig about the rumors or what other people think. And apparently, neither did you when you slept with that woman!" She couldn't believe he was not even going to give her space to think. "What's the problem, Derek? Your agent pressuring you to fix your image? Is this little scandal hurting the team or your ability to play?"

He hesitated. "It's not like that, Syd. You know how it is. This is already public knowledge. We need to counter the accusations."

She shook her head in disbelief. "No, I don't need to counter a damned thing! I didn't sleep with somebody else, you did. I didn't get that woman pregnant, you did. And I really think your priority right now should be taking care of your child. She's the innocent one in all this. I'll be home when I get there. And for the record, home is no longer your house, and we are no longer together, so tell your agent to play another angle." She slammed the phone down before he could say another upsetting word to her.

A knock on the door had her almost jumping out of her skin and she walked with measured steps towards it before using a shaking hand to turn the knob. "Hi," she spoke to Kyle in what sounded to her own ears like a weak voice.

His hands came to her shoulders as he backed her further into the room and kicked the door closed behind them. "What's the matter? Has something happened?"

Normally, she was a strong woman. Growing up in a household of women she'd learned to stand on her own long ago. She didn't fall apart often, and when she did, it was in the solitary of her own room. Very rarely did she lean on her mother or her sisters for emotional support. Instead, she was the one they came running to. But this time was different. She felt stripped of all her defenses, bare to the world and defeated. Before she could stop herself she'd buried her head in his chest and was sobbing uncontrollably.

Something gripped Kyle's heart and held on tightly. He had no idea what had happened before he knocked on her door, but the second he'd looked into her face he'd known something was wrong. The light that usually danced in her warm hazel eyes was gone, replaced by the sadness he'd noticed before at odd moments. Now she was shaking in his arms, crying like her heart was breaking as she stood locked in his arms. Derek Winters had done this to her, he had no doubt. With one arm protectively around her waist, the other stroking her hair, he grit his teeth to keep from cursing the man aloud.

"Shhh. It's okay. I'm here now. Tell me what's wrong."

Hearing his words, Sydney felt foolishness wash over her, and she quickly pulled out of his grasp. She moved to the large window in the living area and swiped at the tears that dampened her cheeks. "I'm sorry. I don't know what came over me. That's really poor hospitality on my part." She tried to joke, but the laughter never made it to her eyes.

Kyle moved closer to her but stopped a few inches away, struggling not to touch her. She needed some space. He had no doubt that falling apart in front of him was not part of her plan. "Don't worry about it. We're past such formalities as hospitality. You want to tell me what happened?" He was startled to find how hard it was to keep his distance from her, but he didn't want to push her too far, too fast. She'd never open up to him if he did. And he realized with a start that he wanted her to confide in him, he wanted her to lean on him. He wanted to be the one to help her through this terrible time.

She took a deep breath and considered telling him it was nothing, but decided against it. She needed to talk to somebody, and right now he was the one available. Sure she could send him home and call Sadie or Selena, but they undoubtedly had enough going on trying to deal with inquiries about her disappearance and Derek's probing questions. Crossing her arms over her chest, she turned to face him. "Derek called."

Those two words confirmed his suspicions. "What did he say?"

She chuckled to keep from bursting into tears again. "He said I should come home so we could form a united front. Apparently, his little indiscretion has gotten out and his agent wants to perform a little damage control. Can you believe that?"

Kyle's jaw clenched. "Yeah, I can." He hated that fact, but understood it well. Derek was a professional athlete, a role model for some and a very public figure. This whole episode would effect not only his personal life, but possibly his game and ultimately his respectability in the league. Not to mention the very real threat of Derek losing not one, but most likely all of his endorsements was also reason for his agent to be in a hurry to clear this up. "It's all about him right now. All about salvaging his career and staying on top. And he obviously doesn't give a damn about you or your feelings after all this."

"So what? Am I supposed to go trekking back to Chicago, suck it up and smile for the cameras? Tell the press and anybody else who cares to hear it the story is fake and I'm standing by my man." She shook her head vehemently. "I saw the test results. I believe her! Isn't that pitiful? I believe a woman that until three days ago I had never seen before in my life over a man that I was about to marry. What does that say about my judgment? About me?" She couldn't help it, tears flowed freely again and sobs broke from her chest.

To hell with this distance crap. Kyle moved quickly, wiping the tears with the pad of his thumbs, then pulling her close for another hug. "It makes you human. It makes you a woman who trusted the man in her life. And it makes him an asshole." He hadn't meant to bash Derek, he'd meant to stay as far away from doing that as possible. But he couldn't help it, asshole was the kindest thing he could think to say about the man.

Holding her in his arms felt right. His chin rested on top of her head as he cradled her, letting her release the anguish he knew was tearing her apart. Rage built inside him, and he longed to get back at Derek Winters. Maybe he'd write that article Randy had called him about. Only it wouldn't be to salvage Winters' career, it would be to expose the lying, cheating womanizer that he was. It would bring him down, hard. Headlines raced through his mind as Sydney's small body shook with the force of her tears. He hated Derek Winters.

What had once seemed to him like a promising NFL career, a man with his head on right, doing the right things, with a successful black woman by his side; was now a disgrace to all good successful men. He'd abused his position and acted foolishly. And in doing so, hurt this woman Kyle had come to care an awful lot about.

But he couldn't write that article. He couldn't print his own personal opinions of the man, and he couldn't reveal the fact that he'd gotten any information from Sydney. That would drag her name through the mud, which was the last thing he wanted to do. No, he'd have to tell Randy it was out of the question. He had no other choice.

When she seemed to calm down Kyle knew the only important thing to him at this very moment was to make her happy. To see her smile again. He couldn't take away the hurt Derek had caused, but he could take her mind off it for a while.

Inhaling the sweet smell of her hair and dropping a kiss on top her head, he finally spoke. "I know just what you need," he told her, keeping his voice upbeat.

Sydney sniffled and pulled away just far enough to look up into his face. He still held her tightly, and she was startled to find she liked it, needed it. "And what might that be? A box of Kleenex?" She smiled tentatively.

Kyle smiled back at the brave face she put on. She was trying to joke when it was obvious her heart was breaking. Just one more thing he liked about this woman. "No Kleenex. You're going to stop crying and drink a cup of that coffee I smelled brewing when I came in. Then we're going out."

"The coffee sounds great, but I don't know that I feel up to skiing today, Kyle."

His grin broadened. "Who said anything about skiing?"

Sydney eyed him suspiciously. Why was he smiling like that? "I know you're not suggesting we go shopping?"

Kyle chuckled. "Are you kidding? I'd have to be pretty desperate and basically out of my mind to offer to take a depressed woman shopping. You'd wear me out." He removed his hands from around her waist because he feared he was getting way too comfortable holding her this close. "Nope, I've got something better planned." Rubbing his hands together, he walked toward the kitchen, knowing she'd follow him.

"You've always got something planned," she said as she entered the kitchen. She reached for a paper towel and wet it slightly before dabbing at her eyes and cheeks. She probably looked a swollen mess after her crying job. But Kyle didn't seem to notice. "So what's on the agenda today, Mr. Jackson?"

Kyle poured coffee into two cups, added sugar and cream then stirred the steaming liquid and handed her a cup. "A good old fashioned snowball fight." He noted her leery expression as he brought the cup to his lips and grinned.

"We're adults, Kyle. I don't think a snowball fight is age appropriate." She took a cautious sip of coffee. Damn, he made it just right!

"Maybe not, but it's a great stress reliever. I remember when I was little and my parents pissed me off, a good old fashioned tantrum always made me feel better. Now, I'm not suggesting we stomp, kick and roll around screaming on the floor." He laughed. "But a vigorous snowball battle where the looser has to give the winner another one of those soothing massages is definitely therapeutic."

Sydney's fingers trembled as she thought of Kyle's hands on her body again, or hers on his. She almost moaned, and she hadn't even won the damned snowball fight yet. "Another massage, huh? What makes you so sure you'll be the winner?" She watched him carefully. Kyle hadn't missed the exchange between them. Without words Sydney had confirmed she was feeling him just as much as he was feeling her. He wanted to leap with joy, but knew that would only add to his childish degeneration. "The last one led to such interesting things that I'm very optimistic."

Sydney shrugged. "I'm thinking the looser will reap some benefits as well." Whether or not she was the giver or the receiver of the massage, being alone and naked with Kyle again was a welcome thought.

Her clothes fit closely over her tight little body, and Kyle's fingers itched to get his hands on her. He'd throw the damned battle just for the opportunity to touch her all over. "Then shall we go?"

"I guess we shall."

Chapter 7

Snow came almost to her knees as they trekked through the cold white stuff in search of a secluded spot for their battle. They'd skirted around the lifts and the entrances to the slopes into an area with trees and privacy.

"This is great. There's enough trees here to provide shelter for the inexperienced snowball combatant," Kyle said, clapping his gloved hands together.

Sydney scooped a handful of snow, cupping her hands until it was a perfect sphere. "And which one of us is inexperienced? I'm from Chicago, remember. Lots of snow every winter," she grinned as Kyle began backing up.

"Touché. I've been warned." Without taking his eyes off her, he bent and scooped snow into his much bigger hands, making a substantially larger snowball than she held. "Any ground rules?"

Sydney grinned. "Yeah, one." When he waited for her to continue a bubble of laughter escaped. "Don't get hit!" Before he could reply, she'd lifted her arm and released her first assault.

Snow splattered with bright whiteness against his black ski jacket, and she laughed as she bent to pick up another one.

Kyle was definitely faster than her, she thought as snowball after snowball barreled in her direction. But his aim sucked. He never hit her in her face like the boys from her old neighborhood always did. Instead, his assaults always landed either in her chest or on her butt when she had bent over to gather her own ammunition. After the first fifteen minutes of the battle, she realized with a heated start that this was his intention. Realizing he was playing dirty she aimed for either his face or his groin, never missing her target.

Kyle took refuge behind a tree to both catch his breath and calm the throbbing need that had grown between his legs. She was agile. She'd bent over to scoop snow into her hands, giving him a clear view of her backside. His thoughts had instantly shifted to his hands at her hips, holding her still while he pounded into her from behind. His erection throbbed.

Then she turned, aiming and landing her shot against his growing arousal. The coolness began to seep through his pants only to be engulfed by the fiery hotness she'd evoked. He found himself targeting the areas he most wanted to touch on her. She was persistent, tirelessly pummeling him with no care as to what she was doing to him. He wanted this battle over with quickly. Whether he won or lost, he definitely planned on getting his hands on Ms. Sydney Mills today.

Across the way from him, she'd grown quiet. He assumed she was gathering her arsenal. He had one snowball left with no intention of making others. This last shot would end the battle, then he'd take her back to the hotel and help her to shed those wet clothes, start a fire, lie down naked and…

A snowball crashed against the tree, inches away from his face. He smiled and shouted. "You've got great aim. You could be an excellent pitcher."

"I don't like baseball," she yelled in return before throwing another snowball in his direction.

It smashed into his shoulder this time as he'd moved from the cover of the tree. She turned to see him approaching and knew with a sinking feeling that this was the final showdown. Quickly, she bent and scooped up her snowballs, plowing him with keen accuracy. But he kept progressing. Her skin hummed with awareness as he closed in on her.

She looked down in haste, only to find she had run out of ammunition. His steps continued, and she wondered if she'd have enough time to make one more. Looking from the snow back to Kyle's approaching form, she regretfully surmised it was too late. With lighting quickness, he reached out and grabbed her by the collar of her coat with one hand, pulling her hard against his chest.

"Looks like you're all out," his voice was husky. His eyes bore into her with fierce intensity.

"You wouldn't assault a poor defenseless female, would you?" Her teeth chattered, but she wasn't cold. To the contrary, her body had become extremely hot.

He smiled devilishly. "Wouldn't I?" With his free hand he held his last snowball up for her to see and watched as she conceded defeat and closed her eyes tightly.

He grinned and pulled on her coat until there was an opening big enough for his hand. Without another word, he dropped the snowball down into her coat and quickly smashed the material against the cool sphere.

Sydney gasped, her eyes shooting open quickly, disbelieving. "Kyle!" she screeched as he held her firmly, making sure the snowball's coldness seeped into her clothes.

"I can't believe…you did…that." She could barely talk as the snow melted against her breasts. "Why did you do that?" Her teeth chattered again.

"I wanted to make sure your blouse was adequately soaked." When she looked at him in confusion, he framed her face in his hands and brought her closer. "That way I could offer to take that off you first. I wouldn't want you to catch a cold from wearing wet clothes."

She opened her mouth to respond, and he silenced her by capturing her lips beneath his in a hungry kiss.

Kyle and Sydney made their way quickly through the doors of the resort, anxious to make it upstairs to either of their rooms. In the elevator they held hands, knowing what await them, but refusing to participate in another heated prelude.

They went to his room again, this time passing through the living room as they stripped of their wet clothes. Arriving in the bedroom, already naked Kyle built a fire across the room while Sydney pulled down the comforter and sheets.

It was quiet except for the noise from their motions. They did not need to speak to each other, as their minds were already thinking alike.

He wanted her.

And she wanted him.

Questions and circumstances be damned.

Kyle crossed the room and stopped at the foot of the bed. "Get on your knees," he said in a slow, ominous voice.

Sydney's body quaked with expectation. Looking at him, she could see his entire demeanor had changed. He was no longer smiling and playful as he had been during the snowball fight. Now he stood, beautifully naked, with the stance of a god looking at her as if he could eat her in one swift erotic bite.

She positioned herself on her knees, then waited for her next instruction.

"Crawl to me."

She did, keeping her eyes on his because she loved the heat they both provided and evoked.

When she was at the foot of the bed, her face level with his magnificent arousal, Sydney could only think of one thing. She reached out a hand and cupped his erection, stroking it until drops of pre-cum moistened her hand.

"Put this on," he said, handing her a condom he'd snagged from his wallet before entering the bedroom.

Savagely, she ripped the package open with her teeth and slid the latex over his thick length.

"Now turn around." She stared up at him in question. "Stay on your knees and turn around. I want to see that ass you've been teasing me with all morning."

Arousal knotted in her stomach as she turned around slowly. And when his large hands grabbed both her cheeks, spreading her almost painfully apart, she moaned with pleasure. Then he released her.

"Show yourself to me. Show me what you know I want." Kyle grabbed his erection, eager to stuff his hot length inside of her, but more excited by watching her willingly submit to his requests.

Not giving it another thought, Sydney leveraged herself so she was still bent forward while grasping her cheeks and opening herself for him to see. She expelled a breath, never having been so intensely aroused before.

"Beautiful," he sighed, jerking his meat a little faster this time.

Her vaginal muscles clenched and subsided, causing her center to cream unmercifully. Her heart hammered in her chest as arousal threatened to overtake her. "Thank you," she whispered.

Kyle took a step closer to the bed, aiming his ready shaft at her exposed cove. "No, Sydney. Thank you for this privilege."

"Kyle," she whispered, wanting him to stop this incessant talking and simply take her.

"Yes, baby. I know," he said and guided his sex inside of her.

Sydney sighed with relief and anticipation. Releasing her cheeks, she fell forward on her hands wiggling her bottom back against him. "Now, Kyle. I can't wait any longer."

At her words Kyle's mind went crazy with desire. Immediately, he began to ride her, fast and hard. Pulling out of her and slamming back into her with all the urgency rumbling through his body. Holding her hips, he looked down and watched as his sex disappeared and reappeared from inside her cushiony warmth, his testicles slapping against her warm backside.

Each time he sank into her dewy depths, Kyle lost another piece of himself. He hadn't known her long, and yet he knew he would never forget her. Something about her appealed to his every need, and he pounded against her in an effort to make her understand. "Sydney," her name was wrenched from his lips as he threw his head back in ecstasy.

Sydney heard her name on his lips along with sound of their sticky flesh making contact. She felt wave after wave of unrelenting pleasure washing up against the shore of her heart. The heart she thought would never be touched again. He'd come into her life at a pivotal time. He'd shown her nothing but consideration and passion. He'd been a shoulder to cry on and an ear to listen. And she was amazed, simply amazed at how well they seemed to fit.

Her heavy breasts swung back and forward as he pumped. She moaned and pushed her hips back to meet him thrust for magnificent thrust. He was implanted so deeply inside of her she wasn't sure she'd ever function again were he to leave.

"You are all mine," Kyle growled and fell over her back, grabbing her breasts into his hands. "All mine," he said again into her ear.

"Yes," she whimpered not giving a second thought to the admission, but knowing no other man could do to her what he did.

He pumped her impossibly harder, putting not only his name, but his mark on her for all to see. Sydney couldn't think, couldn't grasp anything beyond him and what he was doing to her, what he'd been doing to her for these past days.

They panted and sighed, moaned and begged, both pushing each other to impossible lengths to prove that this connection, this thing between them went so far beyond the primal bonding.

Her legs began to shake, her breathing erratic. She called his name, wanting to let him know he'd brought her to that very special place again. He seemed to know without her saying the words because he released her breasts and cupped her cheeks again spreading her as he pistoned inside.

"Mine. All mine," he groaned and thrust and came deeply inside her womb.

For the remainder of the afternoon they slept, made love and slept some more, simply unable to leave that bed.

The sun had already set, and outside the large window on the left wall Sydney stared into the night, lost in her own thoughts.

With a hand to her chin, he turned her to face him. "What are you thinking?"

She'd thought he was asleep again, obviously he'd been up thinking as well. "What are we doing, Kyle?" she asked without preamble.

"We're taking a much needed rest," he joked and leaned forward to kiss her.

She smiled and kissed him back, this time searching for an answer. Resurfacing, she searched his eyes momentarily. "You know what I mean.."

Sometime in the last three days, Kyle had become an essential part of her life. He was like a friend—he listened, offered advice—whether she wanted it or not, saw her at her lowest points and didn't run and hide. But most of all, he made her feel important. Like what she had to say actually meant something to him. She realized she never had that with Derek. With Derek most everything was about his career; what he planned to do after the NFL, all the things he wanted to buy with his money from the NFL, all the luxuries they could have as a result of him playing for the NFL. Until now, it never occurred to her that she really didn't have a place in Derek's life, besides as a trophy wife. He'd even asked her to quit her job after they were married so she could stay home and raise their children.

Kyle never looked away, hardly even blinked before saying, "Whatever it is, I don't want it to end." His knuckles brushed over her cheek.

"I just don't want us to be kidding ourselves."

He sighed. "We live in two different states. We both have professional and family lives we are pretty content with," he continued.

Sydney heard his words and wondered if when she returned to Chicago she would be able to forget him and this time they'd spent together. "I know. But I can't help but think back to your statement about fate and how it seemed right that we met here."

"It does seem right." Kyle nuzzled her neck, aware she was giving their situation great thought. He'd wanted to do the same, but was afraid of what her final answer would be.

If one week with Sydney was all that was meant for him, he'd gladly take it. No matter how much he craved more. "If all I can have is one night," he began.

Her eyes met his. "Will you be satisfied?"

He smiled. "No. But I will accept."

They sat without speaking, the fire blazing and crackling from across the room. Neither one sure of what else needed to be said.

Sydney snuggled beneath strong arms and a warm blanket, her mind vaguely registering it was morning and probably past time for her to get up. But her body protested and stubbornly remained still.

Opening one eye, she saw the fire had long since been banked and the indigo skyline that, along with Kyle's comforting existence, had lulled her to sleep was now a cheery shade of pale blue, artfully adorned with puffy white clouds.

She sighed deeply as she remembered the time she'd spent with Kyle. Along with the hot sex, she remembered the hours they spent just talking. Kyle admitted to wanting to get married someday "to the right woman," he'd quickly added. Sydney had nosily inquired as to the qualifications of "the right woman" to which he'd promptly replied, "someone like you."

She hadn't known how to respond to that and was rescued when he asked if she'd ever consider marriage again. She surprised herself by answering yes, then elaborated that Derek's indiscretions would not make her a bitter, untrusting female.

The ringing phone pulled her away from her thoughts. Without hesitation, she moved Kyle's arm gingerly from around her waist, threw back the softest blanket she'd ever had the pleasure of sleeping under and reached for the phone.

"Hello?" she answered cheerfully.

"Hello?" a bewildered female voice responded.

Sydney felt instant alarm.

"Now I see why it was so easy for him to walk out on me. He already had another honey on the side. And what's your name?"

Sydney smacked her palm against her forehead. She should have known better than to answer a man's phone. "I think you're misunderstanding…I…I mean, I'm not…Kyle and I are just friends."

The moment the words were out, she felt the chill of untruth cascade down her back.

Kyle took the phone from her hand. "Hi, Chantell," he said in a less than pleasant voice.

Sydney mouthed an apology and attempted to climb out of the bed when he caught her at the waist, pulling her backside against his front.

"No, I was not cheating on you. I just met her." Kyle let out a deep breath as Sydney heard Chantell screeching through the receiver.

"It really doesn't matter, Chantell. I've already apologized as many times as I care to. Getting married would have been a big mistake for us."

Even though she knew it was wrong, knew it was selfish, Sydney felt a jolt of relief at Kyle's words.

Kyle sighed. He couldn't believe Chantell had called him again and that Sydney had answered the call. "My feelings for her are none of your business." Especially since he was still trying to grasp the revelation he'd come to only hours earlier as he'd watched Sydney sleep himself. "This is it, Chantell. This is the last time I'm going to entertain this conversation with you. Now, I have a guest to attend to. Goodbye." Kyle hung up before Chantell could continue with her argument.

Wrapping his other arm tightly around Sydney, he dropped a kiss on top of her head. "I guess that wasn't such a pleasant good morning."

Sydney chuckled, loving the feel of being held by him. "I guess not." She turned in his arms until she faced him. "I'm sorry. I shouldn't have answered your phone. Chantell sounded pretty upset."

Kyle kissed her forehead, then her eyelids one at a time. "Yes, she was upset. And no, don't apologize. It's over between Chantell and I. You answering that phone has driven that fact home quicker than I ever could have. So you've actually done me a favor."

Sydney twisted her lips and clasped her hands behind his neck. "In that case, you owe me one," she crooned as she pressed her body closer to his.

Kyle sucked in a breath. The desire that had finally left him alone long enough to catch some sleep last night, was now back with a vengeance. "Whatever you want, I'll gladly do," he vowed.

She nipped his bottom lip. "Promises, promises."

Chapter 8

Just as Kyle closed his eyes and thrust his tongue into her mouth, there was a knock at the door.

Sydney groaned.

Kyle swore.

"What the hell time is it that people don't mind calling or banging on a brotha's door?"

Kyle slipped on basketball shorts and a T-shirt and left the bedroom. Before opening the door he checked to make sure his T-shirt hid the telltale tent in his shorts.

"Hey man," the visitor began. "I'm sorry to bother you, but my wife's been staying in the room down the hall. I just got in this morning, and she wasn't there. I was wondering if you'd seen her?"

Words eluded Kyle as he stared at the six foot two wide receiver. He'd seen his photos a million times and had caught a couple of his games live, but that was before he'd spent time with his…did he say wife?

"Ah, your wife?" Kyle stuttered over the words. He knew Sydney's story was true. It had to be, Randy had called about him writing the story. So what was Derek Winters doing at his door in the Aspen mountains?

Looking for the woman Kyle had so foolishly fallen in love with.

Sydney heard the voice and felt the rage bubbling inside her. She was moving toward the door before it dawned on her that confronting Derek in Kyle's suite may not be such a good idea.

Kyle felt her behind him seconds before she pulled the door open wider.

"Yeah, she's about five—" Derek's words stopped abruptly.

"What the hell are you doing here?" With one hand on her hip and the other on the door knob, Sydney tapped her bare foot on the floor and waited for his response.

Derek looked at Sydney. From her tousled hair to the man's Boston Celtics jersey that barely skimmed her knees, to the equally mussed man standing beside her and saw red.

As a man, Kyle put himself in Derek's shoes, recognized the signs as the slightly bigger man frantically looked from him to Sydney and back to him again. Then he took a step back, craning his head to the side just in time to dodge Derek's hurling fist.

"Derek!" Sydney screamed.

With the narrow miss, Derek grew even angrier. Kyle didn't want to fight this man. Okay, he admitted, he'd like one good punch right across his jaw, but figured it would be best handled without Sydney screeching in the background. He grabbed Derek's arm just as he swung again and twisted it behind his back. "You need to calm down before you come up in here looking for a fight."

"Hell nah, I'm not calming down! You're sleeping with my wife!"

Kyle had no desire for the entire resort to get wind of this, so he pushed Derek further inside the condo, kicking the door closed behind him.

Sydney, who had stepped to the side after Kyle's easy avoidance of Derek's punch, was shocked. She'd never seen Derek get physical with another person off the football field. But that shock ebbed and anger was back full force. "Wife? I thank the good Lord every morning I get up that He spared me from making such a horrible mistake!" she spat the words viciously at Derek who had made his way into the living room.

"Have you been sleeping with him all along?"

Both Sydney and Kyle looked at each other. Kyle felt out of place but was reluctant to leave her alone. "I'll go if you want." His stance said he was prepared to stay.

Her features softened. "Stay."

"That's sweet but didn't I ask you a question?" Derek interrupted.

Sydney turned to face the man she thought she'd be spending the rest of her life with. "The answer to your question is no. I just met Kyle a few days ago."

Derek had a look of pure disgust on his face. "And you've slept with him already? That's pretty crude, Syd."

Kyle took a step closer. "Don't disrespect her again." He kept his fists balled at his sides.

"And what do you know about respect? You're sleeping with another man's woman." Derek looked at Kyle with unrestrained contempt.

"A man doesn't treat a woman the way you did." Kyle knew it was beyond futile to argue with Derek, especially when he'd just broken up with a woman, too, but his growing anger at the man's gall intensified with each passing second.

Derek lunged for Kyle again. This time Sydney stepped between them, her back to Kyle. "Oh please, spare me the hurt boyfriend routine."

Her words halted Derek, and he stared down at her. For a moment she thought she saw a fleck of hurt—an iota of pain in his dark eyes. But she quickly dismissed it. He didn't deserve her pity.

"I was more than your boyfriend. We were almost married," he whispered.

"You're right, Derek. You were more than my boyfriend. So why didn't that fact keep you from having sex with that woman?"

He was about to speak when she put her hand up in his face. "How could you profess to love me while maintaining a relationship with her?"

"Sydney, baby, it wasn't a relationship."

"The hell it wasn't. You got her an apartment, you paid her rent, you saw her at least three times a week. What the hell do you call that?" Selena had called her on Tuesday with this information. Funny how the details of Derek's kept woman had been shadowed by the good time she was having with Kyle.

"It was a mistake, baby. I swear it was just a horrible mistake. Sydney, you've got to forgive me. We can start over. We can put all this stuff behind us," he cut an eye at Kyle. "None of it matters now. I need you, Syd. I love you."

Sydney shook her head, wondering what she'd ever seen in Derek. He was as selfish now as he'd been all the years she'd been with him. He didn't give a damn about her feelings. He'd been with another woman and believed she'd been with another man, but because he needed her, he expected her to take him back. What kind of life would she have had with him? His only concern was his career and the things he wanted out of life—success on the football field, money, a wife and kids—in that exact order. She wondered now if he'd ever really loved her or was she just a convenient part of his plan.

Kyle held his breath as he waited for Sydney's response, praying she wasn't falling for Derek's pleas for her sake as much as his own.

"No, Derek. You made a mistake, a really big mistake. One that cost us our relationship and produced a child. That child, your daughter, needs you now."

Sydney took a step back, knowing Kyle was right behind her. She felt his solid form and drew the courage to say what she'd been holding back for so long. "We were a mistake, Derek. I think I've known that for a long time now. I just never cared to admit it. I thought that once we were married things would be better. You'd be better. But now I see this is just who you are. You're not going to change, and I'd be a fool to take you back just so a few months from now there'd be a different woman or a different paternity test. It's just not worth it."

She shook her head from side to side. It really wasn't worth it, she deserved so much more. She deserved the kind of attention Kyle had given her this past week. The kind of caring support and true desire to make her happy that Derek had never shown. This week Kyle had done everything in his power to make her happy—not make her forget about Derek and her problems with him—but make her happy. When she needed to talk, he listened. When she needed to forget for a while, he made her laugh. When she needed to be held, he held her. That was why she loved him. "I don't love you, Derek." She spoke the words in a clear voice without conviction because she knew in her heart they were truth.

Derek laughed. "You don't love me?" He jabbed a thumb toward his chest. "Do you know who I am?" he asked Kyle. "Can you give her everything I could?"

Kyle knew he was talking about money. And he was pretty sure how rich Derek was. Kyle's personal bank account didn't lack zeros. Neither did his trust fund balance or the monthly reports on his various investments, but that didn't matter. He shook his head because Derek just didn't get it. "I can give her love and loyalty. She needs that much more than material things."

Derek looked at Sydney. "Did you hear that? That means he can't take care of you like I can. With me, you'd have whatever you wanted without ever having to leave the house."

Sydney willed her legs not to shake. Had Kyle just said he loved her? "But I trust him not to cheat on me. I can't say the same about you."

Derek dragged his hands down his face. "Man, you can have her. This is way too much drama for me."

Kyle put his hand on Sydney's shoulder. "Yeah, I can see how pretending to love one woman when you have so many on the side would be tiresome."

Derek ignored the jab. "Come to the room and get your stuff. Since I paid for it, I think I have a say in who occupies it. Get your new man to foot the bill for you, if he can afford it."

Derek walked past her and headed for the door.

Sydney started to say something, but Kyle shushed her and walked behind Derrick.

"Actually, Derek, I think you should get your things and vacate the premises."

Derek turned an angry glare to Kyle.

"Man, please. I paid for that suite. The clerk can vouch for that. What, she's good enough to sleep with, but not good enough to spend money on? You see, Syd, this is what you chose over me. He's a joke." Derek waved a hand at Kyle.

"No. No joke, Derek. But since as of yesterday I became the new owner of this resort, I have the exclusive right to say who stays on my property. I'll gladly refund your money. But I want you gone voluntarily within the next fifteen minutes, or I'll personally escort you out myself."

Standing in the hallway, Kyle watched as Derek gathered his bags and boarded the elevator, leaving the hotel. The man was a colossal jerk, and he was glad he was out of Sydney's life.

Now he was back in his room. To his great relief, Sydney was still there. She no longer stood in the middle of the floor where he'd left her. She now sat on the couch, her legs drawn up, her chin resting on her knees.

She looked like a little girl. A very vulnerable, very frightened little girl.

"Can I get you something?"

She turned to him, her cheek resting on her knee. "How about some glass slippers so Dorothy can go home, because clearly I must be in Oz."

He sat down beside her. "If I get you those slippers, you'll disappear before my eyes." Tentatively, he placed a hand on her head, smoothing her hair down. "And I would surely die if you should vanish from my life."

Sydney closed her eyes to his words. Just last night they'd talked of where this thing between them was going, and just this morning she'd admitted she'd fallen in love with him. But did she really know him? "What else is there I should know about you?"

Kyle took a deep breath, but kept his eyes trained on her. "The most important thing is that I love you."

Her eyes opened, their gazes locked.

"As for the rest, I'm a third generation rich kid. My family's in oil and stock trading. I can give you anything Derek could, if that's what you want. But I'll start with giving you my heart."

A lone tear escaped, making a speedy trail down Sydney's cheek. She lifted her head, letting her feet fall over the edge of the couch. "I don't know. A girl like me prizes herself on possessions. I may need more," she said, remembering the impression Derek had tried to create. She'd never asked him for anything, and she really resented his implications that she was materialistic in front of Kyle.

"I can give you the world, Sydney."

His eyes were so intent on hers she felt the power of his words clear down to her toes. "I wasn't thinking anything that grand. Just the name and number of your friend at Hershey's." She smiled.

Kyle visibly relaxed, then pulled her into his arms. "Don't worry, baby, you'll have all the chocolate you need. As my wife, my connections will become your connections."

Sydney pulled back to stare at him. "Your wife?"

Kyle kissed her nose. He loved her nose. "Yes, Sydney Mills, middle daughter of Naomi Mills, sister of Sadie and Selena, marketing exec and the most intriguing woman I've ever met. I want you to be my wife." Because he believed what they had could last forever.

Sydney stared at him incredulously.

"Keep in mind that if you turn me down, I'll use my connections to cut off your chocolate supply indefinitely."

She giggled. "Oh, you don't have to resort to such drastic measures, a sistah was just stalling."

"Well, quit stalling. I want to marry you right now, today if I could, but I'm willing to wait until you're ready."

She lifted her hands to his face. "When I came to Aspen I was so confused, so unsure of what my future held. But fate had the upper hand. Instantly, I was drawn to you…Wait a minute? You bought the resort? When? Why?"

Kyle smiled as he toyed with a strand of her hair. "The other night when you said you were thinking about taking one of those classes, I got to thinking that if you and we went our separate ways you might be tempted to come back here and do just that. The very thought of you being open and willing with any other man but me was disturbing. So I called my financial advisor and told him to make the owner an offer he couldn't refuse. Then I sent a letter instructing the staff to cease and desist all instruction on the premises."

"All instruction?" Sydney asked cautiously.

"Yes. Why?"

She shrugged. "I was kind of enjoying the things I was learning from you."

Kyle smiled then leaned forward to kiss her sweet lips. "Still stalling?"

She chuckled, then changed to a more serious expression as she cupped his face in her palms. "My friend, my love. I will most definitely marry you, Kyle Jackson, owner of this resort, son of Mathias and Rebecca Jackson, sports writer, novelist and chocolate connection."

He smiled and kissed her waiting lips.

"I love you."

"And I love you ."

About the Authors

Barbara Keaton, a native of Chicago, who thinks its the best city in the world, also enjoys writing. Her first diary is dated December 1975! And since then, Barbara has written articles for *Today's Black Woman Magazine*, Chicago Reader, Chicago Crusader and most recently, True Confessions. In addition, Barbara is an accomplished romance author, having seven titles to her name. Barbara credits her late grandfather, Thomas Hill, and the Oblate Sisters of Providence for instilling in her a love and passion for the written word. Visit her on the Web at **www.bkeaton.com**.

Using creativity and sexuality as her backdrop, **Sapphire Blue** creates stories to entice and arouse.

An event planner and published romance author, Sapphire lives in Maryland with her family. Reading and writing are her passions as evidenced by her work. She was influenced by veteran romance authors at an early age and with time began to add her own level of spice to the timeless tales. Now, thoroughly convinced that a healthy sex life co-exists with a great love affair, she writes what is in her heart and what some are afraid to even imagine.

Writing has always been her dream. Writing strong, witty and sexy characters a must. Sapphire is the culmination of a happily ever after romance novelist and a desire to push the envelope right into the burning flames of passion! Sapphire has been writing for fifteen years and published in romance for four years. Receiving her chance to create new worlds and daring characters by Midnight Showcase, Sapphire is determined to bring a new slice of color to the erotic romance realm.

To Dyanne Davis—my true sistah! Thank you for being the frick to my frack—much love to you!

Maureen Smith is the author of eight novels, including the erotic romance *Taming the Wolf.* She has won the Romance in Color Reviewers' Choice Awards for New Author of the Year and Romantic Suspense of the Year, and has been nominated for nine Emma Awards and two Romantic Times Reviewers' Choice Awards. As a former freelance writer, Maureen's articles appeared in various magazines, newsletters and online publications. She lives in San Antonio, TX with her husband, two children, and a miniature schnauzer. She loves to hear from readers and can be reached at **author@maureen-smith.com.**

Artist C. Arthur was born and raised in Baltimore, Maryland where she currently resides with her husband and three children. An active imagination and a love for reading encouraged her to begin writing in high school and she hasn't stopped since.

Working in the legal field for almost thirteen years now she's seen lots of horrific things and longs for the safe haven reading a romance novel brings. Her debut novel *Object of His Desire* was written when a picture of an Italian villa sparked the idea of an African-American/Italian hero. Determined to bring a new edge to romance, she continues to develop intriguing plots, sensual love scenes, racy characters and fresh dialogue—thus keeping the readers on their toes!

During the course of her writing career Artist has won the YOUnity Guild's Best New Drama and Romance Author Award in 2005/06; been nominated 3 years straight for EMMA Awards, with the fourth time being a charm she took home the 2007 EMMA Award for Favorite Romantic Suspense; and has also received her first Romantic Times Reviewers' Choice Award Nomination for Best African American Romance.

Artist loves to hear from her readers and can be reached via email at **acarthur22@yahoo.com**